Higher Love

JOANNE KUKANZA EASLEY

RED BOOTS PRESS

Publisher-Red Boots Press

Cover Design- Lewis Agrell

Author Photo-Spunky Cloud Photography

ISBN: 979-8-9867133-6-6

LCCN: 2024921175

Dedication

Higher Love is dedicated to the memory of my dear sister, Jeanne Kukanza Cronin. In one of our last conversations, she told me she loved the title of this novel because she loved the song, Higher Love, by Stevie Winwood. I lost her during the writing of this novel and at times, grief overwhelmed me, but I persevered, remembering how Jeanne practiced Higher Love in her daily life for her five children and eleven grandchildren. She is missed.

Contents

Part One

GETTING TO KNOW YOU

Chapter One

LAUREN'S PAST INVADES – AUSTIN 1986

As I primped for my combined sixty-second birthday and twenty-fifth AA anniversary party, I studied my image in the bathroom mirror and concluded no one would guess my age. A few notes from Carly Simon's "You're So Vain" floated through my mind. My lips twisted in self-deprecation as I admitted the habits from my long-ago modeling days had never left me. I gathered my mahogany curls into an updo and spotted another gray hair. I'd have to speak to my colorist. Otherwise, I was quite presentable.

I'd chosen one of my favorite silks, a flowing dashiki in tones of verdigris and periwinkle, adding gold sandals, my favorite necklace, and diamond drop earrings to complete my look. After a spritz of Arpège, my signature scent, I was ready to go.

Brett Owens, my third and fourth husband, knocked on the door. "People are filin' in like you're giving away money. You best get out here."

"Be right there."

Soon, my friends from Alcoholics Anonymous and the food store I owned filled the house. Brett tended to the stereo, and a selection of Texas Blues supplied background music. Iced tea and lemonade flowed. Tubs of cold soft drinks for the coke drinkers were set strategically around the room. With all the delicious food brought by my guests, the dining table didn't have a square inch of open space.

At the height of the festivities, my AA friend Ruth carried an Italian Crème cake into the room and placed it on the buffet. Relieved to see the cake wasn't a fire hazard but bore a tasteful single candle, I smiled. As the guests sang "Happy Birthday," a bedraggled teenage girl wearing a backpack stepped from the entry into the dining room. My guests seemed as astonished as I, given that their voices trailed off one by one until only Brett, whose back was to the door, completed the verse.

Tossing her mahogany curls, the disheveled girl dropped her backpack and approached me, stopping three feet away. I stared into eyes the like of which I hadn't seen since 1940 and realized she had to be related to me. The revelers swiveled their heads between the teenager and me, sharing puzzled looks. No doubt they noticed we shared the same hair color, among other similarities.

My hand flew to my Zuni fetish necklace, a gift from Brett, and I fingered the carved animals as if they were worry beads. Brett came to my side, and I leaned into him.

Jane Renfrew, my close friend despite our twenty-six-year age difference, whom I'd sponsored for years, whispered in my ear. "Who is she?"

My voice shook. "I think she's...my granddaughter. She has Alain's eyes."

Jane's jaw dropped. "Oh my, are—"

"Later," I hissed. Forcing a smile, I approached the girl. Taking a deep, centering breath, I turned to the assembly. "Y'all are gonna have to excuse us for a bit. Please enjoy the cake."

Brett took a step forward, but I gestured for him to remain. "Honey, will you help Jane and Ruth serve our guests?"

On the way out of the dining room, I scooped a soft drink from the tub, figuring the girl was thirsty. As I escorted the surprise visitor down the hall to my home office, my back stiffened when the buzz of speculation reached my ears. Once I'd closed the door to my sanctuary, I gestured toward the deep, rose-colored leather loveseat. "Please have a seat, dear."

The girl remained standing and, in a Boston accent, asked, "Are you Lauren Eaton? Did you give up a baby girl for adoption, like in 1941?" Her words sounded wooden and rehearsed. She appeared tired and road-weary, her clothes far from fresh, and her fingernails dirty. I wrinkled my nose when I caught a whiff of body odor.

"You look dead on your feet. Set yourself down." I offered her the pink can. "Have a coke."

The grubby urchin snatched the can from my hand and popped it open, plopping herself onto the loveseat. "This isn't Coke—it's Tab. I guess you don't have any Jolt." She gulped half the can, grimaced, then burped. I waited in vain for an "excuse me." How had her family failed to instill proper etiquette in the girl? But perhaps she knew how to behave, and her actions were mere teenage rebellion.

Determined to keep my inner turmoil hidden, I sat in one of the matching chairs across from her, folding my hands in my lap to stop them from shaking. "Obviously, you know who I am. What's your name?"

The girl leaned forward and squinted at me. "Stephanie. Stephanie *Babcock* Kingston."

After a pause, I replied, "Of course. The Babcocks. My mother's people. I lived with my Aunt Imogene in Manhattan for a time in the forties." I gulped, my hand returning to the necklace. Like a bomb that for years had failed to detonate, the fruit of my past had landed on the doorstep. As Mama would have said, "Those chickens have come home to roost."

"You didn't answer me. Did you give up a baby girl for adoption?"

I frowned, then realized what I was doing and relaxed my features. "Has no one taught you manners?"

Stephanie burped again. "Still no answer."

Assessing the rude child, I willed my face to show a neutral expression. "Yes. I had a child in 1941, a daughter who was adopted by my uncle and his wife, the Boston Babcocks."

The girl snorted. She screwed up her face and put on an even broader Boston accent. "Grandpa Clark died last year. I still have my granny Evelyn. When my mother died, I found out the truth."

"What? Your mother died?" *The baby I gave up is dead.* Through quivering lips, I stammered, "I-I'm so sorry." And I was—for so many things.

With a grim look, Stephanie crushed the empty can of Tab. "Yeah, so am I. Can I have some cake? It looked delish."

I got to my feet. "Of course. There's plenty of other food if you want something more substantial."

"I'm starving. My money ran out last night in Arkansas. I tried to panhandle at the bus stations we stopped at, but no luck." Stephanie stood and followed me to the door.

I turned to the girl. "I was going to bring you a plate." No need to give my guests more fodder for speculation.

"No way. I can get my own food." The girl's assertiveness surprised me, but I didn't argue with her. "Come along, then."

As soon as we entered the dining room, Brett came to my side. "Darlin', what can I do?"

"Please help Stephanie fix a plate and bring her back to the office. I need to speak to Jane."

I made my way through the gathering, noting the curious faces and intent gazes. Holding my head high, I made small talk and acknowledged well-wishes as I searched the sea of friends for one particular woman.

Glancing into the glass-walled sunroom, I spotted Jane and her husband Joshua in a knot of people. Jane glanced up, and judging by the look of concern on her face, must have seen my distress. She whispered to Joshua and rushed to me.

"How is she?" Jane asked.

"She's dirty and rude, but she is my granddaughter." Almost choking on the words, I continued, "The daughter I gave up for adoption is dead." Saying those words out loud made it real.

Jane gasped and placed her hand on my shoulder. "Oh, Lauren, I'm so very sorry. What a shock! How can I help?"

"Well, would you sit in with us while I try to get this sorted out? Please. I'm in over my head here and could use your expertise."

"Of course. Lead on."

I squeezed her hand in thanks and confided, "When she told me her mother was dead, there wasn't a trace of emotion. That's not normal."

"She may be shut down. It happens," Jane said.

"Could be. Something is off about the child. She doesn't seem to be grieving. In fact, she's quite feisty."

With a somber look, Jane said, "We'll proceed with caution. How are you doing? This has to be a stunner for you."

"I've survived worse."

Jane nodded. "I know."

When Brett reentered my life last year, I had confessed my jaded history to Jane, so she understood the implications of the girl's arrival. In the dining room, I stopped to grab three soft drinks for us.

As we entered the office, Brett got up from the chair. "Kid's all set. I'll get back to the guests."

"Thanks, darling." I blew him a kiss.

Stephanie stuffed tortilla chips, celery, and carrot sticks loaded with dip into her mouth without pause. The girl didn't appear to chew her food.

Unable to look away, I cleared my throat. "Stephanie, this is my friend Jane. She's going to join us while I learn a little about you and your plans."

"Hello, Stephanie." Jane lowered herself into a chair, moving with the care of a woman in the late stages of pregnancy.

With her mouth full, the girl said, "Hi." She licked her fingers and grabbed another chip.

"Since you're still eating, I'll tell you a little bit about myself." Jane smiled at the girl. "I've known Lauren for fifteen years. We're good friends. She helped me when I first got to AA."

The girl's head snapped up. "AA? Like alcoholics?" Finished with her first plate, the girl started in on a huge piece of cake.

I settled in the chair beside Jane. "Yes, Alcoholics Anonymous. You arrived at my twenty-five-year AA birthday, which coincides with my belly-button birthday."

Through guffaws, Stephanie sputtered, "Oh no, Granny. That's so lame. Belly-button birthday. Oh, my God."

Jane's lips twitched, but she held in her laughter.

"Easily amused, ain't you? And please call me Lauren, not Granny." The very term made me shudder.

Stephanie frowned at the new can of Tab but opened it and chugged away.

Recovering a bit from the shock of meeting the granddaughter I didn't know existed, I asked, "Stephanie, how did your mother die? And when?"

The girl drained her second Tab, burped, and said, "Three weeks ago. Mom took her sleazy boyfriend Doyle on a scuba diving trip to Belize. The valve on her air tank got stuck on some coral, then she panicked and drowned. That's the official story. Doyle tried to save her, but he couldn't. At least that's what he said. He wasn't arrested, so maybe it's true."

"What was her name? My daughter's name..." I ran out of words and choked back a sob as the hazy, long-forgotten image of a red, wrinkled baby flashed before my eyes.

"Barbara."

Jane moved to sit beside the girl on the loveseat. "I'm so sorry for your loss. But why are you here?"

"I found out my mother was adopted. And she never knew it. I thought that was shitty and told my fake granny exactly what I thought of her keeping it a secret from Mom. And me. I couldn't stay another minute under that roof, so I threw a few things in a backpack and hit the road."

"How old are you?" Jane asked.

"Sixteen."

Jane winced and leaned toward the girl. "Sixteen. You know, I ran away from home when I was that age too."

Tilting her head, Stephanie studied Jane. "You did? Did you ever go back?"

"Yes. Seventeen years later. Too late. But my story is quite different from yours. Were you and your mother close?"

"When I was younger. But after my dad died, she sort of went crazy."

"What do you mean?" Jane asked.

"After a few months, she started dating a whole bunch of younger men. It was embarrassing." The girl placed her empty plate on the coffee table.

With the name "Barbara" echoing in my mind, I'd been sitting silently while Jane questioned the teenager. Then I rejoined the conversation with the obvious question. "When did your father die?"

"Five years ago. He had cancer, and he died a few months after he was diagnosed. We had to sell our house and move in with my fake grandparents. That gave Mom the freedom to date and leave me with my old-ass babysitter."

I glanced at Jane, whose widened eyes told me she had picked up on the lack of emotion in the girl. "For sixteen, you're mighty jaded. And disrespectful," I said.

Stephanie shrugged. "So?"

Jane and I exchanged a look.

My jaw tightened, and I realized I was grinding my teeth. "Have you spoken to your grandmother since you left Boston? What are your plans?"

"She's not my grandmother. You are! And cool it with the questions. I don't know what I'm going to do." Stephanie folded her arms and leaned back, pouting like a spoiled child. "My goal was to get here and find you. I didn't plan what I'd do next."

"Does your grandmother know where you are?"

Staring at her scuffed boots, the girl mumbled, "No."

I jumped to my feet. "Then you'll call her and let her know. Now."

"No!" Stephanie glared defiantly at me.

"Then I will." I didn't know Evelyn's number and hoped the girl wouldn't call my bluff.

"No way! I'll do it." Stephanie lunged from the loveseat. "Where's the phone?"

I gestured to the desk. The girl stomped over to the phone and mashed the buttons. With the receiver snugged under her chin, she said, "It's way past her bedtime. She'll be pissed."

Jane and I listened to one side of the conversation.

"Hey, Evelyn, it's me."

A squawk could be heard across the room.

"I'll call you Evelyn if I want to. Anyway, I'm fine. I'm in Austin, at Lauren's place. You know, my *real* grandmother."

The girl listened for a moment, rolling her eyes. "I took the bus. They call it 'riding the dog.' Can you believe it?"

Another squawk.

"No, I'm not coming back. And there's nothing in the world you can do to make me." Stephanie's voice rose, and she plunked her hand on her hip. "Take a chill pill!"

My eyebrows rose at the girl's tone. Her attitude and disrespect for her grandmother irritated me.

Stephanie listened again, then held the receiver out. "Evelyn, formerly known as my grandmother, wants to talk to you. She doesn't believe me."

In slow motion, I took the phone to speak to the woman I met only once, forty-five years ago. Uncertain how to address the stranger on the line, I took a deep breath. "Evelyn?"

"Lauren. I don't know what to say. I've been absolutely frantic!"

So, no niceties. Fine with me. "I'm sure you have. Stephanie is safe here. Get some rest. Give me your number, and I'll call you tomorrow." As I jotted down Evelyn's number and stashed the paper in a drawer, Stephanie frowned. She must have realized she'd fallen for my ploy.

Jane rose from her chair. "I'm going to check in with my husband. You two have a lot to discuss."

After the door closed, Stephanie flung herself onto the loveseat, unlaced her clunky boots, and kicked off what I soon learned were called Doc Martens. She curled onto her side and closed her eyes. The girl looked so innocent with her mouth shut.

"By the way, how did you find me?" I asked.

"Got your address from Evelyn's lawyers. They keep track of *all* the Babcocks."

"Oh, right." *Mama told me that years ago.* I winced, dodging the emotions the memory evoked. "I'd forgotten that. But now, I must make an appearance at my party. Would you like to come with me or rest here?"

Without looking at me, Stephanie said, "Rest."

"Okay. I'll be back in a bit." I turned off the overhead light, leaving the soft glow of a tableside lamp for illumination, but waited to leave until I heard her snoring softly.

After easing the door closed, I dashed to my bathroom and assessed myself in the mirror. "Granny? I don't think so." I freshened my lipstick, spritzed more Arpège—the perfume I had used since 1946, when Brett first gifted it to me—and returned to the party.

As soon as I set foot in the dining room, I was mobbed by my guests. I accepted hugs, warm words, and a sliver of the Italian Crème Cake. While I chatted with my friends from AA and Cornucopia, my food store, who were too polite to ask about the stranger, thoughts of the child in my office tormented me. Was Stephanie really as tough and hard as she seemed? Surely she had some emotion about losing her parents.

Brett approached. "There ya are, sweetheart. You're wanted out on the pool deck. I'm told your friends have a present for ya."

I groaned. "But I clearly said no gifts on the invitation. Honey, will you check on the girl? Maybe sit with her?"

He kissed my forehead. "Of course."

I strode out to the patio. The swimming pool glowed with aqua light, and a soft breeze carried laughter and the scent of evening primrose through the mild May air.

Ruth stepped forward with a card. "From the noon Westlake Group."

I smiled as I read the card and scanned the many signatures. "How lovely."

Jane came to my side and gestured to a six-foot-tall potted palm in a huge Talavera planter. "We know you said no gifts, but you were overruled. We know how much you love your garden. Milton provided the plant from his nursery."

Unwanted tears sprang to my eyes. I blinked and turned to the crowd. "Thanks, all y'all. Unnecessary, but deeply appreciated."

After giving and receiving a dozen hugs, I whispered to Jane, "I'm going to check on the urchin."

The unmistakable opening riff of Stevie Ray Vaughan's "Cold Shot" flowed out of the stereo speakers. Several couples cleared a space to dance, and a group of women began to boogie.

The irresistible beat filled me with regret that I couldn't dance with my friends, but the weight of my granddaughter's appearance, and all it implied, hung over me as I hurried back inside.

Peeking into the office, I motioned to Brett to come out into the hall.

"The kid's been snoring the whole time. Ain't so much as twitched." Brett drew me into an embrace. "Got a blanket out of the linen closet and tossed it over her."

"Thank you, honey." I bit my lip. "I need to regroup. This situation is overwhelming, and I hate to end the festivities, but maybe you can gently steer our guests out the door."

"Sure thing."

I stood on my tiptoes, cradled his face, and gave him a heartfelt kiss. Then I made my way past the loveseat, sank into a chair, and recited the Serenity Prayer in a whisper. "God, grant me the serenity to accept the things I cannot change, courage to change the things I can, and wisdom to know the difference." Stephanie's surprise appearance and the drama sure to follow hit me, and I shivered. Overcome, I put my face in my hands. "But God, I gotta ask, what am I gonna do? What's the next right thing?"

Jane knocked softly and entered the room. "Want to talk?"

"Suppose I'll have to. But not right now."

"Do you have a plan?" She jerked her head toward the sleeping girl.

I leaned back in the chair and grasped my necklace. "One day at a time is as far as I can think right now."

"Since I just got my license, my calendar is pretty open. When you're ready, of course." Jane grinned.

"That's right, you'll be seeing clients soon now that you're an official clinical psychologist. I'm so proud of you. And to think, you almost up and quit your schooling two years ago."

"Don't remind me. And remember, you're not a patient, just a friend having a chat."

I recalled how worried Jane was about violating the ethics of her profession when I had sought her advice after Brett tracked me down. "I remember the disclaimer from the last time I asked for your help. Rest assured, I won't turn you into the PhD police."

Jane held up her hands. "Okay, okay."

Stephanie stirred for a moment, then settled.

"How about lunch at Kerbey Lane tomorrow? Noon?" Jane asked.

"Sounds wonderful. By then, I'm certain I'll need a break from the urchin. I'll beg Brett to watch her for a few hours. I have to stop at Cornucopia too. Right now, I'm still processing Barbara's fate, to say nothing of the girl's arrival. Whatever will become of her?"

Cradling her seven-and-a-half-month pregnant belly with her hand, Jane waddled to the door. "More will be revealed. I'd better round up Joshua and head home."

"Yes. Get you some rest. Let me walk you out." I got up and hugged Jane, surprised at how far away I had to stand. "You're not having twins, are ya?"

Jane rolled her eyes.

While I sat in the dim room, visions of the hospital stay in 1941, when I gave birth, played on my mental movie screen. With the aftereffects of twilight sleep scrambling my mind back then, I hadn't formed a reliable picture of events; my memories were vague and incomplete. Evelyn had to have been in her thirties. I did recall the fashionable suit she wore—dusty pink—and the equally fashionable hat. From head to toe, Clark had been a study in gray. Those images dissolved into a red, wrinkled, squalling scrap of life I saw for such a brief moment, I might have dreamed it.

From the hallway, Brett's booming voice interrupted my reverie. "Thanks for comin'. Y'all drive safe!"

A moment later, he cracked the door and whispered, "That's the last of 'em."

"What time is it?"

"Just past eleven. You gonna let her sleep here?"

Stephanie appeared deeply asleep, and I debated whether to wake her. "I'm gonna get her settled in the guest room. She'll get a crick in her neck lying like that. See you in a few."

Brett nodded. "Got it. You want me gone."

"Goodbye, darling."

The door closed, and I steeled myself to wake the girl. "Stephanie."

When she didn't respond, I hesitated, reluctant to touch her—that would make things all too real. I tapped her shoulder. "Stephanie. Let's get you in a proper bed."

With a grumble, she woke and sat up. "Okay. Where?" She picked up her boots and backpack.

"Follow me."

When I switched on the overhead light in the guestroom, the girl blinked. "Nice room. What's that thing hanging on the wall? It's a little scary."

"A multi-media piece done by a friend of mine."

"What is it?" the girl asked.

"You'd have to ask him. I think it's a statement about his upbringing on the reservation. He's Cherokee."

"An Indian?"

I shook my head. "I think he prefers 'Native American.'"

"Oh. Sorry."

"No harm done. You must be exhausted. I'll find you some pajamas—unless you brought some."

"No. I was so pissed when I left, I didn't even think about it."

"Back in a minute. The bathroom is through that door."

When I returned with the nightwear, I heard the toilet flush. Stephanie entered the bedroom, and I handed her tailored cotton pajamas, a gift from someone who didn't know me very well and which I had never worn. "Are you going to shower?"

"Too tired." Stephanie disappeared into the bathroom again, and I turned down the bed, knowing the sheets would need washing the next day.

A few minutes later, the girl padded into the bedroom, clad in the flowered pajamas, and stood in front of me, shifting her weight from foot to foot. "Good night, I guess."

"Sleep well."

She slipped under the covers and sighed as she settled in.

I stood at the door, watching her. "Is it safe to leave you alone?"

Her eyes popped open. "What do you mean? Do you think I'm gonna steal the silver and book?"

I snorted. "Never crossed my mind. You know what I mean."

Stephanie sat up. "Don't worry. I'm fine. Promise."

Given her reassurance, which I chose to believe, I gripped the doorknob.

"Lauren?"

Not having the energy or the inclination to get into any in-depth discussion at this hour, I tried to keep my voice even. "Yes."

"Can I ask you something?"

"All right."

"Why didn't you want my mom?"

My heart galloped. I didn't have the strength to deal with my own pain, let alone Stephanie's. All I wanted was to fall into bed, and when I woke in the morning, discover I'd hallucinated the entire evening. I glanced at my white-knuckled hand on the doorknob and turned to face the girl. "Not tonight. We'll talk tomorrow. Get some rest."

"Okay." Stephanie lay down and snuggled under the covers.

I stood there for a minute or two, but she didn't stir. Thankful for the reprieve, I hustled to our bedroom, breezing past Brett, who was propped up on pillows reading a magazine. "I'll only be a minute."

"I'm good at waiting."

That line always resonated with me. Brett had waited for me for thirty-three years. In the bathroom, I rushed through my bedtime routine, doing just the basics. After donning my silk pajamas, I climbed into bed. Brett closed the *Texas Highways* magazine and tossed it on the bedside table.

When we got back together last fall, I confessed everything about my past to him, all the things I neglected to tell him when we met in Dallas in 1946 and throughout our first marriage. After our shared tragedy—the miscarriage at five months—I'd thrown acid on the wound by insisting on a divorce he didn't want. I never imagined he'd want to see me again, so when he showed up unexpectedly at Cornucopia, so many years after our breakup, I was stunned.

His reappearance forced me to get honest with myself, which I did with the help of my sponsor Helen and Jane. My heart healed, and to my amazement, I agreed to marry Brett for the second time.

Brett took off his reading glasses and patted the space beside him. "Come on over here, Granny."

I scooted over, grabbed his face, and kissed him silly. "Don't you ever, ever call me that again, Brett Owens."

We shared a good laugh that led to a loving embrace. I felt myself relaxing in his arms.

Brett murmured, "Let's debrief."

"Oh, baby. Not tonight. I'm exhausted, worried, confused, sad, and so many other things. My brain is plumb tired."

"All right, darlin'. I understand." He kissed my shoulder and turned off the bedside lamp.

"Night, Brett." We would both need our rest to face the challenge that lay in the guest room.

Chapter Two

STEPHANIE'S SCRAMBLED THOUGHTS

Lauren closed the door softly, and I tried to wrap my head around the fact she was my real grandmother, and I was about to go to sleep in Austin, Texas. When I first saw her, I couldn't believe how much she looked like my mom, except for the nose. I'd think about that factoid later. For being so ancient, Lauren was kind of a Betty, for her age, I mean. The hair color probably had some help from a salon, but she carried it off. But what the heck was that outfit? It looked like a Halloween costume, something a hippie would wear, but wasn't she too old to be a hippie? I had to admit she had a bitchin' bod, not like stooped-over Evelyn Babcock. Of course, Lauren was much younger. There was so much I wanted to know, needed to know. But I should play it cool and figure out these people before I asked too many questions.

Even though I was mega beat, sleep wouldn't come. The bed was comfy, and the room smelled totally awesome, like some exotic perfume, but the old-time pajamas felt weird and scratchy against my skin. Lauren probably thought I was a slob because I didn't take a shower. Whatever.

I turned on my side and tried to relax, but my mind whirred like a blender. The scene at the Babcock family attorneys—when I learned my entire life was a lie—played on a loop in my head. I hadn't thought things could get any worse than losing both my parents. Then they did.

"Evelyn, Clark left a letter to be read in the event of Barbara's passing. If I may?" Cabot put on his reading glasses and cleared his throat.

"Upon my deathbed, I have had time to ponder my life, and I wish to redress a grave wrong perpetrated by me and my wife. When we adopted Barbara as an infant, we swore to each other that she would never know she was adopted. Evelyn, you know I never agreed with keeping Barbara's origins from her, but I bowed to your wishes, much to my regret. However, I do not want that deception to carry forward. Our granddaughter must know the truth."

The woman formerly known as my grandmother gasped and her face became gray. She reached into her bag for a handkerchief, clutching it to the bosom of her Chanel suit.

Cabot frowned, then turned to me. "Miss Kingston, this next paragraph is addressed to you. 'Stephanie, my dear girl, your mother was adopted as a baby. You must know that we loved her as our own. We are grateful to Lauren Eaton, who brought Barbara into the world and gave us the greatest gift.'"

"What!" I flew out of my chair and shrieked at Evelyn. "You fucking lied to my mom for her entire life? And you lied to me too!"

Evelyn reached her hand out to me, but I stepped back. "Don't even. You can't fix this."

Boylston, Cabot, and Lodge rose to their feet and tutted at me. I thought the stuffy old lawyers would have a collective heart attack. Boylston croaked, "Language."

Lodge rushed around the desk and knelt before Evelyn's chair. "Can I get you a glass of water?"

At once, I knew what I had to do. "Who is Lauren Eaton?"

"Lauren Eaton is Clark's niece. Her mother was Rose Babcock, Clark's sister."

"I want her address, my real grandmother's address. Now."

Cabot handed me a sealed envelope. "Her contact information and a copy of Clark's letter are inside."

I snatched the envelope from Cabot's hand and ran out the door, leaving the lawyers to deal with Evelyn. Didn't even look back.

On the street, I hailed a taxi and arrived at the townhouse in minutes. I threw a twenty at the cabbie, dashed inside, and changed from my stupid school uniform into jeans and a tee. Swore I'd never wear plaid again. I shoved some money and a few clothes in my backpack, tied the laces on my Doc Martens, and charged downstairs. The Greyhound bus station was a twenty-minute walk away. Evelyn wouldn't think of looking for me there. Not in a million years.

Wide awake at 2:00 a.m., the words "your mother was adopted as a baby" rang in my ears. Would it ever stop?

My previous life was history. I couldn't go back to that stuffy old lie-filled mansion and that hateful prep school. Rules and expectations up the wazoo. But where could I go? Lauren seemed pretty cool for an old lady, but I didn't know her. Maybe if things checked out, I could ask about staying with her. What other choice did I have? My stomach hurt as I wondered if I'd made a huge mistake running away. Then I told myself: No! You had to leave.

What about that old guy, Brett, Lauren's husband? He seemed okay. The dude was hella tall, and what my mom would have called "distinguished" and Evelyn "dashing." I was dying to get the story about that eye patch but didn't want to ask. He reminded me of the bad guy in that old James Bond movie *Thunderball*, only better-looking and with longer hair.

My mom had crushed on James Bond movies and bought all the VHS tapes. Just thinking about how Mom would make hot chocolate, and we'd snuggle together on the couch on movie night, made me cry. During my dad's illness, we got really close, but that ended when we lost our house because of the medical bills, and we moved in with Evelyn. Then Mom started dating, and each dude got younger. The last one, Doyle, with his slicked back hair, creeped me out. Just thinking about them together made me sick. I'd never know what happened in Belize. Could he have saved her life?

That pregnant chick, Jane, was kinda nice. A little nosy, but nice. They thought I was asleep on the loveseat in the office, but I listened to every word they said. I couldn't believe Lauren called me an "urchin." Wasn't that a word from a Charles Dickens novel, like hundreds of years ago?

Evelyn had threatened to send me to boarding school because I was "a handful." I couldn't imagine how much worse that would be than the heinous day school where I didn't fit in. Already, I missed Allison, my only friend, and an outcast like me because we hadn't known the cool kids since nursery school.

How could Evelyn order me around now that I knew she wasn't even my real grandmother? Lauren was, and I wasn't sure how I felt about that. Did she even like me? Did I like her? And what about my real grandfather? Was it Brett?

I wished I could shut my brain off so I could get some sleep.

Chapter Three

LAUREN'S QUANDARY

The next morning, while Stephanie was still sleeping, Brett and I sat at the kitchen table, and I filled him in on what I'd learned about the girl. He listened and nodded but had nothing to say. What was going through his head? Brett rose and made a much-needed pot of coffee. I figured he was contemplating our situation and gave him space.

Over yogurt and berries, I jotted a to-do list. "Don't forget to wash the sheets in the guest room when she sees fit to get out of bed."

Brett nodded. "And her clothes are gonna need washing. But what we gonna do with her? Ship her back to Granny Babcock?"

I sputtered with laughter. "I may have to forbid the use of the G-word in this house. Had my fill last night."

"Seriously though, sweetheart. She seems downright unhappy living in Boston, and she sure took some drastic action by running away. How about we offer her a place with us?" Brett sipped coffee, seemingly non-plussed about laying out the possibility so bluntly.

Surprised by his question, I bought some time scooping up the last of the berries. "Hmm. That is the ultimate question."

"Yeah, it is. And your answer?" With a grin, Brett reached for my hand.

"How can we make a commitment at this point? The girl's attitude needs adjustment, and her manners are atrocious. And while I feel for her, I just don't know."

The smile fell from Brett's face, and he let go of my hand. "So, what's your plan?"

"I'll call Evelyn to get her side of the story and see how she feels about things. The woman is in her eighties. Is she strong enough to handle all this teenage drama?"

Brett pursed his lips. "And the grief. The kid's tough-girl act could be just a façade."

"Could be. I hope you're right. But right now, she's as prickly as a cactus. Losing both parents and then learning the family secret, well, it's a lot for anyone."

"Sure is. You know I always wanted a family. It didn't work out for us. Maybe it isn't too late?"

Tears welled, and I jumped to my feet and grabbed a handful of tissues from the box on the kitchen counter. Dabbing my eyes, I returned to Brett and bent to hug him. "Oh, honey, you're such a good man. But I'm not sure. Neither of us are spring chickens. Good thing I'm meeting Jane for lunch. I need her advice. And your help."

Brett pulled me onto his lap, and there we sat for a time, contemplating our long-ago losses.

"Hope I'm not interrupting anything, Granny." Stephanie slouched against the doorway, hair in tangles, wearing my tailored pajamas. They would need laundering too.

I stood and beckoned for the girl to follow. "Come with me."

Entering my room, Stephanie glanced around and sniffed. "Is that your perfume I smell? What is it?"

"Arpège. I've worn it for years. Do you like it?"

The girl shrugged. "It's not as nice as Love's Baby Soft."

"I wouldn't know. Now, let's find you something to wear."

Stephanie entered my closet and spun in a circle, mouth agape. "Wow! And I thought my mom had a lot of clothes."

I waved at the hanging garments. "You're as tall as I am, so the pants should fit. Select an outfit to wear while your clothes are in the wash."

"Don't you have any jeans?"

"I do, but they're reserved for me." Judging by the look on Stephanie's face as she worked her way through the closet, she didn't appreciate my wardrobe. "Here. I'll find you something. It's not a lifetime commitment. You'll only wear it a few hours." I handed her a pair of black slacks and a flowered blouse.

The girl grumbled but took them from me. We proceeded to the guest bath, where I issued her marching orders. "Get you in the tub. When you're done, gather up your laundry—bed linens, traveling clothes, the whole shootin' match, and Brett will show you the laundry room and fix you something to eat. I'm having lunch with Jane, so I'll be out for a while."

Stephanie frowned. "You remind me of Judy Benjamin's drill sergeant."

"Who's that?"

"Judy Benjamin, you know, Goldie Hawn."

"You mean the dancer from *Laugh-In*?" I asked.

"What's *Laugh-In*?"

"I'll chalk up that remark to the generation gap."

Stephanie shrugged. "Whatever. Anything else, Sarge?"

"Yes. Wipe out the tub after you've finished."

The girl's mouth opened, and I waited for another smart remark, but she wisely said nothing. As Stephanie turned on the tap and added lavender bath salts, I headed back to my room to call Evelyn and get ready, hoping the girl wouldn't be too hard on my dear husband.

Chapter Four

STEPHANIE DOES LAUNDRY

After wiping out the tub as ordered, I dressed in Lauren's flowing silk trousers and the brightly colored flowered blouse, feeling like I was playing dress up. I gathered the enormous heap of soiled clothes and linens and lugged everything into the kitchen, hoping to find Brett.

"Lauren said you'd show me where to wash these."

Brett looked up from reading the paper and smiled. "Ya got quite the load there. Let me help."

He got up and took the pile from my arms and led me to the laundry room, which was right off the kitchen. "You know the basics?"

I shook my head. "No. I've never had to do laundry."

"That right?" Brett showed me how to separate the clothes, and I wondered if he thought I was a spoiled princess. If he did, he hid it well. I paid attention to everything he showed me because I didn't want to be a burden. Maybe helping around the house would make up for my bad attitude. And maybe I should lose the attitude. If I pissed off Lauren too much, she might kick me out, and then where would I go? The consequences of leaving Boston were really sinking in. How could I survive on my own?

While the first load was washing, Brett gestured to the kitchen. "Let's get you fed. I make a mean omelet."

"That sounds really good. I can make toast. Where's the bread?"

"No need. I got this. Set yourself down."

Brett poured a glass of orange juice for me, and I sat at the table while he cracked eggs. I swiveled in my chair to look out the window and saw a swimming pool sparkling in the sun. Most excellent! Living in this hella cool house could be awesome. I'd have to look for the right time to ask.

A few minutes later, Brett brought me a plate loaded with food. As the aroma hit my nose, my stomach growled, and I grabbed my fork. The cheese omelet tasted pretty delish. Brett tried to make small talk, but it was lame. He was all about school and asked about a zillion questions, like he was trying to get inside my head. No one was getting inside there. Even I could barely stand to be there.

I did my best to avoid answering Brett's questions without appearing rude and secretive, but the way he scoped me out—even with one eye—told me he was onto me. After I swallowed the last yummy bite of toast loaded with strawberry jam, I cleared my plate and followed Brett back to the laundry room. He explained the settings on the dryer, and I loaded it with my clean stuff, then piled the bedding into the washer.

My mind kept returning to the last time I saw Mom, the day she left for Belize with that creep Doyle. She looked real happy, and I hoped she had enjoyed her vacation, at least until she drowned. The reality struck me all over again, and my eyes burned with tears. I was an orphan! And my whole life was based on Evelyn Cabot Babcock's lies. When I thought about how my mother died without knowing the truth, I wanted to throttle old granny. But I also never wanted to see her again.

Brett noticed I was having a hard time. He sat me down at the kitchen table and brought me a box of tissues. "Maybe what you need is a good cry." He was right. I cried. I howled. And through it all, he sat beside me, patting my shoulder. Finally, I ran out of tears. "Can I go back to bed?"

"Sure you can. Let's get some clean sheets." Brett opened a closet in the hallway outside my room and grabbed fresh linens. He helped me make the bed, then drew the blinds. "You come get me if ya need anything."

"Okay. And thanks for breakfast and for showing me how to do laundry."

"You're welcome. Get some rest." He closed the door behind him.

I pulled the covers up to my chin, feeling like a little kid. When would Lauren get home? I bet she and Jane were talking about how to get rid of me, but they'd have to drag me kicking and screaming back to Boston. For the first time since my mom died, I said a prayer, asking God to convince my real grandmother to take a chance on me. If I couldn't stay with her, I didn't know what would happen to me. A frigging orphan with no money.

Chapter Five

LAUREN- LADIES WHO LUNCH

When I strolled into Kerbey Lane at twelve minutes past noon, I made a note never to be late to lunch with a pregnant woman. Apparently, Jane had already polished off a full order of pita and hummus. I said nothing, although I did raise an eyebrow—force of habit. Glad that Jane had snagged a table in a quiet alcove, I settled across from her.

"Where's Stephanie? I thought you might bring her."

"Fat chance of that."

"Where *is* the urchin?" Jane grinned.

"We really have to stop calling her that or it's gonna stick. Still sitting in the tub, I hope. She made an appearance at eleven, and I sent her to take a bath. She needs a good long soak to remove all that road grime. Do they still have finishing schools? I may need to enroll her."

"So, she's staying with you? How long?"

I adjusted my silver bangles and grimaced. "I don't know. Still in the information-gathering phase. Darling Brett is on duty while we lunch. He promised to make Stephanie something to eat once she was clean and to show her how to do laundry. I had to leave. You know how I feel about household chores."

Jane smirked. "Indeed, I do."

The waitress brought ice water and deployed her order pad. "Name's Star. What can I get you?"

"Cobb salad and Red Zinger iced tea, please," Jane said.

I chose the fish tacos, one of my favorite dishes, as well as the refreshing drink.

"Be right back with your tea."

Jane drained her ice water, gulping as if she were dying of thirst.

"Go slow, there. You'll be running to the bathroom every five minutes."

"Don't I know it! The baby's favorite resting place is on my bladder."

Star zoomed back to the table, dropped off two Red Zingers, and left in a flash.

I leaned forward and asked, "How can I help Stephanie?"

Jane stirred her tea. "That's a big question. I need to know more about her situation."

"Of course. I called Evelyn this morning, and she's a mess. Her health isn't the best—early stages of heart failure, so there's no chance of her flying out here. She confided the girl seems out of control and has poor grades when she used to be an 'A' student, that sort of thing."

"What a shame! It's no surprise she's acting out when she's lost so much. But running away—that's extreme. Take it from one who knows. Something has broken."

The waitress approached with our food. "May I have some extra blue cheese dressing?" Jane asked.

"Sure thing." Star glanced at Jane's belly and smiled as she left us.

Jane's shoulders drooped. "These last months of pregnancy are exhausting. I'm either eating, sleeping, or wanting to sleep. And I think he or she is leaching my brain."

Patting Jane's hand, I reassured her. "I doubt that very much."

Star returned with two containers of dressing. "Anything else, ladies?"

"Nothing for me. You good, Jane?"

Because her mouth was full of Cobb salad, Jane could only nod. After the waitress left, I dug into my fish taco.

We ate in silence for several minutes. With half my meal uneaten, I pushed my plate away and tucked a stray curl behind my ear. "Evelyn has so many regrets about the way she handled Barbara's adoption. She justified her actions by saying adoptions were kept a deep, dark secret back in the day because it was thought a child couldn't handle the truth. But I do wonder if *she* was the one who couldn't handle the truth."

Jane gave her fork a rest and said, "That could well be the case."

I nodded. "Giving Evelyn the benefit of the doubt, maybe she thought she was doing the right thing. As for me, I never wanted to be a part of the baby's life or even think about her. Now that decision is eating away at me, especially given Stephanie's reaction to learning about her mother's adoption. What do you think?"

Glancing around the restaurant, Jane murmured, "Let's do this privately." She jerked her head toward the adjacent table populated by three women, who were paying more attention to us than their food. "Can you come to my place tomorrow?"

"Sure. But we can take time for some cobbler and Blue Bell, can't we?" I asked.

"Try to stop me!"

"I wouldn't dare."

After I left the restaurant, I stopped by Cornucopia for a few hours. There were bills to pay, payroll to approve, stock to order, and phone calls to return. My mind circled back to the Stephanie dilemma, and I found it hard to focus, so the routine tasks consumed more time than usual. Once I completed everything on my list, I checked in with the day manager, Jolie, telling her I wouldn't be in that week as much as usual.

She didn't ask for a reason, not that I'd let on about my personal drama. Jolie adjusted her horn-rimmed glasses and nodded. "I've got it covered. If I need anything, I'll call."

I smiled. "I have every confidence."

Driving home, I wondered how Brett and Stephanie had fared. As I entered the house, Frank Sinatra's crooning "Embraceable You" greeted me. I took it as a positive sign. When Brett and I married, he added his extensive record collection to mine, and Old Blue Eyes often serenaded us.

Brett poked his head out of the kitchen. "Thought I heard you. We're starting dinner. Making a stir fry."

Surprised but pleased, I joined them. Stephanie wore acid-washed jeans, the kind all the kids wore these days, and a T-shirt emblazoned "Ramones," as she chopped vegetables. When she turned to the sink, the back of the shirt read "I wanna be sedated," and I almost dropped my teeth.

Much to my surprise, I channeled the strict parent residing somewhere in my soul. "What does it say on the back of your shirt, young lady?"

Stephanie stopped chopping and frowned, hand on her hip. "Don't have a cow, Granny! It's a song title."

"Tomorrow we're going to buy you some new clothes."

Without a word, the girl dropped the knife and stalked out of the room, shooting me a glare that could melt glass.

Chapter Six

STEPHANIE - IT'S JUST A T-SHIRT

New clothes? That should've been a treat, but it sounded like a threat. Without Lauren asking me, I rushed to my room to change. I should have known Granny wouldn't appreciate the Ramones, probably didn't even know who they were. But pissing her off was the wrong move, and I needed to play nice until I could figure out my future.

When I got back to the kitchen, real granny and Brett stopped talking and got busy bringing the food to the table. I knew they'd been discussing me. The aroma of the stir fry made my mouth water and my stomach grumble. Feed me!

Lauren used her chopsticks to push the food around her plate, barely eating. Brett was quiet. Maybe he was all talked out. After I had enough of the silence, I blurted out, "Can I live here? With you? Please?"

I hadn't planned to ask. It just came pouring out. "Boston is the pits. I hate it there. All the snooty kids at my prep school make me feel like a reject. Besides, Granny Babcock isn't even my real relative. You are."

Lauren's face froze in shock. She reached for Brett's hand and squeezed it so hard he winced.

"Stephanie, I don't know at this point. I'm willing to consider it, but there's a lot I need to know before I make a decision."

"Like what?"

"Like everything. How are you dealing with the loss of your parents? What is your relationship with Evelyn like? What about school? What do you want to be when you grow up? I could go on, but you get the picture." Lauren reached for my hand and patted it. "We don't even know each other. That's on me. Also, I think you need to work with a therapist."

"Get my head shrunk, lie on a couch, spill my life story to some old creep? No thanks. I'm doing fine."

"Brett told me you had a bit of a breakdown today."

My eyes burned. I didn't want to cry again, but I really missed my mom, even if she had been more worried about her love life than me. Once again, it hit me. I was an orphan. And so confused about my life. "So what?"

Lauren shook her head. "Oh, you're entitled to a breakdown or two or three, what with life has thrown at you. We're here to help."

"We? Who's we?"

"I'm here for you, and so is Brett."

"What about that pregnant one?"

"Jane is a therapist, but she's working with me." Lauren pushed her plate away and glanced at Brett as if she needed help.

"You? Why do you need therapy?"

"It's not therapy, per se."

I grabbed the last egg roll and took a bite. "Then what do you call it?"

Frowning a little, Lauren searched for words. Her nervousness surprised me. "It's-it's like chatting with a friend, seeking advice, I guess you could call it."

Before answering, I swallowed the food. "I could do that. Chat and seek. Maybe it could help." If I wanted to stay, it was smart to be agreeable.

Lauren nodded. "I'm glad to hear you're willing to see someone."

"Can I ask something else?"

"Sure."

"Who is my real grandfather?" I looked over at Brett. "Is it you?"

The stunned look on his face told me it wasn't him. I hoped my asking didn't piss him off too.

Lauren dropped her chopsticks. Then she cleared her throat and said, "We'll talk later. After dinner."

Brett rose to his feet, looking like he wanted to run out of the room. "Sounds like girl-talk to me."

"Sorry, Brett. I didn't mean to upset you," I said.

"No worries, kiddo. Takes more'n that to get me riled. And just so you know, there ain't no secrets between me and my lovely wife." He smiled, but I still wondered if I'd made him hate me.

Lauren tutted. "He's fine. With our history, Brett can take anything you throw at him and then some."

That made me feel a little better.

Brett said, "I'll clean up while you two chat. Stephanie, do ya want some ice cream? I can bring it to the office."

I was really starting to like this guy, who was so different from my fake grandfather Clark. "What kind?"

"Chocolate chip."

"Sounds good. Three scoops, please."

Lauren rose and said, "None for me, darling. Come on, Stephanie."

I trailed her down the hall, expecting the truth for once in my life. In her office, we sat across from each other in those pretty pink leather chairs.

"You called this meeting, so go ahead and ask me anything." Lauren clenched her hands in her lap, but I could see they were trembling.

Strangely calm, I spit out the first question that came to mind. "How old were you when you had my mom?"

Lauren took a moment to answer. "I'd just turned seventeen."

"Wow! I'll be seventeen next year, and I haven't even...you know." My cheeks burned.

Lauren's eyes narrowed. Did she think I was lying? "Good on you."

"How did it happen?" At once, I realized how stupid I sounded. "I mean, I know how it happened, but where were your parents and who was the guy?"

Lauren's leg jiggled up jand down. She looked like she was about to explode. I waited quietly, though I was dying to hear the whole story.

"When I was sixteen, I lived with your Great Aunt Imogene in Manhattan, and if you know anything about her, you can imagine I wasn't heavily supervised. I fell in love with a photographer, Alain. We had an affair, and

I got pregnant. He was French and returned to fight in the Resistance in World War II."

Goosebumps rose on my arms, and I jumped to my feet. I was legit part French! Lauren gave me just the basics, but I wanted the deets. All the juicy stuff. If only I could tell my best friend Allison about this, but it was better to leave Boston and everything there behind me.

"So my grandfather—and your sperm donor—was French? That's rad!"

"Stephanie! How crude! Sadly, Alain went back to France without even knowing I was having his child."

"Oh! What do you think he would have done if he knew?"

"I have no way of knowing. Of course, I hoped he would have stayed with me, but that didn't happen."

Excited by the awesome drama, I paced in front of Lauren. "Imagine if he had stayed, and you raised my mom. Think about it. If you had, I'd have had you as my granny from the get-go. How awesome!"

Lauren's face fell. "Don't romanticize this! After Alain left, I never considered keeping the baby because I couldn't cope with raising a child at my age—and alone. Imogene swore my mother would never know, but Clark, your grandfather—"

"Not my grandfather, just plain Clark."

Lauren's eyebrows climbed her forehead, but she continued, "—wrote to my mother about the adoption. I'll never understand why." She grabbed a few tissues from the side table and patted her eyes.

"That's crazy, but I can see Clark doing that. Then what happened?"

Lauren took a deep breath and grabbed her necklace with all the little animals on it. When she spoke, her voice shook. "To my amazement, Mama, who wasn't much for traveling and never visited her hometown, showed up unannounced and confronted me." She glanced away. "It was two months after the birth, and I hadn't bounced back, just languished in bed, feeling sorry for myself."

"What did your mother say?"

"She told me if she had known about the pregnancy, she would have sent me to a home for unwed mothers because she didn't want my younger brothers to know." Lauren shivered. "And I had feared she would have made me raise the baby at home and live with the shame. Neither alternative was something I could live with. I knew then I'd done the right thing for me and the baby. Then she insisted I return with her to the ranch."

"So, did you go back?" I asked.

Lauren shook her head. "I refused. That was one of the worst days of my life. After that, our relationship was never the same."

Even though my questions were bugging her, I had more, many more. "What did you do after your mother went home?"

Lauren's mood did a one-eighty. "I got up out of bed and started living again. Now, that's the end of that chapter." She sat up straight and clapped her hands.

I'd better watch my step if I wanted to live with her, but I had to know my grandfather's fate. "Did you ever see Alain again?"

"No. End of story."

Obviously, I better cool it before she got mad at me.

"Sit down, Stephanie. I'm getting a crick in my neck, looking up. I have questions too. Tell me about your childhood."

I sank into the pink chair. "Well, things were pretty good until my dad got sick. Mom and Dad made sure I had everything a kid could want: the best clothes, the best schools, the best summer camps. We were happy, and my parents always made me feel loved. And they loved each other too." I felt tears coming on and changed the subject. "Say, you said you moved to Manhattan when you were sixteen. What was *your* childhood like? What's that about a ranch?"

Lauren sighed. "Didn't the stable of Babcock attorneys fill you in on my history?"

"Nope. They gave me your name and address. That was it. Besides, I want to hear it from you, especially how your parents let you leave home to go to Manhattan." I took off my boots and curled up in the chair.

"Are you deliberately changing the subject? We *will* return to your upbringing, but for now, I'll indulge you. I was raised on my family's cattle ranch near a little town called Mineral Wells. It's not too far from Dallas. And yes, they had mineral wells."

"Okay. So, you're a farmer?"

Lauren made a shooing motion and snorted. "Rancher. But obviously, not any longer."

Brett knocked and poked his head in the door, holding a bowl heaped with chocolate chip ice cream. "Didn't hear any yellin'. Is it safe to come in?"

The tension disappeared. Lauren even chuckled. "I guarantee your safety, darling."

I took the bowl and dug in. With my mouth full of delicious creaminess, I said, "Thanks, Brett."

"You're welcome, kiddo." He left, closing the door softly.

Lauren stared at me as if I was a bug under a microscope, but she resumed her story. "My early years on the ranch were wonderful. I had two older and two younger brothers, and I was the apple of my daddy's eye. I did chores, rode horses, fed the chickens until I got too old for that. Then I was indoors—unwillingly—to learn what I called 'woman's work.' Never did care for it, although I didn't mind baking."

Somehow, I couldn't picture Lauren in an apron, whipping up a cake. While she talked, I scooped the ice cream into my mouth so fast, I got brain freeze and had to stop for a minute.

Lauren tucked a curl behind her ear. "As a child, I did butt heads with my mother, Rose. She left home at nineteen to marry my father, whom she met when his ship landed in New York, returning from World War I. She loved the rural life and never looked back. I, on the other hand, was determined not to end up as a ranch wife in Palo Pinto County. After I spent some time in Manhattan with Imogene, the summer I turned fourteen, I got the idea of escaping that fate. Two years later, I got my wish. I was discovered by a modeling agent and moved to Manhattan for training. You know how that turned out. You wouldn't be here if I hadn't left home."

I sat there listening to every word, fascinated, trying to picture her life. But after the emotional day and the yummy ice cream, my eyes started to close. Then I yawned so big, my jaw popped.

Lauren picked up on that fast. "Get you to bed. Remember tomorrow I'm taking you shopping for some new clothes."

"But I don't have any money."

"You won't need it, dear."

She left the room with my empty ice cream bowl, and I had to pinch myself. She called me "dear."

In my room, I changed into fresh pajamas and slid under the covers, holding onto her words.

Did Lauren actually like me? I fell asleep imagining life with her.

Chapter Seven

LAUREN UNDER PRESSURE

As I rinsed out the ice cream bowl in the kitchen sink, my bones fairly melted with exhaustion. Brett stopped composing his shopping list to kiss me. "You sure do look beat, sugar. Why don't you draw a bath while I finish up here?"

"Honey, I'm going to take a speed shower and turn in. Come talk to me?"

His brow creased with concern. "Be there in a few."

After showering, I drew the silk nightgown over my head and reached for my special night cream. Assessing myself in the mirror, I had to admit, I looked ten years older than I did two days ago. Pretty soon, no one would have a problem believing I was a grandmother. A good night's sleep should help. My lips twitched as I held in laughter. Years of making a living from my looks had forged some indelible habits, and old habits die hard. Didn't someone once say something like, "Woman, thy name is vanity?" Whoever he was, he was right.

Brett strode into the bedroom just as I finished reading my daily meditation. He settled his bulk beside me, drew me close and said, "Tell me."

I sighed from the bottom of my feet. "You know how Jane likes to say I have a 'patented veneer of cool?' Well, if I ever had such a thing, it's long gone. That child is a trial by fire."

"Sure has been lively around here since she arrived."

"Is that all you got to say?" I extricated myself from his embrace and looked him in the eye. "You stole my cool, didn't you?"

Brett chuckled and dragged me to him for an ardent kiss, which made me forget the stress for a few blissful moments.

When I arrived at Jane's the following morning, I steeled myself for the onslaught of Delilah, Jane's young cat. Leaving my silk clothes at home, I dressed in jeans, one of only two pairs I owned and not to be shared with Stephanie, a floral peplum blouse—I'd always been fond of peplums—and the red cowboy boots Jane had insisted I wear at my second wedding to Brett two months ago.

Jane opened the door, and to my surprise, Delilah remained seated right beside her. Nice to see the kitten had developed some self-control. I stepped inside and said, "I didn't see your shingle."

"My shingle is but a dream at this point. Follow me to the sun porch." Jane led the way, trailed by Delilah.

The glass-enclosed room overlooking the Pennybacker Bridge and Lake Austin served as Jane's office. I admired the view, which never disappointed. The crepe myrtles were on the cusp of bursting into bloom, and although the redbuds had lost their flowers, the yellow retama glowed in the sun.

I settled on the loveseat and exhaled, releasing but a fraction of my pent-up tension. "I gotta say, your office sure beats the heck out of my dungeon at Cornucopia."

Sinking into her usual chair, Jane pulled up an ottoman and elevated her feet. The kitten curled up in a splash of sunlight and closed her eyes. "What was all that business yesterday about rethinking your decision not to be involved with Barbara's life? Talk to me."

My mouth dried, and I gulped. "I'm aware the past is done, but regrets are forever. At least she had a loving husband and a child. Now, I think I'd have liked to meet her. Never thought I would, but now that I have Stephanie in my life, I'm sad about not reaching out."

Jane pursed her lips. "You're right; your decision all those years ago is set in stone. But you're just going to have to live with it. You understand that. What's really going on?"

"Evelyn called yesterday afternoon. I was rather taken aback she didn't demand that the girl return to Boston."

"Really?" Jane's forehead furrowed. "I wonder why."

"Evelyn said her cardiologist has recommended that she avoid stress. I'm guessing she means Stephanie."

"Oh! What are your options? Does the girl have any family on her father's side?"

I shook my head. "No. She has no one. Her father didn't have any family, so it looks like it will be up to me. And Brett."

"Are you up for this?" Jane cradled her belly, perhaps thinking about her soon-to-be- born child.

"I'm not sure. In fact, Brett seems more inclined than me, if you can believe it. Stephanie has issues. She's got walls. She acts tough, but I'm not buying her act. Her emotions change minute by minute. She's had several crying episodes already."

Jane frowned. "Isn't that to be expected?"

"Of course it is. But I do think she needs to talk to a professional." I reached for a tissue and found my palms were damp. So much for my cool.

"That might be a good idea. If she's willing, I can recommend a great therapist who works with adolescents."

"You won't see her?"

"Lauren, I can't. It would be a conflict of interest."

I stood and walked to the window, admiring the view, but really wanting to hide my face from Jane's scrutiny. "I guess I knew that. Who do you have in mind?"

"There's an intern in Joshua's office. She's young and might be someone Stephanie could relate to. Let me know when you're ready."

"All right."

I returned to the loveseat and sat. My heart raced. Did I want the girl to stay? Could I handle it?

Jane's raised voice broke through my reverie. "Earth to Lauren. Are you all right? You looked like you were in a trance for a minute there."

"Guess I was." I clamped my lips shut before I revealed too much.

"Care to share? After all, isn't that why you're here?"

Figuring I couldn't slip anything past Jane, I nodded. "The reality just hit me of what raising this girl would mean to me and Brett. She's had sixteen years of life experience I missed. And so much loss." My eyes stung with tears and that wouldn't do. "I'm out of my depth here."

"I get it." Jane leaned forward as much as her pregnant belly would allow. "I'm in the same boat," she said.

"Yes, but you're starting from scratch, and I've got a teenager loaded with baggage."

My friend studied me. "True. However, given your resilience and success in life, I'd put my money on you."

"You flatter me." Heat rose in my face, and I figured it was time to exit before I got more in the weeds.

Jane held up her hand like a traffic cop. "Before you leave, I have to ask if you've checked in with your sponsor."

I grimaced. "Um, no."

"And why not?"

"I didn't want to burden her." As I admitted to myself I'd neglected Helen, my lips quivered. "Helen wasn't feeling up to attending my party. God, was that only two days ago?"

Jane harrumphed and fairly sputtered, "You of all people know the value of a sponsor. You can't count our talks as a substitute for working the steps over this."

Coming from the young woman I'd sponsored for almost ten years, that comment stung. The student had become the master.

"All right, all right. I do need to call her and check in." With a great sigh, I picked up my bag and prepared to leave. "You won't believe this, but I promised to take Stephanie shopping. Better head out."

"Shopping? That oughta be a trip."

"I have no doubt. Say, did you send the kitten to charm school? Her behavior is much improved."

"She has calmed down considerably. But no schooling needed—just time."

"Wonder if that will work with the urchin—I mean Stephanie."

Jane lurched to her feet. "Oof! Time heals. We both know that."

I had to agree.

"How did you leave things with Evelyn?"

"I told her we're going to visit her—that is, if I can get Stephanie's cooperation."

"Wow! Have you ever been to Boston?"

"No, but if you'll remember, I'm familiar enough with big cities in the Northeast. I might be out of pocket for the next few days with the Stephanie show." I headed to the door. "Wish me luck at the mall."

Jane picked up the kitten and walked me to the front door. "You'll get through it. Do you think you'll be able to find the mall?"

I gave Jane a sideways look. "I do."

"Take care. Remember, you have great instincts and a wonderful man to support you."

After hugging my friend, I opened the door. "Well, you're right about Brett. As for my teen-wrangling skills, we'll see. As we say in AA, more will be revealed."

On the drive home, I girded myself for the outing. Right on time, I pulled in the drive and beeped the horn. Stephanie clomped out of the house in those ugly black boots. She hopped in my car and said, "These wheels are ultra! I've never been in a Mercedes convertible."

"Seat belt."

"Yes, Sarge!"

I glared at the girl. "That little joke is just about wore out."

As we drove to Barton Creek Mall, I dreaded this adventure, but Stephanie bubbled over with enthusiasm, such a change from the sullen and volatile child of the past two days. "I can't wait to see if they have Buckle! They probably have The Limited and Contempo Casuals—at least I hope so. Do you know?"

"No idea. We'll find out soon enough."

"No more preppie clothes for me. My fake granny was so uptight and bought me the deadliest clothes. You seem like you're more with it."

Keeping my eyes on the road, I laughed. "Flattery? You may select your clothes—within reason."

"Cool!" Stephanie bounced in her seat and pointed. "Hey, there's a spot near the entrance. Princess parking."

As I pulled into the parking slot, I said a little prayer for a drama-free outing. "Help me get the top up."

Inside the mall, Stephanie raced ahead to the directory and squealed with delight. "Buckle first! It's on the second level."

"I'll be walking, not running. Remember, I have the credit card." I caught up with the girl in the place called Buckle, which obviously catered to teens. She ignored me as she rummaged through the racks. When her arms were full, she acknowledged me and said, "I need to try these on."

I noticed Stephanie had chosen mostly long-sleeved tops even though we were headed into an Austin summer. "Are you aware that soon we'll have months of scorching temperatures? You'll melt in long sleeves."

Stephanie shrugged and charged toward the fitting rooms.

The same scenario played out in four more stores. After leaving The Limited, I dropped onto a bench outside yet another neon-signed shop. "Just let me rest for a minute. Pile up the bags next to me."

"Can I run into Esprit real fast?"

With great forbearance, I dug in my purse. "Why not? Here's my card if you buy anything else."

Stephanie grinned and took the charge card. "I'll be quick."

"Take your time." I leaned back, plotting how to announce the Boston trip.

Twenty minutes later, Stephanie returned with the credit card and more purchases.

"Are you sure you're done? I think there may be one or two stores you've missed."

"No, I'm good."

When we arrived home, Stephanie rushed to her room with her booty. I called after her, "I'll be in shortly for the fashion show."

Tantalizing aromas came from the kitchen, and I followed my nose there. Brett closed the oven door and turned to me. "The lasagna will be ready in about thirty minutes. How'd it go at the mall?"

I stood on my tiptoes to kiss his cheek. "Stephanie has made us much poorer, but she enjoyed the outing. It was nice to see a different side to her—gone was the insolence."

"That's good. Hope she likes Italian food."

"I'll look in on her. Can't wait to see what she bought. Be back in a bit."

As I knocked on Stephanie's door, I reminded myself not to be judgmental about her choices. I knew self-expression was important to teenagers.

"Come in."

I stared at the empty bags and tissue wrappings covering the floor. Garish clothing topped the bed. Stephanie stood in front of the mirror dressed in leggings, leg warmers, and a gigantic sweatshirt that fell off her shoulder. Her updo was crowned with a lace hair tie finished in a bow. She looked like a pop star, one of those current favorites of the young people.

My eyebrows rose. "And where would you wear that getup?"

"School, the mall, anywhere really. Don't you like it?"

"Hmm, I think I saw that fashion statement in a movie poster a while back."

"Yeah, *Flashdance*. My mom took me to see it." And with that, Stephanie's lip quivered, then she began to sob. She dropped to the floor and wailed.

I knelt beside her and awkwardly cradled the child's head in my lap. Because I'd never done anything like that before, it felt unnatural. The girl continued to sob, then gradually calmed until there was only an occasional hitching of her chest. "I can't imagine how you feel. Know that I'm here for you, dear. I'll do the best I can to help you carry on."

Stephanie mumbled, "Thanks, gran-Lauren. Sometimes it hits me like a tidal wave, realizing she's gone. And I didn't even get to say goodbye."

Searching for something to say, I finally found common ground. Loss. "Although I did get a chance to say goodbye to my mother, I told you we were estranged for years. All that lost time haunts me. I could give you the standard lines about grief, but words are small comfort. Grief is a journey, sometimes a very long one. But you won't have to do it alone."

She sat up and wiped her tear-stained face with her sleeve.

"Brett will have dinner ready in a few minutes. Do you like lasagna?"

A faint smile brightened Stephanie's face. "I love it."

"Brett will be happy to hear that. It's his specialty. You do look cute in that outfit. Why don't you get up and show me what else you bought? I love a fashion show."

Stephanie untangled herself and pulled the sweatshirt over her head.

I gasped. "What are those marks on your upper arms?" Alarm bells rang. Recently, a young woman newcomer to AA had shared about her cutting habit. She had been quite frank about the practice, which, until that day, was unknown to me.

The girl lowered her arms, turned her back, and pulled on a long-sleeved top. She turned back to me with a red face. "I can explain. You'll find out anyway."

I got to my feet. "I have an idea what you're going to say."

Stephanie bit her lip, her eyes darting around the room, then she began to speak. "After my dad died, I felt totally numb. Like a zombie. I was only eleven, and Mom was out of it. At first, my friends at school were nice, then they avoided me like I had some disease. I started digging my nails into the underside of my upper arms. The pain let me know I could still feel. And it took my mind off my misery. When I had my physical for summer camp, the doctor ratted me out." She shrugged. "I had to go to therapy, a child psychologist. And I quit doing it."

"I see. Why haven't those marks faded?"

With a bowed head, she answered. "I-I started again when my mom died."

"That's why they're so red. They're fresh."

Stephanie nodded. With tears dripping off her face, she said, "Now you won't let me stay here."

"I said no such thing. But I won't lie. This is cause for concern. And you didn't mention that you'd had therapy in the past."

The girl hung her head. "No, I didn't. I'm sorry." She looked up, and her gaze bore into me. "Will you let me stay?"

"That is yet to be determined. But let me assure you, I know a little bit about self-harm. It takes many forms."

"What do you mean?" The girl plucked some tissue from a box on the nightstand and sank onto the bed.

I sat beside her. "I drank at my problems. You're aware I'm in AA. Haven't had a drink in over twenty-five years. I fully understand seeking to change the way you feel."

Stephanie sniffled and blew her nose. "When will you decide if I can stay? Is it okay with Brett? I think he likes me."

"Before we decide, there's something we have to do."

"What? I'll do anything you say."

"You and I and Brett are going to Boston. I have to meet with Evelyn, get your school records, and see the Babcock attorneys. And now, your therapist."

The girl jumped to her feet. "No way! I never want to see that place again." She folded her arms across her chest and scowled.

"This isn't a negotiation. I'll make arrangements for next week. And I want you to start seeing a therapist here. Jane's husband is a psychiatrist and recommends someone in his office. I'll set up an appointment when we get back from Boston."

Stephanie deflated. "Okay, you win. But I hope it's a short trip. And I hope the therapist is better than the old cow I saw in Boston."

"Jane tells me the therapist is young," I said.

The girl's face brightened. "Cool." She picked up the discarded bags and tissue wrapping from the floor. "I'm starving. Is dinner ready yet?"

"Why don't you change those leggings for jeans? Then join us." I closed the door and headed to the kitchen.

Brett's smile faded as he studied my face. I shook my head and whispered, "We'll talk after dinner." Stephanie trudged into the room a moment later. I guess he picked up on the tension that clung to us like an invisible shroud. "I was just about to go lookin' for y'all. Everything is set out on the patio. Let's eat!"

We settled at the table and filled our plates. Dinner began in silence. Brett cast a questioning look my way, and I shrugged.

Stephanie stuffed half a buttered roll into her mouth and licked her fingers.

Resolutely ignoring her bad manners, I dug into the pasta, promising myself we'd work on etiquette at a more opportune time.

I dabbed my lips. "Brett, honey, this lasagna is delicious."

"Thank you, ma'am. How do ya like it, Stephanie?"

With her mouth full of food, the girl replied. "I haven't had such good Italian food in a long time. It's super delish."

Brett beamed. "Thanks, sweetie."

A moment later, Stephanie dropped her fork and groaned. "My-my dad used to make this." Her face twisted with grief, and she pushed back from the table and fled.

Brett glanced at me. "That child's mood changes faster than Texas weather."

"Second meltdown of the day, and you don't know the half of it. She's into self-harm. Gouges her upper arms. She started after her father died, had some therapy and stopped, but now she's at it again."

"What the hey?" Brett's face contorted with disbelief.

"This type of self-harm is on the rise in young women and teens. It's called cutting. Mostly, they use razor blades to inflict pain, which makes the sufferer feel something other than dead inside. At least, that's what I understood from the woman who shared in a meeting. From what Stephanie told me, she uses her nails rather than a blade. I must call Jane about this."

"You sure must do. The child needs help. When we're in Boston, we got to find out the whole story."

"I added a visit to her former therapist to the itinerary." I placed my napkin down and stood. "Better check on her."

"Good idea."

At the door to the kitchen, I looked back at Brett. "Are you having second thoughts about Stephanie living with us?"

Brett shook his head. "No, darlin'. If anything, I'm more certain we're meant to help her."

I blew him a kiss and headed to the girl's room, saying a prayer of thanks for my husband.

The guest room door was open, so I walked in. Stephanie lay atop the bedcovers with her back toward me, quietly weeping.

"Do you want to talk?" I asked.

Without a word, Stephanie sat up and patted the bed beside her.

I joined her and waited for her to speak. When she remained silent, I said, "You're hurting, which is understandable. For one so young, you've had too much loss. But if we are to make this work, you have to promise me you're not going to do anything more to harm yourself."

Stephanie straightened her shoulders and nodded. "I promise I won't. You know, until I got here, I hadn't cried in ages. Guess I needed to get those feelings out."

Searching her eyes, the sensation of an electric charge passed between us. A connection was forged between me and this vulnerable child. I decided to believe her. "Yes, you must work through your grief. Crying is to be expected." I grasped her hand and squeezed. "Your hair is a mess. Why don't you run a comb through it and then come finish dinner? Brett went to Sweetish Hill and bought brownies for dessert."

"I love brownies."

I stayed on the bed while Stephanie entered the adjoining bath. She didn't close the door, which I took as a sign of trust. After dabbing her face with a damp washcloth and taming those lush curls into a high ponytail, she approached and held out her hand to me. "Come on. I got my appetite back."

As I took her hand, my heart opened to my granddaughter, but the emotional roller-coaster ride was plumb wearing me out.

Chapter Eight

STEPHANIE'S BRAIN IN OVERDRIVE

When Lauren and I walked out to the patio, Brett lunged out of his seat to pull out Lauren's chair and get her settled at the table. He treated her like a princess. Although he looked intimidating, being so tall and wearing that mysterious eye patch, he was turning out to be a real teddy bear. The way he looked at Lauren reminded me of the way my dad used to look at Mom. Maybe someday, someone would look at me like that.

We finished dinner on the patio next to the beautiful swimming pool. No one talked much, and that was fine with me. I ate my fair share of lasagna without tears and stuffed myself with three brownies. Without being asked, I cleared the dishes and headed to the kitchen. At the door, I looked over my shoulder and saw the two of them chatting away. What were they talking about? I just bet they were plotting how to ditch me in Boston. When I was done loading the dishwasher, I went back outside. They both smiled at me, but the hair on the back of my neck stood up. Should I trust them? Instead of sitting down, I gripped the back of my chair. "Are you going to dump me in Boston?"

"No! I wouldn't do such a thing," Lauren said. "But if I were, I'd tell you right up front, not spring it on you."

"What if my fake granny wants me to stay? What will you do?"

Lauren glanced at Brett, then back at me. "I don't think that will be an issue."

What did that mean? And why was Brett so quiet? I pulled out my chair and sat, staring a hole through them. "How do you know?"

Lauren fiddled with her necklace, a sure sign she was uncomfortable. "I'm not going to talk out of turn. We'll take the trip and deal with whatever comes up."

Obviously, Lauren was hiding something. "Do you hate me because of my problem, you know, with my arms?"

"Of course not. Remember, I've been down the road of self-harm. Recovery is possible with the right support."

Finally, Brett spoke up. "Lauren is right. And believe me, we're going to do everything we can to help you."

Were they telling the truth? I really wanted to believe them, but I'd find out soon enough. "Okay, thanks." Keeping my doubts to myself, I said good night and went to my room, where I took a quick shower and got ready for bed. I picked up the tattered copy of *The Shining* I had found on the bus and read until my eyes got heavy. But when I turned off the reading lamp, my heart hammered, and my head started spinning dreadful previews of the trip to Beantown.

I sure wasn't looking forward to seeing Evelyn the ultimate control freak again. Old fake granny would have a cow when she saw my new clothes. Laughing to myself, I planned to wear my flashiest outfit to Beacon Hill. Just imagining her reaction made me laugh.

How I had hated living in that creaky old mansion with all the rules and all the expectations. Five years living in the hideous, gloomy rooms full of dark brown and red velvet everything was more than enough. The place looked like someone had ralphed pizza chunks all over the floors and walls.

And besides, that was where my dad died.

My day school was awful enough, but when I learned about Evelyn's plan to send me to a boarding school, I freaked out. I heard her on the phone telling her precious attorney that I was becoming "a handful." As if. I kept a low profile at the Babcock palace, talking to the housekeeper Clarice more than Evelyn. Usually, the only time I saw her was at dinner. I wracked my brain for what I'd done to make her say that. The only thing I came up with was a dinner conversation about a week after my mother died. Evelyn delicately picked up her soup spoon, babbling about the upcoming symphony season at Tanglewood, the lamest thing ever. Like I gave a crap about the symphony. When I rolled my eyes and whispered "boring," she told me to leave the table. So, I grabbed my plate and charged upstairs to eat in my room.

I guess that was being a handful.

The next morning, she handed me a pile of brochures from boarding schools all over New England, which made me realize she'd been planning my exile for a while. My blood ran cold as I pictured myself parked at an all-girls school in the Maine woods, snowed in for the winter. Visions from Stephen King novels creeped me out. Beacon Hill, Boston, Massachusetts, and all of New England could bite me. Why were there no brochures for schools somewhere warm?

It was so bogus Lauren was making me go back, right after I escaped. But at least I wouldn't have to set foot in that stupid school. On the bright side, I could bring back some of my stuff if Lauren even let me return to Austin with her and Brett. She had to.

But she was going to read the reports from the wannabe dictators who ran the school and Mrs. Doody, my therapist from four summers ago. When I thought about all those miserable hours spent in the beige, over-heated room with dying houseplants, I started sweating. I hated the cranky old woman and called her Sour-Pickle-Face in my mind. She was about a hundred years old. Mom had explained that SPF would help me process Dad's passing. Process? It made me think of the forbidden Velveeta cheese. I loved Velveeta, and at school always traded my lunch with Allison when she brought a Velveeta sandwich. So how do you process somebody dying? Certainly not by sitting on an oversized itchy wool chair under the beady gaze of SPF.

I bet heinous Mrs. Doody would delight in telling Lauren how I had freaked out when Mom informed me, a month after Dad died, she had to sell our home in Brookline. With tears streaming down her face, Mom shouted, "Don't you realize we can't afford to live here now? I'm not about to run out and get a job. And even if I did, I couldn't afford the mortgage." That shocker had been enough to justify several therapy sessions. I guess Mom was too busy with Junior League, Jazzercise, and her pottery classes to think about getting a job. When it sunk in that we would have to move in with my grandparents, and I'd have to change schools and leave my friends, well, Mrs. Doody really raked in the dough that summer. That's when I started scratching my arms, and Mrs. Doody got rich.

Maybe the old bat was dead by now. I wouldn't shed a tear. Death. It was everywhere. Of course, I knew other kids lost their parents. How did they cope with it? How could I cope with losing two?

My only chance to live with Lauren and Brett was to hold it together on the trip.

Although I wouldn't risk calling my friend Allison when we got to Boston, I wished there was someone my age to talk to. Then I started wondering where I'd go to school in Austin. Would Lauren make me go to a private school with plaid uniforms? No, she was too fashionable for that, wasn't she? Besides, she let me buy whatever clothes I wanted. Would she have forked over all that money if she was going to send me to plaid hell?

My emotions were all over the place. I wanted to remember my mom, but whenever I thought about how she blew me off for her boyfriends, I got pissed. Just thinking about her got my stomach tied up in knots. How could I be sad and mad at the same time?

I didn't think I'd ever fall asleep, but knew I had when I woke up screaming from a nightmare. Evelyn, Mrs. Doody, and the Babcock attorneys chased me up and down the halls of the Overlook Hotel with a huge net and bundles of ropes. With my heart pounding, I sat up, listening and hoping I didn't wake anyone. Not a sound. Good. I settled back in bed and closed my eyes.

Chapter Nine

LAUREN FRETS

Twenty-five years sober, and there I sat at my desk in the backroom of Cornucopia, struggling with the most mundane task of figuring out how many vegetables to order for the week. Once I placed the order with the supplier, I picked up my coffee mug to find the brew had gone cold. Nerves shot, I fussed over the list of instructions for Jolie and the other managers while I was in Boston. Although I'd be absent for only three days, I had never before been unavailable for more than one.

Reflecting on that morning's difficult conversation with Helen, I reached for the phone to call Jane, both to assure her I'd complied with her edict to check in with my sponsor—and to tell her about Stephanie's self-harm.

Jane got right to the point. "What did Helen have to say?"

"She was astounded to learn I had a granddaughter. Weren't we all?"

"Yes, of course. But what did she advise?"

"Prayer, meditation, and meetings. I'm going to see her when we get back from Boston."

"Wonderful! How is she doing?" Jane's voice, filled with concern, reignited my own worry.

"Chemo is taking its toll. Her daughter moved back to Austin, which on one level is good, but it makes me wonder about her prognosis."

"Yes, it doesn't sound encouraging. I've always loved Helen, such a remarkable woman and an inspiration to so many in the program. When I first got to AA, her story touched my heart."

Tears stung my eyes. "Mine too. I owe her so much. She talked me off the ledge a time or two. But there's something else."

"Lay it on me."

I told her about Stephanie's history and current self-harm.

Jane gasped. "This is serious stuff. The girl needs help."

"I know that. We're flying to Boston tomorrow. Evelyn made an appointment for me with Stephanie's therapist from when she first engaged in the behavior—after her father's death. She was only eleven."

"When will you be back?" Jane's strained voice made me wonder if she was going into labor.

"Friday. You sound odd. Are you all right?" I asked.

"Just a little Braxton-Hicks action."

"Are you sure? The doctor didn't change your due date, did she?"

After a few huffs and puffs, Jane answered. "No. Still July 10th. So, six more weeks."

"Hang in there."

"Oof! Dang, that was a sharp one." The line went silent for a few moments. "I will. Do you want me to set up an appointment for Stephanie with Joshua's intern, Jenna? He raves about her, and supposedly she's worked wonders with teenage girls."

I needed wonders worked with Stephanie. "Yes, please. His office isn't far from the co-op, and I plan to bring Stephanie to work with me when we return. Brett has gone over and above and needs a break. The girl's self-harm has thrown him for a loop. And he's been chomping at the bit to get back to his work at the recovery ranch."

Jane chuckled. "I see what you did there."

"What do you mean?" I asked, puzzled.

Jane said, "Chomping at the bit? The ranch, the horses, the residents taking care of them for therapy? That whole thing."

I laughed when I realized what I said. "Unintentional. My sense of humor, as well as my sense of equilibrium, have all but vanished. Must run. There're scads of things to do before our trip."

"Safe travels." Jane hung up before I could answer.

Two hours later, with my work tasks complete, I put my face in my hands and took several deep breaths. How could I be unable to navigate my life at this late stage? I'd been through plenty of tough times through the years, but nothing prepared me to deal with the fragility of another human being, and a damaged one at that. With the clock ticking down to our departure, there was no time for an AA meeting, although I sorely needed one.

That evening, after making sure Stephanie had finished packing, I hurried through my bedtime beauty routine and joined Brett in bed. He tossed his book on the nightstand. "Get over here, you." He sighed and drew me into an embrace. "I'm all packed, and I set the alarm."

"Thanks, darling."

"Tell me again how you and Evelyn are related."

Irritated, I sat up and stared at him. "We're not related at all."

"Well, pardon me. I've slept since ya explained the intricacies of your family tree."

"Sorry for the short fuse, Brett. Guess my nerves are getting the best of me." I lay down and scooted closer to him, putting my head on his shoulder.

Brett kissed my forehead. "You're forgiven. But please refresh my memory. Don't want to step on any toes."

"I hear that. Anyway, Evelyn Cabot married my uncle Clark Babcock. He moved to Boston and joined her family's bank. My mother, Clark's sister, believed he was more enamored with the bank and mansion than Evelyn, but who knows? I only met them once when Imogene arranged for them to adopt the baby."

"Right. The bohemian gal." Brett rumbled.

"Yes, my mother's half-sister. I lived with her in Manhattan when I modeled."

My dear husband yawned. "Got it." He turned off the bedside lamp. "Now, let's get some rest so we can be ready to face the gauntlet tomorrow."

The next morning, the three of us trudged out to the taxi with our luggage. We climbed into the backseat, and Stephanie complained about being crushed in the middle between me and Brett. Not the most auspicious start to the journey. We arrived at Mueller Airport fifteen long minutes later.

Brett paid the cabbie, and the two of them unloaded our suitcases. Stephanie's lower lip protruded in a dramatic pout, which I chose to ignore. "Did you even buy me a return ticket?"

"Of course I did." Flying made me anxious, and I dreaded the long travel day. Stephanie's attitude only made things worse.

The girl muttered under her breath as she put her arms through the straps of her backpack and hefted her small overnight bag.

Brett struggled with our suitcases. Had I overpacked for a two-night trip?

"What ya got in here, Lauren? Gold bars?"

"Like a Girl Scout, I want to be prepared."

"Well, ya dang sure are." Brett's grumbling made me think he didn't enjoy flying either.

After checking our luggage, we proceeded to the gate just as the flight began boarding. Not trusting the airline with my cosmetic case, I carried it onboard. If that bag didn't make the connection, I'd never have time to shop for all the necessities it contained. Better safe than sorry.

Brett and I had aisle seats across from each other, while Stephanie clambered over the empty middle seat in my row and turned her face to the window. She muttered under her breath, "Sure hope this isn't the last time I see Austin."

I rolled my eyes. It seemed no amount of reassurance would quell her fears, and I really couldn't blame her. Loss, grief, and abandonment issues—and the self-harm—made for a stew of anxiety. More will be revealed, I reminded myself. Certain this trip would bring answers, I settled in for the flight, taking deep, centering breaths to calm my nerves.

Brett buried his nose in a John le Carré novel. Stephanie stared out the window, a well-thumbed doorstop of a book titled *Dune* clutched in her hand. Yesterday, Brett had taken her to Goodwill, where she bought a huge armload of books. When I asked about her bounty, she mumbled, "Sci-fi," and hurried to her room with her haul. I vaguely remembered the popularity of the book some two decades earlier. Not my cup of tea.

My thoughts churned, and even if I had brought a book, knew I wouldn't be able to concentrate, so I flipped through a few fashion magazines to pass the time. I hoped our luggage would make the connection in Cincinnati. The thought of losing my carefully curated selections for this trip and the uproar if Stephanie's new clothing vanished occupied my mind. So unlike me to worry. Besides the anxiety around flying, the anticipation and dread about dealing with Evelyn and the Babcock attorneys had stolen my serenity. I fretted all the way to Cincinnati, through the layover, and even in the cab to the hotel.

Brett checked us in, and I pointed out our luggage to the bell hop. After depositing our luggage in our room, the young man pocketed his tip and closed the door. I sank onto the bed and took off my shoes.

Stephanie poked her head in from her adjoining room. "I'm starving!"

"I could eat," Brett said.

"Well, I'm exhausted. Let's order room service." While we waited for our meal, I unpacked.

"What time we meetin' Evelyn?" Brett asked.

With the last of my clothing folded, I walked up to Brett and hugged him. "I was told at the civilized hour of 10:00 a.m., and not a minute before."

Brett chucked. "Should be interesting."

"I'm sure it will be."

Chapter Ten

Stephanie's Take on Things

After our room service dinner, Lauren covered her yawn, and I noticed she'd had her nails done. Nice color, some sort of coral. She said, "Evelyn is expecting us at 10:00. We'll breakfast here, then call a cab."

I frowned. "You want a cab to go three blocks?"

Lauren tilted her head. "Oh, I hadn't realized the hotel was so close to her home."

"Yeah, it'll take like five minutes to get there."

"Then we'll walk. Good night, Stephanie."

Brett said, "Get you some rest and don't you worry about a thing tomorrow."

"Night, granny, oops, I mean Lauren." When she shot me a look of disapproval, I smirked and grasped the doorknob to my room. Being back on Beacon Hill brought out the worst in me. "Good night, Brett."

After I shut the door, I put on my pajamas and got into bed, which was hard as a rock. The linens lay stiff against my skin, not soft like the ones at Lauren's. I doubted I'd sleep anyway.

I picked up *Dune* but didn't open it, instead thinking back to my first flight, one I'd rather forget. After I drank two cans of Dr Pepper, I had to pee really bad, which forced me to crawl over Lauren to get to the tiny bathroom. Someone had peed all over the seat and the floor, and unaware, I'd stepped in it. Gross! I threw a wad of paper towels on the floor and squatted over the toilet to pee. Then, like a contortionist, I stood on one foot, pulled off my Reebok and rinsed it in the tiny sink, then I repeated with the other shoe, only this time I managed to drench the whole thing with water. Good thing it was summer, so it would dry fast. When I told the stewardess about the mess in the toilet, she gave me a dirty look. I shrugged and squished my way back to my seat.

Through two flights and the layover, I had worried myself silly about being dumped, and I barely read ten pages of my favorite book. Dad's favorite too. He had always hoped Hollywood would make a *Dune* movie but didn't live long enough to see it. I had mixed feelings about the flick. While the scenery was like what I imagined, it really blew my mind to see Sting starring as Feyd-Rautha. Just didn't compute. During the movie, I had flashed on Sting singing "Every Breath You Take" during the fight scene. My dad had always believed a book was better than the movie version. He was probably right.

Not feeling the least bit sleepy, I started reading, but like on the plane, I couldn't focus on the words on the page. Didn't my life on earth take priority over life on Arrakis?

I shut the book and turned off the bedside lamp. As I struggled to get comfortable in the hotel bed, I burped. The greasy room service burger and soggy fries sat in my stomach like a brick, a Beacon Hill red brick. I missed Brett's cooking. Funny how quickly I'd gotten used to Lauren's house. It only took a few days for her place to feel like it could be my home too.

I turned the pillow to the cool side and pulled up the covers. As I lay there wide awake, the thought of running away crossed my mind, but where would I go? I couldn't show up at Allison's place unannounced, and even if I did, they'd never let me stay.

Could Evelyn have me arrested and make me live with her against my will? I didn't think it was possible but, with the Babcock attorneys, who knew? Then I remembered she wanted to ship me off to boarding school, and I almost barfed up the burger.

Just being near my old school made me nervous. Remembering how the other kids branded me an outcast made my stomach hurt. Apparently, because Clark Babcock hadn't arrived on Beacon Hill until the 1920s, my family didn't have the same status as the natives. Clark married into the

Cabot family, their bank, and their mansion. I hadn't cared enough to tell the snobs at the day school that Evelyn Cabot Babcock was descended from the original Boston Brahmins. That movie that came out last year, *The Breakfast Club*, didn't come close to showing the torture I went through in high school.

Even though I hadn't explored much of Austin, I wanted to live there. A fresh start would be rad. A new school even better. My gut told me to take my chances with Lauren. And Brett. And I believed in my gut. It hadn't steered me wrong yet.

After what seemed like an hour, I still couldn't relax. I tossed. I turned, practically doing an aerobic workout.

My brain kept throwing up images of the day I got brave enough to leave Boston. Had I overreacted by leaving? No. It was totally my only option. Evelyn, alone now in her dreary digs, with only her staff, doctors, and attorneys for company, probably regretted threatening to send me to boarding school. Too bad. Where had I gotten the nerve to hop on the Greyhound? Once I got on the bus and looked around at the grody looking characters, I figured it would be safer to sit near women with children. I stayed alert and barely slept the entire two-day trip.

When the bus finally arrived at the Austin station, I shadowed a family group for cover on the way into the terminal. On the rack of brochures, I found a free map and scoped out where Zilker Park was. I knew from the super-efficient Babcock attorneys that Lauren Eaton, my real grandmother, lived across Barton Creek Road, at the top of a hill. That meant I had to travel to the other side of the river. With only a few coins in my pocket, I figured out a bus route that would get me close, hoping I'd get there by dark.

A long hour later, most of it spent waiting for a bus, I trudged up the hill to her address. Daylight faded, but there was enough light to see I wasn't in Boston anymore. Not a single cobble or red brick. I climbed the flagstone walkway to the front door of a low, modern stone and glass house. Warm light poured out of the windows, and I saw a bunch of people inside. It looked like a party. Was there food? My mouth watered at the thought of tasty snacks. The door was partially open, and I shoved it the rest of the way. A roomful of people gathered around a dining room table singing "Happy Birthday" to a mahogany-haired woman.

Our eyes locked, and I knew I'd found Lauren Eaton.

After my long trip, I was in a foul mood, and I didn't hold back with the attitude. If I was trying to shock Lauren and her friend Jane, I did a wicked good job. I used the granny line on my real grandmother, and man, that pissed her off royally. Actually, Lauren didn't look like a granny, but the name got under her skin. Even at her age, she was more beautiful than my mother had been. It had to be the nose. I bet Mom got hers from her father's side, and boy, color me happy the nose skipped a generation.

Still awake, I wondered if Lauren had any pictures of Alain. Should I even ask her? Rolling over onto my back, the reality of being back in Beantown had my stomach doing somersaults. Under the covers, I grabbed my upper arms but stopped before I scratched myself, remembering my promise.

Chapter Eleven

Lauren Takes on Boston

As we set out for the short walk to Evelyn's, Stephanie lagged behind, clomping her feet in those dreadful boots. Irritated, I spun to face her. "No matter how slow you walk, we'll still get there. Now get a move on!"

The girl brushed past us, glancing back over her shoulder. "Chill, Granny. Let's get this bogosity over with."

Again with the g-word. I hadn't meant to be so harsh to the girl, but stress was getting the best of me. Grasping Brett's arm, I struggled to keep my balance on the uneven cobbled street in my heels. Mere moments later, he gestured to a three-story, red brick home, indistinguishable from its neighbors except for the address. "This is it."

A uniformed maid escorted us to what she called the receiving room. Bulky red flocked velvet drapes sucked the light from the wood-paneled room. The heavy furniture looked like it came from another century, and it probably did. The ambiance was not unlike Imogene's Manhattan residence, the scene of my disgrace and thus familiar in an unsettling way. I shivered.

Evelyn, hunkered on the sofa, wore a black dress with a high collar, the requisite brooch highlighting her scrawny neck. Her face was made up, but the effect was grotesque, with the pink foundation caked in the lines of grief. Or maybe grumpiness caused those creases. Crooked lipstick made her look a bit clownish.

I swallowed my gasp. The forty-five years since our one and only meeting had erased all traces of the eager adoptive mother.

Brett approached Evelyn with a friendly smile. "Howdy, ma'am."

Glancing up at him, she asked, "How do you do, Mr. Owens?"

"Just fine, ma'am. Sorry for your loss."

"Which one?" Her gnarled hand went to her throat. "That was rude of me. Please accept my apology."

"No offense taken, ma'am." Brett retreated to stand beside me.

The interaction gave me time to think of what to say. The woman before me hadn't aged well. She was eighty years old and looked every minute of it. Of course, it wasn't surprising given the loss of her son-in-law, husband, and daughter.

Adopted daughter. My child, although I chose not to know her.

Even though it wasn't, I said, "Good to see you, Evelyn."

"I'd recognize you anywhere, Lauren. You still have that magnificent hair and porcelain complexion." She picked up and rang the bell on the side table. When the maid appeared, Evelyn asked for refreshments. She shifted in her seat to greet Stephanie. "What on earth are you wearing? Are you in costume?"

Stephanie had chosen to wear her Madonna getup: black capri leggings, a pink tiered skirt, and a tight purple top with see-through lace sleeves. Nothing I could say would change her mind. Of course, me in my pink and blue silk Flora Kung and Brett in his beloved jeans and Western shirt must look quite the exotic duo to Evelyn's eyes.

The girl's lip extended in a world-class pout. "Oh, Evelyn, welcome to the Eighties. This is what the kids wear. Not some stuffy old plaid skirt and cardigan."

"So, it's Evelyn, is it?" She shrugged. "It's good to see you despite the outré clothing."

"Outré? I'll take that as a compliment." Stephanie smirked.

Gesturing grandly, Evelyn said, "Welcome to my home. The circumstances are not the best, but please make yourself comfortable."

There wasn't a comfortable seat in the house, but Brett and I took seats on the divan across from where Evelyn was ensconced. Stephanie perched on an armchair.

The maid brought a tray with a pitcher of lemonade and a plate of cookies. Evelyn thanked her and asked Stephanie to serve.

"Sure, Evelyn."

After everyone received their refreshments, Evelyn announced, "I've instructed the family law firm to gather Stephanie's records from her school, doctor, and dentist. They should be here shortly."

I wasn't quite prepared to meet the legendary Babcock attorneys. "Will the records from Stephanie's psychotherapy be provided as well?"

Almost choking on a cookie, Evelyn cleared her throat. "I'm afraid not. Mrs. Doody wouldn't allow the records to leave her office."

Stephanie popped up from the armchair. "What a bitch!"

Evelyn dropped her porcelain plate, which bounced on the immaculate Aubusson rug, unbroken. "Language! If you'll allow me to finish. Mrs. Doody has graciously agreed to meet with Lauren this afternoon at one. As per my attorneys, children don't have a right to privacy regarding their treatment. My expectation is that she will cooperate fully with you, being as you are Stephanie's blood relative."

With a beet-red face, Stephanie sputtered, "Graciously? That old bat doesn't know the meaning of gracious."

I wanted to intervene but frankly, being in Evelyn's presence and knowing I'd be facing the storied Babcock attorneys in minutes intimidated me, so I didn't speak up. Brett patted my knee in silent support.

With a shaking hand, Evelyn rang for the maid to pick up the mess on the floor. "I see you are still out of control, young lady. Please refrain from any further outbursts. My heart can't take it. And sit down!"

Stephanie tossed her head and flounced to the armchair, dropping into it with a dramatic sigh.

I placed my plate on the side table. "Speaking of your heart, how is your health, Evelyn?"

"Not the best. But I have the finest doctors."

"Good. You must take care of yourself. On another topic, Stephanie has asked if she can live with me and Brett in Austin. As her guardian, what are your feelings about this?" I didn't want to let on to Stephanie that Evelyn had already made it clear to me in our telephone conversations she was through with the girl. Hadn't Stephanie been through enough heartache?

Evelyn sipped her lemonade and gently set her glass on a coaster before she answered. "Truthfully, I'm saddened, but Stephanie has been going through troubles for quite a while." Evelyn turned to the girl. "In fact, ever since her father passed away, she's been in counseling for certain…issues, haven't you, child?"

The pout was back on Stephanie's face, and her scowl was impressive. "Child? What bullshit!"

Evelyn leaned back against the sofa cushions and fanned herself with her handkerchief. "Watch your language, Stephanie." Then she aimed her gaze at me. "Lauren, I'm afraid I can't handle the stress of having her live here any longer. My cardiologist insists I have a serene environment."

Worried how the girl would react to the rejection, I stole a glance at her. Stephanie's eyes blinked rapidly, and her chin trembled, but she said nothing. Did the girl care after all?

Evelyn didn't appear to notice. "Are you aware I planned to send Stephanie to boarding school? We had several schools under consideration."

Stephanie snorted and folded her arms across her chest. "We, my ass!"

My eyebrows shot up in surprise, even as I applauded the return of the girl's bravado. "Really? Stephanie hadn't told me." *After losing her mother, shipping her off to school seems cruel.* I studied the girl, who stared as if fascinated at a family portrait over the fireplace. What else was she hiding?

Brett sat ramrod straight beside me. The furniture was far from comfy, and Brett's body language revealed he was ill at ease. Who wouldn't be? I sure was. I could only imagine what was going through his mind. Without speaking, he grasped my hand and squeezed it.

The doorbell rang. Stephanie yelped, and I started. A minute later, the housekeeper led three men to the room. The trio sported gray three-piece suits, subdued ties, and gray hair. No surprise. The three attorneys declined refreshments and remained standing, despite Evelyn offering them seats.

The lead man, distinguishable only by wire-rimmed glasses, set down his briefcase on a console table, opened it, and removed a fat manila envelope. "Evelyn, my dear, don't bestir yourself on our account. This won't take long."

He strode to where I sat and handed me an embossed card with a discreet script announcing "Boylston, Cabot, Lodge." With a phony smile, he placed the manila envelope on the coffee table. "Miss Eaton. Or do you go by Mrs. Owens?"

Before I could answer, he said, "Irrelevant."

How dismissive. And downright rude.

Looking down his nose at me, in every sense of the word, the man said, "We've made copies of all requested documents from Miss Kingston's schools, medical doctor, and dentist. You'll also find copies of the guardianship and trust papers. If you decide to provide a home for Stephanie, guardianship papers will have to be redrawn and filed in Texas and here."

Brett stood and held out his hand. "Hey there, I'm Brett Owens. And who are you?"

The attorney flushed and stammered, "I-I'm Preston Cabot. My colleagues are Mr. Boylston and Mr. Lodge." Cabot briefly shook Brett's hand, wincing at his firm grip.

"Nice to meet y'all." Brett's tone made it clear he wasn't telling the truth.

I hid a smile. Stephanie laughed out loud. Evelyn pursed her lips but didn't bother to correct the girl.

Cabot opened and closed his mouth like a dying fish before continuing with his prepared remarks. "There is also the matter of Stephanie's trust. If Mrs. Owens assumes guardianship, we suggest you hire an attorney to guide you through the agreement. When Clark last revised the terms of the trust, he allowed the fund administrator more latitude in diversifying her portfolio. He insisted on an irrevocable trust, so no changes can be made." By the time Cabot finished speaking, his face had returned to its normal indoor pallor. A smug smile nudged his lips upward.

Evelyn clutched her brooch. "Why would he do that? He was so conservative."

Either Boylston or Lodge responded, "Clark wanted to move into the twentieth century, a little late, but better than never."

Evelyn shook her head. "That doesn't sound like him."

Cabot frowned. "Nevertheless, Clark was clear in his instructions."

"Well, in that case…I suppose it's none of my concern any longer. And because Stephanie has made her wishes clear, I won't fight a change in guardianship." Evelyn drew another handkerchief from her sleeve and patted her brow. "Thank you for bringing the documents by, gentlemen."

Cabot, Boylston, and Lodge nodded and bowed slightly as they prepared to leave. "Never hesitate to call on us, Evelyn," Cabot said. "We're here to serve." He held up his hand. "Don't bother to ring. We can see ourselves out." The three men turned and left. Why was it necessary for all three of them to be present? Must be part of the deluxe service. With their departure, the room seemed a bit brighter.

Chapter Twelve

STEPHANIE'S ROOM

After Evelyn's famous trained lawyers left, Lauren and Brett asked to see my room. Fake granny shooed us away and remained on the sofa. The three of us climbed the stairs, past the beady gaze of Cabot portraits going back to colonial times. At my door, I hesitated for a moment. Had Evelyn thrown away my stuff? When I opened the door, I sighed with relief. Everything looked the way I had left it, down to the dirty socks and school uniform lying on the floor. "Here's my room," I said unnecessarily.

Lauren stepped inside and scanned the room, looking surprised as she took in the NASA posters on the walls, the plastic models of spacecraft, and the constellations painted on the midnight blue ceiling. "What's all this? I didn't know you're interested in outer space."

Brett exclaimed, "Wow! What an interesting room." He picked up a model of the first shuttle Enterprise, the one with the booster rockets. "Who put the models together?"

My eyes stung with tears. "Dad helped me. Until he died." I gulped. "We followed everything NASA did. I remember Mom had a cow when he took me to see the movie *Aliens* when I was nine. He knew I could handle it."

"I bet you could." Brett grinned. "What did you think of E.T.?"

Had Brett actually gone to the movies to see that flick? "It was cute, but not very scientific."

Brett stood in front of the poster of the Challenger crew. "All these folks died in the shuttle explosion. Terrible thing. Tell me you don't want to be an astronaut."

"Not anymore. Anyway, the space shuttle isn't flying now. I'm more interested in aeronautics and finding ways to make sure a disaster never happens again."

Lauren gestured at the pictures on the wall. "Who's Sally Ride?"

Hurrying over to stand beside my hero, I said, "I guess you'd call her my role model. She's an astronaut and a physicist. She went to Stanford, and I told my dad that's where I wanted to go to college. At first, he tried to get me interested in MIT, but I convinced him that Stanford was way better. And he promised me I could go to college there."

Lauren and Brett exchanged a look, then turned back to me. "This is the first time I've heard you mention college," Lauren said.

"Yeah, well, guess I've got more immediate problems than college applications right now."

"If I remember right, you just completed your sophomore year in high school," Brett said. "When do kids apply to college?"

"Maybe in junior year. I don't even know where I'm going to school in the fall." Staring at them with wide eyes, I hoped they would catch my drift. "Sure don't want it to be here, or a boarding school."

Lauren smiled. "If you really want to live with us, Brett and I are willing to give it a try. Of course, we must review your school records and meet with your therapist—and there will be conditions."

"Therapy? I know I have to go." I tried not to show my unhappiness about the prospect.

Brett said, "Chin up, kid. It's meant to help you."

"Yeah, I suppose. Hey, can I bring some of my things back with me?"

"I think we can arrange that. Let's start with your wardrobe." Lauren marched to my closet, threw open the door, and took a step back. "You weren't kidding about the plaid. I see nothing but plaid skirts, white Peter Pan collar blouses, and umpteen cardigans. Do they really make you wear these things?"

"Oh, yeah. They insist on it. Check out the shoes."

Lauren's face said it all. "I haven't seen shoes like that since the forties. We'll leave all this here. Do you have any casual clothes?"

"You saw them. All I had, I shoved in my backpack." I bit my lip so hard, I almost yelped. "I never want to come back here. But there are some things I can't bear to leave behind—like my models and posters. Oh, and my books."

Lauren patted my shoulder. "Don't worry, dear. I'll make arrangements to have them packed up and shipped home."

I perked up at hearing her say "home." "That would be fantabulous! You know, my mom always zoned out when Dad and I talked about space. Even though he was a banker, he told me his first love was aeronautics. He wanted to study that instead of finance, but his family was in the money business."

Brett nodded. "So he went with the flow. People do that."

"Yeah, but he wanted me to do what I wanted in life." My vision blurred, but I refused to cry.

My real grandmother took my hand. "Mine did too. Seems we both had wonderful fathers. I asked you a while back what you want to be when you grow up. Now I know."

I guess she approved because she gave me a dazzling smile. She pointed to a shelf of VHS tapes and read the titles: *Close Encounters*, *Solaris*, the *Star Wars* trilogy. "I don't believe I've seen any of those films."

"Probably not." I struggled to keep a straight face, trying to imagine Lauren as a sci-fi fan.

Brett picked up one of Mom's James Bond videos. "I love these Bond flicks."

"Yeah, me too. My mom and I watched them over and over. Do you want to bring them back with us?"

Brett nodded and winked at me. It was sort of weird being winked at by a guy with one eye.

Happy that my stuff would be shipped to Austin, I dreaded what was next. "Do you want to see my mom's rooms? She had two."

"Lead the way. Why two rooms?" Lauren asked.

"You'll see." What would Lauren think when she saw the shrine?

As we walked down the hall past more portraits of ancient Cabots, I said, "Evelyn keeps my mother's childhood bedroom just like it was when she left to get married. Actually, my fake granny never redecorates or changes anything. You got a taste of that in the receiving room."

Lauren stopped mid-stride and clasped her Zuni necklace. She always wore it, and I wondered if she bathed and slept in the thing. "Although I never knew Barbara, I'd like to get a sense of who she was. At least I think I do."

Brett put his arm around Lauren's shoulders. "You sure about this, babe?"

She looked at him with her amazing turquoise eyes wide. "Yes, darling, I am."

I opened the door to Mom's room, letting Lauren and Brett enter before me.

Lauren gasped. "It's a time capsule—takes me back to the fifties. I bet there's a poodle skirt in the closet."

The pink-checked canopy over the bed set the tone for the whole room. Pink, my mom's favorite color, covered the walls. The shag carpet and fluffy bedding featured various shades of the color. Clark and Evelyn had indulged my mom's every whim—her wish was their command. Probably because of all the guilt from living a lie.

When we moved to Beacon Hill after my dad died, Mom wouldn't sleep in this room and insisted on taking over one of the guest rooms. She acted like a spoiled teenager and sounded like one when she said to Evelyn, "Mommy, I want to leave my childhood room just the same as it ever was. That way, I can relive my fondest memories whenever I wish." Even at eleven, I almost couldn't believe my ears and thought that was a little bizarre.

Lauren stepped around the room as if she were walking on eggshells. She ran her hand over the ruffled bed covers, opened the closet, inspected the dresser drawers, sat at the vanity table, and picked up mom's hairbrush, clutching it to her chest. It was kind of spooky. Brett just stood near the door, arms folded, watching her.

What did she expect to find? What could she learn from thirty-year-old relics? For God's sake, it was almost as if she were visiting a museum.

After several silent minutes, Lauren stood and blinked her eyes. "Thank you for showing me this. It gives me a glimpse into the young woman I never knew."

Was Lauren going to cry? Did she have regrets? It was way too late for that. Brett took her in his arms, and they hung onto each other like they'd never see each other again. It was kinda uncomfortable to watch, and I shivered, breaking the spell. "Excuse me. If you're finished hugging, Mom's grown-up room is at the other end of the hall. Do you want to see it?" Then I got goosebumps. "No, wait. I don't think I can go in there."

Lauren stared at me like I'd just grown another head. "I understand, dear, but I do need to see it."

Then I changed my mind. This might be the only chance I ever got since I had no plans to visit Boston again. "Okay. I'll go with you." Walking past the creepy Cabot gallery, I swore Samuel Junior's eyes followed us. We entered Mom's bedroom, not that she had spent a lot of nights there.

Brett took a step back. "Wow, that perfume is strong! It's not the Arpège you wear, darlin'."

"No, it's not. I think it's Shalimar. Imogene gave me a bottle once, but I switched to Arpège, you know when."

Brett put his arm around Lauren and kissed her cheek. "I sure do."

The PDA was a little much, but whatever. "That's right. Shalimar. My dad gave her a bottle once, and she loved it. After that, Dad always bought it for her birthday."

Lauren glanced around the room. "This-this is so impersonal, almost like a hotel room. I can't get a sense of Barbara here." My real grandmother sank to the bed and shook her head.

A memory of Mom rushing around getting ready for a date and telling me to find something to do, like homework, made me angry—and sad. "Yeah, she wasn't here much. She never bothered to decorate it."

Brett leaned against the doorframe, observing silently. He treated Lauren like she was a precious jewel. I wondered if Alain had treated her that way. I was dying to know the story of their romance. If she had my mom when she was seventeen, that meant she was getting it on with a Frenchman when she was my age. I hadn't even had a single date.

Mom and I never got to the stage of those cozy mother-daughter talks, so I had no clue about my mom's teenage dating history or what advice she might have given me. By the time I was old enough for those chats, she was all about the dating scene—hers, not mine. Going on trips, staying over with "a friend," whatever. Losing that closeness—and her—hit me all over again, and the tears I'd been holding back dripped down my face. I turned and ran from the room, almost knocking down Brett.

Chapter Thirteen

LAUREN CONFRONTS STEPHANIE'S PAST

With Brett on my heels, we rushed after Stephanie to her room. She'd already thrown herself on the bed, a fistful of crushed tissues in her hand.

"Maybe you weren't ready to go into your mom's room." I sat on the bed beside her.

Stephanie sniffed and wiped her nose with the tissues. "It's not seeing her things. It's knowing that we'll never talk again. Once she started dating, she didn't have much time for me. And when she met that asshole she went scuba diving with, well, I hardly ever saw her."

I filed away the revelation about Barbara's dating. "I'm sorry, Stephanie. Grief has a way of rearing its ugly head when you least expect it. Time will help. So will therapy. You often seem angry or detached, then I see a sad, lonely child at other times."

"Don't call me a child!" The girl sat up and glared at me with a red face.

"There you go, proving my point." I put my hand on her shoulder, and she didn't pull away. "I promise to do my best for you. We must build trust."

The girl calmed down and wiped her eyes. "Okay. I'll try to do my part."

Brett stepped forward. "How about you show me around town while Lauren visits your therapist?"

Stephanie's face brightened. "I know just the place. The Planetarium." She leaned her head against my shoulder. "Sorry you have to meet with Sour Pickle Face, Lauren."

"You mean, Mrs. Doody?"

"No. I mean Sour Pickle Face. You'll see. Don't believe everything she tells you. And remember, I haven't seen her in two years."

"I'll keep that in mind. Think on a good place for dinner later."

The taxi dropped me off at a nondescript mid-rise office building. Inside, I found Mrs. Doody's office and, after ringing the bell as directed, sat in the waiting room. I didn't have long to wait until she appeared.

Mrs. Doody stood in the door to her inner sanctum, like an implacable statue. "You're on time. Good." Turning her back, she hobbled into her space. Wondering why, at her age, the woman hadn't retired, I followed. She directed me to a worn gray tweed armchair. The room was stuffy and the cloying odor of sour milk, either from SPF or some forgotten food item, wafted to my offended nose, and I was forced to breathe through my mouth. Before I could say anything, she launched into a speech.

"I never allow my files to leave my office." She glowered at me. "And I don't allow anyone to read them, either." With that challenge, she sat back with her flabby arms crossed over her concave chest and jutted her chin at me.

Stephanie was right—her face does look rather like she just bit into a sour pickle.

Taken aback, I thought a minute before responding to her rudeness. "I have several questions about the therapy Stephanie Kingston received a few years ago."

"I agreed to meet with you at the request of Mrs. Evelyn Babcock. She tells me you are Stephanie's grandmother."

Irritated and faintly nauseated from the odor, I said, "Is that a question?" Giving her my own steely gaze, I waited for her next move.

Mrs. Doody's jaw dropped, which did nothing to improve her looks. She harrumphed and placed her reading glasses on her nose, a move I took as a tactic to bide time—and a sign of weakness. I awarded myself one point.

The disagreeable woman fiddled with a pile of papers on her desk, then snapped, "Of course not. I must inform you I reserve the right not to answer certain questions."

I didn't know how much longer I could remain in the fetid office. And because of her attitude, I decided not to share any details about my granddaughter, especially about the latest bout of self-harm. "Funny, Mrs. Babcock assured me of your cooperation. Your position doesn't seem very helpful and certainly not in the best interests of Stephanie, who, as a child, has no expectation of privacy regarding her treatment."

"Nevertheless, that is my stance. Now, do you have a question?"

"Yes. What idiot licensed you as a therapist?" I stood and left the room, resisting the urge to slam the door. When I reached the sidewalk, I took in great gulps of fresh air.

Back at the hotel, I was delighted to find Brett and Stephanie pouring over a map of the heavens, obviously bonding. Warmth and peace flooded over me. Was it happiness? Brett's and my tragic past flitted into my consciousness, but I cut off thoughts of what might have been for us and relished the sight before me. I kicked off my Ferragamo heels, and Brett looked up, smiling.

"Hey, honey. Stephanie and I had a great old time at the museum. How'd things go at the therapist?"

I glanced at Stephanie, who gritted her teeth and clutched the arm of her chair, obviously apprehensive.

"Well, I found the woman unhelpful and insufferable. Her office needed a good cleaning, or maybe she did. After a grim standoff, I up and left."

Stephanie let out a whoop and rocketed from her chair into my arms. "Thank God! I thought she'd make me look like a nutcase."

Brett came to my side and gave me a hug. "Good on you, babe. You never were one to suffer a fool."

"With all the excitement and drama today, I didn't get lunch, so I'm starving. Where shall we dine?"

"I made a reservation at a seafood place that Stephanie tells me has the best clam chowder and sourdough bread in Boston. Why don't you freshen up? I'll call a cab."

The hostess raised an eyebrow at the sight of us, no doubt because of our attire. Stephanie channeled *Flashdance*, while I wore one of my favorite dashiki dresses in shades of indigo and plum, with golden sandals on my feet. Brett tossed on a jacket over his Western wear. With a tight smile, the hostess seated us at an out-of-the-way table. It couldn't be more obvious that she sought to hide us from the proper Bostonians in the room, and I chuckled to myself. *This is one stodgy city.*

After we ordered, I turned the conversation to my plans for Stephanie upon our return to Austin. "Jane's husband Joshua—you haven't met him yet—has scheduled an appointment for you with his summer intern. His office is just a few blocks from my store, where you'll be working for the summer."

Stephanie choked on the water she was drinking. "What?" After she finished coughing, she asked, "I'm going to work? At your store?"

I found it interesting that Stephanie hadn't commented on the therapy appointment, instead focusing on the job. "Welcome to the real world. You need to learn some workplace skills to prepare you for life. And while Brett has enjoyed getting to know you and will continue to support you, he does have other commitments."

Brett placed his napkin on his lap. "I volunteer at a rescue ranch. Recovering alcoholics live and work there."

"Why can't I go to work with Brett instead?"

"The ranch is no place for you, honey. It's all men and they're all goin' through a rough patch."

"Oh." The girl's face reflected disappointment, which I tried not to take personally.

The waitress brought round, crusty bread bowls filled with steaming New England clam chowder and served each of us. "Enjoy." I doubted she meant it.

Without delay, Brett picked up his spoon and dug in. "This looks mighty fine. Smells terrific too."

"Yeah, it does." Stephanie scooped up her first bite. "This is the one thing I miss about Boston."

After a few minutes, Brett wiped his mouth with his napkin. "Sure is delicious. Tell you what, I'll look for a recipe, and we can try our hand at it. What do ya say, kid?"

Stephanie's smile lit her face. I noticed there was no objection to Brett calling her "kid." As I watched the two of them together, I couldn't help but wonder what my and Brett's son would have been like. The miscarriage, which led to my abandoning Brett and insisting on a divorce he didn't want, haunted me, especially since Stephanie's arrival. If he had lived, our son would be thirty-five years old. I had to stop myself from going down that road and instead focus on the future with the three of us.

Brett rubbed his hands together. "Lookin' forward to the Dover Sole, but I sure could do with a little more of that sourdough."

The waitress appeared with a covered basket, the aroma of fresh-baked dough permeating the room. "Your entrees will be out shortly." She gathered the plates from our first course.

"Thank you, ma'am," Brett said to her retreating back. He reached for a roll. "Being prim and proper sure builds up an appetite."

Stephanie and I laughed at Brett's clowning.

I decided to keep to neutral topics around Stephanie. "Darling, what do you think of Boston?" Later, I planned to chat with Brett about the girl's future.

"Have to admit, I was impressed with the planetarium, but the noise and bustle of a big city doesn't set well with me the older I get. So, I'm thinkin' I can't wait to get back to Texas. Good call to stay just the two nights."

Stephanie added, "Yeah, I'm glad we have an early flight."

Nodding in agreement, I said, "Can't wait until stodgy old Beacon Hill is but a memory."

"My butt is still sore from sitting on that ancient furniture." Brett shook his head. "Must be stuffed with wood."

Stephanie giggled. "It's the worst."

I shuddered. "The atmosphere reminded me of Imogene's place on the Upper East Side. When I first saw her place as a teenager, I remember being impressed by the opulence, but now the decor seems like something you'd see in a museum. Hard to believe people still live that way."

The waitress arrived with a tray and wordlessly served our Dover sole entrees.

Brett beamed and picked up his fork. "Sure looks good."

I couldn't finish the fish, but between them, Brett and Stephanie cleared our plates. After declining dessert and settling the tab, we headed back to the hotel.

While Stephanie packed her things, I drew Brett onto the bed in our room. We sat beside each other and shared a look. His slight smile encouraged me to start.

"Are we really doing this?" I asked.

Brett understood what I meant. "Yeah. Looks like we are. After I heard Evelyn was gonna ship Stephanie off to boarding school, I knew we had to step up. But I ain't wearin' rose-colored glasses. I know there'll be bumps in the road. The girl needs to trust us. And she's gonna have to listen and stay on the straight and narrow."

I threw my arms around him and gave him a heartfelt kiss. "I have no illusions this will be easy."

Brett nodded. "Some folks might be scared off because of her problems, but I like a challenge. That little girl is a sweetheart. Even though she's in a world of hurt right now, I believe we can help her. Besides, I think she's got a lot of potential."

"I'm sure she does, but the pain goes deep. She's got wounds from Barbara's neglect and Evelyn wanting to send her away."

"Yeah, that was an eye-opener. Stephanie plays it a little close to the vest. I hope she gets on with her new therapist. Opens up."

"As do I. Then there's the issue of school, which will start before we know it. While the cab was stuck in traffic this afternoon, I had a chance to review Stephanie's school records. Until recently, she maintained an excellent grade point average in all her classes. In the latest report, her math and science scores were still good, which doesn't come as a surprise after seeing her room, but her English and Social Studies grades were just average."

"We're gonna have to be mighty particular about what school we send her to."

That decision loomed large in my mind. "You're right. I'll ask Jane for some suggestions."

Brett rose and pulled me to my feet. "Let's pack and get some shuteye."

"Let me check on Stephanie. Be right back." I blew him a kiss.

Chapter Fourteen

Stephanie's Mind Churns

Just as I finished stuffing my clothes in the suitcase, a knock came on the door connecting to Lauren's room.

"It's not locked."

My real grandmother stepped inside and pointed at my suitcase. "I see you're all set for tomorrow. We'll have time for breakfast before the flight. Be ready by seven."

I studied her, trying to guess what she was thinking. What had she and Brett said about me in their room? If they changed their mind about custody, I didn't know what I'd do.

Lauren tilted her head. "You look a little frazzled. What's up?"

"Not much." I sat on the bed. "Just a little nervous about school in the fall."

"If you want to get into a top-notch college like Stanford, you're going to have to improve your grades. I saw how much they fell off this spring." Lauren didn't look pissed, so that was good.

"Yeah, but I promise to do better. You saw I used to get As in science and math, and I'll do it again!"

She bent down and hugged me. "I know you will. Now get some sleep."

When a harsh ring woke me at 6:45 the next morning, I fumbled for the phone.

"Rise and shine!" Lauren's upbeat voice was too much this early.

"Yeah, yeah." Yawning, I crawled out of bed and pulled on my jeans and blouse.

When I walked into the suite's living room, room service had already arrived. The smell of breakfast sausage woke up my appetite, and I lifted the lid on my platter without saying anything to Lauren and Brett. The pancakes were burnt, and even after I doused them in syrup and butter, they still crunched. I scarfed down the sausages even though they were barely warm.

Lauren sipped coffee and nibbled on a sweet roll. "Too bad you weren't hungry, Stephanie."

It took me a minute to realize she was kidding because my brain was still asleep.

Brett put down his fork and patted his belly. "I've had better, but time to get this show on the road." He called for our luggage to be brought downstairs, and I ran back to my room to brush my teeth.

As we rode down in the elevator, I did a happy dance, so glad to be leaving Beantown, Beacon Hill, and my fake granny. I enjoyed the hell out of the ride to Logan, vowing never to return to Boston. My new life in Austin would be awesome. I just knew it.

I buried my nose in *Dune* on the first leg of the flight home. We had to change planes in Cincinnati again, which was so lame. When the connecting flight was delayed, I was beyond annoyed. Bored, I wandered down the concourse, checking out the magazines and paperbacks. The candy display caught my eye, and I dug in my pocket for cash. Three Snickers later, my stomach felt full, but I couldn't concentrate on my book, so I people-watched until it was time to board. I fell asleep on the second flight, and Lauren had to wake me up to get off the plane.

When we got home—yes, Lauren's place was my home—Brett fixed us grilled cheese sandwiches.

Lauren poured apple juice, and we ate at the kitchen table. "Are you excited about your new job?" she asked.

I swallowed a bite of my yummy sandwich and shrugged. "I wouldn't say excited."

"Well, what would you say?" Lauren asked.

Aggravated, I shrugged again, not sure how I felt about working.

Brett patted Lauren's hand. "I think she's a little tired from the trip, honey. We all are."

We finished our meal in silence. Brett gathered our empty plates and stood. "Why don't ya turn in, Stephanie? I'll tend to the cleanup."

I pushed back from the table and headed to my room. Brett had put my suitcase on the bed, but I shoved it to the floor, too tired to unpack. After I found a pair of fresh pajamas and brushed my teeth, I fell into bed. But tired as I was, sleep wouldn't come.

How would my first day of work at Lauren's grocery store go? What if I hated it? Maybe the other workers would resent me because I was the boss's granddaughter. I had no idea what to expect at Cornucopia, and that made me nervous. My hands were itching to go to my upper arms to get some relief, but I stopped before I broke my promise. Would that impulse ever go away? I sure hoped my new therapist would be better than that old hag Mrs. Doody.

On the trip, Lauren and Brett got tons of information about me, but there was still so much I didn't know about them. How long had they been married? Why didn't Lauren have any more kids after my mother—or did she? I turned onto my left side and snuggled under the covers.

While I slept, Lauren and Brett tiptoed into my room, emptied my closet, and carried my stuff out to the hallway. Even though they whispered, their words were loud enough to wake me up.

Brett said, "It's a damn shame we have to send Stephanie away."

"What else can we do, darling? We need the room for our son and his family. We can take the girl to a hotel. Or maybe we should send her back to Evelyn. What do you think?"

I woke up moaning, with tears on my face. Even though I knew it was just a bad dream, my stomach felt like rats were gnawing on it. The green glow of the bedside clock radio announced 3:05 a.m. I sat up and punched my pillow into a ball, then lay back down, hoping to get back to sleep.

Chapter Fifteen

LAUREN SHOWS STEPHANIE THE ROPES

The next morning, I was surprised to find Stephanie up and dressed. Brett poured a half cup of coffee for her, and she filled the rest of the mug with milk.

"Thanks, Brett. I kinda like coffee if it's watered down."

I kissed Brett's cheek. "Pour one for me, darling? I need a caffeine jolt this morning. And a yogurt."

Stephanie wrinkled her nose. "Yogurt? Barf me out. I'll just have cereal."

Brett brought her a bowl and a box of granola. "Got some strawberries. Want some?"

"That'd be great. Thanks, Brett."

Once we finished eating and cleared the dishes, I announced, "Time to leave." I took a closer look at Stephanie and was appalled to see her wearing the same pair of jeans and T-shirt she wore on the flight home yesterday. "Is that what you're wearing?"

Stephanie rolled her eyes, "Duh!"

"Change into fresh clothing. You have five minutes." Was this what it would be like every day?

With her lip protruding a good inch from her face, Stephanie flounced out of the kitchen. When she returned, in fresh jeans and a T-shirt without a logo, I smiled. "That's better." I kissed Brett and whispered, "Wish me luck."

We walked out to the driveway. After settling into the passenger seat, Stephanie slammed the door. I had to wonder about the change in attitude, a sharp contrast to how agreeable she'd been in Boston.

Deciding to let her stew a little, I said nothing as I fastened my seatbelt and checked my lipstick in the rearview mirror. Glancing sideways, I wasn't surprised Stephanie sat with her arms folded across her chest and her face turned away. "Buckle up, kiddo."

An exaggerated gasp, which Brett probably heard in the house, escaped Stephanie's mouth as she complied. Ignoring the dramatics, I turned on the radio to an oldies station. Stephanie squirmed in her seat and sighed like the weight of the world had descended on her shoulders, still dishing out the silent treatment. As I drove down the hill, past Zilker Park and across the river, Stephanie craned her neck, taking in the sights.

While I navigated my way up Lamar, I pasted on a pleasant smile. It took fewer facial muscles to smile than to frown, I reminded myself. "Lose the attitude before we get to the store. I expect you to be pleasant to the staff and, most importantly, the customers. My manager Jolie will orient you to your duties."

No answer.

"We're almost there, buttercup. Put on a happy face."

At last, a reaction. An eye roll, but it was something.

We entered through the back door, and Stephanie scrutinized the space, taking in the stockroom, cold storage units, and my workspace, and at last deigned to speak. "Is this where you work?"

"Yes, it is."

"It's pretty drab. No pink loveseat, just some ugly metal office furniture. I guess I expected something nicer."

"Did you now?" I handed her a green Cornucopia apron, and she had the audacity to ask me if I was going to wear one.

"No. I don't need one to sit in my drab office."

The girl had the grace to blush.

"We have a few minutes before opening. Today, there will be a general orientation to the store. After I introduce you to the staff, Jolie will take over from there. I'll be in my office, paying bills, ordering produce and so forth. I usually work full days on Monday and Wednesday and half days on Tuesday, Thursday, and Friday. But your schedule is full time, except Thursday, when I'll take you to your therapy appointment."

With her lips in a tight line, Stephanie glared at me. "Why do I have to work full time?"

I tried to keep my voice level. "One day, you'll thank me for this fantastic opportunity to learn about running a business. Follow me."

In the store proper, the three staff members on duty gathered around us, and I launched into the introduction, which I kept short. "My grand-daughter Stephanie recently moved here from Boston and will be working here all summer. Possibly longer." Even without looking, I was certain Stephanie's face wore her pout.

Jolie shoved her glasses up her nose and smiled. "Very nice to meet you, Stephanie."

I was relieved to see her smile in return, even if hers appeared a tad forced. Colton, a new stock boy, and Shondra, the assistant manager, were polite and welcoming, as expected. But I noticed Colton eyeing Stephanie with a silly grin on his face and made a mental note to keep close tabs on him. Shondra, as usual, was all business and got right back to work.

Since I rarely mentioned my personal business to my staff, I expected there would be much talk and speculation about my granddaughter. Human nature.

Stephanie turned to Jolie. "Lauren says you're going to show me around."

Jolie's jaw dropped, perhaps because the girl called me Lauren instead of the "g" word. She stared at me, a question on her face.

I shrugged. "Have a good morning. Make sure to have Stephanie review and sign the employee expectations document. I'll check in with you two later." As I headed back to my office, I tossed a wave over my shoulder and said a little prayer of thanks for the slight improvement in Stephanie's attitude. I'd ask her about that morning's behavior at lunch—give her a surprise break from her first day of work.

Four hours later, a timid knock came on the office door. "Come in," I called.

Stephanie opened the door, trudged in, and plopped down in the chair across from the desk. "God, I'm tired."

"Haven't you ever worked before?"

"No. Why would I?"

"Someday, you'll understand. At least I hope so. Are you hungry? There's a great hamburger joint down the street."

"Yeah, I could go for a burger." Stephanie stood and took off her apron. "Let's eat."

After we ordered, I dove right into her early morning conduct. "Why the attitude this morning? You were much more agreeable in Boston. Do you think I'm gonna put up with insolence?"

With reddened ears and downcast eyes, Stephanie's contriteness seemed genuine. "Sorry. I guess I woke up in a bad mood."

"Do you want to talk about it?"

The waitress approached with our cokes. "Here ya go. Your order will be up real soon."

After the waitress walked away, Stephanie opened a straw and shoved it into her drink. "You'll think I'm stupid."

My patience was wearing thin. "Just spit it out."

The words came out in a rapid stream. "I had a dream—no, a nightmare—that you and Brett packed my bags and were taking me to a hotel so your son could have the guest room."

"My son?" A sense of unreality overcame me. That was the last thing I expected her to say. I stalled for time to figure out how much to tell her. "What on earth?"

Stephanie twirled her finger around a stray curl, a gesture all too familiar to me. Could such a thing be genetic? "I know it's crazy."

I cleared my throat and adjusted my silver bangles. "No. It's not."

My granddaughter's eyes widened. "So you actually do have a son? Any other kids I need to know about?"

With a dry mouth and wet palms, I struggled with what to say. I leaned forward and spoke softly. "I don't have any other children. But I did lose a baby—a boy. Long ago. I'll tell you more at the appropriate time."

"I'm so sorry." Stephanie's furrowed brow made me think she was indeed sorry.

The aroma of hot, juicy beef preceded the arrival of our lunch. Stephanie ate like a starving stray dog, but my appetite had faded.

I watched in horror as half the burger disappeared in mere moments. "Slow down there before you choke. We have time."

Stephanie put down her food and took a breath. She gulped her drink and wiped her mouth. "I know you were a model. So, why did you decide to open a food store?" She dragged a fry through a puddle of ketchup.

Watching Stephanie eat with such gusto, my appetite returned, and I picked up the luscious hamburger and took a nibble. It went down just fine. Grateful for the change in topic, I rallied. "That is a very long story, so I'll give you the condensed version of my journey to Cornucopia. After my career in modeling, I dabbled in retail for a brief time, then turned my hand to advertising. After I divorced Brett, I decided to try another path."

Stephanie stopped eating. Bug-eyed, she asked, "What? You divorced Brett? But you're married now, aren't you?"

"Much to my amazement, yes! Another long story, but this is not the time or place."

With a scowl, the girl sat back in the booth and crossed her arms. "You know everything there is to know about me, but when I ask you something, it's always 'I'll tell you later.'"

Our eyes locked, and I channeled the soundtrack from the showdown in *The Good, The Bad, and The Ugly*. If I weren't married to Brett, I might could look up Clint Eastwood. After several moments of silence, I ended the confrontation. "And when the time is right, I'll provide more details. But you asked about Cornucopia. I wanted to try my hand at something different. One day, while grocery shopping, the idea of getting into the food business caught my interest. First, I got some experience, then used the nest egg I had from an inheritance to start Cornucopia."

Stephanie gaped at me. "What? Inheritance? Who else died?" Her eyes gleamed with unshed tears.

Was she going to cry? The last thing she needed to hear about was more death, but I answered. "My first husband was killed in Italy in World War II. We'd only been married a matter of months. I was nineteen."

Stating the cold, bare facts didn't have the impact they used to, and for that, I was grateful, but my heart still ached when I remembered Ben, mostly because of the way I acted in the last few days of our time together. I hadn't wanted him to go to war, and with his deferment, he didn't have to but go he did. And he never came home. His final gift to me, the inheritance, provided the funds to open my store. Even through the worst of my alcoholism, I never spent a penny of that money, which still seemed like a miracle. Maybe it was.

Stephanie's face drained of color, and she shook her head. "I can't even…" A tear tracked down her cheek. "I'm so sorry."

I blinked a few times. "It was a long time ago."

We finished our meal in silence. I paid the tab, leaving a generous tip. "We'd better get back to work."

On the sidewalk, Stephanie asked, "When are you going to tell me more about your life? I really want the whole story."

We strolled the short distance back to the store. "The whole story? Well, perhaps just the highlights." Although I understood Stephanie's curiosity, I struggled with how much to reveal to her, especially as she navigated through the loss and grief she faced. With her emotions turning on a dime, was she mature enough to handle my outrageous past?

"Oh, come on, more than the highlights." Then Stephanie smiled at me, and her face transformed from a sullen teenager to a lovely young woman. She held the door for me as we entered the store, where she returned to her duties, and I went to my office to call Brett.

He answered on the first ring. "If you're calling to remind me to start dinner, I've got it covered."

Just hearing Brett's deep rumble made me smile. "I'm sure you do, darling. Just wanted to give you a report on Stephanie. She survived the morning at work without incident. And she ate a hearty lunch."

After a moment, Brett said, "There's something you're not telling me. I can hear it in your voice."

Adjusting a stray curl, I sighed. "Can't fool you. Under Stephanie's relentless questioning, I let slip that we'd lost a baby when we were married the first time. She's determined to know every last bit of my past."

"Are you surprised?"

"I shouldn't be. How much should I tell her?"

"We can figure that out later. Don't dwell on it, sweetheart."

"I'll try not to. See you around 4:30."

Promptly at four, I summoned Jolie to my office. "Tell me how Stephanie did today."

Jolie shifted her weight from side to side. "Well, for one thing, she's smart."

I leaned back in my chair and raised an eyebrow. "How do you figure that?"

"She catches on real quick."

"What about her attitude?"

"She was quiet but polite," Jolie said. "She took the greeting policy seriously. Everybody who entered the store received a smile and hello."

"Hmm. That's good. Thanks."

At the door, Jolie turned back. "There is one thing. Colton asked for more hours."

"That new boy?"

"Yeah, he stared at her all day. But he's shy and didn't even talk to her beyond 'hello.'"

"And how did my granddaughter react?" The last thing Stephanie needed at this point was a romance.

"She didn't seem to notice."

"Keep an eye on them. Let me know if any 'noticing' happens. And please put Stephanie on the schedule Monday through Friday, except for half the day on Thursday. She'll have to take the bus home when I'm not here."

Jolie knew when she was dismissed and nodded.

Half an hour later, Stephanie trudged into my office, wadded up her apron and tossed it on my desk. "I didn't think 4:30 would ever get here. Can we go home now?"

"Hang your apron on the hook, please." After I straightened my desk, I led her to the exit and held the door for her. As I seated myself behind the wheel, Stephanie dropped into her seat with a sigh and lay her head against the passenger door window, appearing exhausted.

As I merged onto Lamar, I stole a glance at her. "What are your thoughts after your first day?"

"It was okay."

I swallowed my irritation. "Care to expand on that?"

"I didn't mind stocking the shelves or greeting the customers. Just felt kind of stupid when I didn't know the answers about where to find whatever."

"You'll learn. We'll eat about six, so you have time for a nap if you'd like."

Stephanie didn't answer because she was fast asleep.

During dinner, Brett tried to lure Stephanie into conversation about her first day on the job, but she responded with one-word answers and shrugs. He pushed his empty plate away and said, "Got a meeting at the ranch in the morning. We need cash, so I got to plan a fundraiser."

Stephanie's interest piqued. "Tell me more about the ranch. What do you do there?"

"Mostly management stuff like keepin' the books, fundraising. Although I did swing a hammer when we put up the bunkhouses and cross fencing. The real work is done by the therapists and the horses."

"Horses!" Stephanie's face lit up. "I love horses!"

Brett took pleasure in explaining the workings of the ranch to Stephanie. She listened raptly as he told her how the ranch rescued horses, and they, in turn, rescued the men. "I know you said the ranch was no place for me, but can I go sometime? See the horses?"

Brett frowned. "'Fraid not. Like I told you, it's no place for a young lady. But I might could take you trail-riding if you'd like."

"Like? I'd love it. I used to take riding lessons in Boston."

"Probably you rode English. At the place I'm thinkin' of, you'd be ridin' Western."

"No problem." Without being reminded, Stephanie rose and started clearing the table. "Once, when I was little, Mom and Dad took me to a dude ranch in Colorado. We had a great time!" Her enthusiasm and smile evaporated in a heartbeat.

I reached for her hand. "Keep thinking of the happy times. Your memories will bring comfort over time, not sadness."

Stephanie glanced at me, eyes shining with unshed tears. "I sure hope you're right."

Chapter Sixteen

STEPHANIE JUST WANTS TO HAVE FUN

After slaving away for three full days at work, I looked forward to my half-day, even though I'd have to go to therapy. Lauren invited me to her office for a chat after dinner. Even though I was exhausted, I really wanted to get some answers from her—about her life—and about my future.

Once I got comfortable on the loveseat, and Lauren settled in her chair, she spoke before I could say a word. "I know you have questions. You may think you want to know everything about me but be careful what you ask for."

I unlaced my Doc Marten's and took them off, snugging my feet underneath me. "I guess the thing I wonder about most is your relationship with Brett. Oh, and how many times you've been married altogether?"

Lauren grabbed her necklace, a sure sign she was nervous. After a few moments, she started talking. "I've been married four times. I told you about my wartime marriage to Ben. Then, I had a very brief, very disastrous marriage to a man I won't name. So, Brett is my third and fourth husband."

"Wow! It's super interesting you didn't marry anyone after Brett until you married him again."

My real grandmother twisted her lips. "That does say something, doesn't it?"

"Well, duh!" Even I figured out she had never gotten over Brett. "How did you and Brett get back together anyway?"

"First, a little history. After I left him in 1952, I moved from Dallas to Austin—to hide. For ten years I did the rhumba with demon rum, then I finally got sober in 1961. My long-time dream of owning my own business finally came true in 1965—that's when Cornucopia opened."

"That gets me to 1965, but how did Brett find you when you were hiding out in Austin?"

Lauren actually blushed. "Last fall, thirty-three years after we parted, he showed up at Cornucopia out of the blue. He'd seen an article in the Dallas newspaper about me buying out my investors in the store."

My mind boggled. "Well, that's totally random."

"Yeah, it was. We got married just this past March."

"So, you're newlyweds. That explains the PDA."

"PDA?"

I snickered. "Public display of affection. You need to get out more."

Instead of getting bent out of shape, Lauren threw back her head and laughed. Her laugh reminded me of my mom. "What more do you want to know?"

"Did you have a big wedding?"

"No, dear. But it was spectacular in its own way. We got married on the top of Mount Bonnell at sunset."

"That sounds really romantic. Where's Mount Bonnell?"

"Right here in Austin. I'll take you there sometime. We climbed, no, trudged, up those 106 steps to the outlook over Lake Austin—plain stunning. On the way up, we had to stop and rest a few times for Jane. Our timing was perfect. The setting sun flooded us with golden light." Lauren sighed and closed her eyes for a moment.

"Okay. Golden light. Got it."

Lauren stared at me, but it looked like she was seeing something else. "Right. The thing I remember most is how Brett's vows made me cry. And I think I saw a tear in his eye too. After we were pronounced man and wife, the guests showered us with rose petals. Then we trekked down those 106 steps, got in our cars, and drove here, where my AA friends had prepared a lovely buffet."

"Hmm. I'm trying to picture you in a bridal gown, and I can't."

"At my age? And marriage number four?" Lauren shook her head. "No. No bridal gown for me. I wore a knee-length ivory silk column of a dress, long-sleeved, with a lace overlay covering the entire thing. Bet ya a dollar you'll never guess my footwear."

"Well, I don't think you wore those high heels of yours or Doc Martens. Did you wear Reeboks to climb all those steps?"

"Nope. At Jane's insistence, I wore red cowboy boots." Lauren shrugged, as if to say she couldn't believe it herself.

"No way! I need to see pictures."

Lauren chuckled. "No pictures, I'm afraid. Now that's enough about me."

I set my feet on the floor and leaned toward her, shaking my head. "No, it's not."

"For tonight, it is. But there's something I'd like to understand. You've told me how shocked you were to learn the truth about your mother's adoption, but leaving at the spur of the moment the way you did—it was a huge risk in so many ways. Why did you do it?"

Surprised by the question, I took a moment to think. "Well, the issue of my school was a biggie. My mom let Evelyn make the decision about that—and everything, actually. When she pulled the boarding school stunt, right after my mom died, I wanted to book but didn't have the nerve. The day I found out the truth about my mom's adoption, and the lie we were living, that sealed the deal."

"So, you hopped a bus? Cross country and alone."

Looking her square in the eyes, I said, "I had to meet you. See what you looked like. When I saw your hair, the same as mine, the same as my mom's, I got chills."

Lauren nodded, patting her curls. "Yes, the fabulous Babcock hair. Imogene was blessed too."

"But it's not only the hair. No one in my family has eyes like mine."

"You have your grandfather's eyes. Peridot green with cinnamon rays. The minute I saw you, I knew who you were."

"Oh wow! I always wondered."

Lauren stood and stretched. "Time to turn in. Tomorrow is your first day of therapy, and I want to hear all about it when you get home."

Even though I had a whole bunch more questions, it looked like the truth-telling was over for the evening. "Well, maybe not everything. Be careful what you ask for."

With her eyebrows raised, Lauren smirked. "I see what you did there."

I grinned. "How will I get there?"

"I'll drop you off on the way to my AA meeting."

I'd been so focused on learning my job, I hadn't spent any time studying the staff. Most of them were students at UT and didn't give off friendship vibes, even though they were polite, probably because I was the boss's granddaughter.

That morning, I was stuck with Colton, stocking bags of dried peas and other legumes. Cornucopia was big on legumes. Colton kept to himself at work, and I knew nothing about him. He had to be over six feet tall but looked taller because he was so skinny. His black hair was cut long on top and skinned on the sides. Different. I liked that. His smile was crooked, and he had nice teeth. Teeth were very important. On closer inspection, Colton was kind of cute.

The dude hadn't said two words to me before that morning, so I was surprised when he got chatty, telling me all about Le Fun, this cool arcade he went to after work.

"Where is this Le Fun place?" I asked.

"It's right next to the dollar cinema on the Drag."

"What on earth is the Drag?"

"Oh, that's right. You're new here. It's what they call Guadalupe Street across from UT. I mean the University of Texas. Le Fun has the best games. Galaxian is my fave. They have Pac-Man and Frogger too if that's more your speed. You ought to go sometime."

Colton was usually quiet, but he went on and on about the games. It was kind of like listening to a foreign language. I'd never been to an arcade but didn't tell him. "Maybe."

Colton grinned. "Come on, you'll like it. I get off at one."

Making sure no one was around, I whispered, "Cool. Meet me in front of 2212 North Lamar. Do you know where that is?"

"Sure, it's not all that far from the arcade."

Ten seconds later, Lauren appeared over Colton's shoulder with her arms folded and her eyebrows raised. If she heard our plans, she didn't let on. "Time to go, Stephanie." She led the way, and I followed her like an obedient child, not looking back at Colton.

Lauren dropped me off in front of a medical office building on Lamar, giving me instructions for the bus ride home. "I have several stops to make after my meeting, so I won't be home until dinnertime."

As she drove away, I wondered how the session would go and if my therapist would be okay. Entering the building, I found the listing for Joshua's practice, took the elevator to the third floor, and reported to the front desk.

The receptionist reminded me a little of Mrs. Doody, but then she smiled, and the resemblance disappeared. "Miss Kingston. Your grand-mother has completed all the paperwork." It took me a moment to realize she meant Lauren, not Evelyn. "Just take a seat and Jenna will be out shortly."

I sat on a slippery black vinyl couch and picked up a *Glamour* magazine. But before I could read it, a door opened, and a tall blonde who looked about my age called my name. How could she be a college intern? She was dressed in a suit with massive, padded shoulders, maybe trying to appear older and more professional. It didn't quite work.

As I followed her through the door and down a brightly lit hallway, she said, "Stephanie, I'm Jenna Steele, Dr. Renfrew's summer intern. I'm at Medical Branch, and I'll be graduating next year. Can I get you a coke or a water?"

"No, thank you." I entered the room she indicated and sat in a com-fy-looking chair, then realized I was really thirsty. "Can I change my mind? I'd like a Dr Pepper if you got one."

Jenna smiled. "Be right back."

When she left, I exhaled from the soles of my feet, relieved because Jenna seemed like someone I could relate to. At least I hoped so. Maybe this time therapy wouldn't be so awful.

Jenna returned with a glass full of ice and a cold can of Dr Pepper. She sat in a chair across from me and folded her hands. I guess she wasn't going to sit behind a desk furiously writing notes like Mrs. Doody had done. Cool.

"Why don't you tell me a little about yourself?"

Forty-five minutes later, Jenna walked me to the elevator. I was amazed that after spilling my guts, I didn't feel judged or ashamed. Jenna was a good listener, like a therapist should be, although someone needed to tell Mrs. Doody that. I'd been mega nervous about doing therapy again, but it wasn't bad at all. We brainstormed strategies for avoiding self-harm, nothing I hadn't heard before, but that was okay.

When I exited the building, Colton was there waiting, and we walked over to Le Fun. I needed some fun.

Chapter Seventeen

LAUREN'S BUSY DAY

After dropping Stephanie off for her appointment, I hightailed it to my regular AA meeting. Because I was a few minutes late, I didn't greet my friends but slipped into a chair near the door. I sat through the meeting in a daze, mind wandering to the many demands raising a teenager entailed. Dating, school, driving, all fraught with risk. Did Brett and I take on more than we could handle? Startled from my reverie by the scraping of chairs, I stood for the closing prayer, then hurried to my car, so I didn't get caught up in socializing.

Luckily, Jane's home was just a couple of miles down Bee Cave Road from the meeting, and it took mere minutes to get there. I rang the bell and was greeted by Jane and Delilah. The minute she saw my face, Jane asked, "Was the Boston trip that bad?"

"Is that a backhanded way of saying I don't look my best? Let me in, and we'll talk."

"Can't wait to hear what you've learned."

Jane and Delilah led the way to the kitchen. "Let's wait here. Joshua is bringing us sandwiches from Thundercloud." She cradled her very pregnant belly.

I brought glasses and a pitcher of tea to the table overlooking her backyard. "The crepe myrtles are glorious."

Jane carefully lowered herself into her chair. "Yes, they are. Now, spill."

"Well, Evelyn's family mansion was dreary and stuffy beyond belief." Taking the seat across from Jane, I said, "It was like traveling back in time to the Victorian era. Evelyn is eighty now but not a well-preserved eighty. Her health is poor, although her mind is intact. Kinda sad to end your life in a maroon velvet mausoleum with only servants, doctors, and attorneys for company."

"Sounds depressing. Not a fun place for a teenager to live."

I tucked a stray curl into my updo. "Of course, I had to see Barbara's rooms."

With a puzzled look, Jane asked, "What do you mean?"

"Turns out Barbara had two rooms. Evelyn made a shrine of her childhood room, perfectly preserved circa 1958. Poodle skirt in the closet, Elvis pictures on the wall, the whole kit and caboodle."

Jane clutched her belly and howled with laughter. "Kit and caboodle? Who says that?"

With an icy stare, I said, "I do."

"Yes, you do! No wonder Stephanie calls you 'granny.'" Gasping for breath, Jane plucked a tissue from the box on the table and dabbed her eyes.

"If the hilarity is over...when Barbara was home and not off gallivanting with one of her beaus, the bedroom she used could have been a hotel suite. No personalization at all. I couldn't get a sense of who she was in the space."

With all traces of levity gone, Jane reached across the table and patted my hand. "What about Stephanie?"

"She was less than respectful to Evelyn, but I can't blame her after a few unexpected revelations. As I've mentioned, Stephanie detested her stuffy prep school, then we learned Evelyn wanted to ship her off to a boarding school—and the girl hadn't even told me—so that pretty much sealed the deal for me and Brett. How could Evelyn do that after the child lost both her parents?"

Jane's jaw dropped. "That's cold. How are Stephanie's grades?"

"A mixed bag. Math and science are her strong suit or were until this spring. As for the rest, she has little interest, which her grades reflected."

"Interesting."

"Another surprise—her room is an homage to Star Wars. She plastered the walls with posters of space movies and astronauts. The bookshelves were loaded with models of spaceships that she and her father built. They bonded over all things celestial, especially aeronautics, and she wants to study it in college. Honestly, I never would have guessed, but she's certain of her life path. Amazing at her age."

Jane shook her head. "No kidding. When I think of where I was at sixteen, it boggles the mind. Running away from home and hitchhiking to Monterey Pop. It's a wonder I'm here today."

"I hear that." I stirred my tea and traveled back to my misspent youth. "All I cared about was modeling, the latest fashions, and dining at El Morocco."

"All I could think about was Jeremy." Jane pursed her lips. "The decisions a teenager makes aren't the wisest."

"Those were different times. It took me until I was over forty to get my act together and open my store."

"Beat ya. I was a mere thirty-four when I made up my mind to finish my PhD."

We shared a good laugh at our past follies. "But enough about us. I'm here for advice on schools."

Jane looked at her watch. "Joshua should be here any minute. He better hurry. I'm starving!"

As if on cue, Delilah bounded from the room. "I think he just got here. Delilah is my early-warning system, just like Tallulah." Jane's face fell, and I thought she might cry as I recalled how much she had loved that cat. But she rallied and rose to greet her husband—and the food.

Joshua, followed by the kitten, strode into the room holding a bag of sandwiches. "Hi, honey. Hey, Lauren." He hugged Jane with one arm. "Subs from Thundercloud as promised. I don't have much time because I've got afternoon sessions."

"Let's eat. I was about to faint from hunger." While Jane poured sweet tea, Joshua parceled out the sandwiches and took a seat.

As I unwrapped my roast beef sub, I turned to Joshua. "Do you have any leads on schools for Stephanie? She's interested in aerospace or aeronautics." I bit into my sandwich, realizing how famished I was.

Joshua brushed his long black hair out of his eyes. "Impressive. I huddled with several of my partners with high schoolers and got a variety of opinions. Some of their kids go to St. Stephen's, some go to Huntington-Surrey—both are private schools. The other option is Austin High. I'm told they have the best science curriculum and the most hands-on resources."

Setting down my sandwich, I considered the possibilities Joshua had outlined. "I really have no frame of reference. Never finished high school back in Mineral Wells."

Jane sipped her sweet tea. "Same here. I left Odessa in my junior year and have a GED. Here's a suggestion—why don't you call the schools and set up tours, maybe meet with the principal or whomever?"

I nodded in agreement. "Sounds like a good idea. Do I bring Stephanie with me?"

"Of course!" Jane said.

Joshua wiped his mouth, wrapped the rest of his lunch, and rose from the table. "I'll finish this at work. Got to go. Lauren, you don't want to leave Stephanie out of this process. This will be a perfect opportunity to cement your bond. When is she seeing my intern Jenna?"

"She's there now. Sure hope it goes well."

"Me too." Joshua bent and kissed Jane on the cheek. "I'll see you around six, babe."

After finishing our food in companionable silence, I cleared the table for Jane. "I'm headed to Helen's for a long overdue visit."

"Give her my best."

"Don't get up. I know where the door is."

As I drove to Helen's apartment complex on South First Street, I dreaded the visit, knowing I'd neglected her. The last time I saw Helen was at my wedding party in March. Since she no longer felt up to attending meetings, several members brought the meeting to her, but I hadn't taken part in a single one. When I recalled how Helen had mentored me through the steps and no doubt saved my life, I stopped at the florist and bought an enormous bouquet of irises, not sure if I did so out of gratitude or guilt.

I parked and hustled up the walk to the door of Helen's garden apartment. Francine, her daughter whom I'd met many times, opened the door and waved me inside. After we exchanged pleasantries, I leaned in and whispered, "How is she?"

"Today is a good day. She had her final chemo last week and seems to be rallying a bit."

Helen, bundled in a quilt despite the warm room, nestled in her favorite chair placed in the bay window. She beamed when she saw me and tried to stand.

I handed the bouquet to Francine and rushed forward. "No need to get up." I perched on a padded bench across from her and smiled. "You have some color in your cheeks. That's good to see."

Helen coughed and grimaced. "I'm getting a little stronger too. But I don't want to talk about me. I'm sick of the subject. Tell me everything about your surprise granddaughter."

Francine excused herself, and I gave my sponsor a blow-by-blow account of the past two weeks. An excellent listener, Helen refrained from commenting until I'd finished catching her up on events.

"My, what a whirlwind! And you've stayed sober through it all. When did you last get to a meeting?"

Relieved that I'd just been, I said, "Today."

"Good." Helen's smile faded as a coughing spell overcame her. My heart clenched in fear for her, and I struggled not to let it show. After she recovered, she said, "You must bring Stephanie to meet me."

"I will. Maybe on Saturday, if that works for you."

Helen chuckled. "I expect I'll be right here. Come after eleven, please."

I stood. "That's perfect. See you then." I bent to hug her and headed home. It had been a day.

When I arrived home, I followed my nose to the kitchen. Brett had fired up the barbecue, and the grilled rib-eyes resting on the counter smelled divine. "Thanks, Brett darling." I stood on my toes to kiss him. "Where's Stephanie?"

"In her room. She just got home a little bit ago."

"Really. Her appointment ended at 1:15. Where has she been? Did she stop for a snack or take the wrong bus?"

"She didn't say anythin' like that." Brett took a salad out of the refrigerator. "Honey, the rolls need to come out of the oven. Can you bring 'em to the table?"

"Of course. Then I'll fetch the girl."

"What did Jane and Joshua have to say? Did ya get the lowdown on schools?"

After placing the rolls in a basket, I grabbed the butter dish. "Yes, Joshua was helpful. We'll talk at dinner."

Just as I was about to go to Stephanie's room, she strolled into the kitchen, yawning. "I took a nap."

Feeling like a caricature of a disciplinarian, I put my hands on my hips and stared at her. "Must have been a short one since you just got home. Care to explain?"

With red ears and a hang-dog expression, Stephanie asked, "Can I help with the salad?"

Brett and I exchanged a look. I let her non-answer pass—for the moment.

Once we were settled at the table with full plates, Brett asked, "What all did ya do today, honey?"

I sighed. "Ran myself ragged. After I dropped off Stephanie at therapy, I made the noon meeting at Westlake, even though I was a little late. It was nice just to sit and listen. Then I headed over to see Jane and Joshua. The dear man brought us sandwiches for lunch. He asked around at work for some names of schools to check out."

Stephanie dropped her fork. "Without me?"

"You'll be very much included in tours and the final decision."

The girl took a bite of the luscious steak and, with a full mouth, said, "That's good."

I bit my lip, so I didn't launch into a Miss Manners lecture. What was happening to me? It seemed like I was becoming a mother or grandmother or something. "Joshua gave me three suggestions, two private schools—"

"No way!"

"—and one public school, Austin High." Despite Stephanie's outburst, I finished the sentence with a pleasant tone of voice. "Jane suggested I call and see who's in during the summer and schedule visits."

Stephanie stabbed another enormous piece of steak. "Gee, I sure hope I can fit it in, what with my work schedule." Then she flung the loaded fork onto her plate with a clatter.

Brett smacked his hand on the table so hard, the dishes jumped. "That's enough! Lauren is going out of her way to make sure you get a good education at a school we all agree on. Stop the sass."

Silence descended, and we concentrated on the meal. When I felt ready to continue, I kept my voice composed. "Joshua seemed to think that Austin High School is your best bet for a math and science curriculum."

At once, Stephanie's attitude improved. "Cool. Where's it at?"

"We drive past it every time we cross the bridge on Mopac on the way to work. Just over the river, on the right."

"Oh, okay. Colton graduated last month. I can ask him where he went."

Pushing my plate aside, I placed my hands in my lap. "Colton. My employee and your co-worker. You seemed quite engrossed in conversation this morning."

Stephanie's eyes shifted as she avoided my glance. "Yeah, he was telling me about this cool arcade, Le Fun."

"Arcade? Like a pinball parlor?"

The girl snickered. "Not even. It's a place filled with all the best video games like Super Mario, Pac Man, Galaxian, and Space Invaders."

"And where is this amusement palace located?"

"On the Drag."

I grasped my napkin and folded it into a teeny tiny little square. "Have you been to this establishment?"

"Um, yes. Today, with Colton." Stephanie drained her glass of water in one huge gulp.

Speechless, I turned to Brett. He cleared his throat and said, "Young lady, you were instructed to take the bus home after your appointment today. When I got home from the ranch at 4:00 pm, I was a bit surprised you weren't here but figured you might could have had a time with the bus. Turns out that's not the case. What do you have to say for yourself?"

Stephanie's lower lip quivered as she answered. "Sorry I didn't come right home. But no one gave me an actual time I should be here. But I'm not sorry I went to the arcade. I had fun at Le Fun!" She stopped to take a breath, then raised her voice to a near shout. "This is the first time I've hung out with anyone my age since I got here. I need friends. It was the best time I've had in months. I even got a higher score than Colton on Galaxian. It was totally rad!"

I winced at the slang, then figured I better get used to it. "I understand you need friends. And I also see that you need clear directions and boundaries, since you were at a loss about what time to be home. From now on, if you plan to go somewhere after work, a therapy appointment, or any other time, you'll ask for permission in advance." I softened the words with a smile.

"Who do you think you are? My mother?" With that, Stephanie shoved back from the table and ran down the hall. A thunderous door slam followed.

Chapter Eighteen

STEPHANIE APOLOGIZES

I threw myself face down on the bed, rolled over, smashed a pillow into my face, and screamed. Was I mad at Lauren and Brett or myself? They had a point, but so did I.

Didn't my rulers understand I needed friends? I really missed Allison but knew I'd never see her again. Was it so wrong to want to experience being a teenager in Austin? But if I was honest, it was sneaky meeting Colton and going to Le Fun. That should have been a warning sign, but I ignored it.

My conscience bothered me about what I'd said to Lauren. It was real shitty to throw that mother business in her face, especially knowing she'd lost both her children, the baby and my mother. Would she ever forgive me?

After a while, my tears dried up, so I crawled out of bed and went to the bathroom. I blew my nose and threw some cold water on my face. When I looked in the mirror, my splotchy face stared back, and I didn't like what I saw. There was only one thing to do: go back to the kitchen and apologize.

Brett and Lauren were outside on the patio, sharing the padded bench. I took a deep breath and eased up to them.

Lauren glanced at me, silent and obviously waiting for me to say something. Brett held her hand and gave me his one-eyed stare.

A little nervous about how they'd react, I stood there for a moment. "I'm sorry. Really sorry. Can you ever trust me again?"

"Pull up a chair, dear," Lauren said. "To tell the truth, I was quite taken aback by your anger. But you have a fair point about meeting people your own age."

I sank into a lounge chair facing them. "Can you forgive me for what I said?"

"Are you referring to the comment that I'm not your mother?"

"Um, yeah. Actually, I kind of like that you want to know where I am. It shows you care. And I could use a little mothering."

Brett let go of Lauren's hand and stood. "I'm right proud of you for owning up, Stephanie. Now, I'll just head inside and leave you two to talk."

After Brett left, Lauren and I talked for an hour. She wanted to hear all about my therapy appointment, so I told her a few things, without giving away a lot.

"I'm glad you feel safe with Jenna. Joshua can't say enough good things about her."

"Yeah, she's way nicer than old Mrs. Doody. And way younger."

Lauren raised an eyebrow, something she did when she wanted to make a point. "Age aside, as long as she helps you, I'll be happy. Tomorrow I'm going to arrange tours of the three schools. I know you're not interested in a private school, but I want to explore all the options available here in town."

It wasn't what I wanted to hear, but being agreeable was the smart thing. "Okay. Just so you know, the thought of wearing plaid again makes me want to hurl. Public school sounds awesome. And didn't Joshua say Austin High has a great math and science curriculum?"

Lauren stood and stretched. "I hear that about the plaid. And about the academics."

"So, Austin High?" I jumped to my feet.

"Not so fast. As I said, we're going to visit all three schools. After we do that, I think the answer will become clear."

My shoulders slumped, and I dragged my feet as we walked into the house. I'd do everything in my power to go to Austin High. "Good night, Lauren. I'm beat."

She turned to me and said, "Oh, I almost forgot. Brett asked around about family law attorneys, and one of his ranch buddies offered his wife's help. We must take care of custody and guardianship matters. I have an appointment next week. Sweet dreams, dear."

Hearing about the lawyer really got me psyched, and I let out a whoop and booked it to my room. After a fast shower, I got in bed with *Dune* and read until my eyes got heavy.

An hour later, I still hadn't fallen asleep. My stupid brain kept churning out negative thoughts about school and guardianship, even after everything Lauren said. What if Evelyn decided she wanted me back? What if Lauren and Brett made me go to a private school with plaid uniforms? How could I be at my best tomorrow for work if I couldn't even sleep?

Chapter Nineteen

LAUREN DEVISES A PLAN

When I entered our room, Brett was already in bed with a book. "Be back in a few." I blew Brett a kiss as I hustled into the bathroom. After I showered and donned my silk nightgown, I climbed into bed beside him, and he tossed the novel on the nightstand.

"Hey, darlin', how'd it go with the girl?"

"Fair to middling. She's got her heart set on Austin High. I hope it pans out. How are you feeling about things? Any regrets?"

"Nope. After seeing the situation in Boston, I knew we had to step up. But remember, I said it wouldn't be smooth sailing. Turns out I'm right." He pulled me close. "I know it's not the same thing as us having our own child, certainly not at our age, but this girl is part of you, and I love her just for that."

"Oh, honey, thank you, that's so sweet."

Brett kissed my forehead. "I think we can provide a loving, stable environment for her. And we'll have to find the right school. Keep on top of things, without clippin' her wings."

"That will be tricky. I remember how headstrong I was at her age. She'll be pushing the boundaries, and we're gonna have to get used to it. When she's in school, I think things will calm down. She'll make friends."

"I'm already worried about boyfriends," Brett said. He chuckled. "Is that a cliché?"

"No, it's reality." I snuggled into his side.

"You know, I didn't ever imagine I'd be sleeping with a grandma."

Taking that as a challenge, I leaned over and kissed him silly. "Is that how a grandma kisses?

We had a good laugh that led to more kisses. Our passion ignited. After thirty-three years apart, we had a lot to catch up on.

"Whew! You still got it, darling." After putting my nightgown back in order, I lay back and drew the covers to my chin, luxuriating in the afterglow of intimacy.

Brett donned his pajamas, slid under the covers, and kissed the top of my head. "Love you."

"And I love you."

As I was about to drift off to sleep, a knock came on the door. Realizing I'd forgotten to lock it—something I'd never do again—I called out, "Come in."

Stephanie opened the door and stuck her head in the room. "I can't sleep. Can I borrow a sleeping pill? Mom used to give me one."

Did I hear right? I fumbled for the bedside lamp and turned it on, then launched myself out of bed. "We don't use drugs in this house. They are poison to an alcoholic."

"Oh sorry, I didn't know." The girl rubbed her eyes.

"I'm stunned to hear that your mother would give prescription medication to a child."

Stephanie stared at her feet and mumbled, "It was only once or twice."

"That doesn't make it right."

Brett sat up and swung his legs over the side of the bed. "Anything artificial that changes the way you feel can lead to addiction—and addiction ends one of three ways: insanity, jail, or death. You gotta find a better way to cope. Read. Warm milk. Count sheep. Hey, I'll even get up and make you some hot cocoa or chamomile tea."

"No, thanks. I'll go back to bed and hope for the best." Shoulders slumped, Stephanie turned and left.

I snatched my robe from the foot of the bed and followed my granddaughter to her room. The too-bright overhead light made me squint. "Turn on the lamp, would you? I'm going to turn off the ceiling light."

Without making eye contact, Stephanie perched on the bed, and I sat beside her. "Tell me what's bothering you."

"I worry Evelyn wants me to come back to Boston, that she changed her mind about giving you and Brett guardianship. And I keep worrying about school. Please don't make me wear plaid again." Stephanie grabbed a handful of tissues from the bedside table and dabbed her eyes.

"Oh, Stephanie, have a little faith. I'll take care of the guardianship. Believe me, Evelyn isn't about to change her mind." At that moment, I felt every bit a mother.

The girl rested her head on my shoulder. "If you say so."

"I do. And sweetheart, the school thing will work out." We sat like that for a time, until she lay down. I drew the coverlet over her and kissed her cheek, leaving the room with a full heart.

I tiptoed into our room, thinking Brett might have fallen asleep, but his deep rumble greeted me. "Everything okay?"

"For now." I climbed back into bed and reached for his hand. "Darling, I've got an idea."

"I'm listening."

"How about we create a bedroom for Stephanie, something of her own, where she can pick the décor?"

"Great idea, but where we gonna put it?"

"There's only one possibility—my Pilates studio."

"What're ya gonna do with your mats and stuff?"

"We'll make it work. I can put some gear in my office and move the loveseat into her new room. That way, we'll be able to keep our offices and have the guest room available again."

"Not sure why you insist on keeping a guest room, but it sounds like a plan. Having her own space will reassure Stephanie. Good thing you bought this big old house, my dear." Brett switched off the lamp. "Sleep well."

I turned my pillow to the cool side. After a jaw-cracking yawn, I said good night. But, like Stephanie, I couldn't sleep. Brett, however, had no such trouble. Envious, I sighed and tried to meditate but couldn't achieve the tranquility I sought. Stephanie's upbringing was still a mystery to me. The girl insisted on delving into my past but was far from candid about her own.

Chapter Twenty

STEPHANIE'S SCHOOL DAZE

A week later, as I got ready for my school tours, I plotted how to get Lauren to agree to Austin High. Because Brett had an interest in outer space stuff, I hoped he would be my secret weapon. Checking myself out in the mirror, I remembered how the kids at the arcade had reacted when I asked about schools. St. Stephen's got eye rolls and barf sounds. Huntington-Surrey got shrugs. One Goth girl, dressed in black from head to toe, asked, "Why'd you want to go to a private school when you can go to Austin High?" Exactly.

My rulers were waiting at the front door when I left my room.

"Change your clothes." Lauren said.

"Why?"

"Short shorts and a tank top aren't appropriate. Now go change and make it fast. We'll be in the truck."

Brett shook his head and opened the door for Lauren.

My choice of clothes was totally appropriate because it was hot as hell. I was psyched the marks on my upper arms had faded so much they were almost invisible, and I could wear sleeveless clothes again. But whatever.

I hurried back to my room and threw open the closet. Even though I wanted to wear my acid-wash Jordache jeans, I went with a straight-leg dark blue pleated pair instead. They made my waist look tiny. Knowing Lauren would have a cow if I wore a crop top or anything with a logo, I tossed on a plain white tee.

Then I ran into the bathroom to recheck my hair and saw a tangled mess. I gathered my curls, trying to make a decent ponytail. As I pulled my hair through the rubber band, I recalled how the mean girls at the snobbish academy in Boston either ignored me or snickered when I walked past them in the hall. In a big school, and Austin High was huge, I might have a better chance of finding friends, kids who shared my interests. Just one more point for public school.

With no time to spare, I rushed out to the driveway and squeezed into the backseat of the pickup.

Lauren glanced over her shoulder. "Much better. We're going to St. Stephen's first."

We drove down Bee Cave Road to Loop 360, passing a humongous display of pink flamingo lawn ornaments on the corner, and a few miles later turned into a massive campus. The sign said St. Stephen's Episcopal School, and I groaned. "Episcopalians. Again."

Brett eyed me in the rearview mirror. "Problem?"

"My last school was Episcopalian. You know how I feel about that place." I leaned forward and pointed at what looked like student housing. "Hey, are those dorms?" Was Lauren trying to dump me at a boarding school?

"Some students board, but most are day students," Lauren said.

"Oh. Okay." I shut up but steeled myself to resist this place.

We met a smiley woman who enthusiastically sang the praises of the school. I moped along, hoping Lauren picked up on my body language. It seemed really far from town, with no shopping or arcades along the route. How would I get to school here anyway? Get chauffeured by Lauren or Brett every day? No thanks.

When we got back in the pickup, I started talking first. "It's way too far, and for such a ginormous campus, there're not many more students than my old school, which I hated, in case you forgot. And they're Episcopalian."

Brett snorted and shook his head. "Don't know what you got against Episcopalians, but I don't think this is the school for you."

Lauren said, "They are known for their academics, but we need a school closer to where we live."

Awesome. They agreed with me. "Austin High gets my vote. But, hey, do I even get a vote?"

My guardians glanced at each other, then Lauren swiveled around to look at me. Her eyebrows were raised, and I knew what that meant. "And skip the other tour?"

"Well, duh. Why bother?"

"Because we have an appointment, and it would be rude to cancel mere minutes before the scheduled time. Don't you agree, Brett?"

"You betcha. Always keep your word."

We drove across Pennybacker Bridge and took 2222 into town. Huntington-Surrey had an even smaller enrollment than St. Stephen's. When I learned class was only half a day, I got a little interested but guessed Lauren wouldn't go for that. Or maybe she would and make me work after class was over.

The lady giving us the tour looked like an old hippie with her dreads, scarves, and beads. "We at Huntington-Surrey don't teach our students what to think, we teach them how to think."

I barely endured her super boring speech without hurling. The science lab was even worse than my Boston school. No way. I wanted to book, but Lauren and Brett insisted on finishing the tour.

Back in the truck, I said, "That's a no for me. I need a better science program."

Brett nodded. "Okay, then. We'll grab some lunch and get to Austin High right on time."

"Good idea, darling. I've got a taste for some Tex-Mex. How about The Ditch?"

Did I hear wrong? "The ditch?"

Lauren laughed. "Sorry, El Arroyo. It's not far from the school."

"I still don't get it."

"An arroyo is a gulch or gully, hence the sobriquet 'ditch.' Did you study a language at your old school?"

"Yeah, Latin. Real handy."

"Living in Austin, you'll pick up a little Spanish in no time. Right, Brett?"

"*Sí, Señora!*" Brett smacked the steering wheel and chuckled in appreciation of his lame joke.

We pulled into the lot, and I laughed when I read the billboard: *Did it bother anyone that the guy from the Operation game was clearly awake?*

Lauren remarked, "That one's a bit obscure if you ask me. I've seen funnier messages."

"I think it's hella funny," I said. Inside the restaurant, the walls were half blue and half orange and the windows had green trim, very un-Boston-like. Plain wooden tables and chairs filled the space. I couldn't imagine what Evelyn would think of this place, but if the food tasted as good as the smell coming from the kitchen, I'd be happy. As the hostess escorted us past the other diners to our table, I checked out what they were eating. I wasn't really familiar with Mexican food besides tacos but was willing to learn. My stomach tightened in hunger.

The waiter brought menus, but Brett waved them away. "Already know what I want—beef enchiladas."

"Good choice. I'll have the same," Lauren said.

"Hey, I don't know what I want. And I'm starving."

"Please make that three orders." Lauren smiled at the waiter.

So much for having a choice. Would I get to choose my school? Maybe it'd be smart to save my opinion for when it really counted.

A few moments later, the waiter brought us chips and salsa and sweet tea. I'd never had that kind of chip before or any kind of salsa either. But once I tasted it, I couldn't get enough. "Oh, my God. The chips are still warm. Delish!"

With full bellies, we climbed back in the truck. Brett started the engine and headed to our last stop. "Lauren finagled us a special tour of Austin High with the head honcho of the science department. I think Joshua had a hand in makin' it happen."

"Correct, darling. Mr. Contreras will meet us at the entrance."

"Cool beans. The main science dude is just the guy I want to talk to."

When we drove up to the campus, I couldn't believe the size of the parking lot. No way did they need that many spots for teachers. Did kids drive to high school in Texas? I couldn't wait to find out. The big gray building was kind of ugly, but the important things were inside.

A short man in a tweed jacket and a bow tie stood in the drop-off zone. Wearing tweed at the height of summer gave him a mad scientist vibe. His round glasses glinted in the sun.

Brett parked, and we exited the truck.

"Welcome! I'm Leo Contreras, director of the science department. Come in out of the heat, and we'll start the tour."

Lauren introduced us, and we followed Mr. Contreras up the steps to the entrance. Inside, he pointed out the main office, and then we climbed the stairs to the science labs. The first classroom was huge, with row after row of tall benches, each one with a sink. He opened the cabinets to reveal scads of gear: microscopes, Bunsen burners, scales, all kinds of glassware, everything neatly lined up in rows. The school had dropped some serious coin on this stuff.

I hung on Mr. Contreras' every word as he showed us around the science wing. "I hear you're interested in aeronautics."

"Yes, sir!"

"Then you'll be pleased to learn that UT has a fantastic program right here in town."

"That's cool." I didn't mention that I planned to go to Stanford.

Mr. Contreras bragged about all the achievements at UT. What was he, their personal recruiter? But I listened and couldn't help being impressed when he told me a UT alumnus, Robert Crippen, piloted the first space shuttle. That really got my attention. The sales pitch continued: many UT graduates went on to big time jobs at NASA and Lockheed Martin. I wondered how my experience stocking shelves at Cornucopia would prepare me for a job in the space industry. But the most important piece of information was that UT's aeronautics school actually had women in it.

"Students, a few of whom graduated from here, helped build a subsonic wind tunnel at the Experimental Aerodynamics Lab." Mr. Contreras talked about low thrust trajectory analysis, orbital mechanics, and other juicy topics. "And five years ago, the center of space research was established. We're mighty proud of that here in Austin."

Lauren's eyes glazed over at all the science talk, but I was pumped. Brett paid as close attention as I did.

After thanking Mr. C. for the tour, we got in the truck and buckled in. "This place is awesome! Please tell me I can go to school here."

My rulers smiled at each other, then they turned to face me. "Yes, dear. I think Austin High is perfect for you," Lauren said. Brett winked at me. I had a feeling he steered Lauren in my direction. He really was a cool dude.

Chapter Twenty-One

Lauren Plans the Fourth of July

For two weeks, life chugged along peacefully and predictably, something I never would have expected after the Le Fun incident. With the school issue settled, and Stephanie's fear of plaid allayed, there hadn't been a single emotional outburst since the tantrum the day of her first therapy appointment. Serenity reigned in our household, but for how long?

Cornucopia ran smoothly under the management of Jolie. She gave Stephanie's work ethic and competence glowing reports. Knowing Jolie as I did, I knew she wasn't just shining me on.

Satisfied that life was back on track, I addressed the items on my to-do-list: guardianship, outfitting Stephanie's new room, and planning my annual Fourth of July bash. The visit with the family law attorney went well, and I left things in her capable hands. The transfer of guardianship was fairly routine, I was told. While the management of the girl's trust fund was out of my control, monthly statements would be provided. My jaw almost hit the floor when I learned the amount in Stephanie's trust fund. The kid was wealthy and could attend the college of her dreams. As she stated ad nauseam, she had her heart set on Stanford. Even though she knew UT had a well-respected aeronautics program, the girl wouldn't hear of applying there. Already, I recognized her inevitable departure from our home would gouge a big hole in my heart. But that was two years away. I ought to enjoy our time together and not think that far ahead. The wisdom of the old AA adage, one day at a time, resonated with me. So simple, but so vital.

The shipment of Stephanie's belongings had arrived intact. She was thrilled to see the boxes, especially because the creation of her new room was underway. The only things in Stephanie's new bedroom were the pink leather loveseat from my office and twenty or so cardboard cartons filled with her treasures. We had work to do.

On a steamy June morning, Stephanie and I set out to buy bedroom furniture and paint. John-William Interiors carried the finest selection of solid wood furniture in town. On the drive to the store, I emphasized the importance of hardwood to a bored Stephanie. But when she chose a lovely suite in the palest maple, a stark contrast to the dreary dark brown furniture she'd lived with at Evelyn's, I was pleased. At the paint store, I tried not to cringe when the girl chose a shade of purple for her walls that reminded me of a nasty bruise. We lugged two gallons of the obnoxious color to the car, along with a bag of supplies. By the time we reached our final stop, a custom home décor store, I was exhausted and gratefully accepted the offer of a chair. The girl rifled through every sample swatch containing purple, violet, or heliotrope, hunting for the perfect fabric for curtains and a bedspread. She chose a loud tropical print—not what I would have selected, but I didn't have to sleep in her room.

"Isn't it fantabulous?" Stephanie asked as she stroked the fabric.

Being diplomatic, I said, "I'm glad you're happy with your choice."

"I can't wait for everything to be delivered."

"It will be a few weeks, but Brett promised to paint the room this weekend, so when the furniture arrives, we'll be ready.

At last, I turned my mind to the Fourth of July extravaganza for my AA friends. My home was a magnet for the party because of the fabulous view of the fireworks at Zilker Park. No need for my guests to fight traffic and the crowds. My invitee list stayed the same, but each year word of mouth increased attendance. I relied on Ruth and Debbie to coordinate the dishes of the invited guests, so I'd have some idea of where there might be gaps, but there was a level of unpredictability as to who would show up and what, if anything, they'd bring.

Then it hit me. Jane. She would be six days away from her due date on the Fourth. As her sponsor, I owed her a phone call, but I'd also ask if she intended to be at the party. When we met for lunch two weeks ago, she lacked her usual energy and complained about the heat.

I dialed, and Jane answered on the second ring.

"Hey, Jane. How you feeling?"

"Very fat, thank you very much."

One thing I loved about Jane was her self-deprecating humor. "Reason I'm calling, the Fourth will be here before you know it. You're due date too. I don't guess you and Joshua will be comin' to my party this year."

Jane gasped. "Why do you say that? Of course, we're coming. I'm not due until the tenth and besides, first babies are often late."

"What does Joshua have to say about this?"

"Actually, I haven't asked him. It's my decision."

I rolled my eyes. "I think he may disagree."

"Look, we're coming. You know how I love the fireworks display, and South Austin Medical Center is just five minutes away if anything happens."

I hung up, shaking my head.

When I heard Brett's truck pull in the drive, I glanced at the time and hustled to the kitchen. I'd promised to make dinner tonight. All the fixings for Cobb salad sat in the fridge, right where I'd left them when I arrived home, and then promptly forgotten. With no time to waste, I gathered lettuce, olives, tomatoes, hard-boiled eggs, chicken, blue cheese, and got to work chopping the tomatoes.

Brett's footsteps approached. When he kissed the nape of my neck, a frisson of pleasure traveled through my body. I dropped the knife and turned into his embrace.

"How was your day, my love?" Brett whispered.

"Better now that you're here." Corny, but true.

"Aw, honey. Need any help?"

"No, sir. Get cleaned up. Stephanie should be here any time now. The salad's almost done. I'm going to pop the bread in the oven, and we'll be ready to eat soon."

Not five minutes later, Stephanie called from the hallway, "I'm home! Is dinner ready?"

"I'm putting it on the table."

During the meal, we discussed the logistics for the Fourth.

"Brett, honey, this is your first year at the summer event of the season, but I do need your help, both with the planning and on the day of."

"Love a good party, so I'm happy to help," Brett said.

"Zilker Park becomes a zoo on the Fourth. Perched on this hill, we have one of the best views in town of the festivities. We can even hear the strains of the Austin Symphony if the breeze is just right. Of course, we tune into the radio broadcast for the full effect of the music. It's a magical evening."

"Am I invited?" Stephanie asked.

"Of course you are."

"What are we gonna eat?" the girl asked. Stephanie helped herself to more bread and slathered it with butter.

"I always provide hamburgers and hot dogs. But the guests will bring side dishes and desserts."

Brett grinned and patted his stomach. "Sounds like a good old time. Lemme see if I can wrangle Trey and Milton to man the grill, so I'll be free to circulate and put out fires. I'll lay in a big supply of ground beef for burgers and several dozen hot dogs. I can make the burgers early in the morning, so they'll be ready. What else do you reckon I need to do?"

"Last year we ran out of ice. With it being so danged hot, we don't want a repeat of that. I'll pick up a couple of extra ice chests. If you can fill the garage freezer with bags of ice, we should be good."

Brett took another helping of salad. "What about soft drinks, honey?"

"We'll make a couple of gallons of sweet and unsweet tea and lemonade. The big dispensers are stored in the garage rafters. They'll need a good cleaning."

"Unsweet?" Stephanie frowned. "I never heard anybody say that before."

Brett chuckled. "Won't be the last time you hear it."

I turned to Stephanie. "Do you want to ask Colton to join us?"

The girl blushed to the roots of her hair. "I-I-guess."

"You don't have to," Brett said.

Stephanie glanced at Brett. "No, I think I want to. Can I invite some kids I met at the arcade?"

I needed a moment to think. "That depends."

"On what?"

"Do you think they know how to behave if they aren't in front of a video game?"

Stephanie made a face. "I think they can break away from Galaga for a while. Especially if there's food and a good view of the fireworks."

Brett stepped in and said, "It'll be good to have some young people around. I kinda like this one, and I'm sure her friends will enjoy the evening."

I gave my husband a look that said, "whose side are you on anyway," but graciously agreed. "If you're judicious about whom you invite, I think we can handle a few more guests. But keep it to four. Six teenagers ought to be plenty."

The girl squealed in delight. "Awesome!"

"Be sure they know it's a sober party. And the pool is off-limits."

"Of course." Stephanie flashed a smile, which lit her face.

"I'm closing the store at noon on the fourth, so we'll have plenty of time to prepare. Ruth and Debbie will arrive early, around three. They'll be keeping track of who's coming and what food item they're bringing, otherwise we might end up with chips but no dip or all desserts."

"Can't have that!" Brett exclaimed.

Stephanie laughed. "I think all desserts could be awesome."

"Let me tell you, there are always surprises. Folks bring everything from soup to nuts. Literally. Once, someone brought hot and sour soup. Not your normal July fare. People also bring their own cokes, so we shouldn't run out of beverages."

Stephanie said, "What else do you think we'll need?"

"I provide cups, paper plates, plastic forks, and such. Also, the buns for the burgers and hot dogs."

"Sounds like you've got it under control, sweetheart." Brett started clearing the table.

"It's never under control, darling. You'll see. You know how word of mouth spreads through AA. My finite guest list is but wishful thinking."

Chapter Twenty-Two

STEPHANIE'S FIRST ROMANCE

Working was a huge adjustment, but to my surprise, I didn't mind it. At least I got some encouragement from Jolie, who showed me how to run the cash register, display the sale items, and stuff like that. She called me a quick study. Well, yeah. And having my own money was the best.

Lauren had a sweet schedule, working two full days and three half days, but she had me working four full days. The only time I got off was on Thursday for my head-shrinking, but that was cool because Lauren agreed to let me hang out with Colton after therapy as long as I was home by five.

Even though Colton and I hung out every week, I couldn't really call it a date. So far, he hadn't made a move on me, not even a kiss. But I believed there was something there because I didn't get friend vibes from him. And of course, I'd noticed him scope me out the day I started work.

Because I'd never had a boyfriend, I didn't have a type. On second thought, maybe I did. Last week, I saw an ad for a new movie, *About Last Night*, with my fave actor, Rob Lowe. I couldn't wait to see it. Rob Lowe was majorly hot. Colton didn't look a thing like Rob Lowe, however. Well, they both had the good teeth thing going.

On the days Lauren took off at noon, I had to take two buses to get home, which was lame and took way too much time. I didn't know how to drive but wanted to learn. Maybe someday. I bet I could talk Brett into giving me lessons, just not in his huge truck. And I somehow couldn't imagine tooling around town in Lauren's Mercedes convertible.

One Thursday, when I walked out of the therapy appointment, I was astonished to see Colton waiting for me on a motorcycle. Walking around the shiny black cycle, I admired every detail. "That bike is hella wicked. When did you get it?"

"Saturday. It took all my savings. Now I'm broke, but it was worth it. Get on."

"Please go easy. This is my first time riding on one of these." I hopped on the back of his Kawasaki and almost fainted when I realized I'd have to put my arms around him. When I finally got up my nerve to touch him, I noticed his ears were red. Was he as nervous as me?

He revved the engine but didn't blast out of the parking lot as I feared. Actually, he went pretty slow as we headed over to the Drag. Even though it was almost July, the rushing air chilled my arms, so I leaned into his back to keep warm. I hoped he didn't read anything into my boobs pressing against him.

That afternoon, we didn't stay long at Le Fun. While I was crushing it on Galaxian, someone pinched my butt. I jumped in the air and squealed, letting go of the controls. Game over. Pissed, I spun around to confront Colton, but he wasn't there. Instead, I saw this guy named Jared grinning at me. Colton had warned me Jared was trouble, and now I knew why.

I wanted to smack him but settled for words. "Bite me, you poser!"

Jared's smirk fell off his lips, and he put his hands up as he backed off. "Chill, little princess." He turned and stalked away.

Colton rushed to my side. "What happened?"

When I told him what Jared did, he frowned and smacked a fist into his hand. "Where'd he go?"

"Don't! Anyway, I think he left."

Colton grasped my shoulders. "Are you sure you're okay? I mean..."

"I'm fine. But I would like to get out of here."

He held my hand as we walked to his bike. "I'm giving you a ride home. No bus today."

"This time, you can keep up with traffic. I'm not scared."

Colton grinned. "Cool."

Because I'd already survived the contact thing on the ride to the arcade, I wasn't as nervous about holding onto him. As we zoomed down Lamar and crossed the river, I caught a glimpse of the boaters on Town Lake and hoped I'd get a chance to do that. A few minutes later, he pulled into Lauren's driveway, and I climbed off the cycle. Then I stood there like a dweeb, unable to think of anything to say. He swiveled in the saddle to face me. "You okay, Steph?"

"Oh, no one calls me Steph."

He blushed bright red and said, "Sorry."

"Oh, I didn't mean it that way." Warmth rose from my neck to my face—I was probably as red as him. "Don't be. Actually, I kind of like it."

Then he smiled.

I took a step back and waved. "Thanks for the ride. See you at work."

"Okay." He looked like he was about to say something else, but he took off.

I watched him peel out and wondered if I could be any more awkward. But Colton was shy and awkward too. Maybe we were a match. When I got to my room, I lay down on the bed, wanting a nap. Random thoughts floated through my mind, mostly about romance. Thinking about Lauren getting pregnant at my age made me want to keep my knees squeezed together if I ever got the chance to make out with a guy. Would Colton be that guy? My French grandfather sounded like a smooth operator, like Sade sang about in that song that was out a while ago, but I didn't think Colton was.

At last, the Fourth of July arrived! Getting off work at noon was awesome. Already, it was a toasty 93 degrees. Lauren said it wouldn't touch 100 today, but it would come darn close. What a treat to ride home with her instead of taking the bus.

Colton was stoked about the invitation to the party, saying it would be great to see the fireworks without all the hassle. When I asked who we should invite from the arcade, he suggested two couples, Eric and Jessica, and Tony and Marie. Did that mean he thought of us as a couple?

As we drove home from work, Lauren said, "You might want to take a little lie down. We'll start setting up at three, when Ruth and Debbie get here. When I called Brett this morning, he was busy making hamburgers. I swear, he's as excited as a kid on Christmas morning."

"It's hard to think about Christmas when it's so hot. Colton is coming at six. Is that too early?"

"No, he can lend a hand. The official start time is 7:00 pm, but hosting a sober party is like herding cats. Plan all you want but be flexible. What happens, happens."

"Is your friend Jane coming?"

Lauren sighed. "Yes. She is one stubborn woman. Joshua will be on high alert with her being so near her due date."

"When is that?"

"July 10th."

I didn't say anything. I was too busy planning what I'd wear. Lauren had been right about not wanting long sleeves in the summer. Thank God, the marks on my arms had faded. I'd die if Colton knew about my problem.

After a nap, I showed up for duty in the kitchen, planning to quit at five, so I could get ready for the party. Lauren introduced me to her friends. I'd seen them before, on the night I arrived on Lauren's doorstep, but hadn't spoken to them.

Ruth, a cheerleader type with bouncy blonde curls who had to be in her forties, jumped up from her chair and gave me a bone-crushing hug. Was that really necessary? I forced a smile. "Nice to meet you," I squeaked.

I gave the much older Debbie a sideways look. To my relief, she stayed seated and nodded.

Lauren handed me a copy of the guest list. Beside each name was a dish. I'd never been to a potluck dinner and was interested to see what people brought. Reading down the list, I saw several items I'd never heard of. What the heck were samosas?

Ruth took charge. "Stephanie, you're on iced tea and lemonade duty."

"How much should I make?"

"Gallons. Be sure to make both sweet and unsweet. It's hot as Hades. Brett, please fill two or three ice chests from the garage freezer."

"Yes, ma'am."

Ruth turned to Debbie. "Can you help Lauren with the plates and such?"

Lauren brought paper plates, cups, and eating utensils to the counter, and Debbie carried them out to the patio.

Brett gave Lauren a one-armed hug. "Got my marching orders. I'll check in with you later."

Lauren kissed Brett on the cheek. "Thanks, honey."

I watched them together, being so loving. They reminded me of how my parents used to be before everything went bad. Tears stung my eyes, but I blinked them away and got back to work.

Chapter Twenty-Three

LAUREN - DRAMA ON THE FOURTH

Leaving things in Ruth's capable hands, I slipped from the kitchen and sought refuge in my office. With the loveseat now in Stephanie's room, there was plenty of floor space for my meditation practice. I rolled out my mat and sat in lotus position, breathing deeply, intentionally. All I needed was a few minutes alone. I lay back on the mat and recited my daily litany of prayers. Of course, I included the Serenity Prayer and the St. Francis prayer, to which I aspired but knew I'd never attain the level of selflessness it spoke of.

After ten minutes or so, I sat up and blinked. Feeling more centered, I checked on the party preparations. Ruth told me that Debbie had taken care of arranging the serving tables, and Stephanie had finished the tea and lemonade. I hurried outside to see if Brett had everything he needed.

As Brett watched me approach, a slow grin spread over his face. "There you are, darlin'. Trey and Milton just showed up and started the coals in the grills." The scent of lighter fluid and hot charcoal wafted through the air, the very essence of a summer party.

Three long tables formed an open square around the patio. Debbie arranged the drinks table with ice chests positioned strategically around the space. She'd even made signs for each cooler: "coke, water, ice."

Stephanie lugged a gallon of tea to the drinks table. The burble of a motorcycle caught my attention—and hers. She grinned and dashed into the house. I followed and peeked out the sidelight window at the front door. To my horror, the rider was Colton. He rolled the vile machine around the side of the garage where it would be out of the way. Stephanie, wreathed in smiles, walked beside him, chatting away. Had the girl been on the motorcycle? I'd have to address the dangers with her later.

Parking would be at a premium. There was space for four more cars in the driveway and some room along the street. As far as I knew, I was the only one on the block throwing a house party that evening. As many Austinites did, several of my neighbors had headed out to cooler climes for the summer. Three of them granted me permission to park in their drives, which would alleviate overcrowding. I'd encouraged my guests to carpool, and I hoped many of them would do so.

Then a brilliant idea occurred to me. I'd assign Colton to direct guest parking, and I'd make sure Stephanie helped in the kitchen and the serving line. I checked in with Ruth to clue her in on my plans for my granddaughter and then found Brett again.

"Colton arrived on a motorcycle," I fumed.

"Really, what kind?"

"Are you kidding me? Is that what you want to know? *I* want to know if Stephanie has been on the darned thing."

"Okay, sugar. I hear you. Just remember you hired Colton, and I know you don't hire anyone without a thorough check and several recommendations. I'll have a little talk with the boy later. Right now, it's party time!"

Realizing I was frowning, I nodded and relaxed my face. "You're right. Anyway, I have a plan to keep him busy out front with the parking logistics. And I'll keep Stephanie occupied elsewhere."

Brett leaned down and kissed the top of my head. "I knew you'd be on top of things. Just relax and enjoy the evening. Guests will start arriving before you know it, so I'll get the fellas started grilling."

The aroma of hamburgers and hot dogs drew the crowd to the patio, where the serving tables awaited, loaded with a variety of eclectic ethnic treats. Those whose tastebuds favored south-of-the-border fare had guacamole, queso, and several types of salsa from which to choose. From pizza to petit fours, there was something for everyone.

I spied Stephanie and Colton at a table with four other youngsters. With plates piled high, they ate enthusiastically, joking and laughing together. Seeing Stephanie enjoying her friends brought a smile to my face.

Jane and Joshua arrived late. He hovered around Jane as if she were made of fine china and might break. I rushed to her side. "I thought you'd changed your mind. It's almost time for the concert. Can I fix you a plate?"

Under the strings of sparkling white lights, Jane's face paled. "No, thank you. I ate at home."

Joshua snorted. "When? You haven't had a bite all day. You should be at home, resting."

"I'm fine." Jane's mouth tightened. "Let's get a seat for the show."

I'd rented thirty chairs and six tables, which were mostly full. There was space on the low stone wall that overlooked Zilker Park, which would be uncomfortable for Jane, so Joshua went in search of a cushion for his beloved to sit on. When her husband returned, Jane sank into her place with a grunt. Brett tuned the radio to the simulcast promptly at 8:30, when the concert began.

After a few minutes, I left my friends and mingled with the other guests, many of whom I hadn't had a chance to greet. I missed Helen's presence. She so loved the Fourth. Thinking back, I realized her last public event was my wedding in March. Her diagnosis came shortly after that night, and she'd been too ill to come to my birthday party. Helen had enjoyed meeting Stephanie and later told me how impressed she was with the girl's thoughtfulness and intelligence. I'd have to visit Helen soon.

Although I didn't get an exact headcount, it sure seemed like there were more people than last year. Stephanie and crew pitched in to help Ruth cover the leftover food. I headed to the kitchen, where Debbie washed the casseroles and platters so guests could take a clean serving dish home.

A loud boom and oohs and aahs signaled the start of the fireworks. "Come on, Debbie, leave the dishes for later. The show is starting."

We hurried out to the patio and joined Brett, Jane, and Joshua. The fireworks lit the sky, and the smell of gunpowder stung my nose. In my opinion, that night's spectacular display rivaled that of the bicentennial.

Appreciative exclamations and enthusiastic clapping reinforced that belief. After an especially vibrant spectacle, I glanced over at Jane, who had cried out, but her outburst had nothing to do with the fireworks. As Jane started to slide off the cushion, Joshua caught her. He knelt on the ground, holding her close. "I have to get her to the hospital. Her water broke. It looks like she's been hiding the fact she's in labor. Damn, I should have paid more attention." His brow knitted with worry.

Brett said, "Is there time? And ain't you a doctor?"

Joshua tossed his long black hair out of his eyes. "Yeah. I had to become a medical doctor before becoming a psychiatrist, but I never practiced. My one obstetrics rotation is but a dim memory. If we leave right away, I think we can make it in time."

Brett helped Joshua lift the protesting Jane. Together, they half-carried her to the house and sat her in a chair. Ruth and Debbie rushed inside to help, and I asked Debbie to bring some towels.

Wringing her hands, Ruth said, "I'm so excited to see the baby, but it's better if the birth takes place at the hospital. If you don't make it to the car, give me a holler, and I'll help Joshua deliver."

"God willing, that won't be necessary," I said.

Joshua yelled out the phone numbers for Jane's OB and South Austin Medical Center. I made the calls.

Colton and Stephanie must have seen the commotion. They burst into the kitchen. "Can I help?" Colton asked. Stephanie froze, staring at Jane.

Joshua tossed him his car keys. "Find my car. It's a black Saab, a stick shift. Bring it as close as you can to the driveway. I parked on the street, so you should be able to get to it."

"Good thing I can drive a stick." Colton grabbed the keys and ran.

Jane cradled her belly and groaned. "I forgot everything I learned in Lamaze. I'm supposed to breathe and pant, I think."

I brought Joshua a cool cloth to wipe Jane's brow. "Thanks, Lauren. We better get going."

Joshua and Brett carried Jane out the front door. I followed with towels. As they loaded her into the back seat of the waiting Saab, I flashed back to the birth of my daughter forty-five years ago. Such a blessing they didn't use twilight sleep anymore on young mothers. My throat thickened as I remembered the day I lost Brett's son.

After Joshua drove off, Brett turned to me. "That was some other kinda fireworks. Let's go watch the rest."

As we were about to enter the house, a racing engine sounded, and a motorcycle drove right up the terraced stairs. A tall young man in a hooded sweatshirt jumped off, ditched the bike, and ran into the house, trailing a distinct odor of alcohol.

Astonished, Brett and I gave chase. The hoodlum knocked over the dining room chairs, then stormed through the house and out the back door. He flung open the coolers. "Where's the booze? Where's l'il princess?"

He threw the cooler into the pool, then began tossing chairs and the trash containers in too. Several of the men ran up, with Brett leading the way. The vandal shoved Trey into the pool and charged the others. Before Brett and the much younger Murry tackled him to the ground, the thug landed a roundhouse punch on poor Milton's jaw. Brett yelled, "Call the cops!"

Without missing a beat, I rushed inside and dialed 911. Ruth was right behind me.

As the final cymbal crashes filled the air during the grand finale, I put my face in my hands and sank to the floor. Ruth sat beside me. "This sure will be a night to remember. First Jane goes into labor, then that hooligan busting in. My Lord!"

"I have no words."

By the time the police arrived to relieve Brett and Murry from detaining the thug, the party was over in spirit. Most of the guests had already left, offering subdued thanks on their way out.

Debbie hustled into the kitchen and helped me and Ruth to our feet. "You won't believe this! That nasty drunk didn't go easily and fought the police when they hauled him to his feet. Before they got him cuffed, he head-butted the smaller officer in the stomach."

Stunned and angry at the turn of events, I shook my head. "Unbelievable! I wonder how he chose our house to attack."

"That's not all," Debbie said. "The arresting officer is booking him for assault and battery and resisting arrest. Told him he's going away for a while."

"Well, good." I couldn't be more pleased.

Brett stormed in the door and came to my side. I threw my arms around him. "Where's Stephanie?"

"Good question. Who the hell was that crazed maniac?" Brett asked.

"I don't know, but maybe Stephanie does." Although I hated to think so, my suspicions were aroused.

"You might could be right." Brett pursed his lips. "He did ask about 'l'il princess.' Wonder who that is."

An officer entered the kitchen and approached us. "You the homeowners?"

After giving our statement to the police, my darling husband took hold of my shoulders. "You look beat. Tell you what, go on and get you in the tub."

"Thanks, darling. That's just what I need. What are you going to do?"

"First, I gotta make an ice pack for poor old Milton, then find Trey some dry clothes. Murry stuck around to help me pull everything out of the pool. And don't you worry, I'll call the pool service first thing Monday."

I groaned. "The pool."

"It'll be good as new, I promise. Say, I wonder if Jane had her baby yet."

"Probably not yet. I can't wait to find out if it's a boy or a girl." I leaned in for a hug.

Ruth and Debbie gathered their things and stood at the counter, looking like they'd rather be somewhere else.

I summoned a smile. "Good night, you two. Thanks for all your help. Couldn't have done it without you. Talk soon." As I headed to my bathroom sanctuary for a long hot soak, Brett said, "Ladies, let me walk y'all to your cars." I called over my shoulder. "Honey, let me know when you sort out the Stephanie situation. You know where I'll be."

Chapter Twenty-Four

STEPHANIE FACES THE MUSIC

When the maniac ran out on the patio and shouted, "Where's l'il princess?" I knew it was Jared, and my life was toast.

Colton muttered, "What the hell?" He grabbed my hand, and me and my friends hid behind a shrub and watched the craziness and arrest. It was only a matter of time before I'd have to face the music, as my dad used to say.

I had to ask my friends the obvious question. "Did any of you tell Jared about the party?"

Five shocked faces stared at me. "No way! He's heinous," Jessica said.

Eric patted my shoulder. "That loser probably overheard us talking. We never even talk to him."

They all denied it, and I believed them. With the party ruined, the two couples beat feet.

Colton shook his head. "What are you gonna tell your folks?"

"The truth."

"Which is?"

"That Jared is a creep who hangs out at the arcade even though he should have a job and hang with people his own age."

"That's a fact. But how did he find out about the party?"

I shrugged. "I think Eric nailed it. Jared spied on us."

"Yeah, that's gotta be it. Can't think of any other explanation." Colton shrugged. "Sure hope you don't get in trouble."

"Me too. I'll walk you out."

Colton's bike was right where he left it. He stood next to his bike and raised the kickstand. "Stand back, Steph. It's too narrow here. Wait a minute, then follow me." He pushed his bike to the street and hopped on. I met him under the streetlight.

"That jerk really tore up Lauren's flower beds." Colton scanned the yard. "I don't see Jared's Harley. Cops must have taken it."

"Yeah, I'm sure it's evidence." Not that I was an expert or anything, but I watched my share of *Night Court*, *Miami Vice*, and *Moonlighting*.

With one arm, Colton pulled me to him and surprised me with my first kiss. He tasted like grape soda. As he drove away, I stood there, touching my tingling lips, but not feeling much else. Where were the butterflies I heard so much about?

Brett came out the front door with Ruth and Debbie. He spotted me and said, "Wait for me in the kitchen."

With a racing heart, I did as he ordered. Unable to sit still, I paced like the animals I used to watch at Franklin Zoo. A bead of sweat slid down my face, burning my eyes. Brett would ask tough questions, and when he found out I knew the perp, I imagined my punishment: being packed off and sent back to Evelyn or grounding forever. It seemed like an hour until Brett returned.

Before he could speak, I asked, "Where's Lauren?"

"Taking a nice relaxing bath to relieve the stress. She was fairly undone by all the drama."

I gulped. "Oh. Sorry."

"We're wondering how that criminal idiot came to find our party. Know anything 'bout that?" He fixed me with his single-eyed gaze. The intensity was more than enough for two eyes.

"I-I know who he is. His name is Jared, and he hangs out at the arcade."

"Friend of yours?" Brett put both hands on the counter and leaned toward me.

"No way! No one likes him. He's a lot older than most of the kids. He creeps me out. I swear I didn't tell him about the party."

"Well, he found out somehow." Brett's frown made his eye patch scrunch up.

I tried not to stare. "My friends think he overheard us talking about the party. It's dark in the arcade, so we might not have noticed him." Worried about my punishment, I shivered. "Is Lauren mad at me?"

"Lauren is too tired to be mad, but if what you say is true, it ain't your fault. Now get you to bed, and we'll talk in the morning."

I practically ran from the room.

At breakfast the next day, I apologized all over the place to Lauren. She looked like she didn't get much sleep last night.

"Stephanie, I don't want to dwell on last night's incident. The authorities will deal with that...cretin. We'll get the pool cleaned and fix the landscaping and go on with life."

That was a relief because I didn't want to think about it either. "Not to change the subject or anything, but do you know if Jane had a boy or a girl?"

Lauren smiled, making her look more like her usual self. "The proud Papa called this morning. Jane had a little baby boy, well, not so little. Nine pounds and change. And long too—twenty-two inches."

"Awesome! Is she okay?"

"She's doing well and said she'd be ready for company next Saturday. Want to come with me to visit?"

"I guess. What did they name him?"

"Will. Will Renfrew. It has a nice ring."

By the time Thursday rolled around, I was actually looking forward to my therapy appointment. Probably had something to do with seeing Colton afterward. With the usual instructions about being home by five, Lauren dropped me off. After Friday's disaster, I was sure she'd forbid me from going to Le Fun or riding on Colton's motorcycle, but she didn't.

The air conditioning in the office must have been set on arctic. Good thing I'd brought my denim jacket, so I'd stay warm on the motorcycle. I didn't have long to wait until Jenna appeared, wearing a long-sleeved striped dress with a bowtie at the neck. It looked like something her mother would wear.

We entered her office, which didn't feel as frigid as the lobby, and took our usual seats.

"Today, I'd like to delve into when you started engaging in self-harm."

Even though I knew the topic would come up, that didn't make it any easier. Crossing my arms, I leaned back in the chair, not saying a word.

Jenna let the silence drag on for a minute or two.

Of course, I folded first. "It started a few months after my dad died. I was eleven." I gulped several times, feeling tears fill my eyes.

Jenna waited.

"When Dad was diagnosed with cancer, my mom took it like a champ. She was confident he'd beat it, and so was I. He had to be okay. He just had to." Tears spilled, and I had to stop talking. Like Mrs. Doody's office, and probably every shrink's office in the world, there was a box of tissue in easy reach. I grabbed a handful.

"Before they wheeled him to surgery, we kissed him goodbye and tried to smile. Only thirty minutes later, the nurse came to the waiting room to tell us he was in recovery. Mom and I looked at each other. I remember the stunned look on her face. My stomach hurt, and I started shaking. Mom asked the nurse, 'Why is he done so soon?' The nurse stood there with her hands folded in front of her. 'The doctor is on his way to Mr. Kingston's room to speak to you.' Then she walked away."

Jenna asked, "Do you need a break?"

"No. I want to get this over with." I dabbed my eyes. "Mom and I waited in Dad's room. He was still in recovery. The doctor came in and gave us the worst possible news. He said something like, 'When we opened, we saw the cancer had spread throughout his abdomen. We closed immediately.' There was nothing they could do for my dad."

I crushed the soggy tissues in my hand. "Mom and I cried and cried. When they brought Dad back to his room, we tried to hold it together, but as soon as we saw him, we lost it. Dad was so brave. His only concern was for us."

"That is very tough stuff for a child of eleven."

"Yeah." I blubbered a bit, then took a deep breath. "Dad couldn't work, and the medical bills were monster, so they had to sell our house. We moved in with Evelyn and Clark—my fake grandparents."

With her eyebrows raised, Jenna said, "You mean your adoptive grandparents."

Well, that kind of pissed me off. Wasn't Jenna supposed to be on my side? "Maybe that's what *you* call them."

"I didn't mean to offend you. Feel your feelings."

"Dad died in that dusty, dreary old house. The hospice people came and set him up in a room off the kitchen. He faded away a little more each day. The smells coming from that room were awful." I stopped for a minute, not sure I wanted to continue. But I had to get it out.

"I didn't recognize him at the end. He looked like a skeleton covered with gray skin. Then one day, I walked through the door after school and just knew. Can you feel an absence?" I glanced at Jenna. "Is that even possible?"

Jenna's forehead wrinkled. "Yes, I think it is."

"Anyway, the air felt different. And I knew I'd never see him again."

Everything about that time came back to me: the sights, the sounds, the smells. I buried my face in my hands and wailed. When my tears ran out, I sat up and sniffled. "The funeral was awful. It rained. I didn't have any black clothes. There was a reception back at the house, but I couldn't make myself go, so I stayed in my room and cried."

"Are you okay with finishing the session?" Jenna's eyes were a little too shiny. Was she tearing up?

"Might as well." I blew my nose and grabbed some tissue. "My life was ruined. My dad had spent a lot of time with me, encouraging me to study aeronautics when I got to college. We both loved outer space. He never got to see the launch of the first Space Shuttle."

"You will always have your memories. When you feel down, think about those wonderful times."

"Yeah, the standard advice." I glared at her—anger was better than tears. "But I missed my old house, the kids from my neighborhood, and my school, but most of all, I missed my dad. Evelyn enrolled me in private school, and I hated it. I had one friend, Allison. She was a scholarship student, so the minute we became friends, I was shut out by the popular girls and the cliques."

"That must have been painful."

"Yes. Very."

"How were things with your mother after your dad passed?"

An excellent question, but tough to answer. "Mom and I got close at first. We watched movies—James Bond movies mostly. She didn't care anything about outer space like my dad did. Most evenings, we made popcorn and hot chocolate and hung out together. We were both so sad, at least for the first few months."

"What changed?"

"Her friend Kelly had been bugging Mom to get out there and meet someone and convinced my mom to go on a blind date. I didn't think she'd go, but she was super excited. She'd lost weight after Dad died and had to buy new clothes. She came home with bags and bags of flashy clothes, too flashy for someone's mother. Then she went to the salon, got a haircut and had highlights put on her hair. I didn't know who she was anymore. That date didn't work out, but there were plenty more, and I hardly saw her. She went out to bars at night during the week and on dates on the weekend. When I told her I wanted to spend more time with her, she asked, 'Don't you want me to be happy?'"

I stared at Jenna. "Can you believe that? Of course I wanted her to be happy. But she obviously couldn't see *I* wasn't."

"It seems like your mom coped with her grief differently."

I snorted. "You might say that!"

"I didn't know how things could get worse, but they did. When I needed my mother the most, she wasn't there for me. Right after I turned twelve, I got my period and rushed to her room to tell her. She was getting ready for a date and said, 'There's some tampons in a box in my bathroom. Read the instructions first.' I turned away before she could see my tears, not that she'd care. That was the day I started hurting myself."

Colton was in his usual spot when I walked out of the medical office. The smile dropped off his face when he got a look at me. "What's wrong?"

I guess my swollen eyes gave it away. After reliving Dad's death and how Mom abandoned me, I felt lower than dirt. "I don't feel like going to the arcade today. Can you just take me home?"

"Got a better idea. Let's go to Nau's for ice cream."

After a short ride to a part of town I'd never been to, he parked the bike in front of an old-timey-looking store. "They have the best chocolate malts. Or maybe you'd like a coke float."

Inside, the U-shaped counter, lined with orange stools, looked like something from the fifties. We sat at the counter and ordered two chocolate malts.

"Want to talk about it?"

"Talk about what?"

"Whatever happened at your appointment. You look so sad."

"Nope. I'm all talked out."

Colton shrugged. "Okay, I'll back off."

The soda jerk slid two malts in front of us and gave us a little salute. I had to admit, my drink was delicious.

As we sipped our cold treats, Colton took my hand, like we were a couple on that old TV show *Happy Days*. I laughed out loud.

"What's funny?"

I told him.

"Huh, I never watched that show."

"It's set in the fifties, just like this place."

"Oh, got it."

When I slurped the last of my malt, we hopped off our stools and Colton paid the tab. We browsed the candy section for a while, then went outside and got back on the cycle. "Still want to head home?" Colton asked.

"Not really. What do you have in mind?"

"Ever been to Barton Springs?"

"No. Is that near Lauren's house?"

"Sure is. It's totally awesome. You'll see."

With the wind in our faces, Colton gunned the bike onto Mopac, zoomed across the river, and exited at Bee Cave Road. He hung a U-turn under the bridge and in minutes, we parked and walked down to the coolest place I'd ever seen. A big outdoor swimming pool.

"I can't tell if it's natural or man-made."

"A little of both."

We watched the swimmers. Colton convinced me to sit on the edge and stick my toes in the water. It was a little chilly but felt good on a hot summer day. When the shadows started getting longer, I asked him to take me home. That day he didn't kiss me, and I wondered why.

Chapter Twenty-Five

LAUREN REGAINS HER FOOTING

Determined to forget the stressful Fourth of July, I forbade any talk of it. With the pool cleaned and the landscaping repaired, there was nothing to see. Stephanie seemed to blame herself, even though I did everything possible to reassure her it wasn't her fault. She'd been quite subdued since that night.

Perhaps a girls' dinner and a trip to the mall would perk her up. When she got home from work on Friday, I suggested we have a meal at Chuy's and then stop at the mall.

Stephanie groaned. "Do I have to go?"

"Have you got something better to do?"

"Nope."

"I'd like to shop for baby gifts for Will. Remember, we're meeting him tomorrow."

"Oh, yeah. I forgot." The girl's lack of enthusiasm couldn't be more obvious.

As casual as could be, I asked, "This won't cut into your time with Colton?"

Stephanie frowned and narrowed her eyes. "No."

When Stephanie confided to me she was a virgin, I was astonished, given we were two decades past the sexual revolution. I wondered if she still was.

Maybe the shopping trip would give me an opportunity to broach the subject. "Well?"

The girl shrugged. "Okay. I'll go. Let me change."

I closed my eyes, and visions of Madonna and Cindy Lauper danced through my head. Until Stephanie arrived and made a plea for MTV, I'd been blissfully unaware of the songbirds. I wandered into Brett's office where he was doing paperwork.

"Darling, you'll have to fend for yourself tonight. I'm taking Stephanie to Chuy's, then on to the mall."

He glanced up from his desk and smiled. "See y'all later. Have fun."

"Not sure if fun will be on the agenda, but I'll give it a try."

As usual, the restaurant was packed, but we got lucky and were shown to a table right away. With wide eyes and her head on a swivel, Stephanie trailed behind me, staring at the unique interior decorations.

"What a wild place! What's with all the Elvis stuff?"

I tutted. "Elvis is the King of Rock 'n' Roll, and the owners rightfully give him his due."

"There are pieces of cars hanging on the wall. How crazy is that?"

"Not even a blip on the screen of crazy. This is Austin. Let's order."

The girl chomped on chips and salsa while flipping through the menu. "Ha! I'm going to have the beef Big As Yo' Face Burrito."

"Good choice. I'll have the same. I recommend getting it smothered in queso."

"That melty cheese?"

"That's right. You should up your game on menu Spanish."

The waitress brought our sweet tea and took our order. Service was usually fast, and tonight was no exception. Within minutes, the tantalizing aromas of sizzling beef and spice announced the arrival of our meals.

"Wow, they weren't kidding about the size of this thing," Stephanie said.

We ate in companionable silence for a while. With only half my big burrito finished, I pushed my plate away. Stephanie devoured her burrito, beans, and every last grain of rice. For a moment, I feared she might lick her plate.

"Now that you're finished, why don't you tell me what's on your mind? You're not still feeling guilty about the incident on the Fourth, are you?"

Stephanie flicked her eyes at me. "Nope."

"Then what is it?"

"Nothing."

My eyebrows rose to their full height. "I doubt that very much."

"Okay. You'll bug me until I tell you. This week, I had a really tough therapy session."

"Do you want to talk about it?"

She looked at me with eyes way too old for a sixteen-year-old girl. "Not here."

I glanced around the bustling restaurant. "That's probably wise. Let me know when you want to talk."

Stephanie nodded while avoiding my eyes.

Wondering when and if the girl would open up to me about her therapy, I settled the tab. We wove our way through the packed crowds to the door, got in the car, and headed to the mall. Stephanie had quickly become a pro at handling the convertible roof. After the top was secure, I locked the door, and we strolled inside to Dillard's. "What do you think we should get for the baby?"

"No clue. What do you think Jane needs?"

"She's well-stocked with newborn items. Because she and Joshua didn't want to learn the sex of the baby beforehand, the décor and baby clothes are all green and yellow. I say we go overboard on the blue. And maybe we should think ahead and buy larger clothing for the winter."

"Do we even have winter here?"

"Well, we call it winter. It varies from year to year, and sometimes we don't even get a freeze."

"That's awesome!"

"Yes, for the bugs."

Stephanie wandered from display to display, checking out the baby clothes. I hadn't even thought about such things when I was pregnant with Barbara, knowing Clark and Evelyn were adopting her. With my second pregnancy, Brett's child, I miscarried at five months and hadn't even started planning a nursery. Even though my sad history with babies still weighed on me at times, I felt nothing but joy for Jane and Joshua.

Overwhelmed by the selection, we asked the advice of a lovely saleswoman. She took her time with us, and we settled on several outfits sized six to nine months. While we waited for our purchases to be gift-wrapped, I drew Stephanie to a quiet alcove and asked about Colton. "Is there a budding romance in the air?"

The girl gave me a sideways glance. "What are you really asking?"

I fixed her with my no-nonsense look. "You know what I'm asking."

"Oh my God! Gag me." Stephanie guffawed. "We haven't done anything except kiss. Believe me, after you told me what happened to you at sixteen, I swear it won't happen to me."

Taken aback, I couldn't think of a suitable response, so I kept my mouth shut. At last, Stephanie stopped chortling. We picked up our packages and drove home. Neither of us turned on the radio.

When we arrived, Stephanie placed the packages on the dining room table, then rushed to her room without a word. Within seconds, the sound of MTV leaked through her door. Resigned to the noise that had become part of our daily lives, I entered the kitchen and spotted Brett on the lighted patio.

Once outside, I took a deep, cleansing breath. "I'm home, darling."

"How was your evening?"

"Dinner was fine. We had a successful and expensive bout of shopping for Jane's little one." Then I told him what Stephanie had said about not repeating my mistake. "Tell you the truth, it kind of stung."

"Oh boy." He held his arms out to me, and I joined him on the chaise lounge. We sat for a time, watching the night sky and listening to the tree frogs. Brett always brought me peace. He didn't have to say a thing.

Saturday afternoon, Stephanie and I set out for Jane's. "There's a florist on the way. I'll pop in and pick up some flowers."

When we pulled into Jane's driveway, the girl said, "Wow! What a cool-looking house." The rusticated Austin limestone exterior and copper metal roof were impressive. We got out of the car, and Stephanie grabbed a loaded shopping bag. I scooped up the flowers and the other bag of gifts.

Before I could stop her, Stephanie rang the doorbell. I cringed, hoping we hadn't disturbed a peacefully slumbering infant.

An unshaven and disheveled Joshua answered the door and took the packages, placing them on the hallway console. Loud wailing came from within. Stephanie and I followed him inside.

I handed him the flowers. "For the new mother. Did we wake the baby?"

"No, he's been fussy since he woke up at five. If we're lucky, he'll settle down, so you can see how handsome he is with a closed mouth."

With his uncombed hair and dark circles under his eyes, the poor man personified exhaustion. He trudged to Jane's office, where we found her rocking the baby and making cooing sounds. Joshua showed Jane the roses. "I'm going to put these in water, then brew a pot of coffee." He left the room.

Delilah, who uncharacteristically hadn't greeted us at the door, sat beside Jane's feet, and I wondered if the kitten was jealous or just fascinated with the newcomer.

Stephanie knelt next to Jane's chair, not to see the baby, but rather the cat. "What a gorgeous cat! What's her name?"

Jane smiled. "That's Delilah."

"Can I pick her up?"

"I'd let her come to you. She hasn't left my side since we came home with the baby."

The girl rose to her feet. "Oh. Okay."

"Motherhood agrees with you, Jane," I said. "Joshua looks a little worse for wear, but you look marvelous."

My friend grinned. "The secret is napping when Will does. Poor Joshua is on a hair trigger. He jumps awake at any sound during the night. I hope he calms down, so he catches up on his sleep. He only took two weeks off work and must go back a week from Monday."

Will's cries decreased in volume, then he snuffled a little and fell silent. Stephanie asked, "Is he asleep?"

"Yes, he is. Come close and get a look at him."

"He's a cutie. Is it all right if I hold him?" Stephanie asked.

"Do you know how to support his head?" Jane's concern was palpable.

"Sure do! When I was a freshman, my friend Allison's mom had a baby. Was she ever embarrassed! Allison spent so much time babysitting that if I wanted to hang out, I had to go to her house. So, I picked up a few things."

"Okay, but be very careful," Jane cautioned.

"I promise." Stephanie leaned down and tenderly lifted the baby in her arms. "He smells so good."

Jane nodded. "Yes, he does. By the way, good job. Perfect technique." She gripped the arms of her chair and began to stand. "Can I get y'all a cold drink?"

I patted Jane's shoulder and shook my head. "Oh, no, you don't. Set yourself back down. No need to play hostess today. We came bearing gifts. They're in the hallway."

Settling back with a sigh, Jane said, "We can get them later. Let's visit."

"Do you want to hold him, Lauren?" Stephanie asked.

"Maybe later. Let me take a peek." Completely out of my element, I girded myself to view the baby. Stephanie brought the sleeping Will close. "What a beautiful child! That mass of dark hair is stunning. I swear he has Joshua's nose, but his skin is creamy, like yours." Unwanted memories of Barbara's birth and my miscarriage rocked me. Had I said the right things?

Jane gave me a searching look, as if she could sense my roiling emotions. "Unfortunately, he'll lose that hair."

Stephanie handed the baby back to Jane and then joined me on the loveseat. Delilah's curious nature prevailed, and she came over to sit at the girl's feet, then she pounced, landing in Stephanie's lap.

"Her fur is so fluffy. What kind of cat is she?" the girl asked.

"A doll-faced Persian."

"Cool." Turning to me, Stephanie asked, "Can I get a cat?"

I shuddered. "That's not in the cards, dear. I grew up on a ranch where animals were not pets."

"Well, you don't live on a ranch now."

Irritated with my granddaughter, I clenched my teeth. "I said no."

Joshua stuck his head in the doorway and whispered, "Anyone want coffee or something else to drink?"

Stephanie and I declined the offer.

"Is he actually asleep?" Joshua asked.

Jane grinned at her husband. "Yes, at last. He must be exhausted from all the hours of fussing. Will you put Will in his crib and turn on the baby monitor, honey?"

"Of course, babe. So glad he's finally settled down. Keep your fingers crossed he doesn't wake up." Joshua leaned down and took the baby in his arms. We all held our breath as he left the room.

Stephanie placed Delilah on the floor and stood. "I'll go get the presents for Will." She brought back the bags of prettily wrapped packages, laid them on the coffee table, and plopped herself in a chair, choosing not to sit beside me. Delilah hopped into her lap, which put a smile on the girl's face. "She likes me."

In a moment of weakness, I actually considered getting the girl a cat, but sanity prevailed.

I handed a gift to Jane. "Go ahead and open it. I know everything you bought for the nursery is either green or yellow, so we brought you some relief. The saleslady said you'd appreciate getting some larger-sized things as Will grows."

Jane grinned and tore into the packages. She held up a blue onesie with an applique of a cat. "Perfect!" After all the presents were opened and exclaimed over, Jane thanked us. "I knew you'd go overboard, Lauren."

"It was my pleasure. We're going to head out. You should be napping while the little one is quiet. We'll catch up later."

When we arrived home, Colton sat astride his motorcycle in the driveway. He got off the bike and opened the car door for Stephanie. "Hey."

"Hey," she replied.

Colton nodded to me.

"Do you want to come in, Colton? You can join us for dinner if you'd like."

Stephanie's jaw dropped, and she blushed bright pink. Not sure what that meant, I looked a question at her. She nodded and smiled. The boy grinned from ear to ear. I'd never noticed what good teeth the boy had, such an important attribute.

We filed into the house and through the dining room to the kitchen. Brett sat at the table reading the Chronicle. "Say, honey, you ever read the classified ads in this here rag?"

I laughed. "Once or twice. Very entertaining. We have a guest for dinner. Colton, you remember my husband, Brett."

Brett rose to his full height to shake Colton's hand. "Thought I heard a motorcycle. Good to see ya, son."

"Same."

"Good eye contact. Firm handshake. Guess you can stay for supper."

Stephanie tugged on Colton's sleeve. "You have to get used to his sense of humor. Come on, I'll show you my room. Lauren let me pick out everything myself."

Brett called after them. "Keep the door open and your feet on the floor. Dinner on the patio at 5:30."

I kissed Brett. "Darling, I owe Helen a call. I've been so busy I haven't had a chance to visit in weeks."

He bent to kiss me back. "Make sure you find the time to see her. I'll start dinner soon. Come join me?"

As I left the room, I glanced back at him. "Of course, darling." In my office, I sat at the desk and dialed Helen. Francine answered.

"May I speak with Helen?" I asked.

"Not at the moment, I'm afraid. Hospice is here."

"Oh, no!" Stunned by the news, I managed to say, "I'll keep you and Helen in my prayers. I'll call back later."

Numb, I hung up the phone. Helen had been my sponsor for twenty-five years. What would I do without her?

Chapter Twenty-Six

STEPHANIE'S BREAKTHROUGH

Sometimes, I had to pinch myself when I woke up in my awesome room. I couldn't believe how radically my life had changed in only three months. My escape from my fake granny and Boston was the smartest thing I'd ever done. Freedom to wear the clothes I wanted and having MTV at long last was a massive upgrade.

Soon, I'd start my junior year at Austin High without knowing a single person—that was a little scary, but I still couldn't wait. For one thing, I wouldn't have to work except on Saturdays. Of course, I'd have a boatload of homework to keep me busy during the week. Colton asked Lauren to change his schedule so he worked on Saturday, but I'd definitely be seeing him less when school started. Our budding romance, as Lauren called it, stayed a closed bud. When I talked to him about my plans for Stanford and asked him if he planned on going to college, he just laughed. I wondered if he planned on stocking groceries and going to the arcade until he retired.

What should I wear on my first day? I asked Lauren to help me pick out an outfit. "Of course, you know I love a fashion show," she said. While I modeled every single item in my wardrobe, she sat on the bed and voted down each combination. "If I were you, I'd be a teeny bit conservative on the first day. I doubt your peers are going to show up in Madonna garb."

"Garb?"

"You know what I mean."

"Can you take me to the mall?"

"Of course."

The mall crawled with people buying stuff for back to school. I checked out what the other girls were buying and ended up with bags of Jordache and Guess jeans and tons of cute tops. Lauren was right about toning it down. With my new clothes, I felt more confident I'd blend in with the other kids.

Bonus, no more worries about Lauren sending me back to Boston because she was now my official guardian.

The only downer was Lauren insisting I write to Evelyn every week. I'd rather just make a phone call, but Lauren wouldn't budge and bought me a box of baby blue stationery and a booklet of stamps. At first, I didn't know what to write. Evelyn didn't know the first thing about Austin. Then it hit me; I'd tell her all about my new city. Each week, in my finest handwriting, I wrote two pages of news. After three weeks, I got a letter back from her. All she wrote about was her doctor's appointments and the flipping opera. Since Evelyn took so long to write back, I would too. Maybe she'd stop, and then so could I.

At our last session, Jenna gave me homework. She told me to write down three things I loved most about my parents. The list for my dad was easy. The list for my mom wasn't, and I dreaded the next appointment, so of course, Thursday rolled around too fast.

Lauren waved and tooted the horn as I stepped out of her car. Her good mood pissed me off. I stuck a hand in my pocket to make sure I had my assignment and entered the lobby with my feet dragging.

Jenna was back to wearing her power suit with the big shoulder pads, but it wasn't my place to give her fashion advice. I asked for a Dr Pepper and took my seat.

She handed me the cold can. "Got one right here. Did you do your assignment?" Jenna asked with a smile.

"Sure did."

"Great!" She acted surprised that I'd done what she asked. She needed to be more confident.

"There are tons of things I loved about my dad, but here's the top three. One, he told me he loved me every single day. Two, he spent hours helping me build models of spaceships. Three, he told me I could be anything I wanted to be." Although tears stung my eyes, I couldn't help smiling, remembering the good times.

"Lovely. He sounds like a wonderful father."

I nodded. "The best."

"And your mother's list?"

"About that." I took a sip of my coke, as Lauren called it. "It took me forever, but I finally found three things. One, she never yelled at me. Two, she loved James Bond movies. Three, she gave me five bucks for each 'A' on my report card." When I finished reading, I glanced at Jenna, whose mouth hung open.

She snapped her jaw shut and blinked a few times. "That's quite a bit...less personal than your dad's list."

"Yeah. So what?"

Jenna crossed her legs and tugged at her skirt hem. "Just an observation."

"You know I've been in therapy before. When I had my physical for summer camp the year after my dad died, the doctor ratted me out about the marks on my arms, and Mom freaked. Marched me right to a therapist if you can call her that. We didn't get along at all. You're a lot nicer."

Dimples appeared on Jenna's cheeks. I hadn't noticed them before, but I guess she kept her serious face on during our sessions.

"After a few months, I stopped the self-harm, mainly because if I did, I wouldn't have to see Mrs. Doody anymore."

Jenna had just taken a gulp from her water bottle and choked. Water gushed from her nose. She dabbed her face with tissues while I tried not to laugh. "Was that really her name?"

"Yeah, but I called her Mrs. Sour Pickle Face."

Jenna bit her lip, trying to hide her smile, but I saw. She sat up straighter, put on her serious face. "Let's move on and talk about when you started hurting yourself again."

"It was after my mom died." I tried to sniff the tears back, but they fell anyway.

Jenna handed me the tissue box. "Tell me what happened." Jenna never took notes during our session, and I didn't see any sign of a tape recorder. I thought that might be illegal anyway. More TV wisdom. I imagined she furiously wrote notes as soon as I walked out the door, but maybe not.

"Once Mom got a taste of dating, she didn't stop. We never got close again. For four years, it seemed like her only concern was her social life. Then she met Doyle, the king of hair gel. Doyle—what an asshole! He mostly ignored me, and that was fine with me. I heard him give my mom loads of compliments that melted her heart and gave me the creeps. Once, I asked her what he did for a living, and she told me to mind my own business. But I overheard her talking to Evelyn, something about lending him money for some stock. That made me think he was a gold digger. Oh, but Mom wouldn't hear a word against him."

Jenna held up a hand. "You sound angry with your mother."

"Well, yeah. Wouldn't you be?"

"This is about you, Stephanie."

I crushed the empty can of coke and snorted. "I get that. Anyway, Evelyn didn't give him any money, but mom convinced her to pay for the trip to the Caribbean—the trip where she died. When we got the phone call from Belize, I couldn't believe I'd never see her again. Evelyn called the attorneys, and I ran to my room and started scratching my upper arms until they bled. It was like I'd never stopped." Looking down at my hands, I saw they were curled into claws, so I sat on them. When I peeked at Jenna to see her reaction, she wore her professional face.

The words poured out of me, and I couldn't stop even if I wanted to. "I'll never get a chance to make up with Mom. That's the worst. Then I realized I was an orphan, stuck forever in that creaky old maroon velvet prison of a house with only Evelyn for company. Evelyn, old, cranky, hypochondriac, Tanglewood-obsessed, Boston royalty, opera-going Evelyn, as old-fashioned as a—a—a buggy whip!" As I sat there, my hands itched to hurt myself again.

"What about your friends?"

I glared at Jenna. "Friends? Allison, my only *friend*, tried to cheer me up, but nothing she said helped. A week later, right after Evelyn presented me with a pile of brochures for boarding schools to dump me in, the attorneys summoned us to their offices. I learned that before Mom went on the trip, she signed a paper making Evelyn my guardian." I stopped to take a breath. "They told me Clark set up a trust fund for me I couldn't touch until I was eighteen, as if I cared about money. Then they read Clark's letter, and all hell broke loose."

Jenna tilted her head. "What do you mean?"

"That's when I learned my whole life was a lie. My fake grandparents adopted my mom when she was a baby, so Evelyn wasn't really my grandmother. And get this, Clark, who died a year earlier, wasn't my grandfather, but he was my great-uncle. And they never ever told my mom she was adopted. How rotten is that?"

Jenna's forehead wrinkled. "Lots of people don't—"

I held up my hand. "Nope! Stop right there! I don't give a shit about what lots of people do. I care about my mom never knowing the truth. And the way I found out."

"Take a breath. I can imagine you were in shock, but your whole life isn't a lie. Your own mother and father raised you."

As the truth of that hit me, I shut up for a minute. But I wasn't done with my rant. "That may be true, but right then, I didn't even think about that—or give a shit. My head was about to explode, and I had to get out of there. While Evelyn had the vapors, I demanded my copy of the letter and took off. I kept a twenty-dollar bill in my shoe for emergencies, so I hailed a cab. When I got home, I shoved some clothes in my backpack, then hiked over to the Greyhound station and hopped a bus to Austin to find my real grandmother, Lauren Eaton."

Jenna's face went through some changes as I finished my story. No more professional poker face. She sipped her water and after a moment, said, "That was a little rash, don't you think?"

I shrugged. "Maybe. But that's what I did."

"That's all the time we have today." Jenna uncrossed her legs and leaned forward. "I think you should take a look at your anger and consider if it's misplaced. You might want to examine if you're angry with your mother for dying."

Oh, my God! Was Jenna right?

Chapter Twenty-Seven

Lauren Wears Many Hats

The camaraderie we shared at the end of AA meetings lifted my spirits every time, and the recitation of the Lord's Prayer comforted me. With the final words, "It works if you work it!" suffusing me with warmth, I filed out onto the porch for the meeting after the meeting. Ruth, whom I hadn't seen since the eventful Fourth of July party, hugged me with enthusiasm. She finally released me but hung onto my hands. "Want to grab lunch?"

"Can't today. I have a salon appointment." I'd seen another gray hair and that wouldn't do.

Still clinging to my hands, Ruth asked, "Whatever happened to that crazy guy who trashed the party?"

Gently extricating myself from her grip, I sighed. "I don't know, and I don't care. Because he was booked for resisting arrest and battery of a police officer, we didn't have to get involved. Why would I press additional charges and have to appear in court? He's in the system now, and the authorities can handle it. As far as I'm concerned, I'd rather forget the whole thing. The damage has been repaired. Life goes on. Speaking of that, have you been to see Jane's baby?"

"No, I haven't, but I should visit her. I heard she had a boy."

"Will. He's adorable. He's got Joshua's warm brown eyes and his nose. My granddaughter is interested in babysitting for them."

"That's great experience."

"Actually, I think she really wants to babysit Jane's cat."

"Don't tell me—"

"No! You know me better than that—no pets allowed at my place, but Stephanie can visit Delilah all she wants." I waved goodbye and started walking backwards. My stylist wouldn't be pleased if I were late.

Freshly coifed and relaxed, I put up the roof on the car before driving home. Mandy gave the best scalp and neck massage in Austin, besides being a marvelous colorist. A sense of well-being infused me as I drove up the hill to the house. Brett's truck was in the drive. Excellent. The girl wouldn't be home for an hour or two. I had plans for Brett.

An hour later, I gently poked Brett to rouse him from snoring. "Get up, sleepyhead. Stephanie will be home soon."

"Did you remember to lock the bedroom door?"

"You betcha, but let's get dressed and head to the kitchen. I'm starving."

Brett chuckled and kissed my bare shoulder. "Exercise tends to do that."

"You're a good man, Brett Owens."

"Yup. I'm a peach. Guess that's why you keep me around."

"Darling, there are many reasons I keep you around." I hopped out of bed, grabbed my clothes, and hurried into the bathroom to dress and put my hair in order. When I emerged, Brett was pulling on his socks. I sat beside him. "I wonder what changes the school year will bring. With our summer routine gone, I sure don't look forward to more turmoil."

"Who said there'd be turmoil?"

I put my head on his shoulder. "You're right. No need to borrow trouble. I just hope the girl adjusts to Austin High. It would be disastrous if she didn't like it."

"There you go again, being negative."

"I don't know what's gotten into me. Why am I so apprehensive these days? I shouldn't be, especially after the day I had. Things are pretty darn copacetic. The store is running smoothly, I hit a meeting, had my hair done, and spent a blissful hour with the man I love."

"Aw, shucks."

We rose and strolled into the kitchen, planning our dinner. Brett took a chicken from the fridge, which he cut up for stir fry. I buttered a loaf of French bread and chopped vegetables.

My ears picked up the roar of a motorcycle, and a minute later, Stephanie flounced into the kitchen. "Just so you know, I broke up with Colton."

I dropped the knife and steeled myself for more teenage angst. "Really? Want to talk about it?"

Stephanie shrugged, grabbed a carrot, and took a bite. "Not really. We just don't have that much in common. I'm way more serious about the future than he is. Colton thinks college is a waste of time, and I don't. It's as simple as that."

"How will it be working with him?"

"Um, I was hoping you'd take him off the schedule on Saturday, so I won't have to see him at work. Even though it shouldn't be a big deal. We're still friends." With that, she turned and left the kitchen.

Brett and I grinned at each other. "That was easy," he said.

"Yes, it was. Amazing!" Stephanie's handling of the breakup was mature and reasoned, a vast improvement given her past behavior. I offered a prayer of thanks that Stephanie appeared to be on the right path. But why did I have a nagging feeling that trouble lay ahead? Was this what grandmotherhood did to a person?

After dinner, Brett left for a meeting, and I headed to my office. As I passed Stephanie's room, strains of some pop star's caterwauling assaulted my ears. I knocked on her door. "Turn down the volume, please."

"Well, if you insist, granny." So much for mature and reasoned, but despite the sass, she complied with my request.

In my office, I turned a lamp on low and sat in silence, contemplating Stephanie's journey over the last three months. Last evening, Jenna phoned me with news about the girl's progress in therapy. The intern explained she was leaving for her final semester at Medical Branch and would hand off Stephanie's care to another therapist. She also said Stephanie no longer needed weekly sessions and checking in once a month should suffice. She would be thrilled at the news.

Ten minutes later, I stood and stretched, wincing at the tight muscles in my neck and shoulders. I found my yoga mat, rolled it out, and settled into downward dog for several minutes, then I lay back for shavasana, which I refused to call corpse pose.

The next day, I overcame my dread about seeing Helen and visited her on the way home from work. Francine answered the door. Her long face and red eyes told me how things were going. "Please don't stay long."

I patted her shoulder. "Of course." When I walked into Helen's room, she rallied and tried to rise. It hurt my heart to see her looking so frail, every vein visible under her transparent skin.

"Please don't get up. Let me help you sit up a little." A stack of pillows on the window seat provided what I needed. I leaned down and supported her shoulders, then placed two behind her head. "Comfy?"

Her voice was so weak, I barely heard her. "Good." That single word took a lot of effort, and I understood why Francine asked me to keep the visit short. I sat in the chair beside the bed and forced a smile.

"Have you heard about Jane's baby?"

Helen nodded. "Someone told me she had a boy. Nice." Her eyes closed as a coughing fit overtook her.

My heart twisted in my chest as I watched her struggle. When she recovered, I said, "Will is a beautiful baby, and Jane is an excellent mother."

"I knew she would be. How is...your granddaughter?" Helen asked. She paused, then cleared her throat. "Stephanie, right?"

"Yes. Stephanie just started Austin High and loves it, especially the science labs. At sixteen, she has her life planned out. She wants a career in the aerospace industry and has her heart set on the program at Stanford University."

Helen smiled. "That's...good." She took several labored breaths, then settled into a normal breathing pattern.

Not wanting to tax her, I stopped the chatter and reached for her hand, holding it for several minutes. A soft snore let me know she'd fallen asleep. I stood and tiptoed from the room.

Francine rose from the couch when I appeared. I hugged her goodbye and promised to visit again soon.

As I drove home from Helen's, I tried to wrap my head around the fact she'd be shuffling off this mortal coil sooner rather than later. She would be missed in the AA community—and by me. Selfishly, I groaned at the prospect of finding a new sponsor, but I'd leave that for another day.

With the girl in school, I had been able to breathe a little easier and focus on my day-to-day activities. While at work, I sometimes forgot for hours there was a vulnerable teenager for whom I was responsible. My morning commute wasn't the same without her. For one thing, I could enjoy my classic blues station without her commentary, but I had to admit, I missed seeing her face.

On a toasty September morning, I pulled into my parking slot and hustled inside Cornucopia. After I had my first cup of coffee, I summoned Jolie to my office.

"Have a seat, dear."

"Is everything all right?" Jolie's glasses slid down her nose. She really should get them adjusted.

"Yes, all is well. I'm changing Colton's work schedule. He'll no longer be working on Saturday. Please let him know. I'll post the new schedule shortly."

"Okay. Anything else?"

"I'm expecting the first shipment of a new line of whole grain crackers. It should arrive this afternoon. I'll probably be gone by the time it comes, so keep an eye out for it."

Jolie stood. "Will do."

As she left the office, I got to work on the schedule and the quarterly taxes.

On the drive home from the store, my thoughts turned to Jane, as they often did since our new roles as mother and grandmother coincided. We both navigated uncharted waters. From what I'd seen, Jane had effortlessly embraced motherhood, which was surprising since she didn't have much of a role model. A childhood spent dealing with her alcoholic mother and absent father took its toll, but she'd overcome those disadvantages.

In comparison, my early years on the ranch were spent with a loving family, although I often got sideways with my mother, when we should have been allies in the otherwise male household. It seemed like we both had mommy issues.

When I arrived home, the driveway was empty. Brett must be at the ranch. I changed into my workout clothes and began a strenuous Pilates session in my office-studio. The phone rang while I was in an awkward floor pose, and I struggled to my feet, picking up a towel. I grabbed the receiver, heard Jane's voice, and sank into a chair.

"I was just thinking about you. How goes it?" I asked.

Jane chuckled. "It goes pretty darn well. Will naps like a dream, but it will be a while before he sleeps through the night. I was wondering if Stephanie would babysit for us, and thought I'd run the idea by you first."

Despite my happiness for Jane, thoughts of my long-ago losses often intruded on the present when we discussed her baby. It seemed I hadn't healed properly from the trauma of giving up Barbara and the miscarriage. In the past, I would have turned to Jane for advice about my uneasiness but couldn't do so in this case.

"Hey, Lauren? You there?"

I closed my eyes and took a breath. "Oh, sorry. Funny thing. Stephanie asked me if you were looking for a sitter."

"You're kidding! That's great."

"Yeah, it might could work. At the moment, she's without a boyfriend. Can you believe she broke up with Colton because he wasn't interested in going to college? I'm right proud of her."

"Good for her. That's quite mature. Shows growth."

"I agree. When would you want Stephanie to start?" I dabbed the towel at the sweat along my hairline.

"Even though she has some experience with a baby, I'd like her to come to the house while I'm here, so I can make sure she can handle things. If it goes well, we can schedule a Saturday or Sunday evening. Joshua has been begging me for a date night at a restaurant. He's tired of frozen food and casseroles. He also wants to go to the movies, but I won't do both on the same night."

"When she gets home from school, I'll tell her."

"Great! Can she come by for the test run tomorrow?"

"I'll let you know. Got to run." I needed a shower.

Brett brought a pizza home for dinner. The three of us gathered on the patio.

As I passed around paper plates and napkins, I said, "Stephanie, I'm sure Jenna told you she's going back to school, and you'll be seeing Maggie, another therapist. How do you feel about that?"

The girl shrugged and reached for a slice of pizza. "No biggie. I already met Maggie, and she's cool. But the best news is I only have to see her once a month!"

"Jenna must think you've made good progress," Brett said.

"Yep! This pizza is delish. We should have it every week."

I placed a piece on my plate. "Not every week, but we'll do this more often. Jane called today and asked if you'd consider babysitting for Will."

Stephanie broke into a huge smile. "I'd love that! And I'd get to see Jane's cat. What was her name?"

"Delilah. Jane lost Tallulah, her first cat, several months ago, and Joshua surprised her with the kitten. The little thing was quite rambunctious at first, but she's considerably calmer now. You do realize your main responsibility will be the baby and not the cat?"

Stephanie rewarded me with an eye roll. "Of course!"

"She'd like you to stop by for a test run while she's home. Would tomorrow work? Brett or I can run you to her place after school."

The girl helped herself to another slice of pepperoni. "Absolutely!"

"How're things goin' at school?" Brett asked.

"Great! I made a friend in chemistry class. Her name is Becca. She's wicked smart and wants to be a doctor. We're lab partners, and I bet we both get an 'A.'"

"Is she a junior like you?" I asked.

Stephanie took a huge bite of her pepperoni slice and answered with a full mouth. Another reminder to discuss manners. "Uh-huh. She just turned sixteen and already has her driver's license."

"Is that so?" I hoped she wouldn't pursue the topic, but she did.

"Yeah. She took driver's ed this summer. I didn't even know that was a thing. Can I sign up?"

Brett and I exchanged a glance. I sipped my sweet tea while I framed an answer. "What does it entail?"

"They have classroom instruction and actual cars you can practice in. Can I?"

My dear husband came to the rescue. "We'll think on it, but I'm sure Lauren agrees we want to see your grades first."

Why didn't I think of that? At least there was a reprieve from the issue for a few weeks.

"Well, if I can't drive, can we go horseback riding like you promised?"

"You betcha. I know just the place."

Stephanie flew out of the chair and threw her arms around Brett.

I, for one, would not be joining them on their ride. Miss Priss, my childhood ranch mare, was the last horse I rode, and I wanted to keep it that way.

Should we think about getting her a car of her own? Just the thought made me break out in a cold sweat. For one thing, Stephanie was unfamiliar with most of the city. Her world extended from the store, located north of the river, to Barton Springs Road, and, of course, the mall. Just when I thought we'd reached a period of relative calmness, another problem arose—Stephanie behind the wheel of a car.

Chapter Twenty-Eight

STEPHANIE BABYSITS

When I got to Jane's for my trial or interview or test or whatever it was, Jane came to the door holding Delilah. I think the cat was happy to see me because she meowed.

Lauren shouted from her convertible. "Call me when you're ready to come home." She backed out of the driveway and sped away.

"Come on in. So glad you're here. Joshua is asleep, as is Will. Let's go to my office and chat."

I followed Jane to the room that overlooked Lake Austin. It was the skinniest lake I ever saw. She told me it was actually the Colorado River, and then it made sense.

Jane sat in her favorite chair and pointed me to the loveseat. "Have you ever babysat?"

"Sort of."

"What does that mean?" Jane's puzzled look was hilarious.

"Well, I told you about my friend in Boston, whose mom had a surprise baby. It was like Allison was perpetually grounded, she had to help her mom so much. Anyway, I learned how to change a diaper and give a bottle. So, I don't actually know if I can claim I babysat, but I have some experience with a newborn."

Jane nodded. "That's good."

"Also, I'm very responsible. Before this summer, I never even had a job, but I learned fast, and my manager would give me a recommendation."

"No references required." A squawk blared from the baby monitor, and Jane jumped out of her chair like her butt was on fire. "Follow me."

Jane rushed upstairs to the nursery with me and Delilah trailing her. "Joshua barely slept last night so I don't want to wake him. He's in our room next door." In the baby's room, Jane bent over the crib and picked up Will, soothing him, humming a lullaby that seemed familiar. Had my mom sung the same song to me? With a last whimper, the baby settled.

"What can I do to help?"

"I need to change him. Can you grab a diaper and the wipes? He'll need a fresh onesie. Look in the top drawer."

Jane worked quickly, showing me her technique, then moved to the side. "Go on, pick him up."

I held him close, trying not to squeeze too tight. "Now what?"

"I'm breastfeeding, but when I'm out, you'll have to give him a bottle. Let's go to the kitchen, and I'll show you what you need to do."

Careful that Delilah didn't get under my feet, I took my time coming down the stairs with Will. After we warmed the bottle, we sat at the kitchen table, and I fed him. He fussed a tiny bit at first, but once he got the nipple in his mouth, he chugged away. A lesson on burping followed.

"Are you comfortable doing everything I showed you, Stephanie?"

"Yeah. I think I can take care of this little sweetie for a few hours."

Jane nodded. "I think you'll do fine. Sunday night, Joshua wants to go see *Stand By Me*. I checked, and it only runs for an hour and a half, so we'll be gone for three hours tops."

Sunday, Brett drove me to Jane's house and dropped me off.

"Jane said Joshua will bring me home, so you won't have to come back."

"Okey doke, maybe I'll take my lovely wife out for a meal." He waved and drove down Cicero Lane.

Joshua opened the door. He looked tired but was smiling. "Jane's in her office. She just fed Will. He's still awake and in his bassinette."

Delilah greeted me at the door to the office. Jane wore the cutest wrap dress covered with tropical flowers. No one would ever guess she had a baby a few weeks ago. "We're ready to go. I'm a little nervous about leaving him. Nothing to do with you, just first-time jitters."

"Joshua said you just fed him."

"Yes. He will need a change before you put him in the crib. If he wakes up crying, warm up a bottle of breastmilk and see if he'll take it."

"Okay. If it makes you feel better, I can stay in the room with him after I put him to bed. I brought a book, and there's a comfy-looking rocking chair."

Jane let out a whoosh of air. "You'd do that? That's wonderful. Now, don't be surprised if I call. Nerves. There's an extension in the guest room across the hall from the nursery."

Baby Will was the cutest, lying in his bassinette, staring at the mobile hanging over him. Delilah kept me company, an added bonus. She stayed right next to me when I sat down to read. Will woke up about two minutes later. I carried him upstairs, changed him, and placed him in his crib. Within minutes, he was asleep. I hurried downstairs to get a Dr Pepper and my book, then tiptoed back to his room, Delilah following my every move. Will was still quiet. After I got comfy in the rocking chair, I opened my book, *Foundation's Edge*. Jane called it a doorstop of a book. I wondered how my dad would have reacted to know Asimov continued the Foundation series after thirty years. The new one coming out soon, *Foundation and Earth*, wasn't nearly as long. I had to admit, *Edge* dragged a little bit. Delilah hopped into my lap.

Almost exactly two hours later, Will woke up and wailed like someone stuck him with a pin. I dropped my book and picked him up. His face was red, and his mouth stayed open in a prolonged yowl. Delilah joined in, and the noise was ear-shattering. Then I understood why Joshua needed a break.

I gathered the supplies to change him, remembering to grab an extra onesie just in case. Poop. Almost gagging, I got to work, determined to clean his tiny body properly. When he was dressed in a fresh outfit, I carried him downstairs, still wailing away, snagged his baby seat with one hand, and took him to the kitchen. I strapped him in the chair and took a bottle from the fridge. While the bottle warmed, I tried talking to Will, telling him his mom would be back soon, and food was on the way. He stopped crying and peered at me. Then he got the hiccups.

After he finished the bottle, I changed him again. No poop this time. With the baby back in his crib and asleep, I picked up *Edge* and read, with Delilah purring in my lap.

The cat's ears pricked, and thundering steps sounded on the stairs. Jane and Joshua rushed into the room. When they saw the peaceful scene, they relaxed.

"Did you have any trouble?" Jane asked.

"Not a bit. I thought you might call, but you never did."

"Joshua had to restrain me, but we made it through the movie. Good movie, by the way. We stopped for some take out. Do you like Chinese?"

"I could eat." We sat in the kitchen and shared beef with broccoli, Kung Pao Chicken, and a couple of other dishes. Amazing how comfortable I felt with them, chatting away as we ate. If anyone had told me I'd be friends with a shrink and a psychologist, I'd never have believed it.

Brett came through on his promise of horseback riding. I knew he would. Lauren refused to go.

"When I was a young girl, I had a horse named Miss Priss. She threw me once, and I've been horse shy ever since. You go on and have fun. I'm getting a manicure."

Brett and I climbed into his truck and headed to the stables. "There's a little place on Bluff Springs Road that has trail access. We'll have to cross live water, though. Ever do that?"

"What's live water?"

"A crick."

"What's a crick?"

Brett burst out laughing. "Okay, I'll spell it. C R E E K."

"Oh, a creek, like a river. No. I've never been riding out in the country."

"This ain't what I'd call country, but it's as good as we got here in Austin."

I didn't have any cowboy boots, but Brett said my Doc Martens would do just fine. I couldn't wait to meet my horse.

We pulled into the lot and walked into the office.

"Howdy, Ma'am. Name's Brett. My granddaughter and I would like to take a couple of your horses for a trail ride."

Awesome—he called me his granddaughter. Warm fuzzies.

Carlene, the lady who ran the place, led us over to the pasture where six horses stood in the shade of an oak tree. It was hot as usual, and I asked if the horses would be okay.

"Sure thing, honey. They do this every day. The creek's about four foot deep at the crossing, so that'll cool 'em off some. You got any experience riding?"

"I took lessons when I lived in Boston."

"Boston, Massachusetts?"

"Yes. I rode English in an arena. Oh, and I went to a dude ranch when I was little. I'm pretty sure we rode Western there."

"Sir, what about you?"

"I been around horses in one capacity or another most of my life. This ain't my first rodeo."

Carlene tilted her head and squinted at me. Was she looking at my Jordache jeans or my Bon Jovi t-shirt? "Okay, come back to the office and sign the waiver, then I'll help you saddle up."

I picked a beautiful chestnut mare with a white blaze named Savannah. She nickered and nudged my hand, and I knew we'd get along.

"Now, Savannah is getting up in years, so go easy on her. She knows the trails like the back of her hoof." Carlene slapped her knee and cracked up.

Pretty lame, but I smiled.

Brett's horse was black as midnight, and that was his name. He stood a couple of hands higher than Savannah, which made sense because Brett was so tall.

Carlene knew her stuff. We were saddled up in no time and headed down a lane past more white-fenced pasture to the creek. Midnight crossed first. Savannah stopped for a minute, and I thought she wasn't going to go. I gently touched my heels to her side, and she set off. The water came up past her belly, and I lifted my feet, so I didn't get soaked. The water made no difference to Savannah, who was surefooted and didn't have any trouble. I held my breath until we climbed up the steep bank on the other side. I knew enough to let her have her head.

Once across the creek, we trotted a little way in the sun, then the horses slowed once we reached the shade. The trail wound through a mile or two of trees, and we came up on a subdivision of new houses. Brett was right. We weren't in the country. There was a sort of hill behind the homes that blocked the view of the trail, but the illusion we were on the frontier sort of evaporated.

"Brett, what's going to happen in the future? Will they build houses where the trails are?"

He shook his head. "No tellin' what they'll do, but I sure hope not. This little stretch of land is an asset if you ask me."

When we came to a park where kids were playing on the swings and slides, the horses turned around and slow walked back to the crossing. I leaned way back in the saddle as Savannah stepped down the steep bank, counting the seconds until we were on dry land again.

After I dismounted, I didn't want to leave. Carlene was happy that I wanted to stay and hose off Savannah, get the saddle sweat off her pretty coat.

On the way home, Brett asked how I was enjoying my new room. The furniture had arrived two weeks ago. Lauren helped me hang the curtains and make up the bed, but that was as far as I got. Looking at the stack of boxes piled against the wall was getting old. Why couldn't I unpack them?

I knew why. The memories. Worried I'd break down and cry, I put off settling in. I glanced at Brett, but he was paying attention to the traffic and didn't notice. "Actually, I haven't really unpacked all those boxes from my old room. The bookcase is empty, and I haven't put up my posters or displayed my models."

"What ya waitin' for?"

I turned to look out the passenger window. "I'm afraid."

"Afraid of what?"

"That I'll cry when I see my models and other stuff."

"You're allowed to cry, sweetheart. Just remember, you can always ask for help with whatever you need. When we get home, we'll get you settled in right quick."

I smiled at Brett and relaxed a little. "Thanks." It felt good to have a home.

Chapter Twenty-Nine

LAUREN TAKES STOCK

With Brett and Stephanie out horseback riding and my nail polish set, I made a pitcher of hibiscus iced tea and carried a frosty glass out to the patio. I sat on the side of the pool and dipped my pretty Chilly Rose toenails in the cool water. Maybe I'd take a swim. Maybe not. The sun on my face felt wonderful for about five minutes, then I retreated to the covered patio to relish my alone time, which soon came to an end.

Brett came to the chaise lounge I had been trying to lounge on and bent to kiss me. "Darlin', our girl needs help."

Swinging my legs over the side, I sat up and asked, "Did something happen on the trail ride? Is she okay?"

He chuckled. "Nothing like that. Have you been in her room lately?"

"Not since I hung the curtains."

"Seems she's havin' trouble gettin' settled. None of the boxes have been unpacked. And she asked me to give her a hand."

I stood and stretched. "Let's go. She needs to feel comfortable, moved in, and at home."

Stephanie's door was open, and we found her on the bed, leaning forward, clutching her middle. Two opened cartons sat at her feet. She looked up with teary eyes. "I know I've got to do this, but it's too hard to do it alone."

Brett said, "I'll get a couple of chairs from the dining room, and we'll get right to it."

"Thank you, honey." I sat beside Stephanie and pulled her to my side. "Don't you know you can always ask us for help? No need to go it alone. You're part of our family now."

A sob escaped her lips, and she rested her head on my shoulder. I smoothed her hair, amazed at how easy and natural it felt to soothe the girl, so different from the first time I comforted her. In my heart, I knew my experiences as a young woman lost in alcoholism had stunted my emotional growth and killed my ability to love. The estrangement from my family, a chasm that never healed, the shallow relationships with men, the geographical cures, were all wounds that took decades to heal. With the return of Brett and then my granddaughter, the bitter ruined walls around my heart dissolved completely. And I was vulnerable. Loving others does that to you. I didn't ever plan on being vulnerable.

My darling husband entered the room, a chair tucked under each arm. How did I get so lucky? While Stephanie's tears had stopped, mine were threatening to fall.

"Lauren?" Brett knelt on the floor in front of me.

With a shuddering breath, I composed myself. "I'm fine. Just marveling at our little family."

He took my hand. "Me too."

Stephanie stood and wiped her eyes with her sleeve. "Let's get to work."

Brett and I each sat in a chair. Stephanie used scissors to cut the tape on the boxes, and we each took a carton. "I've got plenty of space on the shelves. Just hand me the books and tapes, and I'll arrange them."

Working together, we made quick work of Stephanie's treasures.

Brett asked, "What you gonna do with the models?"

"Could you put them on top of the bookcase? Except the Challenger. I want that one on my desk."

"You got it."

After we'd finished, Stephanie and Brett carried the empty boxes out to the garage. I slipped into my office, needing to regroup after the emotional stew I'd wallowed in. Three months of having Stephanie in my life changed me in ways I couldn't have imagined.

Part Two

THE CALM BEFORE THE STORM

Chapter Thirty

LAUREN CONTEMPLATES THE FUTURE

Two months into the school year, all signs concerning my granddaughter were positive. Stephanie's disposition could be described as sunny, a stark contrast to the disagreeable and rude urchin who landed on my doorstep only five months ago. She enjoyed choosing her own clothes and hadn't mentioned her hatred of plaid in weeks. Her delight in her purple room and having access to MTV might have something to do with the turn-around in attitude.

For the first time in ages, I had the time and mental energy to focus on my business in a way I hadn't been able to since Brett walked back into my life last November. Our reunion, whirlwind romance, and wedding spun me into turmoil for a time. Then, just as my equilibrium returned, Stephanie landed like a Texas tornado and dumped me into chaos once more. At last, the stress lessened to a manageable level.

My peaceful morning commute gave me time to think about future plans for my business. After I arrived at work on a sweltering October morning, I settled behind my desk with a cup of fresh coffee. Cornucopia had succeeded beyond my wildest imagination, and it was time to consider a second location. At this point, it was only a dream, but I luxuriated in the possibility. Our current spot, not far from UT, was a hike from my place in Zilker, so it made sense to have a location south of the river, closer to home. Pouring over the financials, it appeared I might could start scouting potential sites next year. Jolie had proven to be an excellent manager, with a take-charge attitude, so giving her primary responsibility at the original store didn't give me palpitations, as it once might have done.

To begin, I made a list of the most pressing considerations about expanding, and staffing was at the top. As I recalled the trials and failures of hiring and training the employees for Cornucopia's opening and for the past twenty-one years, my confidence crumbled. I tabled the idea for the present. Would I ever find another Jolie?

I addressed more practical matters, such as the schedule for November, although I dreaded having to deal with the many conflicting requests for time off during the holidays. But my mind returned to my ambitious plans; I was no quitter. Remembering how long it took me to forge my path to having my own business and the many detours along the way, I had faith that events would unfold in due time.

With the mundane task of the day completed, I drove to my regular AA meeting. I sat with Ruth and listened to a newcomer spout his drunk-alogue. We shared a glance and a rueful smile as he recited his litany of woe. Newcomer meetings were a good reminder of my tortured journey to sobriety. I hoped his recitation would prove cathartic and perhaps healing for the man. Even though the meeting would turn into a stream of drunk-alogues, mostly stories I'd heard many times before, it was important to remember the meeting wasn't about me but rather helping others in the throes of the disease.

After the closing prayer, Ruth and I walked out together. "Do you have time to grab a bite? I'm thinking El Gallo," she said.

"Sounds good. We haven't really had a chance to catch up since the summer."

"Honey, it may be October, but it's still summer," Ruth said. "Just look how I'm glowing!"

"You say glowing, but I believe it's more commonly known as sweating. Let's get in the air conditioning ASAP."

As I drove home from El Gallo, I hoped my husband planned on a light dinner because I was stuffed with carne asada and too many chips. We'd been married over six months, yet it still thrilled me to say or even think, "my husband." Such a good, kind man. After I succumbed to his charms last winter, he'd been nothing but a loving, committed partner. Even though he spent many hours each week at the recovery ranch, he still found the time to be present for me. And the way he accepted Stephanie into our home was nothing short of remarkable. My eyes filled with tears. I'd have to do something special for him. But what? I'd have to think on that. While we were still in the honeymoon phase, inevitably that time would come to an end, and I wanted to delay it as long as possible.

When I pulled up to the house, Brett's truck sat in the driveway and darned if I didn't get butterflies, just like a teenager. I strolled into the kitchen, where Brett was reading the financial section of the newspaper. "Hey, handsome." I sat on his lap and kissed him. We snuggled for a while, then I rose and poured two tall glasses of hibiscus iced tea.

Back at the table, I said, "Stephanie's grades should be coming out soon. Have you given any thought to having her get her driver's license?"

Brett frowned. "Not sure I'm ready for that milestone, although it would relieve me of chauffeur duty."

"I agree. I've done my share of carting her around too. She really hates the bus, as she routinely reminds us."

"First off, she needs some driving lessons, but I doubt she can handle the truck. Are you okay with her learning in your little coupe?"

"I'm not ready to put Stephanie behind the wheel of my sweet ride, as she calls it. She did mention the driver's education program at school, but I don't know the first thing about it."

"Let me call the school and learn more," Brett suggested.

"Sounds like a plan, but I'm not bringing up the topic or making any decisions until we see her grades." I stood and stretched.

"Hope you're hungry 'cause I'm making beef curry for dinner."

"Oh, honey, I ate a late lunch. Although it does sound delicious. I'm sure Stephanie will bring her appetite. And her terrible table manners. You know, it's past time I spoke to her about it."

"Good luck with that."

As I left the kitchen, I called back, "I'll need it. I'm going to change clothes and relax for a while."

Brett rose and opened the refrigerator. "See ya later, honey. Ya know where I'll be."

In my closet, I selected a summery Norma Kamali pants ensemble. While I dressed, I rehearsed what I'd say to Stephanie about her eating habits. Although I should have addressed the issue with her when she first arrived, there were so many other pressing concerns, I let it slide. Would she get upset? I hated to disrupt the current period of peace.

There was some time before Stephanie arrived home, so I headed to my office for a bit of meditation. While I sat in lotus position, the aroma of cumin, coriander, and other warm Asian spices wafted through the air and made my mouth water. I pinched my waistline and decided a yogurt would have to suffice for dinner.

The front door slammed, and loud clomping from those atrocious Doc Martens sounded in the hallway. Stephanie called out, "I'm starving!"

I sighed and followed my nose to the kitchen, where Stephanie was setting the table. Brett served curried beef with sticky rice, which tempted me, but I stuck to my guns and joined them with a carton of plain yogurt.

"Aren't you eating?" Stephanie asked.

"Yes, I'm having yogurt."

"Well, duh, but why?" The girl piled her plate with food.

"I had a late lunch. But enough about me. How was your day?"

Stephanie shoveled a forkful of curry into her mouth and answered, "Fine."

Brett shook his head. "Might be a good idea to swallow your food before talkin'." His remark indicated he was as annoyed as I was about the girl's manners.

Stephanie swallowed and narrowed her eyes. "What do you want, a minute-by-minute timeline?"

My face froze in disbelief. "That's uncalled for, young lady. Mind your manners, table and otherwise."

"Oh, wow! Well, excuse me." Stephanie put down her fork and folded her arms across her chest. "Okay, there was a small, tiny incident in the lunchroom today." She demonstrated just how small it was with a slender space between her thumb and finger.

"Want to tell us about it?" I asked.

"It's not worth mentioning." Stephanie looked down at her plate.

I patted her shoulder. "Tell us anyway."

"It's the cool girl clique. They invited me to sit with them, but I said, 'no.' Then Tiffany, she's the leader, said, 'I guess you prefer sitting with that brainiac Becca.' Everybody started laughing at me, so I got away as fast as I could. Someone made fun of my Boston accent too."

"That's plain rude. By the way, I think you're losin' that accent. Soon enough you'll be talkin' Texan," Brett said. An exaggerated eye roll was the girl's response.

Knowing how the crowd mentality operated, I said, "In any setting, there's a circle of snooty girls. Because they're inadequate individually, they band together to make themselves feel superior. Good on you for walking away. Be true to yourself, dear, and you won't go wrong."

Stephanie shrugged. "Yeah, it was embarrassing, but I'm not going to let it bother me. Oh, before I forget, I'm going to stay over at Becca's on Friday night."

"You askin' us or tellin' us?" Brett had become quite the father-figure lately.

"Oops. Can I go? Please?"

I met Brett's gaze, and we both nodded. "That's fine. As long as you get yourself to work on time."

"No problemo." Stephanie took another helping of curry.

The girl ate like a longshoreman but never gained an ounce. Those days were over for me, and I glumly finished my yogurt.

Chapter Thirty-One

STEPHANIE'S BOYFRIEND BLITZ

I loved most everything about Austin High. Tiffany's crowd was the one thing that bent me out of shape. When the clique took an interest in me, I was sort of flattered, but they were all about partying and I wasn't. And there was the "brainiac" comment, which still pissed me off. So, I avoided them, which was easy because the school was huge. While the size intimidated me at first, the good thing was if I felt overwhelmed, I could just melt into the background. Also, I loved my chemistry class. Becca was my lab partner, and we always sat together during lectures.

That morning, a cute guy in my English class asked me out. I couldn't wait to tell Becca. Although I was bummed no one had asked me to the homecoming dance, the possibility of a date made me happy.

Becca and I took our seats in class, contemplating that day's assignment: chemical reactions. There would be a test next week, which I had to ace. I much preferred lab days to lectures but resigned myself to the reality of listening to Mr. Oliver's high-pitched, nasal whine for the next hour. We had a few minutes before class started, so I shared my news.

"Becca, you'll never guess! I've got a date! A really cute guy asked me out to a movie on Friday."

"Wait. I thought you were coming over on Friday." Becca sure didn't look happy.

"Oh, yeah." Thinking fast, I said, "I can still come over after the movie. Would that work?"

"Whatever." Becca shrugged. "Who's the guy?"

"His name is Dylan. Tall, with long brown hair parted in the middle and crazy blue eyes. Do you know him?"

Becca tilted her head and frowned. "No. Is he a junior? Can't think of anyone by that name in our class."

"Oh. Well, he's really cute. And I kid you not, he wrote an actual poem about me. I thought it was so sweet. No one ever did that for me before. I just about freaked out."

"A poem?" Becca snapped her fingers and then started giggling. "I know who you're talking about. His name isn't Dylan. It's actually Jimmy, and he goes around trolling new girls with that line. If you look at the liner notes on Bob Dylan albums, that's where you'll find your 'poem.'"

"What? That's totally bogus!" My ears burned, and my cheeks got hot. Embarrassed, yes, but more angry than anything. "Well, he picked on the wrong new girl. Help me figure out a way to get back at him."

Just then, Mr. Oliver plodded in and started writing on the blackboard.

Becca shushed me and whispered, "We'll figure something out at lunch. Jimmy's been pulling this stunt since he was a sophomore. It's time someone stopped him."

After class, we hurried to the lunchroom, where we plotted Jimmy's downfall over a meal of hard-as-a-rock meatloaf and lumpy mashed potatoes. I'd accept the date to meet "Dylan" at the movie theater Friday night to see *Jumpin' Jack Flash.* Becca offered the services of her older brother Ryan to help with the plot, which was a little surprising since I barely knew him. We'd come walking up to the theater holding hands, and when I saw "Dylan," I'd say, "Did you really think I'd go out with you, *Jimmy*?" Then Ryan would kiss me. The only part I wasn't sure about was the kiss. Becca assured me Ryan would love to pull the prank, and she knew at least four girls who swore he was an excellent kisser.

"Why do you think Ryan will help me? He hasn't ever said a word to me." I'd run into him at Becca's house a few times, but he looked right through me.

Becca shrugged. "Maybe not, but I heard him talking to his buddies about how cute you are."

"Get out! He did not."

"Um, yes, he did."

I couldn't hide my amazement. Ryan graduated last year and attended UT while living at home. And he was really handsome, even though with his shaggy blonde hair, he looked nothing like Rob Lowe, although he did resemble Jon Bon Jovi.

Becca picked up her lunch tray. "I've got to get to Biology."

"And I've got World History." As we dumped our uneaten food in the trash, I said, "Thanks, Becca. This is a brilliant plan, and it won't take long. Ryan can bring me back to your house in plenty of time to watch a movie."

Friday night, Ryan picked me up at home in a 1972 Chevy Caprice, a big boat of a car. I'd already gotten permission to stay over at Becca's and told Lauren he was driving me there, which wasn't a total lie because we'd go back to their house after the Jimmy prank.

We parked near the theater entrance, and Ryan got out of the car and said, "Sit tight." To my amazement, he ran around to the passenger side and opened the door for me. He took my hand and helped me out. It started to feel like I was on a real date, but I didn't have time to think about that then.

I hoped I'd be able to pull this stunt off, because being so close to Ryan made me nervous and tongue-tied. On top of his hunky muscles, he smelled wonderful. It must be some sort of aftershave, which reminded me of cedar and leather. "Thanks," I managed to squeak.

"No problemo." He squeezed my hand and asked, "You ready?"

I nodded and peeked up at Ryan, who was grinning at me.

"It'll be cool. I know this joker Jimmy, so I'll be able to spot him right away."

We headed to the mall entrance, and sure enough, Jimmy was leaning against the wall next to the entry doors.

He spotted us, and I enjoyed the shocked look on his face. As we approached Jimmy, Ryan threw his arm around my shoulder.

Jimmy frowned. "Stephanie? What the hell! I thought—" The huge gaping mouth wasn't a good look on "Dylan."

I put my hand on my hip and sneered. "What did you think, *Jimmy*? That I would actually go out with a poser like you? 'Eyes like smoke,' you creepazoid Bob Dylan rip-off artist."

Ryan went chest-to-chest with Jimmy. "This little nimrod bothering you, sugar?" He poked Jimmy in the chest. "You're out of your league, bud."

Then Ryan swept me into his arms and laid a kiss on me. Wow! It made Colton's kiss fade into oblivion. I think I kissed him back, but I wasn't sure of anything at that point. When I regained my senses, I got a fine view of Jimmy's back as he ran into the night.

Ryan laughed and grabbed my hand. "Let's get outta here."

Once we were back in the car, Ryan turned to me. "You really want to go see my kid sister, or do you want to have some fun?"

Without a second's hesitation, I said, "Fun, please."

"You got it, sugar. I'm taking you to the coolest record store."

"Most excellent!"

Ryan zoomed out of the parking lot and jumped on Mopac. A few minutes later, he pulled up to a little stone building with a dinky front porch. The sign on the roof read: "waterloo records." I was not impressed and wondered why Ryan thought this place was so special.

"Doesn't look all that cool."

"Wait 'til you get inside." Ryan opened the car door for me again. Surprised he was continuing the fake date mode, I took his hand. Then he helped me out of the car and kissed me.

I pulled away. "You don't have to keep pretending we're on a date."

"Who's pretending?"

I had no comeback to that line.

Inside the store, which was half the size of the one in the mall, people milled through the racks of vinyl, but I was in a daze. Ryan was a big metal fan. He raved about a local band called Watchtower and put headphones on me so I could listen to them. The music was too frantic and didn't appeal to me. I preferred Bon Jovi and Van Halen—that was as metal as I got. But Ryan was so cute as he talked about the band that I didn't say anything.

When we left the record store, we drove to Zilker Park—and parked. But when Ryan climbed on top of me and shoved me down on the big bench seat, I panicked and pushed him away. Despite the butterflies in my stomach from his kisses, I wasn't ready for that much action. "Please don't. Just take me to your house. Becca is expecting me."

He held up his hands in surrender and backed away. "Sorry. Guess you're a little too young for me."

"Yeah. Guess I am." I leaned against the passenger door with my arms folded across my middle. The butterflies had died, replaced with a sick feeling.

Ryan drove in silence, staring straight ahead. As he pulled into their driveway, he said, "Look, we don't have to tell anyone about this."

"Right. This was a mistake. Becca doesn't have to know." I couldn't face losing my only friend over Ryan's horniness.

As I got out of the car—no help with the door—Ryan called after me. "Good night." He peeled out, going to find his next victim, I supposed.

I just kept walking up the path to Becca's front door. I'd have to tell her about the record store, but I'd take the rest to my grave.

The incident with Jimmy and Ryan, but especially Ryan, left me turned off to romance. There were more important things, like getting into Stanford. But three weeks later, when Doyle from my World History class asked me to a concert, I jumped at the chance. He was more my age and really cute, with his long hair and crooked smile. Also, he had good teeth.

Doyle didn't say what kind of music, and I didn't even think to ask. Guess I'd find out on Saturday. I had to turn Jane down for a babysitting job but told her I could do it on Sunday, so that worked out.

Music filled Lauren's house, everything from Brett's big band stuff to Lauren's old time Texas blues, but I liked my MTV. When Lauren agreed to buy me a TV and get cable, I couldn't thank her enough. "Just not too loud," was all she said. I loved the awesome music videos. Robert Palmer was my current favorite because of his awesome videos. Stevie Winwood was ancient, but I still liked his song, "Higher Love." It reminded me of my mom, who told me she had a crush on him in the sixties, when he was in a bunch of bands.

I didn't tell Becca about my date because I didn't want her to mention my name to Ryan, even by accident. Lauren and Brett asked me a million questions about Doyle. They insisted he come into the house to meet them. I guess they didn't do that with Ryan because he was Becca's brother, but I wasn't looking forward to the inquisition and hoped they wouldn't embarrass me.

When the bell rang, I rushed to the door. Doyle leaned against the doorjamb, grinning. "Hey, Stephanie. You ready?"

"Can you come in for a minute to meet Lauren and Brett?"

He pushed his long hair out of his eyes and stepped into the foyer. "Who are Lauren and Brett?" he whispered.

"My grandmother and her husband."

"Okay, cool. Where they at?"

I led him to the patio, where Lauren and Brett were enjoying the view of the Austin skyline.

Brett got to his feet and held out his hand. "Brett Owens."

Doyle shook hands with Brett. "I'm Doyle." He nodded at Lauren, "Nice to meet y'all."

Lauren smiled. "Are you and Stephanie in school together?"

"Yes, ma'am. We got a class together. World History."

Brett asked, "Where you off to?"

"We're going to hear some music. I'm a drummer, so I like to scope out who's rockin' Austin."

Lauren asked, "What type of rocking might that be?" I wanted to sink into the floor.

"Actually, I like the blues." Doyle stuck his hands in the back pockets of his jeans.

Lauren perked up. "Oh, really. Now you're talking about my kind of music. I've tried to get my dear husband to share my enthusiasm, but he's lost in the Big Band Era."

Brett chuckled. "She speaks the truth."

I zoned out while Lauren and Doyle talked about their favorite blues guitarists. They didn't mention anyone I knew. As I was about to give up hope we'd ever escape, Lauren rose and walked us to the front door.

Doyle didn't open the car door for me, but no biggie, even though it would have been nice. He drove a Volkswagen Beetle that was missing trim work and painted with three different primer paints. When I sat on a protruding spring, I jumped and squealed. Doyle burst out laughing. "I shoulda warned you about that. But don't judge. This fine automobile gets me from point A to Point B."

"And where is point B?"

"You'll see."

Ten minutes later, he parked across the street from Waterloo Records, and my stomach sank. Not again! I prayed Ryan wasn't inside. "I thought we were going to hear some music."

"We are. A couple of fellas I know are playing in the parking lot."

"That's a thing?"

"Yup."

Doyle walked around to my side of the car and opened the door. He grasped my hand and yanked me out of the low car. And I'd thought he didn't care. With his arm around my shoulders, he hustled me across Lamar to where dozens of kids were pouring into the parking lot of the record store. I only hoped Ryan didn't like the blues.

The music reverberated in my bones, and I found myself getting into it even though it was a lot different from Van Halen and Bon Jovi. The crowd clapped like crazy after each song.

Communication wasn't possible during the concert and, it turned out, afterward either. Doyle left me and shouldered his way to the musicians. Stranded, I followed and watched him and the band members having an intense conversation. Feeling like a fool, I hung out while Doyle helped the band pack up their instruments. At last, Doyle seemed to remember he had arrived with a date and scanned the lot. When he spotted me, he grinned and waved me over. He introduced me to the guys. "You'll never believe this. Blues Heaven is going on tour next month and their drummer can't make it, so I'm fillin' in! Ain't that something?"

I didn't know what to say. Doyle was a junior in high school. How could he just drop out? Wouldn't his parents stop him?

The grin fell from his face. "Well, ain't you got nothing to say?"

I blinked. "Yeah, that sure is something. I'd like to go home now."

"What? The guys are having an after-party. Don't you want to go?"

"No. Please take me home."

Even in the faint light from the storefront, I could see his frown. He wasn't happy, but neither was I. As he drove me home in silence, I wondered what was wrong with me. Why was I O for four in the boyfriend game?

Maybe I'd mention it to Maggie, who had replaced Jenna as my therapist. Or maybe not. She was okay, more self-assured than Jenna, and, of course, a thousand times better than Mrs. Doody, who I only thought about when I went to an appointment. I only saw Maggie once a month and would have my final appointment in December, so why get into anything new with her? It would be awesome to put all the soul-searching and sharing behind me.

So, it was back to my studies. Forget romance. I had to keep my grades up, and if my grades were decent, I'd work on getting Lauren to take me to Stanford next summer for a tour of my future college.

Chapter Thirty-Two

LAUREN LOSES HER ROCK

One gloomy day in early November, I got the phone call I'd been dreading for weeks. Francine informed me Helen had passed away in her sleep the night before, her thick voice revealing the depth of her grief.

I felt physically ill on hearing the news. "Oh, Francine. I'm so sorry. Your mother will be missed."

After a pause, Francine said, "You won't be surprised to learn Mom pre-planned all the arrangements and paid the bill in advance. God bless her, she was thoughtful to the end. I've called my brother and nieces and nephews. Many of them will be able to attend the funeral. I hope you'll be there. I'd like you to speak."

Taken aback, I didn't reply at first.

"Lauren, are you there?"

"Yes. Sorry. I'm a little numb from the news. Of course, I'd be honored to celebrate your mother. She was the best." My eyes stung, and I blinked away tears.

"Thank you." Francine choked out the words. "I have to go. Lots more calls to make."

"Of course." As I hung up the phone, tears ran down my face. I rushed to Brett's office to give him the news.

The morning of the service, we dressed in somber clothing appropriate for the funeral. Stephanie had to borrow a pair of black slacks and a blazer from me. We drove to Oakwood Cemetery, where Helen would be laid to rest. Her instructions specified no wake or visitation, just a graveside service. This didn't surprise me because Helen never wanted a fuss made over her. But, in my opinion, she deserved more fanfare because of her legacy in the AA community, sponsoring dozens of women through the years and inspiring many others.

The huge live oaks held onto their leaves, and we took shelter under them to get out of the wind. When the Renfrews pulled up and parked, Stephanie rushed over to help. Joshua assisted Jane out of the car and moved the seat forward so he could lean into the back for Will. After the stroller was ready, and Jane placed sleeping Will inside, Stephanie took over. I observed the girl's interaction with Jane and the baby, pleased at how simpatico they seemed. Perhaps the girl saw Jane as a mother figure, although Jane was barely old enough to fill that role. Regardless of the reason, their friendship made me happy.

A sizeable crowd had gathered, probably sixty or seventy people. Francine and the family sat in a row of chairs set up under a canopy. For many, it was standing room only. Brett and I stood to the side, nodding at familiar faces from our home group. Handkerchiefs and tissues abounded. Soft sobs from a group of women, most of whom Helen had sponsored, reached my ears, and I clenched my jaw, so I didn't start weeping. Brett noticed my struggle and held me close.

Helen had chosen Evan, one of our members, who had a small congregation in a storefront church on the east side, to conduct the service. Despite his small stature, Evan possessed a booming voice that conjured memories of the fiery preacher at the Methodist church I'd attended as a child. But I had to say, the man was eloquent. He had known Helen for years too and spoke from personal experience about her character and worth as a human being. By the time Evan wound up his eulogy, there wasn't a dry eye in the house, as the saying goes.

Then Francine rose and turned to face the mourners and spoke briefly about her mom. Fighting tears, she wiped her eyes and had to stop several times. Her final words resonated with many in the crowd. "Even though I knew the end was near, nothing prepares you for losing your mother."

When it was my turn, I squeezed Brett's hand, took several deep breaths, and walked to my place. Because of my long-ago public speaking training as a Powers Girl, I had no fear of addressing the gathering, just a fear of not giving Helen her due. I'd stayed up late the night before, writing my eulogy. Even with the depth of gratitude I had for Helen's friendship and sponsorship, I struggled to find the right words.

I stood tall, clasping my hands at my waist, and began the homage to my dear friend. "My name is Lauren. Many of you know me from Alcoholics Anonymous. Helen was not only my sponsor, but a friend. I still haven't come to terms with her passing, and probably never will. Life is not going to be the same.

"I'll never be able to walk into an AA meeting without remembering the first time I heard her speak. It was the summer of 1961 at Bouldin. After hearing her story, I wanted what she had and hoped she'd sponsor me. She said some powerful words that stuck with me: Let us love you until you can love yourself."

I glanced at the crowd and saw several people nodding in agreement. Those words were an often-expressed sentiment in the program. "That day, we went out for coffee, and my hand was shaking so badly, I spilled hot coffee all over the table. As I mopped up the mess, I got up the courage to ask Helen to be my sponsor. Before agreeing, she had one requirement: that I read the Big Book first. I'd been gifted a copy of the book years ago but never opened it, because I wasn't ready. Sadly, it took almost a decade before I hit bottom. For some reason, I kept that book and knew right where to find it. Once I'd finished reading, I met with Helen and my journey to sobriety began."

I'd sworn I wouldn't break down during my tribute to Helen, but I was darn close. "Helen had forty-five years of sobriety when she passed. Forty-five years during which she selflessly helped others. She sponsored countless women, some of whom accepted the gift of sobriety, some who didn't.

"Helen's was a life well-lived. Her kindness and compassion will long be remembered. Goodbye, my friend, until we meet again, in a place where there are no goodbyes." My voice caught, and I swallowed a sob as I made my way back to Brett. His strong embrace comforted me, and I leaned into him. We stood together as several of Helen's sponsees spoke of their love for that good woman. At last, the memorial service was over. Interment would be private.

Francine approached me with a stack of invitations, complete with a map, to the reception at Helen's apartment. "Please pass these out to everyone you can catch. I sure hope we get a large crowd because of all the food people donated. My neighbor is there setting up and will let you in."

"Of course."

Stephanie approached and hugged me. "Your speech was beautiful, Lauren. It almost made me cry. Well, actually, I did cry a little thinking about my mom and dad."

"Oh, honey. I understand. Are you okay?"

Stephanie nodded. "Yeah, I'm fine. What's in your hand?"

"Maps to Helen's reception. Francine asked me to hand them out."

"Let me help. Then I'm going to catch a ride with Jane if that's okay."

"That's fine, dear." I glanced around for Jane, who waved, then turned to greet Murray, the young man who'd been such a help at our dramatic Fourth of July party and would soon celebrate one year of sobriety. He'd adored Helen and said more than once he wouldn't be sober without her.

"Nice job, Lauren."

"Thanks, Murry. I hope we'll see you at Helen's."

"You will." He shook Brett's hand and headed to his car.

Once we distributed the invitations, Brett and I returned to his truck, too late to avoid the mass exodus and traffic jam.

"That speech of yours was might good, honey."

"Thank you, darling." Not in the mood to chat, I closed my eyes and leaned my head against the window.

Twenty minutes later, we arrived at Helen's apartment and had to park down the side street because the lot was full. The woman who opened the door introduced herself as Connie, Helen's neighbor. After exchanging pleasantries, I said. "I see there's already a crowd. Put me and Brett to work." I was desperate to have something to do because I wasn't inclined to mingle. Brett took over coffee brewing duty. Connie asked me to restock plastic utensils and carry casseroles to the table. The chores took my mind off the fact I'd never see Helen again.

Chapter Thirty-Three

STEPHANIE'S THIRD FUNERAL

Even though I had met Helen only once, her death made me sad, probably because it reminded me I was an orphan. I tried not to think about my parents' passing. Too depressing. That was why I took over caring for Will at the funeral. Nothing like a baby to make you focus on the present. And the future.

Will slept through the memorial service, but when we got back in the car, he woke up and started wailing. Jane dug in her baby bag and handed me a bottle of breast milk. "Give him this before I start leaking. We probably won't stay long at the reception."

Joshua started the Saab, then glanced over at Jane. "Should we just head home?"

"No, honey. I'm good. I'd like to have a bite and catch up with some of my friends from Bouldin, whom I haven't seen in a while."

"Whatever you want, babe." As he pulled out of the cemetery, he said, "I'm thinking about trading in my car. This two-door isn't exactly the car for a family man."

Jane reached over and put her hand on his, which rested on the stick shift. "Is that what you are? A family man?"

"Yes, babe, that I am."

Watching how they were together made me hope that someday I'd be that happy with my future husband. But why was I even thinking about marriage with my lame romantic history? I had big plans for college and a career. Who knew if I'd ever have one successful date? If by some miracle I found someone, he'd have to support my work, just like Brett did for Lauren.

Jane told me she planned to see patients for therapy after the first of the year but hadn't found a nanny yet. If the job weren't during school hours, I'd consider taking it. Even with the occasional dirty diaper, I preferred babysitting to stocking groceries because I could read while Will slept and raid the pantry for yummy snacks.

When we got to Helen's apartment, there weren't any parking spots, so Joshua dropped us off and went to hunt for a place to park. Inside, I thought I recognized a few people from the Fourth of July party. Some of them greeted me by name and smiled, which felt pretty weird because they knew who I was, but I didn't really know any of them except Debbie and Ruth. Jane carried Will into the spare bedroom to check his diaper, so I was free to hit the buffet. I fixed a plate of goodies but couldn't find a place to sit, so I had to eat standing up.

After I chowed down, I went looking for Lauren and Brett. I saw his gray head towering above everybody and squeezed through the crowd to reach his side.

How weird was it for a teenager to hang out with AA people all the flipping time? Pretty lame.

Brett spotted me and smiled. "Did you get you some food?"

I nodded. "When are we leaving?"

"That's up to Lauren. I think she's helping with the food. Let's go track her down." The crowd thinned out as we got to the kitchen. My eyes popped at the sight of Lauren wearing an apron and washing dishes—by hand. At home, she helped with the cooking once in a while, but I'd never seen her wash a dish or wear an apron. Brett had one that said: "Kiss the cook." I was pretty sure he bought it to entice Lauren.

"Can we leave now?" I asked.

Lauren dabbed her forehead with a towel. Was she actually sweating? "After I finish here. Brett, can you see if there are any dishes in the living room?"

"Sure thing. Come on, Stephanie, give me a hand."

At least helping with the cleanup gave me something to do instead of listening to funeral conversations. When I came back to the dining room from carting in a bunch of empty plastic cups to the trash, I spotted Jane, who was eating while Ruth held Will. When Jane finished her food, the baby started to fuss, so Jane took him and looked around the room. "Joshua, honey," she called.

Joshua rushed to her side. "I'll go get the car. Be right back."

Bored out of my mind, I offered to help.

"Can you get the diaper bag from the guest room?" Jane asked.

"Of course." When I got back, Will's little face wore a frown, and then he burst out in an ear-splitting wail. Heads turned, and Jane's face flamed beet red. "I think we've outstayed our welcome."

"Let me walk you out." I held the door and followed her outside. Joshua pulled up and got Jane and the baby settled, then took off for home.

I stood on the tiny porch. People poured out the front door, and I had to wait until I had an opening to go back inside. Since everyone was leaving, maybe we could finally go home. I headed to the kitchen.

Lauren removed her apron and put it on the counter. She tucked a loose curl behind her ear and hugged Francine. "You have my number. Call me if you need help with anything."

Helen's daughter nodded and thanked Lauren.

On the ride home, Lauren didn't say a word. Brett kept glancing over at her, but she stared straight ahead. "You okay, darlin'?"

"Hmmm."

"Don't feel up to a chat?"

She turned to look at him, and there were tears on her face. "Maybe later."

I'd never seen Lauren so sad. And I'd been to enough funerals to last me forever. I closed my eyes and saw mom's and dad's shiny caskets covered with flowers and almost lost it. With so many depressing thoughts swirling through my brain, I needed to veg out with a little MTV. As soon as we got home, I rushed to my room. Van Halen or Robert Palmer sounded good. I turned on the tube and grabbed the Stanford pamphlets the guidance counselor gave me. Propped up on pillows, I studied the pictures of smiling students at various campus events—none of them funerals—imagining my life at college.

My grades were coming out next week, and I really wanted to get my driver's license. How awesome would it be to drive to California in my own car? By then, I'd get my trust fund money and could buy some wheels. Just thinking about it cheered me up. Like the song said, "the future's so bright, I gotta wear shades."

Chapter Thirty-Four

LAUREN -THE HOLIDAYS

When we returned home from the funeral reception, my grief over Helen consumed me. Ignoring Brett and Stephanie, I retreated to my office, called Jolie, and told her I wouldn't be in for a day or two, leaving the store in her capable hands without a twinge of guilt. I searched the bookshelf for a particular book, "On Death and Dying" by Elizabeth Kuber-Ross. It was a gift from Jane after my father passed away, and I'd never opened it until that night. Between bouts of tears, I read a few passages. Unable to concentrate with all the woulda, shoulda, couldas tormenting me, my guilt ratcheted up to astronomical levels. I tried to rationalize my neglect of Helen during the past six months with the need to care for Stephanie, but my heart wasn't buying it. Guilt and regret cloaked me.

Brett knocked on the door to announce dinner. "Supper's on the table. Fried chicken."

"Not tonight," I answered.

"I'll save you some." Brett's footsteps retreated, and I was glad he didn't intrude. But, two hours later, my darling husband strode in, took the book out of my hands, and pulled me out of my chair. With a firm grip on my shoulders, he said, "I know you gotta work through your sorrow, but honey, Stephanie needs you. I need you."

I stepped back from him, but he enveloped me in his arms. Spent from the tears, I leaned into him. "I wish I'd spent more time with her at the end."

"Don't do this to yourself."

"But I feel so guilty."

Brett kissed the top of my head and said, "Ya hear that?"

"What?"

"I do believe it's Helen saying, 'Life is for the living.'"

"Oh, Brett."

"C'mon, honey, let's hit the hay. Unless you want a piece of my famous fried chicken?"

"No, darling. Just hold me tonight."

When Brett suggested we celebrate Thanksgiving with brunch at the Driskill Hotel, I agreed. Although I'd returned to my daily routine, my mood was still low, and the outing was just what I needed. Dolled up in my new Flora Kung, I felt more like myself. I'd even convinced Stephanie to wear a dress, a not insignificant victory. Brett surprised me by wearing his one and only suit, which he'd worn twice: once to our wedding and once to Helen's funeral.

The atmosphere of the hundred-year-old hotel evoked more gracious times with the high, coffered ceilings, elegant columns, mahogany wainscoting, and tall, leaded-glass windows. Of course, the food was marvelous. Although I didn't much care for buffets, I made exceptions for the Driskill and Fonda San Miguel.

After we were seated, Stephanie left the table without waiting to place a drink order. "I'm going to order an omelet."

Brett chuckled. "I'd tell her to slow down, but she's already gone."

"The seafood selection looks wonderful. You know how partial I am to shrimp."

"Sure do, honey. Me, I'm more of a carnivore, so I'll be hittin' up the carving station."

We ordered coffee and a coke for Stephanie. The waiter hurried back with two steaming cups and the soft drink. While I was stirring the robust brew, Brett ruined my day.

"By the way, have you found a new sponsor yet?" he asked.

"No," I snapped.

"Touchy, ain't ya?" Brett grumbled, his face reddened.

Immediately, I kicked myself for my misplaced anger and reached out for his hand. "I'm sorry, darling. Forgive me?"

"Always." But his downturned mouth and lack of eye contact told a different story.

Obviously, I was stuck in the anger phase of grief. I wondered how long it would take me to reach acceptance—and to find a new sponsor. Determined to enjoy the outing, I firmly pushed those thoughts to the backburner.

Stephanie returned to the table with her omelet and a pile of bacon. Brett and I rose and joined the ranks of hungry diners. Back at the table, we began our Thanksgiving feast. I had much to be thankful for: a loving husband, a granddaughter, and good health. I needed to remember that.

On the day of Stephanie's first report card, Brett and I waited in the kitchen, not sure of what to expect. When she arrived home, she slammed the door and dragged her feet as she entered the room. One look at her face, and my heart sank.

She handed me the report card and stood with her arms folded as Brett and I read it. Her grades in math and science met our expectations of straight As, but her other grades did not. A "B" in English and a "C" in World History wouldn't help her grade point average or get her into Stanford, and the girl obviously knew it.

While I gathered my thoughts, Brett commented, "A very fine effort, but you're gonna have to ace all your courses if you expect to get into the college of your choice."

With clenched fists and a mighty frown, Stephanie snarked, "Tell me something I don't know. I've already figured out I'm not getting my driver's license. And probably never will!" She turned on her heel and fled.

"Well, that didn't go very well." I sighed. "At least she brought up the license, so I didn't have to."

"Dodged that bullet, but are her grades so bad you don't want her to get one?" Brett asked.

"No, darling. She was more upset about her grades than I was, but that works in our favor. My concerns have to do with letting her out on the roads. I'm not ready to take the risk just yet."

Brett pursed his lips. "Will ya ever be ready?"

"Probably not."

"What're we gonna do?" Brett asked.

"Let her sulk for a bit. Why don't we go out for dinner tonight? That should cheer her up."

Brett came to my side and put his arm around my shoulders. "I see why folks look forward to an empty nest. Never thought I'd say that. Growin' up ain't easy for teenagers, honey."

"And it's not easy for the parents, or grandparents, as the case may be. The faint of heart need not apply."

"I hear that." Brett held me tight. "Maybe she can sign up for that driver's education course she was talkin' about."

"I'll think about it."

An hour later, I knocked on Stephanie's door.

"It's not locked," she yelled.

I cautiously opened the door to find Stephanie lounging in bed, watching MTV with the volume off. "Want to share your thoughts?"

The girl wiped her eyes with her sleeve. "I don't know if I'm more angry about my grades or not getting my license." Eyes blazing, she whined, "I'm the only junior who doesn't have a license!"

"I doubt that very much, Stephanie."

The girl lay back against the headboard, seeming to deflate. It appeared the tantrum was over. "I'm going to bring up my grades. I know what to do."

"Good. Now, how about dinner at Chuy's?"

She jumped to her feet. "Yes!"

Tex-Mex—an excellent motivator.

As Christmas approached, it was time to plan the annual Christmas potluck dinner at Bouldin, which Helen had organized and managed. The event held special meaning for me, both because I wanted to honor Helen's legacy, and at last year's event, Brett and I rekindled our relationship.

I set the kitchen table with coffee cups and silverware. "Ruth and Debbie will be here any minute. Will you join us?"

"Sure will. I'll set out the coffee and a plate of those cookies you like."

"Thanks, darling."

Once we were settled at the kitchen table, Debbie took the lead, since Bouldin was her home group. "After the 10 a.m. meeting, people will start arriving with their dishes, so let's plan on serving at eleven. I expect a rush, then attendance will taper. We'll need all hands on deck by 10:30."

"Last year, there was a sore lack of gravy, and not a scrap of cornbread," Brett said.

Debbie scribbled in her day planner. "Noted. I'll revise the sign-up sheet to ask for the items we had a shortage of last year. Hope it helps. Tomorrow, I'll post it right next to the coffee machine, so no one will miss it."

Ruth reached for another cookie. "I do believe these are homemade. Good for you, Lauren."

I shook my head. "Not me. Brett is the chef."

Debbie tapped her pen against her coffee cup. "Yes, the cookies are delicious, but back to business. We'll have a good two weeks to talk up the potluck and encourage donations. But as we all know from experience, you can never predict what people will bring."

"That's the truth," I said.

"Last year, you could barely see the table with all the pecan pies. Y'all know you can never have too much pecan pie," Ruth said.

Brett grinned. "You're right about that!"

"Are we going to provide the turkeys again?" Ruth asked. "I can roast at least two."

"Yes, I'll get four big ones." Debbie made another note. "We'll need more money to buy cokes and serving items."

"Let me get you a check." I pushed back my chair, fetched my purse, and rifled through it for the checkbook. "Brett and I want to increase our donation this year, in memory of Helen."

When Debbie looked at the check, her eyes popped. "Very generous. With this, we'll be all set."

The meeting broke up, and after our friends left, Brett pulled me into his arms. "I'm right proud we're carryin' on Helen's legacy."

I lay my head on his chest. "It's the least we can do."

That night, after dinner, I asked Stephanie to join me in my office for a chat.

Her shoulders slumped. "What did I do now?"

"Nothing that I know of. Do you have something to confess?"

"Heck, no! I'm a paragon of virtue."

"Just as I thought." I hid my smile as we entered my office and settled in my lovely pink chairs.

"Stephanie, Christmas is coming up. We'll be spending the day at the Bouldin AA group's potluck supper."

"We? You mean I have to go?"

"Yes. Your presence is required. You can help serve."

Stephanie folded her arms across her chest and stuck her lip out.

I ignored the pouting and body language. "We keep Christmas very low key, but is there something in particular you'd like as a gift?"

The girl thought for a moment. "Yeah, there is one thing. I'd like a Nintendo."

"Okay, but what is a Nintendo, and where do I find one?"

A snicker preceded her answer. "It's a video game thingy you hook up to your TV. They have them at the mall. I don't go to the arcade anymore, so I'll be able to play my games again."

"Done." I swallowed my irritation with her attitude and asked, "On another note, your final therapy session is next week. Are you ready for that?"

Like a thespian, Stephanie threw her arms open with great drama. "Am I ready? Yeah, you could say that."

"Do you think the sessions have helped you?"

The girl slouched in the chair, her eyes on the ceiling. "I guess so. When Jenna left, Maggie took over without missing a beat, so I was glad I didn't have to repeat myself. Both of them were easy to talk to. So, yeah."

"Don't get mad, but I gotta ask, have you had any thoughts of wanting to hurt yourself?" I studied her face.

As if surprised by the question, Stephanie's eyes widened. Then she frowned and rubbed her chin. "Nope. Nada. I can't even remember the last time I felt like using my nails in an inappropriate manner."

The finger quotes when she said, "inappropriate manner," were a bit much, but still my heart rejoiced, and I said a prayer of gratitude. With the ordeal of self-harm over, I wanted to imagine a wonderful future for my granddaughter, but I was a realist. There would be trying times ahead, of that I was certain.

Chapter Thirty-Five

STEPHANIE TAKES ANOTHER SHOT AT ROMANCE

Even though my feet itched to leave during my last therapy session, I sat politely, listening to Maggie's farewell speech.

"I have every confidence that you've overcome your urge for self-harm. And the work we did on grief has really helped you to process the loss of your parents. But if you ever feel the need to talk, I hope you'll give me a call."

Nodding and smiling, I said all the right things to Maggie, but as soon as I hit the street, I danced all the way to the bus stop. There was no way I'd ever go back to a shrink. Staring out the bus window, I imagined the future when I'd finally get a car and could go anywhere I wanted, whenever I wanted.

My first Christmas with Lauren and Brett was super quiet. I really didn't mind because the holiday brought up so many memories with my mom and dad that it just made me sad. Hanging around the potluck dinner was probably the most boring time I'd ever had, except for the people watching. There were people dressed up like they were going to church and others who looked really rough and smelled bad. But the food was delish, and I did pig out on the desserts. I wanted to get home to open presents and fire up my Nintendo.

I tapped Brett on the shoulder. "Hey, I'm done eating. Can we go now?"

Brett frowned at me. "We'll let you know when it's time."

Twenty endless minutes later, we left.

But when we got home, and I tore into the large rectangular box that was obviously a Nintendo gaming system, there weren't any games. Lauren probably didn't know you had to buy them separately. But I smiled anyway, planning a trip to the mall to buy Mario Brothers and see if they'd come out with any space games.

Resigned to the fact I wouldn't be driving any time soon, I threw myself into my studies. I thought about asking Lauren if I could stop working on Saturday but decided that was a bad idea. A work history would look good on my college application.

I had to get accepted at Stanford—there was no other option. When I met with my guidance counselor, she gave me a list of things to do before I applied. One item made me groan: join school clubs. The only one that appealed to me was the Astronomy club, but I needed more activities to make my application shine. Half-heartedly, I joined *The Maroon* student newspaper as a staff writer, although no one said I had to actually write anything. I signed up for the finance club too, thinking I might need the skills to manage my trust fund. My counselor suggested the debate club, but I did all my debating with Lauren and Brett and lost every single time, so I passed.

To my relief, my GPA just barely got me qualified for the National Honor Society. I figured it was a must for anyone to go to Stanford. When the application packet arrived last month, I got choked up just thinking about how proud my dad would have been if I actually got in. Then I ripped open the manila envelope, kissed the Stanford brochure, and began reading. I'd just about worn out the pamphlet I had, so I was psyched to have a new one.

One early January afternoon, I sat on my bed watching MTV, stressing over what to say in my admission essay. Gently folding my treasured brochure once again, I wished they had included a spare in the envelope. The other information Stanford sent, which I read about a hundred times, didn't give me any ideas about what to write. My essay had to be perfection, and I didn't have a clue how to make it stand out from everybody else's. I turned down the volume on Steven Tyler and Run DMC rocking "Walk This Way," so I could concentrate on writing down my ideas. But getting accepted was only a dream if I didn't raise my GPA and write a kick-ass essay.

With school, club activities, and work, I fell into bed exhausted at night. Thank God my therapy sessions were history. Even though I'd been asked out by a couple of guys this month, I refused. I hadn't had much luck in the romance department, and besides, there'd be plenty of time once I had my aerospace engineering degree. Then Eric, a fellow brainiac, asked me out, but remembering my failures with Colton, Jimmy, Ryan, and Doyle, I almost said no. But he was so sweet and shy, I decided to try one date.

At first, I couldn't figure out how I'd overlooked Eric in my chemistry class. Guess I was too focused on the subject matter to notice him. He was my height, which wasn't ideal, but his eyes behind his horn-rimmed glasses shone with intelligence, and that sealed the deal. For once, music wasn't on the agenda for our date. Instead, he invited me to a lecture at UT, telling me the speaker was "right up my alley." My mind turned immediately to aeronautics, and I couldn't wait.

That January evening, Eric pulled up on a motorcycle, and I cringed at the memory of Colton but reminded myself Eric was way different from the arcade dude. Even though the thermometer hit seventy during the day, it still got chilly at night, so I looked at my dress, which I wore because it was appropriate for going to a lecture in a car, and knew I'd better change. "Eric's here! Can you answer the door, Brett?"

Brett got up from the couch. "Sure thing."

"Thanks. I need to change my clothes." I dashed to my room and quickly put on jeans and a velour top, layered on a sweater and leather jacket, and grabbed gloves and a scarf.

When I got back to the foyer, Lauren and Brett were quizzing Eric. I rushed in to save him. "We better get going." I grabbed the doorknob and nudged Eric.

"Be home by midnight," Lauren called after us.

Eric kept me guessing about the program we were about to see. "It's a surprise," was all he said. He took my hand as we walked into the Thompson Conference Center. It felt right.

The first thing I saw was a poster of Robert Crippen, the UT graduate who piloted the first space shuttle orbital flight. I gasped and got goosebumps. "Are you kidding me?" When I turned to Eric, his grin said he knew he'd made me happy. I was going to hear from one of my heroes. Best date ever.

Mr. Crippen's lecture kept me mesmerized. Of course, I knew he flew the first Space Shuttle test flight of Columbia. That night, I learned his last shuttle flight was on the Challenger in 1984, two years before the disaster. He also worked on the recovery of the seven dead astronauts after the Challenger tragedy. Crippen believed the space shuttle program would fly again and promised to do everything in his power to make it happen.

I left the auditorium full of wonder and excitement. Eric again held my hand as we walked to the parking lot. He was just as jazzed as me about the space program. We both wanted to work in the aerospace industry. Our only disagreement was about college. He was going to MIT, and I wasn't. Then he commented on my Boston accent, which I was doing my best to lose. That lost him a couple of points. "I know you lived in Boston. Why aren't you applying to MIT?"

"It's a long story."

"I'm a good listener."

To my surprise, my eyes burned with tears, and I almost choked when I answered. "My dad wanted me to go to Stanford, so that's where I'm going."

"Your dad? Is he still in Boston?"

I bit off each word. "He died when I was eleven."

Eric stopped in his tracks. "Oh, I'm so sorry. Is that why you live with your grandparents?"

I yanked my hand out of his. "Enough with the questions! My turn. Why is a Texas boy set on going to MIT?"

"My dad graduated from there."

"Maybe now you understand." I put on my gloves and thought about taking the bus home.

Eric pushed up his glasses. "Guess I touched a nerve. I'm sorry. Why don't we head over to Les Amis? We can walk."

"What's Les Amis?" Did I even want to finish the date? My mind whirled with thoughts of my dad, his dreams for me, the program I just heard, and Eric, who shared my interests but was way too nosy. Still, I kind of liked him.

"It's a way cool hangout spot. I've never been, but I heard some of the cool kids talking about it."

"Well, if the cool kids like it, by all means," I said, waving my hand in a grand gesture, which made him chuckle.

"Do I detect sarcasm?"

I laughed. "Maybe a little. Okay, I'm game."

The crowd at Les Amis could only be described as eclectic. Eclectic was one of Lauren's favorite words, and I found myself using it a lot to jazz up my vocabulary. That made me think about my essay again. My English teacher gave us the Word Power test from *Reader's Digest* to help us on our college boards. I knew that would also help with writing my essay, if I ever got around to it.

Eric waved his hand in front of my face. "Hey, Stephanie. You zoned out for a minute. Welcome back. I see a table in the corner. Let's grab it."

We sat and ordered coffee and hot fudge brownies. The buzz of conversation in the space made it difficult to hear each other, so we shrugged and people-watched instead of talking. When we finished, Eric paid the check and put his arm around me as we walked back to his motorcycle, chatting about our career plans. The ride home chilled me to the bone, so I leaned into his back. At the door, Eric dove in for a quick kiss. Disappointing. So, I threw my arms around him and gave him a kiss to remember.

He stepped back with a big grin on his face. "Wow!"

I opened the door and said, "You're welcome."

I was ultra busy, and Lauren and Brett were absorbed in their own lives, but we came together in the evenings for dinner. Brett was teaching me how to cook, so I usually helped prepare the meal with him. He explained each dish and helped me through the steps.

One warm, sunny day in mid-February, I got up the nerve to ask him about his missing eye. As I chopped celery and green pepper to add to the sizzling onion in the skillet, I just spit out the question. "Hey Brett, do you mind if I ask how you lost your eye?"

He rinsed his hands and dried them. "You just did."

"Oh." Feeling like an idiot, I turned to see his face.

"Just joshin' ya, kiddo. I lost it at Bastogne, in a brutal battle in World War II. You may have read about the Battle of the Bulge in history class. Took some shrapnel. The medics sent me to a battalion aid camp and from there to a field hospital. Then I headed stateside to recover. My warrin' days were over."

"Does it hurt?"

"Not anymore."

"Did you ever think about getting a glass eye?"

Brett shook his head. "Too much damage for that."

"I'm so sorry."

"For what? There're hundreds of thousands of men who didn't make it home. The way I look at it, I got off easy."

"Wow! I can't even imagine. Well, for sure, I'm glad you made it back."

Brett added the chopped vegetables to the pan. "Me too." He stirred the mixture, and the heavenly aroma made my mouth water.

"What are we making?"

"Shrimp Etouffee."

"Sounds French."

"Cajun. My mother used to make this dish. It's one of my favorites."

My curiosity about Brett and Lauren's history kept me probing into their past. "Lauren told me she lost her first husband in Italy." As soon as I said the words, I regretted them. Brett probably didn't enjoy hearing about the other men in Lauren's life, even if they were ancient history.

Brett sighed. "Yep." After a few seconds, he continued, "I also lost my first wife. She sent me one of those 'Dear John' letters."

I picked up a big spoon to stir what Brett told me was the Holy Trinity of Cajun cooking. "Those are real?"

"Sure are. Believe me, I'm not the only fella who got one."

"That's wicked mean. Both you and Lauren have had your share of heartache."

Brett patted my shoulder. "As have you. Life can dish out some pain, that's for damn sure. The key is being grateful for what you do have."

As we finished cooking dinner, I thought about what Brett said. "I should do what Lauren does and make a gratitude list."

Brett busted out laughing. "Looks like AA is rubbin' off on you."

I cracked up. Maybe he was right, but I'd never have to worry about needing the program.

Chapter Thirty-Six

LAUREN'S NEW SPONSOR

In March, I asked Debbie to be my sponsor. I needed someone who was close to my age and had stable, long-term sobriety. With so much going on in my life, I craved a sounding board besides Jane, not that we had seen each other much lately. She was busy with the baby, while I had my hands full with my many responsibilities.

When I told Brett I found a sponsor, he had one question: What took you so long? Although I was miffed, he had a point. No doubt he'd noticed that not having a confidante made me cranky and drowning in self-defeating introspection.

I invited Debbie to my home for our first weekly session. After a quick trip to Restaurant Row for Chuy's takeout, I set the table. The doorbell rang as I finished pouring tea.

As Debbie stepped into the foyer, her face broke out in a smile. "Do I smell Mexican food?"

"I ran over to Chuy's."

"Yum! My favorite!" The way to Debbie's heart was through her stomach.

"Follow me. Our feast awaits!" We sat at the kitchen table and dove right into our beef enchiladas.

"Delicious as usual." Debbie patted her lips with her napkin and took a sip of sweet tea.

"Indeed. I'm going to finish the whole thing."

A few minutes later, Debbie looked at her empty plate. "I didn't expect lunch. Is this a bribe?"

"No, but I may take up most of your afternoon with all I want to discuss."

Together, we cleared the table, and I refreshed our iced tea. "It's a glorious day. Let's sit out on the patio."

"Lead the way," Debbie said. Once we settled on chaise lounges, she turned to me. "Okay, Lauren. What's on your mind?"

"Well, at the moment, I'm a bit overwhelmed with any number of things."

Debbie pursed her lips. "That's nice and vague. As long as I've known you, you've been supremely confident and a champion multi-tasker. But you do seem tense. Why so uptight?"

"Uptight?" I burst out laughing. "Am I in a time warp? Haven't heard that one in ages!"

At first, Debbie glared at me, then she began to chuckle. When the hilarity died down, she said, "Guess I'm stuck in the sixties. Seriously, tell me what's eating at you."

I ran my fingers over the stone figures on my Zuni necklace. "My confidence has fled. I'm second-guessing myself at every turn, especially about Stephanie."

Debbie's brow wrinkled in concern, and she patted my hand. "I can tell you from experience the teenage years are difficult—"

"Difficult?" I barked a laugh.

"Okay, hellacious."

"That's more like it."

"I survived three teenagers. Two of them, girls. Thank God I was sober by then, or I couldn't imagine. Now, is there something specific?"

"Let's see. Boys, driver's license, college, for starters." I shifted in my lounger. "Stephanie's been dating a boy who's her intellectual equal, something new for her. They've been going out for months, much longer than anyone else she's dated, and that concerns me. I pray she has better sense than I did at her age. As for driving, how can I turn Stephanie loose on

Mopac—ever? Also, I may be having empty nest syndrome a year and a half before she goes to college."

Debbie held up her hand. "Whoa! That's a lot right there. I do believe you're living in fear. False evidence appearing real."

Struck my Debbie's insightful comment, I blinked. "Oh! You're right. Why didn't I realize that?"

"Lauren, you're too close to the situation. That's why we need sponsors. I'm happy to help. Let's tackle each fear, one at a time."

After Debbie left, I needed a good workout session, but after doing The Hundred, I cursed Joe Pilates and threw my towel on the floor. My body refused to continue with the rest of my usual routine. I got up to light a jasmine-scented candle, then lay back on the mat and practiced deep breathing, hoping to enter a meditative state. No luck. With a groan, I rose and hit the shower.

Brett brought home a generous order of County Line barbecue for dinner. Given my indulgence at lunch, I glumly ate yogurt, watching him and Stephanie enjoy the luscious brisket. I adored their version of cole slaw and potato salad and hoped there would be leftovers.

Perhaps my lectures about table manners were having some effect since Stephanie swallowed her food before asking about visiting Stanford this summer. She'd been relentless in pursuing the topic for weeks, and I knew it couldn't be avoided much longer.

"Here it is March, and you haven't planned a trip to Stanford. I'm getting sick of waiting. Are you even going to take me?" Stephanie's whiny voice irritated me—and Brett.

Brett put down his fork and said, "You mean, if."

Stephanie's face reddened. "No, I mean, when." She smacked the table and glowered at Brett.

I rolled my eyes. Did Brett think he was setting boundaries? If so, he was going about it the wrong way. "All right, you two. That's enough!"

Brett's head swiveled to me, a surprised look on his face. Stephanie's lower lip protruded, but she remained silent.

"Tomorrow, I'll look at my work calendar and block out some time in late July or early August." I made eye contact with Stephanie. "Then I'll contact the travel agency and have them make reservations. When everything is in place, I'll give you the details."

Stephanie pumped her fist into the air. "About time!" Belatedly, she added, "Oh, and thanks, Lauren." She helped herself to more potato salad, dashing my hopes for leftovers.

My dear husband nodded. "That'll work."

That night, while I applied body lotion after my bath, a rustling noise and Brett's chuckle came from the bedroom. What was he up to? Finished with my nightly beauty ritual, I entered the bedroom to find a naked Brett propped up in bed, wrapped in a gigantic white bow.

"Oh, honey, our anniversary isn't until tomorrow," I said.

"I wanted to surprise you."

"Well, you sure did." I made a running leap onto the bed to accept my early anniversary present.

Three weeks later, while I was putting my desk in order before heading home from the store, the phone rang. It was Jane, and I gave thanks the call wasn't work related.

Jane's voice was rushed. "Hey, I'll make it fast. Got to feed Will. I'm inviting you to lunch. It's been ages."

"Love to! Where shall we dine?"

After a moment, Jane said, "I hope you don't mind if I bring Will."

"Oh!" Though I wasn't pleased with the prospect, Jane sounded desperate to get out of the house. "All right, but I have one condition. It must be someplace outside, in case the baby erupts into howling."

Silence.

"Have I offended you?" I asked.

"Not at all. I know just the place. The Oasis, on Lake Travis. The deck is huge. They can stick us in a corner, way far away from civilized people, so we don't disturb anyone."

"Do I detect a hint of snark?"

Jane chuckled.

Even though it was almost an hour's drive, I agreed. "I'll come out to you, but you'll have to carry on from there because my two-seater won't accommodate the baby."

"Does Tuesday work?"

"I'll be there at eleven."

"See you then!"

The breathtaking views at the Oasis were worth the time on the road. A cool April wind rippled the water, and the sun peeked out from behind fluffy white clouds. Perfect weather.

Will fussed a bit on the drive but settled into a deep slumber under a shade umbrella. We ordered lunch and sweet tea from a young waiter who introduced himself as Antonio.

"It's occurred to me I haven't been a very attentive sponsor lately, Jane. Sorry about that."

"Believe me, I get it. We've both had big life changes."

I squeezed a lemon into my tea. "Truth. I haven't run into you at Westlake. Have you been going to meetings?"

"Yes, in fact. Joshua has been a doll, watching Will on Saturdays, so I can get to the noon there."

"Wonderful! You picked a good one."

"Yes, I did," Jane said.

Antonio arrived with our shrimp tacos and refilled our glasses. "All good, ladies?"

"Would you bring us more lemon?" Jane asked. When the waiter was out of earshot, she glanced at me. "Anything new with you?"

"Debbie agreed to sponsor me. Never thought I'd find a replacement for Helen, although I shouldn't say that. No one can replace her."

"Of course not. But it sure took you a while."

I noticed the waiter headed to our table with a plate of lemon slices and refrained from commenting.

Over lunch, I caught Jane up on the latest about my granddaughter. "I asked Stephanie what she wanted for her birthday and got an earful."

"About what?"

"A car."

"But she doesn't have her license, does she?"

"No, I keep putting her off, but I did agree to let her take driver's ed this fall."

Jane added pico de gallo to a taco. "That's months away. How did she take it?"

"About as well as you'd expect. I'm dealing with it."

"Well, I'll watch and learn, although it will be a while before I have to handle a teenager." Jane polished off one taco, then leaned over to peek at Will, who blissfully slept.

"Actually, the main thing I want to discuss is my business." Between bites, I laid out my plans to open a second Cornucopia location.

Jane's eyebrows rose. "Isn't that a lot to take on? I mean, with Stephanie and all."

I dabbed my lips with my napkin. "Don't think I can do it?"

"Oh, no, I know you can. But should you?" Jane pushed her empty plate to the side. "What does Brett say?"

Gazing out over the water, I said, "I haven't told him."

"What?"

"You heard me. I haven't told him."

"Whyever not? Don't you think he'll have some input?" Jane sipped her tea, watching me over the rim of the glass.

"I suppose he will, but I'll do as I please." A bit surprised at Jane's question, I waved my hand in dismissal. "Forget I mentioned it. I've barely started formulating a business plan."

"Okay." Jane looked as if she wanted to say something but was having a hard time getting it out.

"What's up, Jane? You're looking pensive."

"Does Stephanie have plans for the summer?"

I had an inkling of what was coming. "I'd planned for her to work at Cornucopia. Why do you ask?"

Jane's mouth turned downward. "Oh."

"Out with it."

"I was hoping she would babysit for me. You know I fully intended to be working months ago, but I haven't found anyone I'm comfortable with. I've seen a few clients in my home, but it doesn't feel professional. Joshua told me they'll hold my office space a little longer, but if someone new joins their practice, I'll be out of luck. I really don't want to find another location."

"I see. I'll ask her, but I'm sure she'll jump at the chance. The only thing is, we're visiting Stanford the first week of August, so you'll need someone permanent by then."

Jane sighed and leaned back in her chair. "Right. But if Stephanie helps me for those two months, that buys me some time."

I studied my friend, noting signs of stress. "I can see how torn you are. You want to work, but it's hard to leave Will. It's not easy finding a balance, but you'll do it."

"Thanks, Lauren. I sure hope so. Tell me about this Stanford trip."

Apparently, Will had enough of the outing and started to squall. We paid the check and made a hasty retreat. Like a little angel, Will slept through our lunch, but he made up for his silence on the way home. By the time we arrived at Jane's, I was ready for some peace and quiet—at least the relative peace and quiet of living with a teen.

Chapter Thirty-Seven

STEPHANIE'S EVENTFUL SPRING

Eric asked me to prom. Of course, I expected it but still was psyched for my first formal. For my birthday, Lauren took me shopping for a dress. Together, we tore through the Gunne Sax section at Dillard's. All the girls at school wanted a Gunne Sax dress, and even though the super frilly dresses weren't my usual style, I wanted to fit in.

Why were most of the dresses pink? No way could I wear pink with my hair color. At last, I found a purple dress—size six. I yanked it from the rack and hurried to change into it. Lauren waited for me outside the dressing room. When I came out, she clapped her hands. "Brava! It's perfection!" She went on and on about it, calling it "a lavender confection with a sweetheart neckline and the most darling pleated cap sleeves." Whatever.

As the cashier rang up the dress, I threw my arms around Lauren. "Thanks so much." My excitement faded as I visualized my mother's face. I missed her, even though we'd grown apart. Would she have liked the dress?

On the drive home, Lauren said, "Jane wants you to call her. She still hasn't found a sitter for Will so she can work, although I think she hasn't really tried. She wants to offer you the job."

"Really? How will this work? She knows I have school until the end of May, and then I suppose you'll force me to work at the store this summer."

Lauren whipped her head to glare at me. "Playing the victim, are you? I'm detecting a tad bit of ungratefulness as well."

I sank down in the seat. "Sorry," I mumbled.

"Apology accepted. Give Jane a call and see if you can work something out. I told her we're going to Stanford the first week of August, so she's on notice."

"So, there's a chance I can do this?"

Lauren's profile held the hint of a smile. "Call her, and then we'll talk."

When we got home, I jumped out of the car, scooped up my fluffy prom dress, and ran into the house to call Jane.

"Hey! Lauren said you wanted to talk to me about Will."

"Yes. Let me put Will in his playpen. Be right back."

How awesome would it be to babysit instead of stocking grocery shelves this summer?

Jane took forever to come back to the phone. "My little guy is keeping me on my toes. He's pulling himself up to stand, then falls on his butt. He doesn't seem to mind, though. I think he'll be walking soon."

"Cool!"

"Not so sure about that. It's kind of sad the baby stage is over."

Trying to cheer her up, I said, "There are still bottles and diapers."

Jane chuckled. "Yay! At least there's that. I was wondering if you'd consider taking care of Will this summer while I see clients in town."

"Absolutely. I'm ultra interested, but I won't be able to start until school gets out."

"Of course. Lauren told me you're visiting Stanford in August, so I know it'll only be for two months, but it would be such a help. And I'll sweeten the offer by helping you write your admission essay."

"Oh my God! That would be stellar. Every time I sit down and write, it just gets more lame, so I could really use the help. I'll double-check with Lauren and call you back."

After I hung up, I found Lauren in her office, furiously entering numbers on her calculator. The door was open, so I stepped in. "I just talked to Jane."

Lauren glanced up. "And?"

"I'd like to help her, if you let me off the hook at Cornucopia."

"Consider yourself off the hook. But I may need to call on you for an occasional Saturday."

"I can live with that! Oh, I almost forgot. Jane is going to help me with my college admission essay. It's been eating my lunch."

"Well, I'm glad you're getting some help with it. Now, if you'll excuse me, I'm in the middle of some calculations. Please close the door on your way out."

"Sure thing. Anyway, I want to call Eric to tell him the color of my prom dress and ask him not to get a matching tux."

Eric gave me driving lessons on Sunday nights in the mall parking lot. He borrowed his dad's humongous station wagon with fake wood panels on the side. The cool kids would mock us mercilessly if we were seen in the car, but neither of us cared.

"If you can drive this behemoth, you can drive anything," Eric assured me.

"This isn't as hard as I thought it was. But I need a car of my own. There's no way I can drive Brett's truck or Lauren's convertible. They're both stick shifts.

"I can drive a stick, but I don't have access to one to teach you."

"That's okay. I'm taking driver's ed in the fall. Once I pass that, I bet Lauren will get me some wheels."

Eric got quiet.

"What's the matter?"

"I won't be here. I'll be in Cambridge at MIT. Will you miss me?" He slung his arm around me and pulled me close.

"I will. But we have the summer."

When I answered the door on prom night, Eric stood there with a silly grin, wearing a black tuxedo, and holding a wrist corsage of lavender roses and carnations.

Lauren and Brett hovered in the dining room with a camera. We posed for pictures for a few minutes, then hurried out the door.

Thank God, Eric had borrowed his mother's car, a boring ride, but not embarrassing like the station wagon. When we arrived at the banquet hall, a pastel line of couples headed toward the door.

Inside, the ballroom had a stage for the DJ at one end with a wooden dance floor in the middle. Round tables, each with ten chairs, lined three sides of the ginormous room.

Eric leaned close and whispered, "I wonder if they'll spike the punch."

"I think you've watched too many teen movies, Eric."

Becca waved at us from a table near the middle of the room, and we joined her, her date, and familiar faces from chemistry class.

The DJ spun some choice tunes, and I coaxed Eric to the dance floor. We danced to Prince and Robert Palmer, but when "Keep Your Hands to Yourself" started, he threw up his own hands in surrender. "I'm about danced out." I was disappointed but made the best of it.

We returned to our table, but the loud music made conversation impossible. When the DJ took a break, I told Becca and her date we were heading over to Matt's El Rancho for a late dinner, and they joined us. I only hoped I wouldn't spill salsa on my dress.

I'd been dating Eric since February. Our romance hadn't progressed to anything radically physical. He was a devout Roman Catholic and told me he didn't believe in sex before marriage. I was actually stunned when he brought up the topic, but his boundaries were fine with me because I wasn't ready either. I enjoyed our make-out sessions, but from what I'd read in Cosmopolitan and seen in the movies, there was something missing, but I didn't know what. Or maybe I did, as I thought back to Ryan's kisses, kisses that both scared and turned me on. The more I thought about it, it was time to end things, whatever this thing was. Eric was leaving for Boston while I was in Palo Alto, so this relationship wasn't going anywhere. I had mixed feelings about it. Kinda sad but also relieved. I just had to look for the right time to tell him.

A couple of weeks later, I got my opportunity at the graduation party his parents threw for him. All the brainiacs from Austin High were in attendance, so it was fairly tame—actually, deadly boring.

After the cake was served, Eric took my hand and led me out to the patio. I wasn't sure what I was expecting from him, but it wasn't what he said.

"I can't wait to get to MIT."

Barf me out. "Good luck with that."

"Wow, pretty snarky. You grew up there. Don't you miss it?"

"Not even a little."

"Wow! So, I guess you won't come to visit me?"

Pulling my hand out of his, I stepped back. "Not a chance."

"Oh." He looked down at his feet.

"You know, I have really bad memories of Boston, and I'm kinda sick of you talking about it all the time!"

Despite the dim light on the patio, I could read his facial expression. He was hurt and maybe a little angry as well. "Can't you be happy for me?"

All I could hear was my mom asking me the same thing, and I lost it. Not holding back, I waved my arms like a maniac. "See how happy I am? Whoop-de-do. Enjoy Beantown and your life."

That shut him up. Satisfied with my unnecessary cruelty, I rushed into the house, leaving him standing there with his mouth hanging open. I snagged Becca to give me a ride home. It was way easier to leave someone before you got left. Besides, MIT might as well be the moon, and I would much prefer the moon.

When Brett dropped me off at Jane's for my first official day as a nanny, I guess you'd call it, I was jazzed to spend the day with the cute baby and, of course, Delilah. Jane threw open the door, waved me inside, and rushed back down the hallway with Will in her arms. I followed them and the cat to the kitchen.

Jane strapped Will into his baby seat on the counter, and I went over to him. He waved his arms and made baby noises. I grabbed his little hand, and he squeezed my finger. Cool beans! Jane was a mess, dashing back and forth from the fridge to the counter, fiddling with a boatload of papers that probably contained detailed instructions about Will's care. As if I didn't babysit for him every two weeks so she and Joshua could have a date night. I stood there, watching her unravel, but finally had to speak up.

"Relax. I've known Will since he was born and have taken care of him dozens of times. If anything goes wrong—"

Jane froze and stared at me with wide eyes.

"—but it won't—you're only a phone call away."

She pulled out a chair and sank into it. "You're right. It's not the first time I've left him, but it feels different somehow. I'll be with clients with my attention focused on them."

I undid Will's seat belt and picked him up, surprised to find myself in the position of giving Jane advice. "You're only working a half-day, right? You've been gone just as long on date nights."

Jane straightened her shoulders and tried to smile. "You're right. I've worked so hard for my education and license. This is what I always wanted."

"I'm sure it will get easier."

"Let me hold that boy," Jane said, rising to her feet. She took Will from me and kissed him about fifty times. "Okay, onward!" He handed the baby to me, picked up her briefcase, and entered the garage, pushing the button to raise the door.

I heard the Mustang's engine start up, then listened to make sure the garage door closed.

"Okay, Will. What do you want to do this morning?"

"Gah."

"Gah, it is!"

That morning, Jane called only three times. I guessed that was between each appointment. Did all working mothers act this way? Of course, I wouldn't have to worry about that for many years, if ever. I assured her each time that Will was still breathing and having a wonderful time crawling around chasing Delilah.

"Okay, that's good. He hasn't started walking without me, has he? I'll be home soon, so if he stands up, help him sit down."

"You got it. See you in about an hour."

"I'll bring us lunch and while Will is napping, we'll work on that essay of yours."

"Lunch sounds good. See you soon." I hung up the phone, hoping Jane didn't get a speeding ticket on the way home.

At 1:30 pm, the garage door rumbled. A minute later, Jane raced into the kitchen, dropping a bag of food from Manuel's on the counter and sweeping Will into her arms. After the reunion of mother and son, accompanied by a thousand kisses, she put him down for a nap. While she was upstairs, I unpacked the tacos, beans, and rice and waited impatiently for Jane to reappear. Everything smelled delish. Finally, she joined me at the kitchen table. As we ate our lunch, she asked me for a minute-by-minute replay of the morning. Once she was satisfied, she relaxed and changed the subject to my college education.

"You might not want to hear this, but I think you should apply to UT as well as Stanford. It's smart to have a back-up plan, for college, and for life in general."

I groaned. "Lauren says the same thing. But I suppose you're right. Okay, I'll do it."

Jane cleared the table. "Good. Now, let's get to work on your essay. I know nothing about aeronautical engineering, but I can help with an outline and salient points to cover. The technical stuff will have to come from you."

"Awesome! Thanks a bunch." I grabbed my notebook, and we got to work.

When Brett picked me up at five, I had a decent draft of my Stanford essay. Switching it up for UT would be super easy.

Chapter Thirty-Eight

LAUREN GETS DOWN TO BUSINESS

With Stephanie occupied working for Jane and dear Brett chauffeuring her most days, I was free to concentrate on Cornucopia. My manager Jolie continued to impress me with her handle on the business. One afternoon in June, I spent several hours with her going over my ordering process and the list of vendors I used for fresh produce.

Once finished, I asked, "How would you feel about placing next week's produce order?"

"I think I can handle it."

"Good. As time goes on, I plan to give you even more responsibility. Exciting times ahead."

Jolie leaned forward and grinned. "Interesting. Is there anything you can share with me?"

"Not yet." Gathering the papers we'd gone over, I returned them to the filing cabinet. "I've been impressed with your performance this summer, especially the way you handled Colton's resignation and that customer who always complains about the avocados. There will be an increase in your paycheck next week."

"Oh, wow! Thanks much." Jolie pushed her glasses up and stood. "Better get back out front."

I met with Debbie every two to three weeks, usually for lunch after a noon meeting. Her forthrightness and common sense about handling teenagers boosted my confidence in dealing with my granddaughter. And I made an effort to check in with Jane more often. It felt good to reconnect with my tribe.

The end of June snuck up on me—time to plan my annual Fourth of July party. But recalling last year's hectic gathering, I considered skipping it this once. After dinner one evening, Brett and I sat outside on the patio bench, relaxing.

"Honey, I'm not sure I want to throw a shindig on the Fourth."

"You kiddin' me? You've been hosting on the Fourth for years. Can't stop now! Never known you to be a quitter."

"Do you remember last year?"

"I'll never forget it. But I'm game if you are."

I moved closer to him and put my head on his shoulder. "Hmm. I do think I'd regret it if I didn't. Besides, no one on the guest list is pregnant, and Stephanie won't be there. She and Becca are going to see some sci-fi movie."

"No teenyboppers this year would be good."

"It's also Will's birthday. Let's get a cake for him. Since Stephanie's busy, I'm sure Jane will bring him."

"You think that's a good idea? The little guy might be scared of the noise."

"I'll talk to Jane and go from there."

The next afternoon, I phoned Jane to discuss having a little celebration for Will on the Fourth.

"Oh, Lauren, we won't be there this year."

"Why not? Are you traumatized by the way they hauled you out last year?"

Jane laughed. "Nothing like that. We're driving out to Odessa to see my father. Tom and his family will be there too."

It took me a moment to process the news. Jane had left home at sixteen and didn't return until her mother's funeral two years ago. She came back to Austin, harboring a deep resentment against her father. After realizing how harsh she'd been to him, she asked me for advice. We talked through her issues, and she reached a place of forgiveness, and called him when she learned she was pregnant. Progress, not perfection. I hoped an in-person visit would complete the healing process for Jane and Mr. Jennings.

"Lauren, you still there?"

"Yes. Sorry you'll miss the party, but I'm glad your father will get to meet Joshua and Will."

Jane sighed. "I am too. It's about time."

"Give me a call when you get home. I want to hear all about it."

"Will do. Hope your party is nice and boring."

"Same here. Safe travels, my dear."

The party on the Fourth went off without a hitch, making me glad I'd listened to Brett. Life was good. As our summer routine continued without drama, my serenity blossomed. Brett commented on my sunny outlook. "I kinda like this new Zen Lauren. Looks good on you."

"Zen? I'll take it."

The only cloud on the horizon was the impending expedition to Stanford. I didn't enjoy traveling, especially outside of Texas, but was resigned to the trip.

A few days before our departure, I called Debbie to suggest lunch at Castle Hill Cafe, my favorite new restaurant and where Brett had taken me for our anniversary. She suggested Chuy's instead, but I wasn't having it. "You probably never thought you'd hear me say this, but I'm tired of Mexican food. Since Stephanie arrived, we eat it at least twice a week. Castle Hill is a lot quieter than Chuy's, and I need to talk."

Debbie groaned, then said, "Okay, I hear you. Meet you at 11:30."

The next day, I was delighted to walk up to the restaurant to find Debbie already waiting for me. "I'm starving," she said. She usually was.

After we ordered and had iced tea in front of us, I leaned forward and said, "We leave on the dreaded trip to Stanford next week."

"You don't look too happy about it."

"You know I hate to leave Texas."

Debbie frowned. "Buck up, Lauren. It's only for a few days, and it's not like you're going to be touring other colleges."

That reality check made me realize how selfish I was to complain about taking Stephanie to see the campus she'd been dreaming about for years.

Debbie's pork tenderloin and my red snapper arrived, and the dishes smelled divine. After a few bites, Debbie put her fork down. "You know I visited my daughter in San Francisco in March. It's not too far from Palo Alto. You must get to the city. We had a fabulous meal at Pier 39 on Fisherman's Wharf. As a seafood aficionado, you'd love it."

"Geography isn't my strong suit, and I've never been out west. I hadn't realized the college was so close to San Francisco."

"It's only about an hour's drive. And the shopping is fabulous. The Ghirardelli Chocolate Factory is not to be missed, and it's close to Fisherman's Wharf. They've restored the original location and added tons of cute shops."

I nodded. "I'll add the city to our itinerary. Although, it might be difficult dragging Stephanie away from Stanford." Then I remembered my dream from the night before and shuddered.

Debbie asked, "You all right? What just happened?"

"Oh, I recalled a nightmare—was it only last night—about Stephanie running away during the campus tour. We couldn't find her and had to fly home without her. It was so real. And it woke me up."

With wide eyes, Debbie shook her head. "This trip has you in a tizzy. Just relax and enjoy it. You'll be back home in no time."

"Thanks, Debbie. Now, how about dessert?"

"Have I ever said no to dessert? Where's the menu?"

We ordered two Mocha Toffee Torts and coffee. While we waited for our treats to arrive, I said, "There's something else I need to discuss." Not telling Brett about my plans to open another store made me increasingly uncomfortable. Debbie would be a good sounding board.

"Okay, you have my attention. By the look on your face, you're feeling guilty about something." Debbie clapped her hands together in delight as our dessert and coffee arrived. When the server left, she stirred cream into her coffee and tilted her head as she studied me.

I pushed the tort around my plate, not taking a bite because my mouth was so dry.

"Spill!" Debbie scooped a forkful of dessert into her mouth and stared at me.

"I've been thinking about opening another store, a second location south of the river."

She swallowed and asked, "Why on earth would you want to do that? Don't you ever plan on retiring?"

Her response set me back some, and I took a moment to frame my answer so as not to be rude. "Didn't expect that answer."

"Fair enough. What answer did you expect?"

Taking a moment to sip my coffee, I realized I wasn't used to being challenged—by anyone, if I were honest. "Perhaps something a tad bit more supportive."

Ignoring my comment, she asked, "What does Brett have to say?"

I gripped my fork so hard my knuckles ached. "I haven't told him."

Debbie's eyebrows shot up. "Really? I think you might do an inventory over that."

My two closest friends had similar reactions to my secret expansion plans, and I had to give weight to their opinions. What were my motives for not telling Brett? What was I afraid of? Then it hit me—I knew he wouldn't be pleased. My mind traveled back to the end of our marriage when Brett was planning to open his own advertising agency. I had felt left out and really upped my vodka quota during those days. Then I got pregnant. And lost the baby at five months. After the miscarriage, I had driven Brett out of my life. Such painful memories.

Debbie's voice cut like a knife. "Lauren, where did you get off to? You're a million miles away."

I met Debbie's eyes and gulped. "A trip down memory lane to a place I rarely visit."

"Do you want to talk about it?"

"No, not now. It's ancient history, but I think it gave me an idea of why I'm—not hiding—let's call it not telling Brett. It will be a good start on an inventory."

"Will you share it with me when you're done?"

"Of course."

Debbie's polished plate prompted me to ask for a to-go box for my dessert. "My treat, Debbie."

I settled the bill, and we walked out together. Debbie hugged me. "Call me when you get back."

"Count on it."

Chapter Thirty-Nine

STEPHANIE DOES STANFORD

All the way from the house to Mueller Airport, I could barely sit still because of the excitement. I was finally going to see Stanford University for myself, in person, for real. My studying paid off and my GPA had risen to a most excellent 3.96. No way would Stanford turn down my application.

With my mouth dry and my underarms wet, I paced in the airport lounge until they called our row for the flight to San Francisco. I grabbed my carry-on bag and rushed to the gate but had to wait for my rulers to catch up because Lauren had my ticket.

"Take it down a notch, Stephanie. The tour isn't until tomorrow morning," Brett said.

Finally, we made it on board. "Dibs on the window seat!" I scooted into our row. "Have I told you how grateful I am that you paid for the trip? I'm really, really grateful, and I'll pay you back when I get my trust fund."

"No need to repay us," Lauren said as she squeezed into the middle seat, leaving the one on the aisle for Brett's long legs.

After the flight attendant finished the safety routine, the engines screamed as the plane raced down the runway and took off. Now that I was on my way, I relaxed. How I wished it was my dad taking me on the trip. He couldn't be there, but I hoped he was watching from heaven. I peered out the plane's window, scanning the skies for a sign from him.

The next morning—the morning I'd anticipated since I was ten years old—I jumped out of bed, showered in a flash, and dressed in my most sedate dress. I wasn't sure what the student culture was like, although the brochure showed kids in jeans with backpacks, pretty much the standard student attire anywhere.

Promptly at 8:30, I knocked on the door to Brett and Lauren's adjoining room. Brett opened the door. "Lauren's making herself gorgeous. She'll be ready soon."

A few minutes later, Lauren came out of the bathroom, followed by a cloud of Arpège. My Love Baby Soft didn't stand a chance. "Let's get a bite for breakfast. It's so convenient to have the Menlo Tavern right here in the hotel. We have plenty of time before the tour."

"Do we have to? I'm not even hungry."

"What do you propose we do for the next hour? I'm famished. Brett?"

"I could eat," Brett said, patting his flat stomach.

After we had a breakfast of yummy blueberry pancakes, which I was able to eat after all, I hustled Brett and Lauren to the car and went over the map with Brett. In minutes, we turned into the campus on Galvez Street, drove past the stadium, and followed the signs to the Visitor Center. The campus blew away the pictures in the brochures. Sandstone buildings with red tile roofs as far as the eye could see.

Brett helped Lauren out of the car, and she twirled around in a circle. "I've never seen so many arches. This isn't exactly the red brick buildings covered with ivy scene I imagined. It's beautiful, especially with the backdrop of the hills."

I hopped on one foot, then the other. "Let's go! I don't want to miss the start of the tour. I hope we see the Dish."

"What dish?" Brett asked.

"It's a radio telescope up in the hills, and it's beyond awesome."

"Hills? Think I'll pass," said Lauren, looking down at her high-heeled sandals.

Brett held the Visitor Center door for Lauren, and I practically shoved her inside. About fifteen people milled around the lobby, looking at the exhibits and waiting for the tour guide. The parents huddled together, inspecting campus maps, chatting with each other. Prospective students lounged and tried to look cool, but if they were anything like me, their stomachs were in free-fall. Why did I wear a dress? To please Lauren, of course, but I felt stupid because every kid was wearing jeans.

Just as I was losing patience, a tall young guy walked in and held up his hands. "Attention! I'm David, your guide for this campus tour. We're about to start. Anyone have a question?"

No one raised their hand.

"This is a walking tour and lasts about ninety minutes. We'll cover nearly all the central areas of campus. Don't worry if you didn't bring your Reeboks, we'll be staying on the flat and easily accessible two-mile path."

Lauren clutched Brett's arm. "Did he say two miles, Brett?"

"Yes, my love. Can you make it?"

"Watch me."

I rolled my eyes. What was Lauren thinking when she chose those shoes? Two miles in ninety minutes meant a brisk walk of about one and a third miles per hour. I was certain my granny could handle it.

We filed out of the visitor's center and headed down Galvez Street, hung a right and stopped to gaze at the Oval. Then we made our way to the main quad. I lost count of the number of buildings we passed, each one gold and red.

David had his spiel down cold. He told us that Frederick Law Olmsted designed the Quad, which contained twelve original classrooms from way back in 1891. We viewed a bunch of sculptures from some French guy I never heard of. There sure was a lot of history and commemorative plaques everywhere. It would take a month just to read them all. The library was massive, but it had to be to hold the millions of volumes the University owned.

The clock tower was rebuilt a few years ago. It had originally been on top of the church but fell during the 1906 earthquake. I wondered why it took so long to reconstruct it, but David didn't explain. I tried not to think about earthquakes, but chills ran up and down my spine. Was it worth the risk to study in such an intellectual atmosphere?

After a while, all the buildings and their historical significance blurred into an information overload. I glanced over at Brett, who paid close attention to our tour guide. Lauren was starting to wilt in the sun and glanced around as if looking for an escape route.

I took pity on her. "Want to sit for a while?" I pointed to some outside tables with umbrellas. "The tour is about done."

"Yes, that would be a blessing. My feet hurt." With Brett helping her, Lauren hobbled over to a table. She sank into a chair with a sigh. "I feel smarter just from taking the tour."

Brett said, "I can't believe this place. So many cultural centers and activity hubs. They got all the bases covered."

"They sure do. I just wish my dad was here to see it. And my mom, I guess."

Lauren glanced at me, concern on her face. It looked like she couldn't continue the tour, which was disappointing, but I would be living at Stanford in a year, anyway.

Brett patted my shoulder. "Let's get you some of that Stanford gear you've been wanting. The tour guide said the bookstore was chock full of it. But let's get my lovely wife a cold drink first."

"Yeah, I brought a list of things to get, like a sweatshirt and other stuff."

Lauren raised an eyebrow. "I hate to ask, but what if you don't get in?"

Even though that pissed me off, I stayed calm. "Oh, I'm going to get in, but even if I don't, I still want a few things."

After we brought Lauren a cup of lemonade, Brett and I headed to the bookstore. I planned to get every brochure and pamphlet available and maybe a campus guide, as well as some clothes.

Although I had my own money, Brett insisted on paying. If Lauren had been with us, I'm not sure she would have approved of everything I bought. I loaded up, picking out a microfleece pullover hoodie with pockets, a regular sweatshirt, a long-sleeved tee shirt, and a short sleeve too, a baseball cap, and a pennant. Brett just smiled and pulled out his credit card.

"Thanks, Brett."

"You're welcome, sweetheart."

We found Lauren right where we left her, relaxing at the table outside the Student Union. She chatted with a couple of prospective parents, at least that's what I thought they were, being way too old to be students.

When she spotted us, she waved us over. "These fine folks are from Oklahoma. Their daughter is interested in attending Stanford too." I stood there with my two big bags of gear, bored silly while the adults exchanged small talk. At last, the Oklahomans got to their feet and headed off to find their daughter.

"That's quite the haul. Two bags." Lauren said. She didn't look upset, but I felt guilty about how much Brett spent on me.

Brett helped Lauren to her feet and planted a kiss on her cheek. Embarrassed for them, I glanced around to see if anyone noticed. They sure weren't embarrassed for themselves.

It took about twenty minutes to get back to the parking lot. Lauren said, "I have a blister on my toe. Let's head back to the hotel."

"You got it, darlin'."

"You still up for going to San Fran? Brett asked.

"Of course. But first, I'm going to soak my feet, put on a band-aid, and take a power nap. Then we'll head into the city."

I kept my mouth shut. They'd taken me out to California for my dream trip, so I shouldn't complain about their plans, which didn't sound bad at all. It would be cool to see San Francisco.

On the flight home, as I paged through the Stanford campus guide and munched on a tasty Ghirardelli chocolate bar, I had plenty of time to think. I dreamed of my first day at Stanford. After I settled in my room, I'd hike up to the Dish. But I had a whole year to wait. What would senior year be like? For sure, I'd keep up my grades. One thing I was excited about was driver's ed. Then I thought about what kind of car I'd buy when I got my trust fund money. So far, it was between a Camaro and a Firebird.

As the plane began the descent into Austin, I put my stuff under the seat and thought about Becca. She was dating a guy from Bowie High who was also going to UT Medical Branch in Galveston. I hardly saw her anymore.

It might be nice to have a boyfriend, but I doubted I ever would, with my non-existent social life.

Chapter Forty

LAUREN – BATTLE LINES BEING DRAWN

After the trip to Stanford, I got serious about scouting for a second Cornucopia store. Last quarter had been my most profitable yet, and I felt confident I'd be signing a lease soon. Of course, I searched for an existing building, not wanting to fiddle with construction from scratch. Still, the interior work could be extensive and costly, depending on what I found. Ruth knew a commercial realtor, so I made an appointment to see a place on Congress and another on South First. It was time to tell Brett about my plans. Given the doubts raised by Jane and Debbie, my stomach was in knots as I took Brett by the hand and led him out to the patio.

While Stephanie cleaned the kitchen, Brett and I settled on the bench, as we often did. I leaned into his side and laid the news on him. "Darling, I've been thinking about opening a second store."

"Why would you wanna do that?"

"Because I can." From the look on my beloved's face, it wasn't the most judicious response.

Brett shook his head. "That's no answer. How can ya handle two stores?"

That right there put my back up. "You don't think I'm capable?"

"Don't go gettin' on your high horse. I didn't say that."

"You said exactly that."

"Hey now, take it easy." Brett reached out a hand to me, which I ignored. "Didn't mean it like that."

I rose and paced along the edge of the pool. "Oh? In what way did you mean?" My tart tone caused Brett to raise his eyebrows.

"Look, sugar, I was thinkin' you might could retire soon."

My fists clenched, and I had to unlock my jaw before I could speak. "Did you now? What do you propose I do—take up pottery?"

Brett threw his hands in the air and got up from the chaise lounge. "How long you been plannin' this?"

"A while. I've prepared a budget and looked at a couple of locations."

"I'll be darned. And you never even talked to me about it?"

"I had my reasons." My chin lifted in defiance.

"Wonder what those might be." Brett's tight lips and frown revealed the depth of his anger. "Looks like the honeymoon is over."

As he stalked into the house, I shouted at his back. "Looks. That. Way."

The discussion was far from over, but it was damn sure over for that night. After I cooled off, I said good night to Stephanie, who had finished her kitchen duties and was doing her homework. When I entered our bedroom, Brett had his pajamas and toothbrush in his hands.

"Gonna sleep in the guest room."

"Good," I said, even though I didn't mean it.

So ended the period of relative peace as battle lines were drawn between me and Brett. If I had known what was to come, I might have fled to a commune and taken up macrame.

Part Three

WHEN HISTORY REPEATS ITSELF

Chapter Forty-One

LAUREN'S SACRIFICE

After a day of hurt silence and avoiding Brett, I swallowed my pride and knocked on his office door. "It's open," he rumbled.

I stepped inside and looked him straight in the eye. "Brett, I owe you an apology." He said nothing, so I girded myself to continue. "It was wrong of me not to tell you about my plans." That was all I could muster. Even as I stood there, I knew it wasn't enough.

Brett stood and came around the desk, gazing at me intently. I threw myself into his arms, but he held his body stiff and didn't return my embrace. Startled, I pulled back and studied his face.

"No hug?" I asked. "Won't you forgive me?"

Brett shook his head and took a step back, out of my reach. "I'm still smartin' from yesterday. Tell ya the truth, you keepin' your plans secret set me back on my heels a good bit. And it brought back some painful memories to boot. Figure ya know what I mean."

My heart sank. Memories of the awful treatment I handed out to Brett during our first marriage flooded over me. "So, you need time to nurse your wounds?"

"Well, darlin', you sure can dish it out. And your anger surprised me, goin' from zero to sixty pretty darn fast."

Unable to meet his gaze, I lied. "I don't know where it came from. Obviously, I need some advice. I'm going to call Debbie."

At last, Brett cracked a smile and gave me a one-armed hug. "Good plan."

As I left the office, I mentally kicked myself for hurting him again. With great misgivings about my ability to navigate this marital crisis, I picked up the phone to call my sponsor.

The next day, Debbie and I connected at the noon meeting. She suggested lunch, but I declined. "Not today. I'm not very hungry. Let's just sit outside and talk."

My sponsor frowned. "Must be serious if you're off your feed."

I snorted. "Probably true." The after-meeting crowd melted away, and we sat on a bench in the shade.

"Let's have it." Debbie could be blunt, or perhaps she was hungry and wanted to make this session fast.

"You know I've been considering opening a second store."

Debbie's frown revealed she still didn't care for the idea. "Right. And you've kept it a secret from your husband."

I glanced away. "Not any longer. I finally told him, and let's just say it didn't go well."

"And this surprises you?" Her frosty tone of voice made me shiver.

My face warmed. "Guess it shouldn't have. We had words."

"I just bet you did."

"Well, *I* had words. When he challenged me, I snapped at him, and things escalated fast and got fairly spicy. He slept in the guest room."

Debbie patted my hand. "Have you made up?"

"Not really. Even though I apologized, I can tell he's still hurt."

"You never did get back to me about that inventory I asked you to do on this very subject. It really helps to write down your resentments and fears. Brings clarity."

Had I ever felt so uncomfortable in my own skin? "I know."

Debbie softened her tone. "Lauren, you have to examine your motives."

Embarrassed at hearing what I'd told my sponsees so many times, I nodded. "I have been examining why I lashed out, and it goes back to our first marriage. Brett wanted to open his own advertising shop. He spent months crafting his business plan, with my help, I might add. But I felt excluded, not sure what role, if any, I'd have in his venture. It's just one of many things I drank over."

"That's really old stuff, but it's new information for me. I'm sure you shared this with Helen, but please bring me up to speed."

Dredging up one of the most painful periods of my life made my stomach churn, but Debbie wasn't aware of my entire checkered history. I filled her in on how I lost Brett's baby, then sabotaged our marriage and fled to Austin all those years ago.

Before commenting, Debbie took a full two minutes to process my confession. "Oh Lauren, I'm so sorry for your loss. What a journey you two have taken to get to this point!" She shook her head. "It's a testament to Brett's love that he forgave you and even went on a mission to find you. And you married him all over again. From what I've seen, you've been deliriously happy, until this. If you let your old resentments rise to the surface, you're in for a world of hurt."

I found a tissue in my purse and dabbed my eyes. "Thanks for the tough love. And the reality check."

Debbie stood and stretched. "I've gotta run. Make amends to your wonderful husband, then give me a call."

Humbled and dreading what I must do, I watched her walk to her car.

When I got home, I spied Brett sitting in a chair out on the patio. I poured two glasses of hibiscus mint iced tea for us and joined him.

He glanced up at my approach and smiled slightly, very slightly. "Thanks. I was just thinkin' about going in the house to fetch me a drink."

I handed him the frosty glass and sat on the edge of the chaise beside his chair. After taking a sip, I mustered my courage and began my second request for forgiveness. "Brett, I met with Debbie and talked things out. You're entitled to an explanation for my behavior, as well as an apology."

Brett nodded but said nothing.

With a heavy sigh, I put my glass on the side table. "It all goes back to my old resentments from our first marriage. We talked a little about this when we got back together, but not in depth. You were so kind and forgiving, and I was grateful you didn't dwell on it, so I never really made amends."

"Lauren, you gotta let go of the past."

"Yes, honey, but I need to get this off my chest. When you were planning your own agency, I felt left out and bitter, not knowing if there was a place for me. I drank at my feelings. And stupidly, never told you how I felt."

Brett rose and came to sit beside me, putting his arm around me and snuggling me close.

Relieved, I melted into him. "If I had been honest back then, who knows what our lives would have been like?" Tears stung my eyes, and I blinked them away.

"Hold on, there. No use doin' that to yourself. The past is the past. And I have to own my part. Sorry I was so self-involved. Looks like I never made it clear you'd be my partner."

"Oh, Brett! That means a lot, even after all this time."

"Lauren, honey, let's close the book on all that business. The only thing I care about is loving you now and for the rest of our lives. If you wanna open another store, I'll even help you stock the shelves or work the checkout line. Anything to make you happy."

"That's so sweet, Brett." I held onto him for dear life.

On October 20th, the morning newspaper's headline delivered stunning news: "Wall Street Panic." Because I wasn't invested in the stock market, the consequences for our family weren't immediately apparent. My portfolio held one item—Cornucopia. Brett wasn't much of a gambler, and his money was in savings bonds. He said he was content with collecting interest on a stable investment. While the stock market had lost over twenty percent of its value on Monday the 19th, we were unaffected and congratulated ourselves on our prudence.

The next day Evelyn called. She was so upset I could barely understand her, but the message still came through loud and clear. Stephanie's trust fund was wiped out. Evelyn also faced great losses and would be forced to sell her family's Beacon Hill mansion. Out of the kindness of her heart,

Imogene had agreed to take her in. I couldn't imagine how that would go. Aunt Imogene hadn't mellowed with age, and she continued her bohemian lifestyle even though she was in her seventies. How would Evelyn adjust to life in Manhattan, where she knew no one besides her niece by marriage? She'd need to find new doctors, and I imagined she'd want new lawyers to sue the pants off Boylston, Cabot, and Lodge. At a loss for how to soothe the distraught woman, I got off the phone as quickly as possible.

Two weeks later, I received a formal letter and final financial statement from the Boston attorneys with a small check enclosed. Would that amount even cover a semester's books? Brett and I huddled, trying to figure out a way to break the dire news to Stephanie. There would be no money for her to attend Stanford, shattering her dreams. Knowing she'd be devastated, I dreaded telling her. The girl slept with the Stanford brochure and had mailed her early action application on the first of October. She checked the mail every day, looking for an acceptance letter. Although graduation was six months away, and she wouldn't start orientation in California until August, she had already made a list of things to pack. I braced myself for her reaction.

The one saving grace in the situation was the back-up application to UT. I believed Stephanie had applied there only to please me, thinking I couldn't handle the thought of her departure for college.

Despite the current disaster, I almost chuckled when I recalled our conversation that day.

"Can I come home from California for school breaks?" the girl had asked.

"You better! This is your home, and you'll always have a place with us."

"Are you going to keep my room a shrine?" Stephanie asked with a grin.

"Hardly." I had snorted at the idea, although I knew her departure would be hard on me and Brett.

Bringing myself back to the present, I asked Brett, "How do we tell her?"

"Sugar, there ain't no way to cushion a blow like that. We're just gonna have to lay it out, no sugarcoating. She's a smart kid, and she'll know if we try to minimize this."

I bit my lip. "You're right. When should we tell her?"

"Today. No use delaying."

When Stephanie got home from school, Brett and I corralled her at the front door and told her we had some bad news. "Let's sit in the kitchen," I said.

She dropped her backpack on the floor, and we trooped into the breakfast area and sat.

"Bad news? Did Evelyn die?" Stephanie's face wore an inappropriate smirk.

"That's your first thought?" As soon as I uttered the words, I regretted my harsh tone.

The girl frowned and folded her arms over her chest. "Okay, then what?"

Brett laid it out plainly. "The stock market crashed a couple weeks ago, and the investments made by your attorneys in Boston have lost their value. Your trust fund is gone."

"All of it?" Her wide eyes darted around the kitchen, and then she covered her face with her hands. "No, no, no, no!" she howled, shaking her head. "It can't be true. That was my college money."

Brett scooted his chair closer to her and patted her back. "We're very sorry, Stephanie."

Searching for something to comfort the girl, I blurted out the first thing that came to mind. "Let's go out to dinner. How about Chuy's?"

Stephanie didn't answer, just gave me a blank stare, and left the kitchen. A moment later, we heard a door slam, then screaming and loud thumps. Brett and I rushed down the hallway to her room. He flung open the door. Books littered the floor. Stephanie ripped a Stanford banner from the wall, tore the brochure into confetti, and collapsed on the bed, howling like a stuck pig.

I sat beside her and took her in my arms. Her chest heaved, but the ear-splitting yowls stopped. "I hate them! Those rotten, stupid idiots have ruined my life."

Brett sat on the desk chair, silent, but just having him there helped.

"There's always UT," I said. "Isn't it fortunate you applied there too?"

Stephanie barked a laugh. "Whoop-dee-do. Fucking UT. Can I even afford it? Well, I guess I get in-state tuition, so maybe."

"Come on. Let's get your face washed. I'll brush your hair. That'll make you feel better," I said.

"Nothing—I repeat, *nothing*—will make me feel better."

An hour later, I peeked into Stephanie's room. She was sound asleep. I found Brett in his office. When I entered, he looked up from a pile of financial papers. "Thought I'd take a look at the finances to see if we can help the girl, but tuition and room and board at Stanford for an out-of-state student is mighty dear."

I sank into a chair and studied the figures he'd prepared. "Indeed, it is. I've been wracking my brain for how I can help."

Brett pursed his lips. "Hate to bring it up 'cause we both hate gettin' into debt, but should we look at student loans?"

In disbelief, I raised my voice. "Have you lost your ever-loving mind? Interest rates are astronomical right now. One of the girls at Westlake got a quote of over 12% on a mortgage loan!"

He held up his hands in capitulation. "All right, no need to shout at me. Didn't realize rates were that high."

My shoulders slumped. "Sorry, Brett." I stood. "I'm feeling a bit overwhelmed and need to meditate about this. We'll talk later."

In my office, I rolled out a mat and lay in relaxation pose. After a dozen deep breaths, my mind became focused. There was so much loss in Stephanie's young life. After a rocky start with us, she'd found her bearings and worked hard for her dream. Because I'd done the same in my life, I understood that on the deepest level. But what price success? Could I sacrifice for my granddaughter? Was I too selfish? Full of pride and ego? Never in my life had I put family before ambition. Maybe it was time I did so. As I lay there contemplating what I'd have to do, tears dripped down my cheeks. I let them fall. After a while, I stretched my limbs and sat up. Refreshed and certain of my decision, I returned to Brett's office.

I swept through the open door and settled in the chair I'd recently vacated. He glanced up from his reading and smiled. "Looks like you got your serenity back."

I nodded. "For now. I did a lot of thinking."

"Come to any conclusions?"

"Yes. I have to make sure Stephanie goes to Stanford. And there's only one way to make that happen." I closed my eyes for a moment. "I'm going to sell Cornucopia. It may take a while, so let's not tell the girl until I find a buyer."

Brett pushed back from his desk. "Honey, you can't be serious. You just bought out your investors not that long ago." He paused, and I could see the wheels turning. "And here ya were just thinkin' about a second store. Sure you wanna do this?"

I studied him, assessing his reaction, but didn't see a trace of gloating, only concern for how I'd handle the self-imposed divestment of my life's work. "Stephanie has lost so much in her young life. I must do this, Brett."

Chapter Forty-Two

STEPHANIE REBELS

After I got the news about my personal bankruptcy, I sort of blew off school. A few days after I learned I was a pauper, I cut class for the first time ever. Just walked out the door after US History, went to Zilker Park, and took a ride on the kiddie train. How lame was that? Then I wandered over to Barton Springs Pool and watched the crazy people swimming in the sixty-eight-degree water. Even though it was in the eighties, I shivered just looking at them. Once I got a taste of rebellion, I kinda liked it. I walked home, making sure to get there at my usual time.

No one was home when I arrived, so I grabbed a Dr Pepper and headed to my room to watch some MTV. But even David Coverdale singing "Here I Go Again" didn't improve my mood. Then Heart's song "Alone," came on and really bummed me out, so I got up and turned off the TV.

Whenever I thought about those evil, stupid, worthless Boston lawyers wrecking my future, I got pissed. I didn't know for sure the total in my trust fund, but I overheard Lauren and Brett saying I was freaking rich. That meant I lost more than my tuition money, so yeah, my entire future was toast. Thinking back to the trip to Boston, I remember the Babcock attorneys saying something about changing how my trust fund was invested, but what did I know about that crap? And they obviously didn't know shit about what they were doing. At the time, my big concern was the lie my family had lived since 1941.

Lauren and Brett treated me like I was made out of glass and didn't want me to break. Eventually, I stopped crying every day. I picked up my room, making sure I tossed every last thing with the word "Stanford" on it. When I told Lauren I wanted to quit my Saturday job, she didn't even argue with me, but I could see her disappointment. "Let me know if you change your mind," she said. I felt bad, but not bad enough to go back to work.

Jane called me to babysit, and I refused. "Nope, I've retired from childcare, thank you very much."

"Oh. I see." She sounded hurt, but what did I care? *I* was hurt. My entire life plan had imploded.

Lauren tried to cheer me up. "UT has a great program. Remember what Mr. Contreras told us?" *Blah blah blah.*

I might be able to accept going to UT next fall, but not yet, and I didn't have to like it. And I didn't have to think about it right then because I was too mega-pissed. Lauren told me she'd pay my tuition at UT, which made me cry all over again.

At least Lauren didn't insist I go back to therapy. I had finished my monthly check-ins almost a year ago, and they'd have to drag me back kicking and screaming. Even though I was heartbroken at not going to Stanford, I didn't once think of harming myself.

If only my dad was there to talk to me. Lauren and Brett tried to help, but it just wasn't the same. Dad had shared my aeronautical dreams and supported my choice of Stanford for college. "I checked it out. The school has a fantastic program." And actually seeing the campus in person last summer made it real.

Dead Dad. Dead dream.

Bored and bummed and needing some spice in my life, I drifted to the party-girls clique. Much to my surprise and never figuring out why, the popular girls had recruited me when I started at Austin High, but I hadn't joined the inner circle. Because I wasn't stupid, I stayed on good terms with Tiffany. Then I met Becca in chemistry class and found a real friend. And I happily aligned myself with the brainiacs, never looking back. But now

Becca didn't have time for me because she spent all her time with the dude she met last summer. When I saw her in class, all she talked about was their plans when they went to UT Medical Branch next fall.

I hadn't been on a single date since breaking up with Eric last May. Pathetic! My romantic life was the pits. Why hadn't I ever gelled with the right guy? Maybe because no one could compare to Rob Lowe. Would I judge every guy by him?

About a week after my life plan died a horrible death, I spotted the cool girls in the cafeteria. Tiffany, the leader of the clique and head cheerleader, sat at her usual table, surrounded by Misty, Heather, Kimberly, Jessica, Stacy, and Brandy. Of course I knew their names. Everyone in the entire school knew their names. I had no clue who was who because they were all a certain type with the same big hair and pastel clothes. If they weren't all natural blondes, they were all blondes now. I waltzed up to their table and said, "Hey! I love your new jeans, Tiffany. Where did you get them?"

"Buckle, where else? Hey, y'all usually don't hang with us. What's up?"

"That's what I was gonna ask you. I'm looking for a little fun."

Tiffany grinned. "Well, you came to the right table!" The other girls howled with laughter. You'd think they were watching Dana Carvey on *Saturday Night Live*.

I forced myself to laugh with them. "Yeah, I can see the finish line of school, and I'm ready to par-tay."

Tiffany scooted over on the bench and patted the empty spot. "Cool! Sit with us. There's a killer party Saturday night. I'll tell you all about it."

That night at dinner, I put on an epic performance of a happy camper, burying my anger and disappointment, but Lauren watched me closely. Maybe my act made them suspicious.

Lauren smiled. "I'm glad to see you're in better spirits."

"Me too. Can't stay miserable forever, right? If it's okay with you, I'm going to stay over at Becca's Saturday night." I peeked at Lauren to see if she detected my lie.

Lauren turned to Brett. "That's wonderful, isn't it, darling?"

"Sure is. You should get out and see your friend." Then Brett gave me that one-eyed stare. Had he tuned into the fact I hadn't mentioned Becca in ages?

"Do you need to buy some new clothes? We could go shopping." Lauren looked so hopeful that I couldn't say no. "That would be great, but I'm not sure I need much."

"Whatever you decide is fine, honey." She'd been calling me a lot of pet names since I became destitute. I didn't really mind, although it was a bit much at times.

That night, I lay awake in bed, unable to sleep. I turned the pillow to the cool side and lay back, staring into the dark. My conscience was bothering me for lying to Lauren and Brett, so I thought about what I'd wear to the party instead. I needed to blow off a little steam, and I was so ready.

Saturday night, I dressed in new Calvin Klein's and hid my slinky low-cut gold lamé tee shirt under a long, loose blouse. I loaded my backpack with Love's Baby Soft perfume, makeup, and covered everything with a pair of pajamas, so it would look legit if Lauren peeked inside. Of course, Lauren had never done anything like that, but my nerves and guilt made me feel like I was covering up a crime.

I said good night to my rulers, who were in the living room slow dancing to old records. Whatever floats their boat, I thought. "See you in the morning!" Not waiting for a reply, I hurried out the door. Kimberly was picking me up. I had told her to wait around the corner. When I got to our meeting spot, she waved from a really sweet ride. A red 280Z, low-slung and hot as a firecracker, as Lauren would say. When I got in, it was like I was sitting on the floor. Before I could fasten my seatbelt, Kimberly peeled out, and the car swerved before it hugged the road. The girl had a lead foot, taking the downhill street like a race car driver. Instead of feeling scared, I felt alive for the first time since learning I was poor.

Before we got to the party, we stopped at 7-Eleven so I could use the light from the storefront to put on makeup. I spritzed Love's Baby Soft from head to toe.

Kimberly started coughing and said, "Hey, you're ruining my Jovan Musk!" Then we both laughed.

"But we smell oh so sweet." I put my perfume away and fluffed my hair, wearing it long and loose, loving the way it fell around my face. A few minutes later, we pulled up to a house in a part of town I hadn't been to before. The homes were huge and set far apart. Light blazed from every window, and Van Halen's "Why Can't This Be Love" blared through the open door and windows. Sounded like a party to me. Kimberly said, "Everyone who is anyone will be here."

I opened the car door. "Can I leave my stuff in the car?"

"Sure, just stuff it behind the seat. It'll be fine." I took off my blouse, revealing my slinky gold lamé tee.

"Oh, my God!" Kimberly squealed. "That's gorgeous! I think I saw it in the window at Buckle. Is that where you got it?"

"Where else?" Playing their game was easy because I was a quick study.

As we walked up to the house, I recognized some of the jocks standing around in the yard. Football season was over, and we hadn't made the playoffs this year, so training didn't matter, judging by the beers the guys held and the pile of empties on the ground. Logan Armstrong stepped back from the huddle and strode over to me. "Hey, doll. Haven't seen ya at a party before, but I sure have seen ya at school." His eyes devoured me, stopping at my chest. "Like the top. Name's Logan, but I guess ya knew that." Grinning, he tried to peer down the neckline, and I wished I hadn't chosen such a low-cut tee. My mouth went dry, and my palms went wet in the mild November air.

I gulped and felt sweat bead on my upper lip. Why were my nerves getting the better of me? I told myself to chillax and go with the flow. "Hi, Logan. I'm Stephanie."

"Sweet. Wanna beer?"

Thankful the darkness hid my blush, I shook my head. "No, thanks."

He stepped closer and hooked his arm around me as if he owned me. "Come on in. Jeff's parents are out of town, so we can party hearty. I'll find ya somethin' else."

"Cool." I think my voice squeaked, but he didn't seem to notice. I glanced back over my shoulder at Kimberly, who shrugged, walked up to another jock, and laid a kiss on him.

Inside, the music was even louder. We stepped through the huge foyer and past a staircase, weaving through the crowd. Everyone made way for Logan. I got a few curious stares but ignored them. The dining room table was set up for a sort of game. Guys lined up and threw ping-pong balls into cups filled with beer. Apparently, it was great fun. Logan dropped his arm from my shoulder and took my hand, pulling me to the kitchen where tubs of cokes and a dozen liquor bottles lined the counter. He grabbed a cup, threw in a few ice cubes, filled it halfway with gin, and topped it off with Dr Pepper. "Drink up, babe. It's a party!"

I took a sip and nearly barfed. "It tastes awful."

"Get past it. You're going for effect, not taste."

The next thing I remember was waking up naked in a big double bed with a snoring and equally naked Logan. The bright overhead light hurt my eyes, and I squeezed them closed, but I couldn't shut out the shame. My mouth tasted like I'd chewed on a putrid rug all night, my head pounded, and my thighs were stuck together. I was afraid to look down, and when I did, I gasped at the smeared blood. I'd obviously had sex but couldn't remember anything. As quietly as I could, I rolled off the bed. The last thing I wanted was for Logan to wake up. Just thinking about him coming after me again made me want to barf. I swallowed hard. Crawling around on the floor, I gathered my jeans and top. I had to get out of the room before I screamed. I looked everywhere but couldn't find my underwear or my shoes. When I pulled my jeans up, I winced at the sting in my girl parts. After pulling my soggy top over my head, I slipped out the door.

I tiptoed past two guys asleep on the floor in the hall and hurried down the stairs. Kimberly lay on the living room couch, passed out and snoring, but at least she had her clothes on. I shook her awake. "I've got to get home."

She stretched and groaned, then hurled right on my bare feet. I yelped and jumped back, but it was too late.

"I can't believe you just did that!"

Kimberly gazed at me through slitted eyes. "Sorry." Then she puked again.

"We've got to get you cleaned up." Afraid I'd puke in sympathy, I held my breath and pulled her to her feet, half-carrying her to the bathroom down the hallway. Luckily, no one was in there. I turned on the water in the tub and rinsed my feet and dried them on the rug. All the towels were wet, lying in a pile on the floor. Gross.

Kimberly stumbled to the sink and threw water on her face. "My God, I'm never drinking bourbon again."

I snorted. "I'm never drinking again, period."

She cracked up and had to lean on the counter, so she didn't fall down.

In my opinion, there was nothing funny about the situation. "Do you have your keys?"

Kimberly patted her jeans pocket and nodded. "Think I'm still drunk. Can't drive. Must have coffee."

"Let's see if we can find some." We made it to the kitchen and found Jeff pouring coffee into a mug. He added a generous slug of bourbon. "Want a cup?" He seemed relaxed, not a care in the world, even though he had a heck of a mess to clean up before his parents got home.

Kimberly shuddered. "Yeah, but I'll pass on the bourbon." He handed her a full mug. She drank it down, burped, and asked for another.

I glanced at the clock, after 9:00 already. The sun pouring into the room made me squint. My heart pounded in my chest. Regret for what I'd done, and who I did it with, settled over me like a dirty sheet. So ashamed, I hadn't even looked at myself in the bathroom mirror. How could I face Lauren and Brett? I was sure I looked "rode hard and put up wet," one of Brett's funnier expressions, but I wasn't laughing that morning.

Kimberly hiccupped. "I can drive now, I think."

We said goodbye to Jeff. How would he ever get the place clean again? Not my problem, but I had plenty of others. We stumbled down the walkway to the street and found Kimberly's Z right where she'd parked. But when I reached behind the seat for my backpack, it wasn't there. Great. Add one more problem to the pile. I lowered myself into the passenger seat and cried all the way home.

Chapter Forty-Three

LAUREN GETS A SHOCK

As I stirred a dollop of cream in my coffee, I glanced at the clock and saw it was almost 9:30. Stephanie hadn't come home, and I started to worry. "Brett, don't you think Stephanie should be home by now?" The spoon fell out of my shaking hand onto the counter.

He glanced up from reading the paper. "What time did she say she'd be home?"

"She didn't give me an exact time. I should have asked her or gotten Becca's phone number or something that mothers and guardians are supposed to do, and I haven't." My voice rose with each word until I was fairly shrieking by the time I finished.

Brett lowered the paper and peered at me. "Whoa there! Where's the fire? This ain't like you."

I took a deep, shuddering breath. "Yes, I know. I tell myself there's nothing to worry about, but this niggling sense of unease has me riled up. It can't be mother's instinct because I'm not a mother." Tears blinded me. "Honey, I'm concerned. Just my gut."

"Come on over here, darlin', and set yourself down."

I scooted a chair close to him. Brett put his arm around me and kissed my cheek. His calming presence soothed me. Then the doorbell rang a few minutes later. I jumped to my feet and hurried to the entry, Brett right behind me. When I opened the door, there stood Stephanie, barefoot, wearing a stained gold lamé t-shirt and jeans, hair a tangled mess, with dark smudges of makeup under her eyes. Not wanting to believe what I saw, I gasped and stepped back.

The girl's shoulders shook as she sobbed, head hanging in remorse or shame, probably both. "I'm sorry. Are you going to let me in?" she blubbered.

Brett went to her and circled her with his arm. "Of course."

I stood there stunned, unable to move as a hundred thoughts and images tore through my mind. The overwhelming stench of gin and vomit made my stomach churn, and I remembered the shame, having been there a thousand times. The girl was hung over. Closing my eyes, I whispered the Serenity Prayer. Oh, how I'd need serenity to deal with the disaster in front of me.

Brett led Stephanie into the kitchen with me following, numb and sick at my stomach. I'd never asked my granddaughter about her parents' alcohol use and should have. Did alcoholism skip a generation? Was this my fault? Once again, my lack of experience in nurturing a young human couldn't be more apparent. Brett seemed to handle the situation better than I could, so I decided to stay quiet and follow his lead.

After he guided Stephanie to a chair, Brett sat beside her. "You had a backpack when you left last evening. And where are your shoes?"

In between sobs, the girl answered. "I-I don't know." That admission sent her wailing again, and she buried her face in her hands.

"Let me get you some water," I said, trying to be useful.

"Are your things at Becca's?" Brett's voice was gentle but firm. I had to admire his self-control.

Stephanie lifted her head and gave Brett a sidelong glance. "No. I left them in Kimberly's car. They were gone this morning."

"And who the hell is Kimberly?" I slammed the glass of water on the table. "Stephanie, take a drink of water. You're probably parched from the alcohol."

Stephanie's lips trembled. "How d-d-do you know?" More sobbing ensued.

"Oh, honey, you reek of gin. God knows, I've been there. And I hoped I'd never see you like this."

Brett patted her back. "Did you even go to Becca's last night?"

Stephanie hiccupped and a nauseating odor wafted through the air. "No. I lied. I went to a party. Becca is innocent."

Despite what he said next, Brett's voice seemed to soothe the girl. "There will be consequences for this behavior, but we'll worry about that later. Right now, you go on to your room, take a nice bath, and put on some clean clothes. Then come out to the living room so we can have a chat."

Stephanie gripped the table and hauled herself upright. "Yes, sir." She trudged from the kitchen, the very picture of dejection. I almost felt sorry for her, but my anger and disappointment crowded out the sympathy.

"What are we gonna do, Brett?"

"We'll offer love, understanding, and some heavy-duty consequences, one of which will be her first AA meeting."

"She won't like that," I said.

"No, she won't. That's the point."

"Tough love. I like it." I kissed Brett on the cheek. "Maybe Debbie will have some words of wisdom for me. She left me a message saying she got back to town last night. I'll give her a call."

"Good idea."

Debbie picked up on the first ring.

"Thank God, you're there. I need advice." In a rush, I told her about Stephanie's drinking.

After a moment, Debbie said, "Tough stuff. I've been there, as have many parents. What's your plan?"

"Her first AA meeting. I only hope it will be her last."

"Don't get ahead of yourself. Remember who's in control."

I sighed. "Yeah, and it ain't me."

"That's the correct answer. On another topic, give me an update on your plans to open another store."

"I'm not."

"Really?" I heard the surprise in Debbie's voice. "What changed?"

"Stephanie lost her trust fund in the stock market crash, so I'm selling Cornucopia to pay for her tuition to Stanford." I stretched the phone cord so I could pull out a chair and sit.

Debbie yelped. "Wait a minute! I leave town for a couple of weeks and your entire life turns topsy-turvy. I'm speechless."

"You're never speechless."

"You know what I mean. Do you think losing her trust fund led to Stephanie acting out?"

"Acting out. Sounds so much better than getting drunk. Yeah, I do think that was the catalyst."

"Well, my dear. The cupboard is bare, and I've got to head to the grocery store. Talk later. Remember, deep breaths, prayer, and get to a meeting."

"Thanks, Debbie." Grateful for my friend's support, I hung up the phone, offering a prayer for the strength to help my granddaughter.

Chapter Forty-Four

STEPHANIE - BATH AND CONSEQUENCES

In my bathroom, I pulled off the ruined gold tee. It reeked of gin-flavored vomit, and I stuffed it in the trash. My stomach did a handstand, and I spit out some gross yellow stuff in the sink. Turning on the tap in the tub, I added lavender bubble bath. As I lowered my jeans, I remembered my underwear was gone—as well as my virginity.

When the tub was half full, I got in and turned the faucet to all hot water. Ooh! My privates stung like a bitch. Did I think the water would burn away what happened with Logan? Logan, the football hero wide receiver with a full ride to A&M. Logan, the most handsome boy in school, almost as good-looking as Rob Lowe. Logan, who filled me up with gin and Dr Pepper—and his penis. How could I not remember doing the deed? The only memory which floated just out of reach was a sharp pain, beer breath, and a heavy weight on top of me. The first time was supposed to be special. Last night was anything but.

I closed my eyes and sank under the water, then opened them to discover a world of bubbles. It looked totally awesome. Then I sat up, lunged forward, hugged my knees, and cried.

As the water cooled, I added more hot water. Maybe I'd stay in the tub, never get out. But no amount of time or water could wash away my mistake, and besides, I'd shrivel up like a prune, like the tips of my fingers were already doing. I lathered my hair with Gee, Your Hair Smells Terrific shampoo, unhooked the sprayer and rinsed the suds away. The sweet scent really did smell terrific.

As I dried myself, I was careful around my private area. There wasn't any more blood, thank God, but I was still tender. I dressed in baggy sweatpants and an oversized long-sleeved tee, trying to hide my violated body in fabric.

Would Logan tell everybody what we did? He was between girlfriends, but rumor had it he was *always* between girlfriends. How would I be able to face Kimberly, Tiffany, and the other girls at school? I seriously doubted any of them were virgins, but still.

At the sink, I brushed my teeth about five times and gargled half a bottle of Listermint, not looking at myself in the mirror. Was it my imagination or did I still smell gin? I combed out the worst of the tangles in my hair, leaving it wet. What did I care?

Lauren and Brett were waiting for me in the living room. I had delayed as long as possible before going out to see them. My interrogators sat close together on the couch, so I took a seat in a chair to the side, not wanting to face them head on. I waited for them to say something—anything—but they stayed silent.

Of course, I caved first. "So, I'm guilty as charged. What's my punishment?"

Lauren looked at Brett. It seemed to me she was letting him take the lead, and I wondered why, because she was usually assertive. Not that I'd call her bossy, but definitely a take-charge type.

"Trust has been broken, and it's gonna take a good long while to repair the damage," Brett said.

I gulped. Brett's voice didn't sound angry or mean, but it was full of disappointment. Maybe it would be better if they just yelled at me. Anything was better than seeing the sad looks on their faces. I didn't think I could feel any worse but making them unhappy really did it. My eyes stung, and I wiped them with my sleeve.

Lauren unclenched her jaw. "On Monday, you're going to come with us to an AA meeting. You'll sit there and listen. And learn."

Well, that pissed me off. "Are you kidding me? It was one time. That doesn't make me an alcoholic."

"Not yet." Lauren's turquoise eyes shot fire at me. It was scary.

Was that what they thought of me? My mouth fell open, but no words came out. I clamped it shut and swallowed hard. And waited for more, but Brett and Lauren just stared at me without saying a word.

After a couple of minutes, the silence became unbearable. "Can I go to my room?"

With her eyes still blazing, Lauren said, "I think that would be a very good idea."

I couldn't get out of there fast enough.

Chapter Forty-Five

Lauren Faces her Fears

The next morning, Stephanie didn't come to the kitchen as she usually did. I made pancakes and sausage for breakfast, which were congealing and would soon be inedible, so I headed to her room. Knocking on her bedroom door, I called out in an upbeat voice. "Breakfast is ready. I made your favorite pancakes."

"Not hungry."

"You sure?"

Stephanie raised her voice. "Totally!"

As Brett and I forced down the cold breakfast, we discussed our concern for our girl.

"She has to come out of her room eventually, doesn't she?" I asked.

"'Course she does. My advice is leave her be and check on her later."

I cleared the dishes and scraped the leftovers into the trash. "Okay. I'll let her sulk until lunch."

At noon, I carried a plate with a roast beef sandwich to her door and knocked.

"What do you want?" Stephanie's voice quavered.

"May I come in?"

"You will anyway."

The girl lay in bed, her eyes red and puffy. I laid the plate on her desk and sat on the chair. Filled with dread about the question I was about to ask, I took a deep breath. "There's something I need to know."

"What?" She picked up a pillow and held it to her chest.

I gazed into her eyes, and she stared right back. "Have you tried to hurt yourself?"

Stephanie threw the pillow on the floor, leapt out of bed, and waved her arms about. "No! Is that what you think of me? I'm over that shit. I've got better ways to cope."

"With alcohol?"

Stephanie frowned and clenched her jaw, pacing back and forth in front of me. "Okay, so I made a mistake. One mistake. The gin made me barf so bad, I'll never drink again."

"Brave words. Time will tell if that's true." I folded my hands so Stephanie wouldn't see them shaking. "People with a normal constitution can drink without getting drunk. They know when to stop. Alcoholics don't, so it's worrisome that you drank to excess the first time you tried alcohol. If that *was* the first time."

"It was!" Stephanie shouted.

"Tell me, did either of your parents have a drinking problem?"

She stopped pacing and gaped at me. "No! I don't think so. Maybe."

Frustrated, I shook my head. "Which is it?"

"My dad didn't care much for drinking. Once in a while, he'd have a glass of wine with dinner. But Mom did like her cocktails, especially after Dad died. But I never saw her drunk, not ever."

"That doesn't mean anything."

"Oh, wow! You didn't even know her."

Her words landed like a slap in the face. Of course, it was true. Was I going about the conversation the wrong way? Both of us were hurt. Perhaps the better tactic was to back off for now.

"Brett made you a sandwich."

Stephanie clutched her abdomen. "I guess I could eat."

As I left the room, Stephanie dug into her lunch.

Brett and I decided to take Stephanie to the noon meeting at the Northside 24 Hour club on Monday, even though she'd miss school. There would be a variety of members attending, from those actively detoxing to those with lengthy sobriety. Without a doubt, she'd witness distressing sights and hear raw and painful stories, and we hoped she'd be scared straight.

That morning, a sullen Stephanie trudged into the kitchen. Her sense of style seemed to have abandoned her. She wore gray sweatpants and that darned "I Wanna be Sedated" T-shirt.

"Where's this AA meeting?" she grumbled.

"You'll find out after you change out of that damned T-shirt. It's wildly inappropriate where we're going." I vowed to throw the thing out the next chance I got. "And brush your hair while you're at it."

With an exaggerated eye roll and theatrical sigh, she turned away and plodded out of the kitchen. A few minutes later, she returned in a baggy navy-blue long-sleeved t-shirt and her hair in a ponytail.

"Not very stylish but acceptable. Brett's waiting in the truck." I waved her to the door.

On the silent drive, I had time to think. Of course, I'd called both Debbie and Jane, seeking advice. They agreed that taking the girl to an AA meeting was a good plan, but beyond that, didn't have any brilliant suggestions. I appreciated their support and would need to lean on them in the coming days. The night before, Brett and I had spoken at length, addressing our fears for the girl. As recovering alcoholics, we knew full well the dangerous place Stephanie found herself in. There were many theories about the cause of alcoholism, but what worried me the most was the possible genetic connection.

If Stephanie drank again, her promising future might be derailed. Thinking back to my own problems with alcohol, I shivered and prayed she wouldn't spiral into the hell I'd endured. Would she pull herself together and attend college? Of course, her prospects for college depended on my success in selling Cornucopia. Before I could put the store on the market, there was a lot of work ahead, so I'd better get cracking. But what if I couldn't sell my business in time to pay for Stanford? I doubted the girl would be content to attend UT. But college was months away, and I had to deal with the current problem.

Chapter Forty-Six

STEPHANIE - AA SUCKS

My rulers didn't say a word on the drive. They didn't even turn on the radio, and I sure wasn't going to beg for some tunes, which I'd probably hate anyway. I decided to play their game and kept my mouth shut too. With my arms folded over my chest, I stared out the window. Lauren sure had been mad I put on my Ramone's shirt. But no way was I going to throw it away. It cost $12.00. Why did I wear it? To piss her off, I guess. And it worked.

Bummed about having to go to the meeting, I planned to just sit there, silent. What went on inside those sessions was a mystery, but I'd be finding out.

We drove quite a way up Mopac to an area I hadn't been to. When Brett pulled up to a blue metal and white brick building stuck between a house and some sort of auto shop, I didn't want to get out. Not that I knew what to expect, but it didn't look very inviting. "Is this it?"

Lauren broke her silence. "Yes. There may be people here going through a rough patch. This place is open twenty-four hours a day as a refuge and safe place." We got out of the truck, and Lauren took my hand, which made me feel like a toddler. "Let's go find a seat."

As we approached the door, I dragged my feet. "Can I sit between you and Brett?"

Brett patted my shoulder. "Sure thing." He held open the door, and we followed Lauren to the meeting room. The gray folding chairs and the ratty old couches looked like something you'd see sitting on a curb. I got a whiff of burnt coffee and cigarette smoke, reminding me of Bouldin, where Lauren made me go to that lame Christmas buffet last year.

Lauren led us to a row midway down the aisle. We passed a few men, grody-looking, wearing layers of dirty, stinky clothes. When the odor of vomit and liquor hit my nose, I almost ralphed. I slouched down in the chair and scoped out the place. I was the youngest person in the room by at least twenty years, maybe more. At first, I thought the crowd was all men, but then I saw two women. They sat huddled together, holding styrofoam cups of coffee like their drinks might take flight. Lauren was right—rough patch city. The odor of unwashed bodies made me breathe through my mouth. As if I needed to get nauseous again after the last two days.

An old dude passed out sheets of paper to people near the front, then he started the meeting. "Alcoholics Anonymous is a fellowship of men and women who share their experience, strength, and hope with each other that they may solve their common problem and help others to recover from alcoholism. The only requirement for membership is a desire to stop drinking."

While the old dude kept talking, my attention wandered. Desire to stop drinking? I'd barely started, and I hadn't even liked it. And ending up in that room was the worst.

The leader asked one of the women to read "How It Works." I didn't think she'd let go of her coffee, but she did. Listening to her drone on for several minutes, hesitating over words of more than one syllable, was a real snoozefest. When she got to the part about the Twelve Steps, I was able to follow along, reading them off the huge posters on the wall. I zoned out when another guy read the twelve traditions and almost dozed off when the other woman read the promises. In a way, it was like going to church because God had a major place in the readings. So far, there was nothing to freak out about, but I was epically bored.

Lauren and Brett sat on either side of me, paying attention, although they must have heard that stuff before, probably thousands of times. How did they pull that off?

The leader asked if anyone wanted to "share their experience, strength, and hope," and a few hands shot up. My hope was that Lauren and Brett didn't share their experience with me. Thank God, they stayed quiet while a bunch of people told their sad stories.

How could this hour be ten times longer than any other hour I'd ever lived? At last, the old guy said, "Thanks to everybody who shared. Will y'all please stand and help me close with the Lord's prayer?"

Chairs scraped. Brett led us out to the aisle where the people lined up holding hands to form a square. Glancing around, I sure was glad to be sandwiched between Brett and Lauren. I stared at my shoes, not wanting to make eye contact with the people across from me. From "Our Father" to "keep coming back, it works if you work it," my feet were itching to leave.

When we got outside, I took big gulps of fresh air. "Please don't make me go back."

Lauren stared a hole in me. "That's up to you."

I turned to Brett, who nodded. "That's right. You've got some thinkin' to do, young lady. Now, how about some lunch?"

My stomach grumbled. "I'm starving. And I bet the restaurant will smell a lot better than the meeting." Once we settled in the truck, I asked, "Can we please go to Chuy's?"

Brett leaned over and kissed Lauren on the cheek. "Where ya wanna go, sweetheart?"

"Nowhere fancy. Not with Stephanie dressed like a refugee."

"Wow! That's mean," I said.

Lauren swiveled around to look at me. "Maybe, but it's true. Why are you dressing like that? You were an aspiring fashion plate just last week."

I shrugged and avoided her gaze. "I dunno. It just feels comfortable."

Turning back to face the front, Lauren patted Brett's hand. "Chuy's is fine, dear."

After two days of misery, I was ready for one of those big as yo face burritos smothered in cheese. *Queso.* As Lauren suggested, I had picked up a little bit of menu Spanish.

Chapter Forty-Seven

LAUREN THE DISCIPLINARIAN

After arriving home from Chuy's, Stephanie fled to her room, and Brett and I retreated to the kitchen to talk. "I think allowing our girl to quit her job was a mistake. Do you think she should go back to work?" I asked.

Brett made a pot of coffee and joined me at the table. "Sure do."

I batted my eyelashes at him. "Who's gonna tell her?"

With a chuckle, Brett answered, "That's all on you, darlin'."

My dear husband saw right through me. I reached for his hand and squeezed. "I know, just thought I'd ask. Wish me luck." I rose and headed to Stephanie's hideaway.

She answered my knock. "It's open."

As I entered the room, she switched off MTV and sat on the side of the bed. "What now?"

"Starting this Saturday, you'll be working at Cornucopia again." I stiffened my spine, waiting for her reaction.

"Whatever you say, Lauren."

The girl's puppy dog eyes and meek demeanor did nothing to melt my heart, although I was surprised she took the news so well. Eager for a cup of Brett's coffee, I retraced my steps, recalling the libertine life I led from my teens until I was struck sober at the age of thirty-seven. Was I a hypocrite? If so, too bad. It took me twenty years to escape the dark tunnel of dependency, and I vowed Stephanie wouldn't go down the same path I did.

As I dressed for work the next morning, I realized I'd put on the same dress I'd worn yesterday and chose another. Obviously, the stress was getting to me. I eyed the outsized pile of clothing for the dry cleaners and made a mental note to take it later that week. How had I become so disorganized? On the drive to the store, I prayed aloud, asking for calm and strength.

When I arrived at Cornucopia, I dashed inside and jotted a list of tasks for the day. Then I called Jolie and Shondra to my office. "My granddaughter will be working on Saturdays again. Please keep a close eye on her and don't hesitate to call me if she doesn't toe the line."

"Of course," Jolie said.

"Yes, ma'am." Although I'd tried to discourage her from doing so, Shondra insisted on calling me ma'am.

"Any questions, ladies?"

The two young women shook their heads and left my office. Although I was sure they wondered what had changed given that Stephanie had quit three weeks ago, they wisely didn't ask.

In need of a caffeine boost, I got up and put on a pot of coffee. I had a long day ahead, filled with routine tasks like reviewing time sheets and making the December schedule. Halfway through my lengthy list, I took a break and dialed Jane's number. She picked up on the third ring, out of breath.

"Been running laps?"

"Hey, Lauren. Just got in from work. What's up?"

I flat-out asked why Stephanie hadn't been babysitting for her.

"Um, the last time I asked, she turned me down."

"She never mentioned that to me. When exactly was this?"

"Let me think. It was about a week ago, just before that regrettable drinking episode. She was pretty snippy about it too. Sorry, but even if Stephanie was willing, I just don't feel comfortable having her take care of Will right now."

"I see." And I did, but my heart hurt for the girl.

"Anyway, I found a new sitter who lives just down the street. She's a recent grad who's taking a gap year, so I'm all set. Got to go," Jane said. She couldn't wait to get off the phone.

With a sigh, I tackled the weekly order for produce and dry goods. At six, I called it quits and headed home.

Brett was in the kitchen, stirring a pot of something that smelled divine. When I told him about my talk with Jane, his lips tightened. "That's too bad. Guess I can't fault her for being cautious."

As November plodded on, Stephanie rarely graced us with her presence, preferring to stay in her room. The racket from MTV leaked through the door late into the night. Finally, I told her I would cut off the cable if she didn't turn it off by ten p.m. The resulting quiet was blissful.

Stephanie no longer helped Brett in the kitchen, and I had to practically drag her from her lair for meals. To my surprise, her initial meekness disappeared, replaced by sullenness. One-word answers, eye rolls, shrugs, and deep sighs made her presence at meals a strain on everyone's mood. When grades came out, I was relieved to see she had maintained her grade point average. At least one thing was going right. "By the way, how's your driver's ed class going? You haven't mentioned it lately."

"I dropped out. No money for a car." Even though I was glad Stephanie wouldn't be on the road, I couldn't help but feel bad for her.

Thank the Lord, I'd asked Debbie to sponsor me months ago, so she was up to speed on the trials and tribulations I'd been through with Stephanie. I burned the phone lines calling her for advice. She listened to my concerns and offered understanding and advice, having successfully reared two girls to adulthood. Her steadiness and sense of humor lifted my spirits.

Even though my schedule was packed, I took time away from the store and met Debbie for lunch at Shady Grove. As we waited for our Hippie Chick sandwiches, I unloaded my worry about Stephanie's attitude.

"Sounds all too familiar, Lauren. There were times my girls didn't speak to me for days, so her behavior, while hard to take, isn't all that unusual." Then Debbie regaled me with a comedy routine about raising her daughters. "This gray hair is from when Lydia got a tattoo, and this streak of gray is due to Claire's hippie phase." A good chuckle dispersed my anxiety just a bit.

Thanksgiving arrived, and I thought back to the wonderful brunch at the Driskill last year, but with Stephanie's dour mood, we decided it was wiser to cook at home. Brett roasted a small turkey and prepared the side dishes without Stephanie's help. I made the stuffing and opened the cranberry sauce, but Brett did the rest. Even the aroma of the turkey didn't draw the girl out of hiding. After I set the table for three and helped Brett carry everything into the dining room, I followed the directions on his apron and kissed the cook. "I'm going to fetch Stephanie."

As I turned on my heel and marched down the hall to the girl's room, Brett called after me, "Good luck."

I knocked on Stephanie's door and heard a faint answer, so I entered. She was lounging in bed with a book, one of her favorite sci-fi adventures, no doubt. "Dinner is served."

With a heavy sigh, Stephanie glanced up from her reading. "I'll get a plate later."

"No, you'll get up and join us."

She threw her book on the floor and frowned. "Well, if you insist, granny."

The g-word hadn't been used in months. I gritted my teeth and swallowed the gibe, refusing to take the bait. "Brett has gone to a lot of trouble to prepare our Thanksgiving feast. Please comb your hair and wash your hands. We'll be waiting."

I stalked to the door and turned back to see the girl scoot out of bed and enter the bathroom. Stephanie had been with us for a year and a half, and it seemed to me we were back at square one with a sullen, rude, and angry child.

Joining Brett at the table, I muttered, "Let's hope for the best. It's a far cry from last year, isn't it?"

He didn't answer, just patted my hand.

A few minutes later, Stephanie slouched to the table and seated herself with a gusty sigh. She loaded her plate and ate like a starving person. As usual, the meal was superb, but silence loomed like an uninvited guest. Brett and I tried to carry on a conversation, but our efforts came off as stilted and forced, what Stephanie would call "lame."

I passed Brett the rolls. "Darling, you outdid yourself with this gravy."

"Thanks, honey. How 'bout you, Stephanie, want a refill on anything?"

"I'm good." Those were the only two words the girl uttered during the meal. Once her plate was empty, Stephanie pushed back her chair and stood.

"How's about dessert? Made a chocolate pecan pie," Brett said.

The girl waved her hand dismissively and disappeared back to her lair.

I clenched my fists in frustration. "How long are we gonna have to endure this?"

Brett shook his head. "Don't know, darlin'. Give the kid a little more time to get over her mad or whatever the heck is goin' on."

"Define little. I'm on my last nerve."

Chapter Forty-Eight

STEPHANIE WALLOWS IN MISERY

Back in my room, I regretted not having some chocolate pecan pie and planned to sneak out and grab a piece after my rulers went to bed. Since I lost my fortune and got drunk, I just wanted to be left alone so I hid out, unless I had to go to school or work.

Every afternoon, Brett bugged me to cook with him, but I was in no mood. Would he ever give it a rest? Lately, Lauren worked really long hours, so I didn't have to deal with her as much as usual, which was probably a good thing.

Since my disastrous night with Logan, I hated going to school. I kept the lowest of profiles, avoiding all human contact, hoping to blend into the background. Wearing dark, loose clothes and keeping my head down seemed to work. I stopped going to the cafeteria because I didn't want to run into Tiffany's crowd. Luckily, none of the cool girls were in my classes. I especially wanted nothing to do with Kimberly, and if I saw her coming down the hallway, I spun around and raced in the other direction. How could I make it until graduation? Five months seemed like forever away.

Once, I spotted Logan in the hall, but it was too late to hide. He looked right through me like I wasn't even there. Maybe he didn't recognize me in my ugly clothes, or had I actually succeeded in becoming invisible?

The first two weeks of December dragged. Christmas break arrived, but what did I care? Was it better to go to class or just hide out in my room all day? A toss-up. Bored with MTV—U2 was really getting on my nerves—I dusted off my Nintendo and played Super Mario Brothers until my eyes crossed. I turned the volume to super low, so the sound effects didn't bug my overlords. Although I hadn't played in months, I remembered all the powerups and soon beat my old high score. It was lame but helped pass the time during Christmas break. Without thinking, I picked up the phone to call Becca, but then remembered her family was on a skiing trip in Colorado, and shocker, they brought her boyfriend along. I missed hanging out with her, but her boyfriend took all her free time. But she tried to cheer me up when my trust fund vanished, telling me what a great school UT was and how much fun I'd have there. Fun? Would I ever have fun again?

What happened with Logan had to stay a secret. I didn't want anyone to know, especially Lauren. When she asked me forever ago about my romance with Colton—really wanting to know if I was still a virgin—I said something like, "I swear what happened to you won't happen to me." And now I wondered if those words would come back to bite me in the ass.

One afternoon Brett brought home a Christmas tree, and the piney smell brought back memories from my childhood, when my mom and dad made a big fuss over me. I remembered leaving cookies and milk for Santa and the enormous pile of presents, but that was another life, gone forever. My eyes burned, and I sniffed back tears. I lay on the bed, staring at MTV without the sound on when Lauren knocked on my door.

"What now?" I yelled.

Lauren marched into my room and switched off the television. She stood over me with her hands on her hips. "We're about to decorate the tree. Brett made your favorite peppermint hot chocolate."

"Big whoop."

"I beg your pardon?" Lauren did her usual frown and face relaxation thing.

Pissed off, I sat up and glared at her. "I said big whoop."

Watching Lauren trying to control herself was entertaining, and I almost cracked up.

"I take it that's a no for the hot chocolate. Are you going to help us trim the tree?"

"That's a no for the tree too." I jumped out of bed, ran to my bathroom, and slammed the door. I sat on the toilet, checking to see if I'd finally gotten my period. Nope. Even worse, I couldn't remember whether I had one in November because I never kept track.

Chapter Forty-Nine

LAUREN'S DECEMBER RUSH

December passed in a flash, the days melting one into the other. I neglected my program, missed meetings, and canceled lunches with my favorite people because of all the hours I was putting in at Cornucopia.

One night at closing time, a knock on my office door startled me. "Come in."

Jolie approached my desk with her hands in the pockets of her apron. "Got a sec?"

I pointed to a chair. "Have a seat. What's up?"

Jolie perched on the edge of the chair. "Is there a problem with Cornucopia? A couple months ago, you were training me for bigger things but that stopped." She pushed her glasses higher, an irritating habit. "And you've been spending way more time here."

Reflexively, I reached for my Zuni necklace. Flustered, I swallowed hard and considered what I should share with her. "No, the store isn't in trouble, but I've had to table my plans to open another location. Right now, I'm working through some things and will update you when I know more."

The look of disappointment on Jolie's face made me wince. "Oh, that's too bad."

Although I trusted her, I couldn't confide my plans to sell the store—yet. "Anything else?"

Jolie shook her head. "I'll lock up."

"Thank you." When she closed the door, I closed my eyes and leaned back in my chair. I'd been so wrapped up in the myriad details of listing my business for sale that I failed to see the effect on my employees. Consultations with my bookkeeper and attorney, preparing financial statements, getting an appraisal, and finding the right broker all took time. I wanted the transfer of ownership to be fast and painless, at least a little less painless than the death of my life's work was bound to be.

The Bouldin Christmas AA party organizational meeting snuck up on me. Debbie called to schedule a lunch to discuss our plans.

"So sorry, but I can't spare the time this year. I'm up to my neck trying to get the store on the market." I knew the brunt of the work would fall on Debbie's shoulders, but she was more than capable of recruiting others. "Tell you what, stop by the store, and I'll write you an extra-large check to soften the blow of my absence."

Debbie snorted. "Soften the blow of your absence? A little full of yourself, aren't you?"

"Maybe." I could always count on Debbie to keep my ego rightsized.

"But I'll take the check. And when the store sells, we're going to celebrate."

"You bet we are. Can't wait."

That night in bed, Brett held me in his arms while I vented about my workload.

"At least the store closes early on Christmas Eve, so I'll have a day and a half off."

Brett kissed my cheek. "This too shall pass, as the sayin' goes. Got to say, I do miss our morning chats and our stolen afternoons."

I burrowed into his side. "Me too. What made me think I could handle two stores? These days, I'm exhausted from just one."

"I got some extra time now that the fundraiser at the ranch is in the books. What can I do to lessen your load?"

"You mean besides running the house and cooking me delicious meals every night?"

"Aw, shucks."

"There is one thing. Christmas. I'd like to buy some new clothes for Stephanie, but I don't have time to shop."

"Hmm. Fashion ain't in my wheelhouse. How will I know what to get?"

"Buy *Glamour* magazine and look at the ads. Then shop at Buckle and Contempo Casuals in the mall. I'm sure the staff will help."

Brett let out a gusty sigh. "Guess I could do that. Any other tips?"

"Yes, don't buy anything in navy, brown or gray. Think bright cheerful colors."

"Well, I did offer to help, so I'll get it done." He kissed me goodnight.

I drifted off, imaging Stephanie's smiling face as she opened her gifts. It would be lovely to see her in something other than those dark, ugly sweatpants and shirts.

A week before the holiday, I informed Stephanie her presence would be required at the Bouldin AA Christmas dinner. She snorted in disgust and stomped down the hall. I waited to hear the door slam and wasn't disappointed.

On Christmas Day, as Brett and I enjoyed a quick cup of coffee, Stephanie trudged into the kitchen wearing unflattering brown sweatpants and a matching hooded sweatshirt. "Do I really have to go with you?"

With a grim set to his lips, Brett dumped out his mug in the sink. "Yes."

The girl glared at me. I forced a bright smile. "What Brett said. Let's get going."

On the brief drive to Bouldin, I tuned the radio to a station playing Christmas songs, hoping to spread some holiday cheer.

"Will you turn that crap off?" Stephanie snapped.

If Stephanie was trying to ruin the event for us, she did an excellent job. After I visited with Debbie, complimenting her on the food and attendance, Brett and I helped ourselves to the buffet. We joined Stephanie at a table, where she sat with two plates piled high with nothing but desserts. In horror, I watched as she stuffed pie and cookies into her mouth at an alarming pace. Once she demolished both plates of sweets, she wiped her hands on her pants. "When can we leave?"

We ignored her insolence and finished our meal, then chatted with several friends. Glancing over my shoulder, I observed Stephanie near the door, leaning against the wall with her arms folded and her lips in a pout. I nudged Brett. "Take a look towards the door, honey. Merry Christmas."

He swiveled his head. "Ah, irony."

When we arrived home, Stephanie bolted for the hallway. Brett hustled after her, catching up to her at the door to her room. "Oh no, you don't. Time to open presents."

"Bah, humbug!" The girl shut the door in Brett's face.

Chapter Fifty

STEPHANIE DODGES REALITY

No way was I going to open my presents. I hurried into my bathroom and checked again to see if I got my period. Nope. But the chances I was pregnant after one time had to be tiny, so I blew it off.

That night, after my rulers were in bed, I snuck out to the Christmas tree and brought my presents back to my room. Sitting on the bed, I opened them, prepared to find something Lauren would wear, but was surprised at the gorgeous clothes. I'd seen some of them on display at the mall when I bought The Legend of Zelda. Too bad I wouldn't wear them. Sweats were my thing now, but what would I wear when it got hot? I put everything back in the boxes and stuffed them in my closet.

When I woke up the next morning, I realized it was Saturday and groaned. I threw back the covers and stomped into the kitchen, where Brett and Lauren were drinking coffee and reading the paper. "I quit."

Lauren glanced up and frowned. "What?"

"I'm not going to work. Not today and not ever again. And you can't make me!" Before they could say a word, I ran down the hall, slammed my door, and climbed under the covers. What were they going to do? Drag me out of bed, dress me, and carry me to Cornucopia? I thought I'd feel relieved, but I just felt bad.

Christmas break ended, and I had mixed feelings about going back to school. I didn't want to see Logan or anyone in the clique, but staying in my room all the time was getting old. I'd gone through all the levels of Super Mario and picked up Zelda so fast it wasn't a challenge. And every time I tuned in to MTV, they played videos by Bon Jovi, U2, or INXS that I'd already seen like a million times. Boring. The only bright spot about school was seeing Becca in English class. On the first day after the break, we took our seats. She babbled on forever about her boyfriend and all the fun she had on the ski trip, and I realized we had nothing in common anymore. Was I jealous she was going to her dream school with her dream guy? Maybe. I'd be lucky if I'd be able to afford my backup college.

When I got home from school, no one was there, so I scarfed down some leftover chicken. That's what I did now—ate when I was alone. I refused to eat with them in the evening, lying that I'd already eaten or saying I'd eat leftovers later. After a couple of weeks, they backed off and let me do whatever. My rulers probably wouldn't put up with my behavior much longer, but so what? Since Lauren was my official guardian, she couldn't just get rid of me. At least I didn't think so.

It would take me a really long time to get over not going to Stanford. How do you get over having your life ruined?

A week later, I came home from school and Lauren was waiting for me in the entryway. I tossed my backpack on the floor. "What did I do now?"

"Don't be so negative. You have a letter from Stanford." Lauren gave me a big fake-looking smile.

"So what?" I folded my arms and frowned. "What's the big deal? I'm broke and can't go. End of story."

"Don't you want to know their decision?"

"I guess." We headed to the kitchen, where Brett waited, holding out an envelope like it was a present.

My hands shook when I snatched it from him. I stared at my name on the envelope. "I should just rip this thing to shreds."

Lauren gasped. "No! Don't do that."

I squinted at her. "Why the hell not?"

Brett raised his voice. "Just open it!"

I gritted my teeth, tore into the envelope, and scanned the letter.

"Well?" my rulers asked.

"Not that it matters, but I got in." I burst into tears and ran from the kitchen, letting the letter fall to the floor like so much trash.

The days passed, and I still hadn't gotten my period. So I talked to Becca, the only person I trusted. I still considered her a friend even though she was super obsessed with her boyfriend, and we didn't hang out anymore. Not that I wanted a social life, not after my night of shame with Logan. We walked out together after English class, but I dragged her back into the empty classroom.

"I never told you what happened in November."

Becca frowned. "What are you talking about?"

I confessed what happened with Logan, and Becca dropped her books and leaned against the blackboard. For a minute, I thought she might faint.

"Oh my God, Stephanie. That's horrible."

Tears sprang to my eyes. "It gets worse. I missed my period in December, and I'm late this month."

"No way! Are you pretty regular?"

"Kinda sorta."

"Did you ever miss your period before?"

"Yeah, when I first came to Austin, after I ran away."

"See, that might be it. I wouldn't worry too much." Becca hugged me and picked up her books. "Keep me posted. Got to jet."

"Later."

But as January ended, and I'd officially missed twice, my heart fell to my shoes, as my mom used to say. Wow! I hadn't thought about my mom in like forever. How would she react if she knew what happened? What would old fake granny Babcock say? And worst of all, what would Lauren and Brett do?

Desperate for answers, I took the bus to the public library because there was no way I'd look up information about pregnancy at school. Sneaking over to the card catalogue, I hunched down and looked around to make sure no one was watching me, then flipped through the 570s—biology.

After I found a promising title, I wrote down the call number on my hand and headed over to the Science section. I pulled the heavy book from the shelf and sat down to read. What I discovered sent me running to the restroom, where I barfed all over the floor before I made it to the toilet. The queasy feeling I'd had lately might be morning sickness, which I learned happened at any time of the day. I mopped up the barf the best I could and got out of there fast.

Chapter Fifty-One

LAUREN STRETCHED THIN

In mid-January, I put Cornucopia on the market. The hardest part was telling the staff, especially Jolie. I summoned everyone to my office and informed them that Cornucopia was for sale. The shocked faces and open mouths cut me to the bone. Jolie took off her glasses and dabbed her eyes. Then the questions washed over me in a flood of indistinguishable words.

Standing tall but feeling small, I held up my clammy hands and asked for quiet. "I hope you will stay with me through this period of transition, so I'm offering a cash bonus if you work until the deal closes."

Jolie raised her hand. "Will the new owners keep the store like it is?"

"While I believe the buyer will want to continue with our business model, I can't guarantee it." After I responded to all the queries, I promised each employee a glowing recommendation to the buyers. When no one walked out on me, I was grateful. As the staff returned to their duties, I dropped into my chair and stared at the ceiling, spent.

Store operations continued without a shred of drama—for a week. Then Shondra and two stock boys quit. How naïve was I to think the transition would go smoothly? Brett wouldn't be happy to learn I'd be spending even more time at work filling in for the staff who left.

Demoralized, I called Debbie to complain, but before I could launch into my tale of woe, she lit into me.

"Well, hello, stranger. After you canceled lunch last week, I was wondering when I'd hear from you."

"Sorry about that, but I've been swamped. I finally put the store on the market, but three of my staff quit, so now I'm putting in more hours than ever. I just want this over with."

Debbie took a moment to digest the news. "I hear you and do sympathize. Focus on how relieved you'll be when the store's sold. Remember that nothing lasts forever."

"Truer words." But could I survive the coming weeks?

"Have you been to a meeting lately?"

"Define lately."

Silence.

"Debbie?"

"At a time like this, you need the program more than ever. But you know that."

"I do. And I will try to get to a meeting. Raincheck on lunch?"

"Yes, I'll call you to reschedule. By the way, how is Stephanie doing? She looked miserable at Bouldin."

I realized Debbie couldn't see me shaking my head through the phone lines. "She's still miserable. Thank God school is back in session, so she has to come out of her room."

"At least she's going to school. After losing her trust fund and acting out with liquor, she's bound to take time to heal. Have you thought about having her return to therapy?"

"It's crossed my mind, but I'm sure she wouldn't agree to that. But if this moodiness continues much longer, I might have to revisit that option."

When I told Brett about losing some staff, he said, "Guess I know what that means."

I put my arms around him. "I have no choice. Can't let the business fail when I'm trying to sell it."

"Oh, I get it. Just hope it sells soon. On another topic, I've been trying to tantalize Stephanie into going horseback riding again. She said, 'No way,' and disappeared into her room."

"Oh honey. I feel so bad for her."

Brett's lips tightened. "I do too."

When Stephanie wasn't at school, she lived in her room. Offers of a movie or a trip to the mall were met with a blank stare and a head shake. I waited in vain for a fashion show of the clothes we bought her for Christmas. When Stephanie first came to us, she had been eager to embrace the latest fashions but no longer. She continued to mope around in those dull warm-up clothes. How long would she stay in this funk?

Should I tell the girl about selling the store to pay for Stanford? I feared what would happen if I didn't get an offer, so I kept quiet, but stress was taking its toll on me. Sleep eluded me, and my mind wasn't in the right place to meditate. But I was more concerned about my granddaughter. If I failed in my mission, would she accept UT as an alternative?

I'd been neglecting my sponsorship duties, so I called Jane to catch up. Although I'd been her sponsor for ten years, it seemed our roles had almost reversed.

"Talk to me, Jane."

"Hey, Lauren, strange way to begin a conversation."

"Time constraints, my dear. I've been drowning in work and dealing with a sulky, miserable teenager."

"Did you at least have a nice Christmas?"

As was my habit, I clutched my Zuni necklace. "Has it been that long since we've talked?"

"Yes, it has. Did Stephanie like her gifts?"

Bitter laughter rose in my throat. "No. Actually, I don't know because she refused to open them. But the next morning, the gifts weren't under the tree, so I suppose she put them away. Her attitude has not improved in the slightest."

"Sorry to hear that."

"Brett and I are concerned, but he's busy at the ranch, and I'm filling in at the store for all the staff that quit. Most of the time, Stephanie's in her room listening to that atrocious MTV. After that drinking episode, I put her back to work on Saturdays, but she's quit again."

"What are you going to do about it?"

"About the job? Nothing. She's very prickly, so I'm tiptoeing around her."

Jane cleared her throat. "That doesn't sound like you. Any positive signs?"

"Well, she's attending classes and keeping up her grades."

"Good about the grades, but you need to find a way to get her out of her solitude."

"Oh, we've tried. She doesn't even want to go out to eat. She's refused movies and shopping trips."

"Sorry I don't have any solutions to offer. Maybe try asking someone with teenagers."

"Yes, I have, but nothing works." I could hear the frustration in my voice. "But enough about my problems. How are things with you?"

"We had a lovely Christmas. Will sure loves the ride-on scooter you and Brett gave him. He barrels all over the house on the thing, with Delilah trailing after him like a shadow. I'm getting a workout keeping up with him. Luckily, he's still a champion napper, and I take full advantage when I can."

"You take good care of that boy."

"Yes, ma'am."

"Don't you ma'am me, Jane!"

On that note, we ended the call with laughter, something sorely lacking in my life.

When February arrived with no improvement in the girl's mood, I gathered my nerve and prepared for a confrontation. It was past time to do something. When she came home from school that Friday, I hustled into the entry and followed her to her lair. She actually tried to shut the door in my face, but I wasn't having it. "We need to talk."

"No 'we' don't. *You* need to talk."

"Then I will." I took a seat at her desk while the girl perched on the edge of the bed. "I'll be blunt. I'd like you to try therapy again."

Apparently struck speechless, Stephanie opened her mouth, but no words came out.

"Look, it's been over two months since your...your episode. Do you plan to hide from life permanently?" I struggled to keep an even tone, but the weeks of pouting and attitude had taken a toll on my patience.

The girl's shoulders drooped, and she lay back on the bed. "Yes! Maybe! I don't know!"

"Oh, come on. This has to stop."

"Why? I'm not hurting anyone."

"You're hurting yourself."

Stephanie sat up and grabbed a pillow, cradling it in her lap. "I don't think so. But I'll tell you one thing, I'm not going to see a shrink again, so you can forget it."

Far from surprised at her reaction, I compromised. "Fair enough. But you'll have to rejoin the family. No more of this isolation."

"Deal. I'll sit with you guys at meals. Just don't expect me to like it."

"See you at dinner." I left the room, thinking I'd won the battle.

By the end of February, I still hadn't received a nibble of interest in the store, let alone an offer. I shouldn't have been surprised because the stock market crash had affected many investors. But the balance sheet was solid, and I believed it was just a matter of time. Would a sale come before Stephanie's tuition at Stanford was due?

Stephanie kept her word about joining us at meals but was a reluctant participant. One day she ate like a hungry trucker, and the next, pushed her food around the plate. Brett and I tried to draw her into conversation with little success. The scenario repeated itself at every meal.

Then one evening at dinner, she appeared at the table, dragging her feet in a theatrical display. "Do I have to eat?"

Brett smacked his palm on the table. "Yes. That was the agreement. Take a seat."

Mumbling under her breath, Stephanie plopped herself down.

"Smells divine, honey." I took a helping of Brett's delicious chicken curry casserole.

Stephanie placed a small spoonful on her plate, then pushed back from the table before taking a bite. "Excuse me. I don't feel so good." She dashed from the room.

Brett and I exchanged a look. "Should I check on her?" I asked.

"Wait a bit. Enjoy your dinner. I slaved over a hot stove for ya."

"Okay, darling."

After we finished the meal, Brett stacked the dishes. "Something I've been meaning to ask. The store's been listed for a while now. Why do ya think it hasn't sold?"

I shrugged. "Perhaps I priced it a little too high for today's market conditions. Should I ask the agent about lowering the listing price?"

Brett pursed his lips. "That might do the trick. But I'm sorry you gotta resort to that."

"I am too. But I must face reality." I helped Brett clear the table, then kissed him on the cheek. "Be back in a bit. I'm going to see if Stephanie's okay."

"All right. Let me know how she is."

Chapter Fifty-Two

STEPHANIE FACES FACTS

I locked my door and ran to the toilet, getting there just as I started heaving. Nothing much came up, probably because I'd been nauseated all day and barely ate.

Lauren yelled through the door. "Are you all right? Do you need anything?"

I wiped my mouth and grabbed the counter to pull myself up, and walked to the bedroom door so I didn't have to shout. "I'm fine. There's a stomach bug going around at school. That's probably it."

"Want me to bring you some ginger ale?"

The idea of putting something in my mouth almost sent me back to the toilet. "Um, no, thanks. Maybe I'll get some later."

I pictured Lauren holding onto her Zuni necklace. "If you change your mind, come find me."

"Yeah. Okay." Would she ever leave?

Once Lauren's footsteps faded, I breathed a sigh of relief and changed into pajamas. I put on MTV without the sound and climbed into bed.

Why did my life suck so bad? Was my family cursed? First, my dad and mom died, and then fake granny Babcock wanted to send me to boarding school. Then her stupid lawyers blew my trust fund and my chance at Stanford, and there wasn't a flipping thing I could do about it.

My eyes stung and soon tears dripped down my face. Why had Lauren and Brett been so excited about me getting into Stanford? That was weird. When my acceptance from UT arrived a few days later, they tried to make a big deal about it, but I couldn't care less. When life ripped the grand prize from your hands, second-best meant nothing.

Moving to Austin hadn't turned out so great, but it was my own fault for going to that party. And drinking. Should I have told Lauren everything that happened that horrible night? I couldn't face it then—or now. What would she do if I was actually pregnant? I remember Lauren's sad face when she told me her mom would've sent her to a home for unwed mothers if she'd known about her pregnancy. Would my real grandmother send me away? After what happened with her mom, I hoped not, but the thought terrified me.

It was getting harder to hide my fat waist in my baggy sweats. At least Lauren wasn't home as much to notice. Brett still knocked on my door every afternoon, asking me to help him cook or try a new recipe. I never opened the door, just called out an excuse about needing to study and held my breath until I heard him walk away.

Recalling what I'd read about early signs of pregnancy, I touched my humongous boobs. They were very tender. Lauren hadn't noticed that I borrowed two of her bras because I spilled out of mine.

My stomach grumbled. Some mornings, I threw up right after I woke up and didn't have an appetite. Other days, I was starving and stuffed my face.

When I was getting up to turn off the TV, my left leg cramped. I hopped out of bed, trying not to yell and rubbed my calf until the muscles relaxed. I limped to the bathroom to pee. Again.

Still no sign of my period.

I trudged back to bed and crawled under the covers. If I didn't get my period in a couple of days, I'd talk to Becca.

A week later, I called Becca, hoping she'd be home on a Saturday.

"Hey, Stephanie."

"So glad I caught you."

"Yeah, I'm packing for spring break. What's up?"

"Nothing good. I missed my period again. That makes three times."

"Yikes! Do you have any symptoms? Weight gain, sore boobs, nausea?"

"Yep, you just described my life perfectly."

"I noticed you've been wearing those baggy clothes, but I figured it was to protect yourself from guys bugging you."

"Yeah, no. It's because I no longer have a waist."

I could almost hear Becca thinking over the phone line. "You better take a pregnancy test."

"You mean go to a doctor?"

"Nope, they sell home pregnancy tests at the drug store. If I were you, I'd get one right away."

My hand shook as I hung up the phone. Did I really need a test? I'd done pretty well ignoring the signs, but in my heart, I knew the truth. Still, I stuffed some cash in my pocket and walked down the hill and over to Lamar to buy one.

Chapter Fifty-Three

LAUREN GETS GUT-PUNCHED

Finally, a well-qualified buyer came forward, and on March 15th, I signed on the dotted line before I could change my mind. In a way, it was the end of an era, and painful to let go of my long-sought achievement, but the pull of family overcame my selfishness—for once. And it felt good.

As I drove to the bank with my nice fat check, I gave thanks to Ben, my first husband and second love. If it weren't for Ben and his generous gift, I'd never have been able to open Cornucopia. Through the worst of my alcoholism, I never touched a penny of the nest egg he bestowed on me. Ben, who died in Salerno, Italy in World War II. I'd never gone to Italy to find his grave and wondered if his parents had. If I had made the trip to Europe, I would have been tempted to learn Alain's fate too. Alain, my first love, father of my only child, and Stephanie's grandfather. She had his eyes, a poignant reminder of him.

Goosebumps rose on my arms, bringing me back to the present. No doubt, Brett was happy I'd sold Cornucopia rather than carry on with its expansion, but he never gloated. Instead, he supported me in the decision to finance my granddaughter's college tuition.

After parking near the door, I hurried inside to deposit the check. With my receipt in hand, I drove home, taking care not to get a speeding ticket in my anticipation of delivering the news to Stephanie. I pictured her joy at learning she'd be able to attend Stanford despite her financial ruin.

I parked in the drive and hurried into the house, expecting Stephanie would be in her hideaway. But when I knocked on her door, there was no response. Then I heard loud sobbing from her adjoining bathroom. "Stephanie, I'm coming in."

She sat on the floor, head in her hands, an open box labeled e.p.t. beside her. I gaped at the test tube setup on the counter. The contraption had an angled mirror, and there was a dark circle at the bottom of the tube. What the heck! Stephanie lifted her head and wailed, "I'm pregnant."

The shock knocked the breath out of me, and I bent over double in despair. How and when did this happen? The girl had been subdued and stayed close to home since that one drunken night.

Then it hit me. Of course! That's when it happened. And I was so self-involved, oblivious. At the time, I'd focused solely on the alcohol use, never suspecting she'd had sex. After doing the math, I realized Stephanie was four months pregnant. It became obvious why she'd started dressing like a bag lady. One sign I'd missed. And there were others. The change in eating habits, taking food to her room. I cursed myself for my lack of insight.

When I recovered enough to speak, I asked, "What's in the test tube?"

"Pee. And chemicals. It's a home pregnancy test. Becca told me about it. It reacts with HCG, human chorionic gonadotropin."

Becca the biology whiz, who wanted to be a doctor, and whom Stephanie had confided in, rather than me. "I didn't know such things existed."

The girl wiped her eyes with her sleeve. "Why would you? You're old."

I stepped back, stunned by the impertinence. But impertinence was the least of our problems. "What about college? I was coming to tell you I sold Cornucopia to get the money for Stanford."

Stephanie's eyes widened. "You what? This can't be true! You shouldn't have done that. I can't even go to college now!"

"Perhaps not right away."

"Maybe not ever!"

"Don't say that. Right now, we have to focus on the fact you're pregnant. And you haven't finished high school." My mind spun. What if Stephanie wanted an abortion? Wasn't it too late? I closed the lid on the toilet and collapsed onto it. "How can you make it to graduation?"

"I don't know, but I've done great at hiding it so far."

"Yes, you have. And I've been blind. I wish you'd come to me earlier."

The only response I got was a shrug.

"You must see a doctor. You've had no prenatal care, and you're already four months along."

Stephanie didn't say a word.

"Another thing. You must have missed your period three or four times and only now are you taking a pregnancy test. Why did you wait?" I struggled for composure; the last thing my granddaughter needed was for me to fall apart. "What were you thinking?"

"Guess I didn't want to believe it." She glanced up at me. "Are you going to tell Brett?"

I felt my eyebrows rise to their upper limit. "Are you serious? Of course he has to know."

"He's going to hate me. You already hate me."

"Oh, no, Stephanie. I could never hate you." I sank to the floor beside her, took her in my arms, and held her as she sobbed. Blinking away a vision of pregnant me at seventeen, my heart broke.

Several minutes later, the tears ended, and Stephanie drew a deep breath. "I know you're disappointed in me."

"Hush." I pulled myself to my feet, then reached down to help Stephanie stand. With my arm around her, I guided her to bed and tucked her in. "You take a nap. I'll check on you later."

Stephanie turned onto her side. "Okay."

As I closed the door, the tears I'd held back dripped down my face. I staggered to the living room, fell onto the couch, and wept. Brett would be home soon. I needed his calming presence. We had a lot to discuss.

Chapter Fifty-Four

STEPHANIE PONDERS THE FUTURE

At least Lauren didn't yell at me. But her face aged twenty years right before my eyes, telling me how shocked and disappointed she was. I was shocked and disappointed too. She had to be at the end of her rope, as she would say. Would she let me stay with her? But she said she didn't hate me, so I hoped she would. There weren't any other options unless Lauren sent me to one of those homes. Then I thought about how my parents would have reacted and started crying all over again. And if Evelyn found out, it would kill her.

I put my hand on my growing belly, thinking about the baby inside me. How big was it? Why didn't I feel it move? Tiffany told me that her cousin got pregnant in junior year and had an abortion. She went right back to school as if nothing happened. No way I could do that. And I was pretty sure it was too late anyway, which meant I'd have a baby in August. Every day my body reminded me I was pregnant, but it was still hard to believe.

Could I even raise a baby? When I used to babysit Will, I took super good care of him, but after a few hours, I left. If I kept the baby, I'd never be off duty. My life would be bottles and diapers and nothing else.

Lauren hadn't even asked me who the father was. Probably too shocked. But I'd have to tell her. After that horrible night last fall, Logan ignored me at school. Maybe he didn't even remember what happened. I had to make sure he didn't find out about the baby. Of course, he wouldn't want it, not when he had a full ride to A&M.

What if Lauren wanted me to give up the baby? How could I hand over my baby to some stranger? Lauren knew who was going to raise her child, but I wouldn't. I didn't know the first thing about how adoption worked. But I knew how it had affected my life. My mom never learned the truth, and I wondered what she would have done if she had. Would she have tracked down Lauren? Would she even care?

When I closed my eyes, the drawings of fetuses in the biology text paraded across my mind. I realized my baby was still very small, but all the body parts were already formed, a miniature human. Was it a girl or a boy? Reflecting on how my life had changed made my head hurt and my stomach do cartwheels. And there was another life to think about too. What should I do?

When Lauren knocked on my bedroom door, I woke up, surprised I had fallen asleep with all the guilt and misery I faced. "Come in."

Lauren's eyes were swollen, which told me she'd been crying too. She sat on the bed beside me.

From the look on her face, I wasn't sure I wanted to hear what she had to say. I sat up and leaned on the headboard. "So, what's my punishment?"

"Dear girl, you've been punished enough." She patted my knee.

"Did you really sell the store for me?"

Lauren looked past me. "Yes, I did."

"I can't believe you did that."

"Well, believe it." She leaned forward and smoothed my hair. "I love you, Stephanie."

"Y-y-you do? Even now?"

"You're part of me."

"So is the baby."

"Very true." Lauren's hand fiddled with her necklace. Was she as nervous as me about the future? "Brett will be home soon. We'll bring him up to speed and figure out a plan."

"I'm afraid of what he'll think of me."

Lauren shook her head. "Don't be concerned. Brett's a good man and will cope with the situation. We'll weather this storm as a family. While you were sleeping, I made an appointment for you with Jane's obstetrician, whom she highly recommends."

"So Jane knows."

"Yes," Lauren said. "But there's one thing you haven't mentioned—the baby's father."

I knew we'd be having this discussion, but that didn't make it any easier. "His name is Logan Armstrong, and he's a complete asshole. Big football hero. He's got a full scholarship to A&M. I don't want him to find out I'm pregnant. Since that night, he hasn't said a word to me. Not that I care."

"I see." Lauren looked at the ceiling for a moment, then met my eyes. "Perhaps that's for the best. I'm not clear on the law regarding these things, so I'll call our family attorney and see what she says. Why don't you freshen up?"

"Okay. I'm going to take a shower and wash my hair, so I'll be a while."

Lauren gave me a half smile. "Try not to worry. We'll get through this." She rose and kissed the top of my head.

I didn't mind.

"Take your time, dear." She closed the door behind her.

I sat there for a few minutes, wondering what was going on in my body. Then I got up and went into the bathroom. I stared at my face in the mirror. Was it my imagination or was my face getting fat? I lifted my shirt and turned sideways. My stomach looked even bigger than it did yesterday. Could I make it through senior year, or would my ginormous belly be obvious to everyone? Did pregnant girls go to prom? As if I had a prom date. And what about graduation, which was two months away? By then, there was no way the gown would hide my bulging body.

Then it struck me, what good would a high school diploma do me? College was out. What would my future be like as a high school dropout? One thing was sure, I wouldn't be working for NASA.

I flipped the shower on, stripping while I waited for the water to warm up. When it was ready, I stood under the spray, wishing I could wash away my doubts and fears, and my night with Logan.

Chapter Fifty-Five

LAUREN - HIGHER LOVE

As soon as I heard Brett's key in the door, I flew to the entryway and flung my arms around him. He hugged me tight, then released me, keeping hold of my shoulders. "What'd I do to deserve such a warm welcome?" Then he must have seen the look on my face because his smile faded. "What's wrong?"

No use mincing words. "Stephanie's pregnant."

"Good Lord!" He stepped back, hands dropping to his sides. "How far along?"

"Four months. It had to have happened the night she got drunk."

His eye narrowed. "Bet you're right. Where is she?"

"Taking a shower."

"We've got a lot to hash over. Let's you and me talk first, then we'll present a united front when we see her."

I nodded and took his hand, leading him to the living room couch.

"Say, didn't you close on the store today?"

"Yes."

Brett shook his head. "Complicates matters, don't it?"

"Indeed. But my focus is on my granddaughter right now."

"Our granddaughter."

"Oh, Brett." Tears threatened to spill.

"Honey, I love her too."

"I know you do."

Brett cleared his throat. "Let's get back to business. We need a game plan. Do ya know what she wants to do?"

"No. She's scared and uncertain. And quite emotional."

"Understandable. You gotta hand it to her, the kid's been masterful at hiding it."

"Yes. After that party, she started wearing those loose clothes, and I guess I got used to it and stopped noticing after a while. Now those baggy clothes are hiding a sprouting belly. And there's two months until graduation."

"She's gotta finish high school, for damn sure."

"Of course. But if Stephanie keeps the baby, she won't be going to college." Tears sprang to my eyes, and a sob escaped my lips.

Brett reached into his back pocket for his handkerchief. "Here ya go."

"But I sold the store for nothing. She's not going to Stanford after all."

"You did a wonderful, selfless thing for the girl. Maybe she can get herself to college later in life."

I snuggled against Brett's side, needing the closeness. "I certainly hope so."

To my surprise, Brett began to chuckle.

Astonished, I wriggled out of his embrace and stared at him. "You're laughing? There's *nothing* funny about this."

"Honey, if we're gonna make it through this calamity, a sense of humor is vital. Don't ya think you selling the store is kinda like that O. Henry story, Gift of the Magi?"

Puzzled by the analogy, I studied Brett. "How? In the story, there were two who sacrificed."

Brett shrugged. "True enough, but the sentiment fits, doing something selfless, out of pure love." He helped me to my feet and rested his chin on my head. "We're gonna get through this as a family. Let's talk to Stephanie, and we'll go from there."

We held hands as we walked down the hall to the girl's room. The door was open, and Stephanie, her hair still wet, sat at her desk writing on a notepad. She stared at Brett, biting her lower lip. "You know. Now what?"

"Come on out to the kitchen," Brett said. "We'll talk while I make a pizza."

"I'm starving. You know I'm eating for two now."

Amazed that Stephanie cracked a joke, I broke out in laughter, a great stress reliever. But I wasn't so naïve as to believe this would be a walk in the park.

In the kitchen, Brett took ingredients from the refrigerator and handed Stephanie a grater and a block of mozzarella cheese. She got to work.

Brett rolled out the dough, and I chopped vegetables for a salad. "Stephanie, while you were in the shower, I spoke to my attorney, the same one who helped with your guardianship. She said when a child is born to parents who aren't married to each other, the law doesn't automatically recognize the biological father as a legal parent. Paternity must be established first."

Stephanie's forehead wrinkled. "Um, okay. How can I make sure paternity isn't established?"

"The attorney said you can leave the father's name blank on the birth certificate."

"Then, that's what I'll do. Problem solved."

I thought about all the problems to come but reminded myself to be positive.

"What about school? Will ya be able to finish your classes?" Brett asked.

"Probably not. My belly gets bigger every day. If anyone found out, I couldn't face it. One good thing about senior year is I didn't have to take gym. If I had to, my secret wouldn't be a secret."

Certain the school was buzzing with rumors of Stephanie's pregnancy, I didn't comment, not having the heart to burst her bubble of denial. Instead, I placed my hand on her shoulder. "How would you feel about asking the school if you can test out of your classes or at least finish your coursework at home?"

"Is that a thing? That would be awesome!"

"I'll see if we can make it happen." I tossed chopped tomatoes and mushrooms into the bowl of lettuce. "What have you decided about the pregnancy?" I'd thought long and hard about how to phrase the question and that was the best I could come up with, "the pregnancy."

Stephanie slammed the grater on the counter. "It's not a pregnancy. It's a baby! If you're asking if I'm getting an abortion, the answer is no. I'm having the baby."

"Then what?" I asked.

"I think I want to keep it."

"Think? You're going to have to make a decision." As the words left my lips, I wanted to snatch them back, worried I'd pushed too hard.

"Okay then." Stephanie lifted her chin. "I've decided I'm going to keep it."

Brett added the last of the pepperoni to the pizza. "You don't have to make up your mind right this minute."

Stephanie's face reddened. "I said I'm keeping it."

"Whoa, there! No need to get riled," Brett said.

"Sorry. I'm just a little emotional." Stephanie rushed to Brett and hugged him.

"Understood." Brett kissed the top of her head. "Let me get this pizza in the oven."

"Yes, please. I'm hungry." Stephanie cradled her stomach. "I'm going to wash up. Be right back.

As Stephanie left the room, Brett pulled me close. "She's made the right decision for her, and we're gonna support her every step of the way."

"Darling, the next months are going to make a roller coaster look tame, so buckle up for the ride. Stephanie made a brave choice, and I'm proud of her. She's putting the baby ahead of herself, a true testament to higher love."

Epilogue

STEPHANIE PONDERS MOTHERHOOD

I spend hours in Lauren's pool, trying to stay cool and relieve the weight of carrying my baby. My due date, August 12th, is just three weeks away. Like Jane, I don't want to learn ahead of time if I'm having a boy or a girl, so I made two lists of names. My choice for a boy is Michael and Jeanne for a girl. My baby deserves a clean start and shouldn't be stuck with the name of anyone I know.

With nothing to do but wait, I have tons of time to think. A year ago, all I had on my mind was college life at Stanford. As I float in the pool, with my huge abdomen sticking out of the water, I let the tears fall for what I had lost. Then my baby kicks and brings me back to the present and how drastically my life will soon change. Is anyone ready to be a mother for the first time?

After Brett and Lauren learned about my pregnancy, they spoke to the principal about my situation. I finished my coursework and finals at home, so I wouldn't go through life as a high school dropout. Of course, I didn't attend graduation, but after all, what was that in the scheme of things?

Becca visits me every week, but she'll be heading to Galveston for college soon. She told me everyone at school guessed that I was expecting, which really freaked me out.

But I have more important things to worry about than what the kids at Austin High thought, like giving birth. Because of all the practice I got with Will, my diaper changing skills are wicked good, and I have a boatload of experience with feeding and bath time. But those things are just mechanics. The real challenges will be mental and emotional as I deal with a lifetime commitment. Am I ready for such a humongous responsibility? As Lauren would say, "Time will tell."

Since my grandmother retired, she has plenty of time to shop for baby furniture and something called a layette. My baby is going to be spoiled if Lauren and Brett have anything to say about it.

One evening last week, as I waddled past Brett's office after cleaning up the kitchen, I overheard Lauren telling him, "I became a grandmother a mere two years ago and could have waited a while longer before being promoted to great-grandmother. But such is life."

"And life is good. Got to say, I'm lookin' forward to the little bundle of joy," Brett said.

Warm fuzzies.

I asked Lauren not to tell Evelyn about the baby. Evelyn must be miserable after losing her family's mansion and becoming totally dependent on her niece Imogene. Why should I add to her burden?

In a few hours, Lauren is throwing me a baby shower. It's supposed to be a surprise, but there are just too many clues to ignore. I can almost taste the Italian Crème cake sitting in the back of the refrigerator, hidden behind a large, strategically placed bag of broccoli. Since I'm eating for two, it's only fair I have an extra slice.

Last night, Lauren and I had one of our cozy chats on the living room couch. We talked about what she'd do now that Cornucopia belonged to someone else.

"I've been throwing around a couple of ideas. Debbie and Ruth suggested an upscale children's boutique. And they want to help, which gives me built-in staff. With the way Austin is growing, we think the demand is there."

"Wow! I'd never have guessed."

"At this point, it's only a possibility. Right now, I'm more focused on your baby."

"Me too. I'm so sad my mom and dad...aren't around." My eyes filled with tears, and I dug in my pocket for a tissue.

"Oh, Stephanie, it's heartbreaking you lost your parents, but you found us. Don't forget Brett and I love you."

"I know, and ditto, or 'Back at ya,' as Brett would say." I dabbed my eyes.

"Don't tell me Brett has you talking Texan."

"No way. At least, not yet. But Brett says I've lost my Boston accent. Do you think I have?"

"Most of it." Lauren patted my hand.

"Speaking of accents, there's something I always wanted to ask you. Brett talks Texan all the time, and sometimes you talk like him but other times you speak normally. Why is that?"

Lauren did her frown-and-relax face thing. "Normally? That's one way to put it. As a child, I had quite the country twang, but when I moved to Manhattan to become a Powers girl, that didn't fly. I had to learn to speak like an educated, sophisticated woman. Believe me, I struggled through the elocution lessons, voice training, and vocabulary building, but it paid off."

"Oh, but your country speech comes out sometimes?"

"I suppose so."

I hadn't had much luck getting Lauren to talk about her past, so I tried again. "Now that I'm eighteen, are you gonna give me more details about your wild years?"

"Not if I can help it." Lauren glanced sideways at me.

"Just so you know, I'm going to keep bugging you."

"I'd expect nothing less."

We stared at each other and then burst out laughing. I laughed so hard, I got a stitch in my side and stood up to stretch.

"Are you all right?"

"I'm fine. Just pulled a laughing muscle." I sat back beside her, kicked off my flip-flops, the only shoes that fit me, and tucked my feet under me.

"As your due date approaches, pay attention to your body. Be sure to tell us when the first signs of labor start." Lauren's look of concern was textbook, but I appreciated it.

"Yes, Grandmother."

"At least you've stopped calling me Granny."

"I could start again if you'd like."

That remark earned me two raised eyebrows. "Only kidding."

"Sure hope so." Lauren turned sideways to face me. "With the baby coming soon, I've been thinking about love quite a bit."

"I'm listening."

"When Brett came back into my life, I couldn't believe he'd forgiven me for the past and wanted to try again. I struggled, knowing that if I kept my walls up, I might miss out on the chance of a lifetime. I'd avoided vulnerability, always ran from commitment, but by some miracle, I opened my heart to love again. And then you came along and darned if the process didn't start all over again."

"I'm sure glad you got back together, even if you play Frank Sinatra way too much."

"Dear, there's no such thing as too much Sinatra."

I rolled my eyes. "If you say so." I sat up and stretched my aching back. "Tell me more about this love business."

Lauren stared up at the ceiling for a few moments, then her turquoise eyes met mine. "My life journey has taught me a lot about the subject. Love comes in many varieties. When you mention it, people often think of romantic love, which is understandable. But consider the other types: maternal, paternal, sisterly, brotherly, and the prerequisite for all of them—self-love."

"What do you mean?"

"Well, to me, self-love means self-compassion. It's easy to beat yourself up for your mistakes. It took me a long time to stop being my own worst enemy and start being my best friend."

"How did you do it?" I really wanted to know for myself.

"A lot of what I needed, I found in AA. Healing starts with mindfulness, being aware of what's happening in your life and addressing it, and not letting it fester. Patience, trust, and letting go of negative thoughts helped me. But that's only the beginning of the road to inner peace. I honestly believe self-love is the basis for a tranquil life, but there must be a higher love, a love for others."

"I think I understand."

Lauren smiled. "Are you about ready to turn in?"

My baby kicked, and I put my hand on my abdomen. "Oof, that one hurt. Even though I'm nervous, I can't wait to meet my baby. I'm already in love."

"Me too." Lauren's eyes gleamed, and I hoped she wasn't going to cry. "You know, there's a sort of beauty in our situation. In a sense, our family's story has come full circle, with history repeating itself. But this time, we have the opportunity to do things right."

I scooted over and hugged her. "I'm so grateful you stood by me."

"Of course, my dear." Lauren smoothed my hair like my mom used to.

"Did I ever thank you properly for selling your store for me?"

Lauren kissed the top of my head. "No need. I'd do it again. And you're not so bad at higher love yourself."

Acknowledgements

I would like to thank my beta readers for their invaluable constructive criticism and insightful comments, which helped me in crafting my novel. Much appreciation to the members of my critique group, Lisa, Michelle, Mark, and Billy, who gave excellent feedback along the way.

Joanne Kukanza Easley

A retired registered nurse with experience in both the cold, clinical operating room and the emotionally fraught world of psychiatric hospitals, Joanne lives in the Texas Hill Country, where she writes fiction about complicated, twentieth-century women. Her multi-award-winning debut, *Sweet Jane,* released in March, 2020, was named the adult fiction winner at the Texas Author Project and shortlisted for the Sarton Award and Eric Hoffer Award, among others. *Just One Look*, Joanne's second novel, was a May 2022 Pulpwood Queen Book Club Pick. *I'll Be Seeing You,* her third novel, features characters from *Sweet Jane*. Her prize-winning short stories and poetry have appeared in several anthologies.

SWEET JANE

Sweet Jane

A childhood scarred by her mother's alcoholism drives Jane to flee at sixteen, hitching a ride to California's Summer of Love, swearing never to look back. Seventeen years later, Jane's polished life—marriage, grad school, sobriety—teeters on collapse. When her mother's death calls her back for the funeral, Jane hides her troubled past from her husband and returns to the hometown she swore to forget. Confronting her childhood home and old faces, Jane is thrust into the raw memories that forged her. A shocking revelation forces her to reframe her pain, her family, and herself in a journey of reckoning and redemption.

I'll Be Seeing You

WITH CHARACTERS FROM SWEET JANE

I'll Be Seeing You

A raw, gripping saga of one woman's wild ride through five decades, fueled by ambition, derailed by booze, and haunted by the past.

Lauren's done with ranch life. Spotted by a modeling scout at the 1940 Fort Worth Stock Show Parade, she ditches Palo Pinto County for Manhattan's glitz. But when her dream crashes, she drowns her sorrows in liquor and lovers. By twenty-four, she's a widowed, divorced mess, hopping cities until Austin becomes her last stand. After a decade of chaos, she claws her way to sobriety and builds a thriving business, yet peace remains out of reach.

Then, in 1985, the past storms back: Brett, her third husband, wants her back after thirty-three years. Reeling from old wounds, Lauren turns to Jane, her AA lifeline. The clock's ticking—will she rewrite her story or let it burn?

Just One Look

A STANDALONE NOVEL

Just One Look

In 1965 Chicago, thirteen-year-old Dani Marek falls fiercely in love with John, dreaming of a perfect future. For six radiant years, she builds a future—until Vietnam claims him, shattering her world. Consumed by grief, Dani unleashes a reckless crusade in Rush Street's singles bars, vowing to break every heart she can. Her quest for vengeance traps her in a loveless marriage that ends in heartbreak, leaving her a widowed mother at twenty-four, haunted by ghosts and burdened with a fortune she never wanted.

Set against the vibrant, turbulent backdrop of the Sixties and Seventies, Just One Look traces Dani's raw, turbulent path through sorrow, denial, and the hard-won courage to heal.